Breathless Part 2 - Learning to Love Again

Chapter 1: The Name is Moore. Jon Moore.

I could hear my best mate coming down the road long before he reached my house, the sound of his motorcycle emanating throughout the evening air. Jon has always enjoyed making a dramatic entrance, and was a sucker for all things luxury and flashy. This preference for ostentation extended to everything from cars, to clothes, to gadgets, to vacation destinations, to sexual partners. He was well-read and spoke multiple languages, having traveled all over the world. He was a regular James Bond. In fact, his full name was Jonathan Roger Moore, named after the actor who played Bond for many years. He was born on 4/20, which was fitting, given his love of marijuana.

In addition to being a materialist, he was a daredevil with a smooth and charismatic personality, and annoyingly good at almost everything. He was especially skilled at talking people into doing things.

Here is a list of some of the things Jon has convinced me to do over the years: smoke cigarettes, drink alcohol, smoke weed, snort cocaine, drop acid, eat magic mushrooms, take ecstasy, get a tattoo, get a piercing, fuck him anally, suck his cock, toss his salad, have a threesome, ride a motorcycle, ride a horse, ride an elephant, ski, go zip lining, walk a tightrope, rock climb, bungee jump, skydive, scuba dive, free dive, parasail, ride in a hot air balloon, go white water rafting, take hot yoga classes, run a marathon, compete in a triathlon, try CrossFit, and go on all the thrill rides at amusement parks. He is also the one who turned me on to my favorite fetish: breathplay.

Some of the things Jon talked me into doing were terrifying and/or painful, and some were surprisingly enjoyable and changed my life for the better. One thing was for sure: Jon was brave, and knew how to LIVE. I have known him my entire life, having grown up next door to him and his family when I lived in London. His dad was best friends and business partners with my dad, and before long, Jon and I also became besties.

For as long as I can remember, Jon has been my idol. Even as a young lad, he had a self-assured way about him that let you know he was in control. I began modeling myself after him from an early age. He must have sensed that I was competing with him, because by the time our families had moved us to the states and we were in full blown puberty, he began to one-up me. School grades, athletic prowess, and sexual conquests were all areas of competition. Jon made one thing clear from early on: anything I could do, he could do better.

Jealousies aside, I loved Jon dearly, and was beyond thrilled to see him. I was outside on my deck when I first heard the sound of his motorcycle riding down my quiet street, and was once again hosting a weekend barbecue with Lawrence, Diana, Tracy, Eugene, Daryl, Amy, and Anna in attendance.

Everyone, with the exception of Lawrence, was looking forward to seeing Jon. Lawrence despised my best mate, convinced that he was either an alien or an android. I brushed off Lawrence's suspicions, convinced that he was jealous of Jon for his wealth, good looks, and fearlessness. I admit, Jon's complete lack of nervousness sometimes concerned me, as did the fact that I had never once seen him cry or get angry in the almost 33 years I had known him. However, I still admired and idolized the man. To me, he was the ultimate "alpha male," capable of seducing just about anyone and mastering just about anything he set his mind to.

Before long, the sound of his motorcycle was so loud that it was certain he had arrived at my home. I eagerly ran from my deck to the parking lot to greet him. He appeared almost god-like, sitting atop his luxury chopper, wearing aviator style sunglasses, a fitted white t-shirt that showed off his impressive arm and pec muscles, fashionably ripped jeans, a designer wristwatch, and expensive black leather boots. His golden brown, tousled hair shone in the late afternoon sun, as did his bronze skin. His beard was trimmed to perfection, as usual. He was metrosexual, yet ruggedly handsome. Everything about him screamed, "supermodel." I smiled ear to ear as I ran up to him.

He cut the engine and flashed his megawatt grin when he saw me, his white, perfectly straight teeth contrasting sharply with his flawless, suntanned complexion. He removed his sunglasses, revealing his intense green eyes, which held an air of mischief as well as mystery.

"Hey, bitch!" he called out enthusiastically in his deep, sultry voice as he stepped off his bike, holding out his chiseled, newly tattooed arms for a hug. He was my height, standing six feet, four inches tall. He weighed about twenty pounds less than me, but was just as strong as I was, if not slightly stronger.

I eagerly embraced him, inhaling his unique scent, which consisted of cigarette and pot smoke combined with very expensive cologne. He abruptly lifted me several inches off the ground, nearly crushing my torso with his incredibly strong arms and began to give me an open mouthed kiss, which I discreetly turned my head away from when he attempted to slip his tongue into my mouth.

I chuckled nervously and, with great effort, escaped from his boa constrictor-like embrace. I had told him on multiple occasions that I loved him as more of a brother than a lover, but he preferred the latter. Openly bisexual, he had been angling for me to let him fuck me up the arse for decades. Since I was, at most, bicurious, I had respectfully declined his propositions, reaching a compromise of giving or receiving a hand job, blow job, or tossed salad when he wanted to fool around. It was enough for me, even if it wasn't enough for him. He somehow felt that I "owed him" ever since I had taken his virginity on his 14th birthday. This only happened after much hesitation - and alcohol consumption - on my end. As he kept reminding me over the years, I had let him do everything to me that night except reciprocate the anal sex he had pressured me into giving him. At some point in my twenties, I had drunkenly leaked the details of the encounter to Lawrence, who had half-jokingly advised me to avoid dropping the soap while in the shower. I had laughed. For all his flaws, my brother was tolerant of those who followed alternative lifestyles.

"Hello, Jon," I said warmly. "I have missed you, mate. It's so good to see you!" My voice shook slightly. I admit, his "enthusiastic" greeting had left me feeling on edge, and perhaps a bit victimized. He smiled seductively and grabbed an oversized backpack from the back of his bike, then I walked with him to my deck to greet the others.

"It's so fucking great to be back home, Ken," he said in his deep, somewhat hoarse timbre as he fished into his pocket for his designer cigarette case, pulled out a cigarette, and lit up with his expensive lighter. He took a deep drag before he continued talking, smoke pouring out of his mouth and nose as he did so. "The flight home had a proper shit ton of turbulence. Luckily, I met a foxy brunette in first class who was up for joining the mile high club - and without a rubber, no less. The pilot couldn't fly worth a shit. I do believe that sitting on my ten inch dick is what kept her from falling to the bloody floor."

I tilted my head back and laughed heartily, at once horrified and impressed that he'd fucked a total stranger on an airplane without using protection. With the huge number of partners he'd had over the years, it was a miracle he had never contracted an STD or AIDS. Jon and his ex Lisa had had an open relationship, and the main reason for their breakup was due to Lisa falling in love with another man. Jon had slept with over a thousand people, several of them famous.

We reached the deck, and Jon hastily finished and put out his cigarette then reached into his backpack to hand me a very expensive bottle of single malt scotch. I smiled and thanked him profusely, flattered and a bit embarrassed that he had spent so much money on me yet again.

"You're worth it, mate," he assured me with a wink before turning his attention to the others.

Tracy and Amy rushed up to him for hugs. Then I introduced him to Diana, Eugene, and Anna, who all appeared starstruck upon meeting the man who I considered my first best friend. I couldn't blame them because, character quirks aside, Jon was quite stunning. He and Daryl exchanged awkward hugs and greetings, both knowing it was only a matter of time before an argument ensued. Then there was Lawrence, who stood a bit apart from the others and kept his arms folded across his chest, greeting Jon by nodding noncommittally and abruptly turning away from him to face the ocean. That was when Jon made his first snide remark of the evening.

Jon smirked at me and asked in a voice purposely loud enough for Lawrence to hear, "Is it cold out here, or is it just HIM?"

I couldn't help but laugh, but Lawrence was not amused, and turned around to glare at Jon, who simply smirked back at my brother. Lawrence had a number of nicknames for Jon, including "The Robot," "Mr. Perfect," "Stepford Boy," "The Alien," and, most notably, "The Green-Eyed Monster," since he was convinced Jon was jealous of me.

Eager to diffuse the tension between him and my brother, I handed Jon a beer and told him to get comfortable. Being the show-off and wiseguy that he was, he took a swig of his beer then began taking off his clothes, starting with his tee shirt and rapidly moving on to his jeans and boots. Within seconds, he was standing in his red boxer briefs, which barely concealed his semi-erect member. Lawrence scoffed and turned away.

Jon's body was impressive, although he appeared thinner than the last time I saw him. His abs were very defined, as were the rest of his muscles. He sported tattoos along his left rib cage, which called even more attention to his defined torso. His nipples were pierced. Everyone's jaw dropped at the sight of his tanned, muscular body, except for Lawrence and Daryl, who simply rolled their eyes. He looked like he had stepped out of a magazine. He was primed to take off his underwear, but I put my hand on his shoulder and, with a chuckle, offered to take him inside my house and let him borrow one of my swimsuits. His arse crack was partly visible and his bulge appeared to grow in size. He deliberately lingered before stepping through the sliding glass door into my home, a seductive smirk on his face.

"Jon, buddy, you look like you lost some weight. I hope you've been eating," I said with a smile as we reached my bedroom, where I gave him a choice of several swim trunks. Unsurprisingly, he picked the red ones, wasting no time in taking off his underwear and standing naked in front of me, eyebrows raised. He had no pubic hair whatsoever, electing to get his "mound, sack and crack" waxed on a regular basis. His huge cock, which sported a piercing near his hairless balls, was standing full attention as he spoke, and he stood close to me. Perhaps closer than I wanted him to be. I backed away slightly.

"Of course I eat, mate," he insisted in his sultry voice. "You know me, I have that crazy metabolism." He smirked once again and put on the swim trunks. I couldn't help but feel more relaxed when he was no longer naked, yet I knew it was only a matter of time before he would start pressuring me to fool around. In the meantime, I was determined to keep the mood light.

"Anna and Diana are lovely," Jon remarked with a smile. "And that Eugene fellow is ADORABLE. I love me a tasty ginger boy!" I laughed hard at that. "Does he swing?"

I shrugged. "Tracy mentioned that he's bicurious, but I'm not sure if he's 'out.'"

Jon nodded. "Oh, I will BRING that little leprechaun out, mate! By the time I'm done with him, he will be a full blown switch-hitter, jizzing rainbows and pots of gold!"

We both laughed uproariously at Jon's comment. I told him about the limo incident following Tracy's birthday party, when I had called Eugene a leprechaun and taunted him as Amy blew me. Jon found it hilarious, crediting himself for my drug and alcohol-fueled behavior that evening.

"I've taught you well, haven't I? My little Bitch." He put his arm around me and landed a quick kiss on my lips before I was able to react, then spanked my arse cheek. HARD. I felt my face turn red with minor annoyance but I forced a chuckle.

"I'm nobody's bitch," I argued with a nervous laugh as we walked back outside, my hand rubbing my sore buttock.

"Except for mine," Jon challenged, his green eyes glowing ominously as he looked at me, betraying the lightheartedness of his smile. When he got that look in his eyes, the unspoken message was, "Don't fuck with me." A fucked-with Jon was a dangerous Jon.

He was the most hardcore sadist I knew, in and out of the bedroom. Whereas I displayed a show of force to avoid using it, Jon was a man of action, preferring to speak softly and catch the other person by surprise. For example, where I merely threatened to cut a girl, his tactic was to simply remain quiet for a long time, only to draw the blade against her skin without warning. Jon put it best when he said, "Ken barks, but I bite." He was cunning and sneaky, a true wolf in sheep's clothing. Frankly, I was a bit afraid of Jon...not that I would ever admit this to him.

We stepped back out onto the deck and took seats with the others. Jon took out his cigarette case and lighter, smoking the second of what would turn out to be approximately eighty full-flavor menthol cigarettes imported from Europe, and six blunts full of high potency weed. I bummed an occasional cigarette off of him whenever I was out of my own, and they were unbelievably strong. In fact, the first time I had taken a modest drag off of one, I had coughed, and he had laughed at me, barely flinching as he took a huge drag and inhaled deeply.

It was incredible how much Jon was able to smoke without becoming sick. He didn't even have the slightest bit of a cough, and his stamina was through the roof. Jon smoked up to six packs of cigarettes a day and ten blunts of weed, and had done so for at least fifteen years. Yet, he could still run a mile in under four minutes and hold his breath for at least ten. Like me, he had started smoking at age seven, and it quickly became a daily habit for him. By age nine, he was going through a pack a day, steadily increasing his consumption throughout his teenage years. When I had recently asked if he wanted to cut back, he shook his head and gave his self assured smile. "Nope. I'm in perfect health. No point, mate. Life is too bloody short. Smoke how you want to smoke. Fuck how you want to fuck."

I lit up myself, savoring the taste of clove. Jon's face lit up as he caught a whiff of the clove cigarette and he asked for one. I gladly offered him one of my cloves, and he used the lit end of the ciggy he was already smoking to light it. I watched in amazement as he devoured two ridiculously strong cigarettes at the same time, taking his trademark long drags and holding in the smoke for impressively long periods of time. The guy was a fiend!

Daryl piped up, suggesting we start firing up the grill. Everyone agreed. Jon flashed a Cheshire Cat grin that made it clear he was up to no good, and rose from his chair. He sauntered over to Lawrence, who looked at Jon skeptically. I swallowed, knowing this wasn't going to go well.

"I'll have one of each, please," Jon said in a tone that was a bit too sweet to be genuine, a sarcastic smile spreading across his face.

Lawrence's face turned red with anger. "Um, excuse me. WHAT?" he asked in annoyance, his arms folded across his chest.

Jon appeared shocked. "A hotdog and hamburger," he said, sounding a bit hurt and surprised by Lawrence's attitude. "I'm sorry, I only assumed you were manning the grill because you're such a talented cook. I meant no offense. I can certainly make it myself. Why are you so angry?" Jon appeared genuinely concerned that he had annoyed my brother.

Lawrence swallowed and blushed slightly, appearing a bit ashamed that he had snapped at Jon. "I-I'm not angry," he stammered, in a rare display of sheepishness. "I will make it for you. It's fine." He turned towards the grill and began cooking hotdogs and hamburgers for Jon and whoever else wanted them.

"Thank you, Lawrence," Jon said, his sarcastic tone returning as he sat back down, a satisfied smirk on his face. I could see how Lawrence found Jon to be an obnoxious pain in the arse. Still, he was my friend and I adored him - dick behavior and all.

Lawrence's irritation returned when he noticed Jon's sarcastic tone and facial expression. "Oh and for your information, I'm not a cook. I'm a chef. An EXECUTIVE chef, if you wish to get technical."

Jon smiled brightly as smoke trailed out of his nose, delighting in the opportunity to fuck with Lawrence some more. "Oh, an 'EXECUTIVE' chef. Is that what they call it now? Tell me," he continued as he ashed his ciggies and took another drag, "Do you cook food or do you... CHEF it?" He raised an eyebrow at my brother as he awaited an answer, smoke billowing out of his nose and mouth. I bit my tongue to keep from laughing, mostly from discomfort. The others looked on with amusement.

Lawrence turned beet red, trying his best to hold it together and not blow up at Jon. "Look," he began, "I'm trying to be nice and make you some food. What you just said was unnecessary. Do you think you could quit the rude comments and show some courtesy?" Lawrence appeared sincere, wanting to reach a sort of truce with Jon, who, frankly, was acting like a bit of an entitled dick.

Jon's green eyes glowed hotly as he stared at Lawrence, who appeared a touch intimidated in that moment. I actually began to feel a bit sorry for the uptight prick that was my elder brother, in spite of myself.

A sadistic smile spread across Jon's face. "Fine," he said in a low voice that made it clear he was plotting something. I resisted the urge to smack my best friend at that point. Needing a distraction, I turned my attention to Anna, who was sitting next to me.

"Anna, darling," I began as I ran my fingers through her hair. "Would you like anything to eat?"

Anna smiled and shook her head, insisting she was fine. She wore a lovely black tankini with a low cut neckline that showed off her cleavage. I couldn't help fantasizing about a threesome with her and Jon, and my manhood hardened at the thought of it. There was no question that Jon would be down for it, but Anna had only had sex with me and her ex husband at that point and was still new to edge play. Pitching the idea to her would take a lot of finesse - and a lot of alcohol! Yes, that's what this party needed more of.

"Excuse me for a few moments," I said to Anna. Then I got up from my chair, grabbed the bottle of scotch that Jon had given me, and headed to the kitchen to make some drinks. Jon got up, grabbed his backpack, and followed behind me.

He placed his hand on my arse and spanked me once again, a smug little grin on his face.

"Bug off, Jon," I said, mildly incensed. "Keep your paws to yourself. I'm making drinks. Would you like one?"

"Yes, but I want to make my own," he said. "I have a green smoothie recipe that tastes incredible - with or without booze. I brought the mix and I see you have a blender. Now all I need is avocado, banana, strawberries, lemons, honey, and cocoa powder. Do you have all those things?"

I nodded, excited to try his concoction. I took out the ingredients he needed, then let him do his thing. Meanwhile, I busied myself by making two margarita pitchers, adding plenty of the scotch in addition to the tequila. Jon turned up his nose at my choice of booze, insisting he knew a better brand that was well worth the price. When I argued that mine was top-shelf, he raised his eyebrow and said it "wasn't top shelf ENOUGH." He was a huge snob but had impeccable taste, so I trusted his word. I knew that he acted the way he did because he cared and wanted the best for the ones he loved. Still, part of me wished he wasn't so controlling.

About five minutes later, our respective concoctions were finished and we made our way back out to the deck, armed with pitchers and plastic cups. Jon began pouring everyone some of the green smoothie and I followed with the margaritas. Never a big drinker, Lawrence refused the margarita but agreed to try some of Jon's smoothie. He tentatively put his lips to the cup and took a sip.

"How is the smoothie?" I asked, having taken a sip myself and finding it surprisingly delicious. Everyone else agreed, nodding and smiling in approval at Jon.

"Um, it's... ok," Lawrence offered stingily before putting down the cup. "Jon, your food is ready."

Jon cockily walked up to Lawrence with a cigarette in his mouth, that mischievous grin once again spreading across his face. He then took a drag and blew a heavy plume of smoke in Lawrence's direction. Some smoke got in his face, making him cough. In retaliation, Lawrence held onto the plate more tightly than necessary before letting Jon have it, causing the hot dog to nearly roll off the plate. Jon raised his eyebrows.

"Ketchup?" Jon asked in a cloyingly sweet voice. "Could you pass me the bottle of ketchup, please?"

Lawrence looked ready to kill Jon but thrusted the bottle at him. Jon began squirting ketchup onto his plate, then angled the bottle upward, squirting some onto Lawrence's pristine, white shirt. Lawrence's mouth hung open and he gasped.

"Bloody hell!" Lawrence yelled. Everyone stopped and turned to see what was happening. "Watch what you're doing!"

Jon played innocent but it was clear to me that he had done it on purpose. I was able to read him like a book. I had to stifle a laugh, knowing my neat freak brother hated getting stuff on his clothes.

"Lawrence, I'm so sorry," Jon said in an exaggeratedly innocent tone. "My hand must have slipped. That must go through the wash or it will stain. This means you need to take off your shirt." That smirk again.

Lawrence turned red. He never went without a shirt, being self conscious of his body for whatever reason. Diana walked up to him and put his arm around him.

"Honey, let me put that through the wash for you," Diana began. "Did you want to borrow one of Ken's shirts in the meantime?"

I nodded in agreement but Lawrence refused, saying we were different sizes. He was actually a lot broader than me in the shoulders and weighed over 200 pounds so my clothes didn't fit him well.

"It's a hot day," I said. "Just go shirtless and let Diana wash it for you. Come on. Take it off."

Lawrence felt cornered, standing there in his soiled button down shirt. Then Jon piped up again and began to clap and chant.

"Take it off... take it off... take it off..." Jon repeated, encouraging everyone else to join in. Daryl refused and rolled his eyes at his brother. Diana simply stood there quietly, biting her lip and doing her best not to laugh. She wasn't used to seeing Lawrence so defenseless.

After a few more moments of hesitation, Lawrence began unbuttoning his shirt and flung it off in a fit of anger.

"You all happy now?" Lawrence shouted as he stood there shirtless, looking more at Jon than the rest of us.

It had been years since I had seen Lawrence without a shirt and what I saw stunned me. He was completely ripped, with huge arm muscles and ten pack abs. He was built like a bodybuilder. I couldn't believe it. I knew that he worked out but had no idea he was that muscular. Jon looked at him, impressed.

"Well, well, well," Jon began with a huge smile on his face. "Someone's been lifting the heavy weights. You look great, man. Honestly." Jon took a bite of his burger.

Lawrence stood there for a moment, blushing slightly. The others joined in with compliments, including myself.

He cleared his throat. "Yes, well. I try." He grabbed his plastic cup and poured himself more of the green smoothie, taking several sips.

By the end of the night, Lawrence drank more of Jon's smoothie than any of us but stubbornly refused to ask him for the recipe. When I teased him about why he kept drinking so much of it if it was "just ok," he explained that it was either the smoothie or the margaritas, which gave him a headache.

Unbeknownst to Lawrence, Jon had added a wee bit of tequila to the smoothie, convinced it would help my brother loosen up. Lawrence rarely drank and his tolerance was low, so perhaps the liquor had played a part in his willingness to take off his shirt. It might have also been why he finally caved and asked Jon for the smoothie recipe. When Jon appeared flattered, Lawrence was quick to use the excuse that a friend of his "likes that kind of stuff." Jon and I had smiled at each other, knowing full well that my brother didn't want to admit to liking something of Jon's.

Obnoxiousness aside, Jon was compassionate and sensitive, and had a knack for getting people to like him. He managed to win over everyone that evening, discussing video games with avid gamer Eugene, then impressing everyone with his travel stories. Amy and Anna loved hearing about the museums he had visited, and Tracy enjoyed learning about all the cool European nightclubs. Diana and Daryl asked about the restaurants Jon had been to, and he had everyone laughing over his bout with food poisoning whilst in Paris, having thrown up all over a tourist while riding on a bus. Even Lawrence couldn't help but eavesdrop from the edge of the deck when Jon talked about the time he got bitten by a shark while snorkeling.

As the night continued and the alcohol and weed continued to flow, Jon talked about his various sexual adventures. As experienced as I was, Jon was even more so, having copulated in a number of exotic locales. He had fucked on a Ferris wheel, a phone booth in broad daylight, a church, the top floor of the Empire State Building, a helicopter, the Eiffel Tower, the peak of a mountain in Western Europe, Times Square on New Year's Eve during the ball drop, a planetarium, a rock concert, a cemetery at night, a canoe, a heated yoga studio, a bounce house, and, my personal favorite, a parade float during Mardi Gras. He had even participated in a six-way. When I asked him about the logistics of that, he smiled broadly, happy to share the details. Daryl scoffed, then got up to go inside, having heard enough of his older brother's sexcapades.

"Uptight wanker," Jon mumbled with a smirk as Daryl passed by him, making me chuckle.

Daryl stopped dead in his tracks to glare at his brother. "Why don't you shut your MOUTH, Jon?"

"Why don't you loosen UP, Daryl?" Jon countered in a condescending tone. "It's bloody time for you to dust it off and get it wet, little brother. How long has it been for you now, hmm? Seven months without a shag?"

"Leave me alone and mind your own damn business!" Daryl whined as he stormed off into the house. The rest of us couldn't help but laugh at the altercation, and Daryl's juvenile reaction.

"So," Jon continued as he lit another blunt and took a hearty hit, "The six-way played out like this: I was lying on my back, and a sexy man was underneath me, fucking me up the arse. Then I had one girl ride my dick while another sat atop my face. As for the two other girls? They knelt on either side of me, and I had the pleasure of finger fucking these two lovely ladies at once. In fact," he paused, turning to Anna as he took a big hit from his blunt, "one of them was a gorgeous redhead who looked a lot like you."

Anna blushed and giggled, comfortably drunk on tequila shots.

"Her pubic hair was a beautiful shade of auburn. I loved it. Anna, I hope this isn't too forward of me to ask, but are you a natural redhead?" He raised his eyebrows and took another hit from his blunt as he awaited her answer.

She laughed some more and nodded.

Jon smiled and exhaled a heavy stream of pot smoke out of his nostrils. "Care to prove it?"

Everyone began to laugh drunkenly at Jon's question. But Anna stood up from her chair, walked right up to Jon and, much to everyone's surprise and delight, she pulled down her bathing suit bottom, just low enough to reveal the deep red stubble covering her mound. We all cheered and clapped. A sexy smirk spread across Jon's face as he leaned forward in his chair to get closer to Anna, until his face was just inches away from her crotch. He looked up at her, his green eyes glowing with desire.

"I do love the smell and taste of ginger," he said in a voice barely above a whisper. "And not just the spice." He flashed her his megawatt smile, passed the blunt to me, then lit himself a cigarette.

I took several hits from the blunt and was getting hornier by the second. I knew Jon was too. Earlier in the night, he had admitted to wanting a threesome with "either of the bloody firecrotches" by night's end. Eugene was a lost cause for the time being, appearing rather sullen after spending a good part of the night dealing with Tracy's incessant nagging and arguing. Incidentally, Tracy and Eugene were getting ready to head home, as were Amy and Daryl. Lawrence and his wife had left about an hour prior. In mere moments, it would be just us three. I cleared my throat.

"Anna," I began, standing up from my chair and running my hands over her body. "Would you like to continue the party inside, on the couch? So you and Jon can get...better acquainted? I'm in a 'sharing' sort of mood tonight, and I think the three of us could have a great time together."

Jon nodded excitedly, looking at Anna with a flirtatious gaze. By that point, she had pulled up her swim bottoms. She tilted her head slightly, digesting what I had just asked. Then she grinned.

"I'm game," she finally said.

My cock swelled and I smiled broadly, overjoyed with her answer. My dream was about to come true. Anna was agreeing to a threesome with Jon and me.

Jon and I exchanged goodbye hugs with Daryl, Amy, Eugene, and Tracy before they left for the night, and once they were gone, we retreated inside to the living room and got comfortable on the sofa.

Anna sat between Jon and myself. Jon took a huge hit from the bong that sat atop the coffee table, then passed it to Anna. She took a modest hit then handed me the glass piece. I filled my lungs with as much of the lovely smoke as I could and held it in.

As I have mentioned, Jon was able to hold his breath for at least as long as I could, so our little makeout session doubled as a contest between him and me, to see who could hold in the smoke the longest. We looked at the wall clock at around the same time, and he winked at me. Winking was Jon's way of saying, "game on." He so loved a competition, especially if he came out the winner.

I ran my hands through Anna's hair as Jon ran his hands down her back and nuzzled her neck. She cooed with pleasure, closing her eyes as she smiled. My hands traveled to Anna's front, and I began to massage her breasts through the silky material of her bathing suit, eventually slipping my hand underneath so I could feel her bare skin. Her soft flesh felt so good in my hands, and I loved the way goosebumps formed on her skin. Her nipples hardened and she moaned.

Jon, always the bold sort, glided his hand down her stomach until he reached her crotch, gently grazing her mound through her swimsuit bottom. Anna parted her legs slightly, allowing Jon to caress her inner thighs.

The clock revealed that three minutes had passed, and neither Jon nor I had taken a breath in that time. My lungs tingled pleasantly as I continued to hold my breath, my hands traveling to the hem of Anna's bathing suit top. I quickly took it off, exposing her glorious breasts in all their glory.

Jon quickly helped himself to a handful of one of her breasts, squeezing gently for a few minutes then slapping it slightly, making her giggle in surprise. Jon had a penchant for starting out very gentle with a girl, so she would let down her guard during sex. Then, without warning, he would become unbelievably rough. I once saw him slap a girl in the face thirty times without stopping, and very hard at that. She had wound up with a split lip, bruised cheeks, a black eye, and a nosebleed. It had happened towards the end of a threesome, and my job had been to hold down her arms while Jon brutalized her.

I squeezed her other breast, pinching her nipple hard enough to make her wince. Jon followed suit, using more pressure than I did. Anna gasped. Nipple play and needle play were among Jon's fetishes, and he had pierced, tortured, or otherwise manipulated quite a few nipples over the years. So I was not at all surprised when Jon pulled a roach clip out of his swimsuit pocket and pinched it open, rapidly placing it on Anna's nipple. She squealed in pain, reaching with her hand to remove the roach clip. Jon grabbed her hand roughly and smiled sadistically. After a few more agonizing moments, he removed the clip from her nipple.

Eight minutes had passed, and the need for air began to occupy my thoughts more than it had a few minutes prior. Still, I pressed on, distracting myself with Anna's breasts. I licked and sucked at one of them, letting her soft flesh fill my mouth. Jon busied himself with her other breast, licking and biting at the sore nipple. A vein popped out of his forehead and the color of his face was slightly pink, but he continued to hold his breath, determined to win this little contest.

Anna moaned as we sucked and fondled her breasts, occasionally caressing her crotch through her bathing suit bottom. Jon eventually slid his hand underneath her bottom, running his fingers lightly over her stubble and even more lightly over her pussy lips. She tilted her head back in pleasure as he caressed her ladybits. He smiled gently, pleased to see her so aroused. I couldn't wait to see them fuck.

Ten minutes had passed since either of us had drawn a breath, and I was beginning to feel light headed. I caressed Anna's legs and forced myself to continue to hold my breath, noticing Jon's expression as he watched me. A tiny smirk spread across his ever-reddening face as he saw me struggle. The little bastard was going to beat me, yet again.

By the ten and a half minute mark, I couldn't take it anymore and let go of my breath, gasping for air right away. Jon kept on, grazing his fingers along Anna's inner thighs and half-covered pussy, a smug, "I told you so" grin on his face. Once the clock revealed that eleven and a half minutes had passed, he gently exhaled as if he had only been holding his breath for a short time. He smiled broadly and winked at me, thoroughly pleased with himself. Without skipping a beat, he got on his knees and situated himself between Anna's legs so his face was in front of her crotch. He smiled up at her.

"May I remove your panties, madam?" Jon asked in a low, sexy voice.

Anna nodded. "Yes. But I have a confession."

"What's that?" Jon asked, as he placed his hands on her swim bottoms, ready to pull them off.

"I have my period," Anna admitted, biting her lip shyly.

Jon smiled brightly. "I know."

Anna raised her eyebrows. "You do? How can you tell?"

"When we were outside and you proved to me that you were a natural redhead, I could make out the scent. I find it very arousing. In fact, period sex is a fetish of mine. Are you down for it? Hmm?" He rubbed his hands up and down her inner thighs, kissing her mound gently as he awaited her answer.

Anna looked over at me, and I smiled sexily. She'd had sex with me on her period twice before, but we had been in the shower both times. I knew that she was self conscious about having sex during her period, so I didn't push the issue, or the fact that I had the same fetish as Jon. Still, I so wanted to go down on her during that time of the month, to taste her and feel her warm, sticky blood on my cock as well as on the rest of my body. The thought aroused me to no end!

"If you're not grossed out by it, then fine," she said with a smile.

"On the contrary," Jon said with a huge grin, as he pulled down Anna's swim bottoms with his teeth, revealing her naked crotch in all its auburn glory.

I sighed and began to fondle myself. Sweat broke out on my brow as Jon knelt before her vagina, gently kissing her inner thighs as he took the time to caress her clit. She moaned and smiled as he felt her up. This was becoming too much. We needed to go to the bedroom and start fucking!

"Let's retreat to the bedroom, shall we?" I suggested breathlessly as I ran my hand up and down Anna's back, giving her chills.

Jon nodded. "Yes. Let's."

We all rose from the couch, then Jon abruptly picked up Anna and carried her to the bedroom. She squealed in delight. I followed close behind, smiling ear to ear as I peeled off my swim trunks.

Jon flung her on top of the bed, then turned to me.

"Bitch. Will you take off my swim trunks for me? So Anna can see what I'm working with?" He raised his eyebrows and smirked for what must have been the hundredth time that night. His green eyes glowed once again, giving the clear message that he was aroused and in full dominant mode; to refuse him would be dangerous.

My face reddened in a combination of repressed anger and sexual arousal. Still, I did what he asked, tugging down his swim trunks with more force than necessary, freeing his enormous penis. He was at least as large as I was when fully erect. He stood at the foot of the bed, grabbing Anna's legs to pull her closer to him. Her eyes widened at the sight of his pierced member. He smiled sexily and knelt down on the floor. I got comfortable on the bed, lighting myself a cigarette as I clicked the remote and turned on my stereo system. Sensual music began to play through the speakers.

"Jon? Anna? You don't mind if I watch for a while, do you?" I asked, knowing full well that Jon loved having center stage at the start of a threesome.

Jon grinned ear to ear and nodded, as did Anna, who seemed to be completely at ease in that moment. I'm sure the weed and booze played a part in her relaxed state.

Jon used his hands to spread Anna's legs wider apart and put his face to her pussy. He appeared to be going down on her but, upon further observation, it became clear that he was pulling out Anna's tampon with his teeth. He backed away from her vagina with the string in his mouth, the cotton half saturated with blood. He let the string dangle from his teeth for a few moments before spitting it out onto the hardwood floor. I fondled myself with one hand while holding my ciggy in the other, loving how kinky Jon was. I took a deep drag and continued to watch the little sex show.

Jon's movements were slow and sensual, unhurried. Anna panted with anticipation as Jon ran his hands all over her, following with gentle kisses all over her thighs. Goosebumps formed on her skin and she began to moan sensually, running her hands through his golden brown hair as he seduced her in slow motion from the foot of the bed.

He eventually climbed onto the bed and positioned himself between her legs, his huge dick grazing her inner thighs and pussy lips as he did so. He enjoyed teasing a girl, holding out as long as possible before fucking. His tousled hair hung sexily down his forehead and his eyes glowed like twin emeralds as he kissed and licked every inch of her. She was breathing heavily and running her hands over his chiseled abs and pecs, eventually grabbing his toned arse cheeks. I knew it took every bit of willpower for her to refrain from begging him to fuck the shit out of her.

He placed his hands on her face, gazed at her lovingly, and began kissing her gently on the mouth. As he continued kissing her, he opened his mouth just the right amount and gave her just the right amount of tongue. He ran his hands through her luxurious hair, moaning with pleasure. The intensity of his kisses built slowly, until he was jamming his face against hers and nearly smothering her, just as I had when she and I first kissed. He pulled at her hair a few times, catching her by surprise and making her gasp. I lit myself another cigarette as I watched Jon take Anna's breath away, literally and figuratively.

The head of his penis grazed her opening, which I knew was dripping wet by that point. He slowly backed away from her face, looking at her intensely, his lips curving into the slightest little smile. He thrusted his hips forward ever so gradually, until the head of his cock made its way into her wet womanhood. He tilted his head back in pleasure and a huge grin spread across his face. Anna moaned and wrapped her arms around his neck.

Jon's thrusts were slow and sexy, and his hips moved in sensual figure eights as he entered her more deeply, gently stretching the walls of her vagina. She wrapped her legs tightly around his waist, her breathing becoming heavy as she did so. I loved seeing Anna so aroused. He kissed her passionately on the mouth, grabbing handfuls of her auburn tresses as he made love to her. I knew it was only a matter of time before Jon cut the "vanilla" act and would begin beating the shit out of her, but for the time being, I enjoyed being a voyeur. Jon suddenly took a break from kissing Anna to look at me, a mischievous smile on his face. His green eyes glowed again.

"Ken, my good little bitch," he began in a soft, slightly breathless voice. I felt my face redden. His little joke about me being his "bitch" was starting to really get on my nerves, and I was becoming more convinced he was being serious when he called me that. I swallowed and took a deep breath as he continued to talk. "Would you fuck me from behind? It's been so long since I've had you inside me."

Not long enough for me, I thought, as my heart sped up. Still, I was sufficiently drunk and stoned enough to do what he asked. So I took a final, deep drag off my cigarette and put it out. Then I positioned myself behind him, grabbing his hips as I lined up my erect cock with his arsehole.

"Oh, man," John gasped as he arched his back, bringing his arse closer to me. "You're such a great friend, Ken. I fucking love you."

I spat on my hand several times and slathered my dick with saliva until I deemed myself wet enough to enter him. Anna looked on curiously, appearing turned on at the prospect of me having sex with Jon. I kept my focus on her, pretending it was her that I was fucking. Then, I closed my eyes, spreading Jon's arse cheeks and gradually entering his tight hole. He moaned softly, timing his thrusts perfectly with mine as he fucked Anna, who appeared to be approaching orgasm.

Jon sped up his thrusts, and I did likewise, eager to get this part of the threesome over with. I admit that the friction of Jon's arse felt great against my cock, but I much preferred sex with a woman. I gave in to sex with Jon on account of him being so persistent, as well as the fact that, even though he was a man, the sex still felt good. One day, I would need to stand up to him, and soon. But, for the moment, I enjoyed the physical sensations running through me.

Jon has always rationalized our sexual encounters as "two friends making each other feel good," insisting it wasn't about sex but more about expressing love and affection for each other, a sort of advanced form of hugging. At age 14, I had agreed with his reasoning, and, to a certain extent, I still did. However, I also believed it was ok to say no - a concept that Jon had a hard time accepting.

"Oh my god!" Anna gasped as she rapidly broke into a sweat and gripped Jon's shoulders, her entire body trembling. It was official: Anna had experienced her first orgasm with Jon. I was excited for her. I tightened my grip on Jon's hips and slammed into him harder as he grinded against Anna's clit, determined to make her climax again. I closed my eyes and smiled, looking forward to fucking Anna once my turn with Jon was over. Just then, my right arse cheek exploded with a sharp pain.

SMACK!

Jon had laid one hell of a spank on my arse, having managed to reach around with his long arm when I had my eyes closed for barely a minute. Perhaps he sensed that I had closed my eyes and took that opportunity to smack me. Despite the risk of pissing him off royally, I was tired of his crap and decided he needed a taste of his own medicine. So I smacked him back, whaling him on his left arse cheek as I fucked him. He barely flinched, as his pain tolerance was even higher than mine. He paused momentarily and turned in my direction to speak.

"You won't get away with that, bitch," Jon warned in his deep, velvety voice, remaining as calm as ever. "You best watch your back."

He resumed his thrusts but slowed down the pace considerably, then began to kiss Anna, sweet talking and caressing her. I gulped, knowing full well that this was the proverbial quiet before the storm. That's right, Jon was going to hurt Anna to get back at me for smacking him. After so many years of being his friend and so many threesomes, I knew his pattern.

"Beautiful Anna," he crooned, kissing her tenderly. "Lovely doll. You're so sexy. Making love to you is the best. I just don't want it to end. This is great." He gently caressed, squeezed, and kissed her breasts as he thrusted even more slowly. "Ken is so lucky. Mmmmm..."

Anna appeared to be in heaven, moaning and smiling as she ran her hands all over Jon's toned body. If only she knew what was in store for her. Of course I would pamper her when it was all over, as would Jon. As rough as he was during sex, he was equally gentle and sweet afterwards. Until then? The monster was coming out.

Jon caressed Anna's neck, psyching himself up for the first of what would be many little "attacks" on her. His hand lightly cupped her throat, which led to gentle squeezing. Apprehension was evident in Anna's eyes as her air supply gradually dwindled, Jon's grip on her throat intensifying. Her face reddened and her hands instinctively went to Jon's hand, pulling at it, desperate to breathe normally. Jon would not loosen his grip. She began making choking sounds, her gaze appearing desperate as her eyes locked with mine. I smiled sympathetically to let her know she was safe with me there. Just when I thought she would pass out, Jon let up. My cock softened ever so slightly as I remained inside him, relieved that he had stopped choking her.

"Hmm," Jon began, caressing Anna's face as he thrusted gently. "You're such a delicate, fragile thing. I can tell that Ken has been coddling you. BABYING you."

Anna shook her head in protest. "No he hasn't," she argued. "He's gotten me to do all sorts of things I've never done before. In fact-"

SMACK!

Enter: slap number one. I winced as I saw Anna's head roll violently to one side as she gasped in pain, tears forming in her eyes. He'd hit her very hard, and a red hand print immediately formed on her cheek. Jon leaned closer to her face to talk to her.

"Do not speak to me that way," Jon warned in a voice that was even deeper than his usual one. "I will not tolerate arguing. Understood?"

Anna held her cheek and began to tremble, realizing she was in the hands of a sadist who was perhaps even more hardcore than I was. She nodded as she held back tears.

Jon turned around slightly to address me. "Let's change things up, shall we?" he suggested. "Why don't we have Anna turn over and get on her knees so I can fuck her up the arse, and she can suck your dick at the same time?" He turned back to face Anna. "Doesn't that sound jolly, my darling?"

Anna nodded and agreed, as I did I. "Brilliant idea," I said.

I gradually backed away from Jon until my penis was free from the confines of his tight arsehole, then I thoroughly wiped myself clean with a towel that was next to my bed. I was so looking forward to Anna sucking me off.

"Ken, can you fetch me a cigarette, and get me my backpack?" Jon asked me as he withdrew gently from Anna, who rolled over onto her stomach. "I have to get some... supplies out of there." His tone was suggestive.

I obliged and helped myself to a ciggy as well. Jon grabbed several items out of his backpack, setting them down on the nightstand. One of of the items happened to be a gigantic two-way dildo. The other items were too small to make out in the dim light of the room, but I reckoned that they were drug related. Aside from having an affinity for pot, Jon had a weakness for pills and cocaine.

I took a deep drag off my ciggy before positioning myself before Anna, who got on all fours. We exchanged smiles as I bent down to kiss her. Jon placed his ciggy in his mouth as he climbed back onto the bed, getting behind Anna and gently grabbing her hip as he lined up his cock with her arsehole. I continued to kiss her, then her body jolted forward violently, her head nearly hitting mine. She squealed in pain and surprise, unprepared for the roughness with which Jon had entered her back door. It appeared that he had gone in dry as well; I hadn't seen him wet his cock at all. He took several hasty drags off his cigarette before reaching over and putting it out in the ashtray that was on the nightstand.

Anna began to cry and tense up, but Jon wouldn't let up. In fact, his expression was completely cold as he sodomized her repeatedly, his strong body slapping repeatedly against hers. After perhaps a minute, smoke trailed out of his nose. I held Anna's hand as I locked eyes with her, my expression sympathetic.

"You're safe with me, sweetheart," I whispered, as I ran my fingers through her hair and took a final drag off my ciggy before putting it out.

SMACK!

Jon had actually slapped me in the face in response to my attempt at comforting Anna. Completely livid, I glared up at him.

"What the hell was that for?" I asked Jon as I held my cheek.

His eyes glowed as he stared at me, his expression still cold as ice. "No talking."

My nostrils flared. "You don't want me to talk? Well, why don't you shut me up, then?" I asked, my voice trembling slightly. Jon horrified me when he got this way, but this didn't stop me from defending myself. Plus, I didn't want to look like a wimp in front of Anna.

Jon continued to slam into Anna, and gave a sadistic smile. Before I had time to react, he reached out with his arms and began to throttle me. His hands were so strong, and my throat felt like it was being crushed. My dick hardened immediately, and I decided Jon needed silencing himself. So I returned the favor, wrapping my hands around his throat with considerable pressure.

Anna, perhaps instinctively, grabbed my erect cock and began sucking it. I became lightheaded with arousal as my air supply dwindled. It was quite a sight, Jon and I strangling each other as Anna sucked me off and Jon fucked her anally. It was a veritable triangle of kink, and, despite my annoyance at Jon, I couldn't help but get extra turned on.

The veins in our forearms popped as we choked each other, the blood rushing to our heads as we stared each other down. It was a stalemate in the truest sense, and neither of us would let up until one of us was ready to faint. It was just like our first sexual encounter almost twenty years prior, when he had turned me onto erotic asphyxiation before convincing me to suck his dick and "pop his bum cherry," as he had put it. That time, I had been the first to loosen my grip. Now, it was Jon who let up first, so I mercifully did the same. Then he rapidly grabbed the back of my head and pulled my face close to his, leaning in for a kiss.

Before I had time to protest, he jammed his mouth against mine as he thrusted into Anna, who continued to suck my dick. His beard felt surprisingly soft against my skin, as did his lips. Inevitably, he opened his mouth wide and slipped his long tongue deep inside my mouth, nearly gagging me with it. I did my best to back away but he simply tightened his grip on the back of my head. After several agonizing minutes, he backed away from me, a sexy smile spreading across his face as he gazed at me with stars in his eyes. It was the look of someone in love.

"I've wanted to do that for so long," he admitted in a near whisper. "I've missed it. I love kissing you, Ken."

I gulped and forced a smile, wishing he would just love me as a friend rather than a lover.

Apparently energized by our kiss, Jon slammed harder into Anna, making her grunt with the impact. She continued to suck me off, and I so loved the way her mouth felt on my shaft.

SMACK! SMACK! SMACK! SMACK!

Anna screamed as Jon whaled her on the arse multiple times with considerable force. Before she was able to recover, he pulled her hair very hard, jerking her head back as he did so. His breathing became heavier and sweat broke out on his brow. Within minutes, his body was trembling and he was moaning sensually, having a full blown orgasm as he ejaculated into Anna's arsehole.

"Oh, God, Anna," he panted as he grinded against her. "It feels so bloody good."

He slowly withdrew from her then spread her cheeks and lowered his face to her arse, at which time he proceeded to eat his cum out of her. She was still doing her best to suck me off as this was going on. It was a delightfully kinky scene.

Jon backed away from Anna's arse, his mouth full of semen. He rapidly leaned over to kiss me, once again grabbing the back of my head and opening his mouth to share his cum with me. It was futile for me to refuse so I simply let him fill my mouth with the questionable concoction, which tasted surprisingly sweet. Whether the sweetness was from Jon's semen or Anna's shite was a matter of debate, but in either case, I swallowed the contents with a smile on my face. Jon smiled back.

"Ken, how would you like sloppy seconds with Anna while I take a little 'break'?" He winked at me and nodded at the nightstand, where his drug paraphernalia awaited him.

I nodded. "Of course."

Anna looked up at me with a seductive smile on her face, running her hand over my arse cheeks as she remained on all fours. I leaned down and kissed her deeply, as I ran my hands through her hair.

"Anna, my love," I said between kisses, "Would you turn around on your back, so I can see your beautiful face as I make love to you?"

Anna nodded and turned around on her back. I smiled at her and kissed her some more before fingering her pussy gently. After a few moments, I removed my finger, noticing the slightest bit of blood covering the tip of it. I placed my finger in my mouth, sucking on it and savoring the taste of her secretions. My heart rate sped up as I reveled in the flavor of her menstrual blood. My cock throbbed as I lined it up with her ripe cunt, and I wasted no time in slamming into her. I closed my eyes and allowed myself to get lost in the sensation of fucking her, as I kissed her sweet lips and ran my hands through her luxurious tresses. My revelry was quickly broken, however, by the feeling of something cold against my flesh. My eyes snapped open.

Jon was next to me on his hands and knees, a razor blade between his teeth and a shit eating grin on his face. He had just backed away from my left arm. I was able to make out the slightest bit of white powder lining his left nostril.

I willed my body to remain still as I remained inside Anna, knowing Jon would give me a hard time if I moved too much. He found traditional knife play "too boring and vanilla" so he had developed a fascination with razors. I was impressed with the incredible amount of coordination he exhibited as he held the razor blade between his lips and began grazing it all over my body. Anna watched in wide eyed amazement as Jon gracefully moved his way all over me, the blade teasing my flesh as he did so. This was my first time being on the receiving end of what Jon referred to as the "razor dance." It was nerve wracking enough to watch him do it to someone else, so this definitely pushed me to my limit, comfort zone wise.

Goosebumps formed on my skin from the sensation of the blade against my flesh. When Jon reached my front, I got especially nervous and my pulse quickened even more. I swallowed as Jon made his way over my nipples, then my clavicle, gradually making his way up to my throat. His pace was maddeningly slow, and I could tell from the smirk on his face that he thoroughly loved the suspense. He grazed the sides of my throat, leaving the front for last. I closed my eyes and remained as still as a statue, saying a silent prayer that he wouldn't nick my Adam's apple.

After several more agonizing moments, he backed away from me and focused his attention to Anna, who closed her eyes. I held her hands and squeezed them to assure her that she was safe, however relative that safety was.

Jon started with her arms first, gently gliding the blade along her soft, pale skin. She whimpered slightly, unable to contain her apprehension. Next were her legs, and goosebumps quickly formed all over her body as he glided the razor along her shapely gams, slowly working his way up from the tops of her feet. I saw how much effort it took her to remain still, her head trembling ever so slightly.

By the time Jon made his way to Anna's torso, she was hyperventilating and swallowing, tears forming in the corners of her closed eyes. I continued to hold her hands, trying to calm her. Jon moved his way down to where our bodies were joined, grazing her mound with the razor and taking some of her stubble with it in the process. Anna whimpered again, and I knew it took every bit of her willpower to avoid having a total meltdown. Jon moved onto her stomach, then her breasts, where he deliberately lingered around her nipples. Tears fell down her face as she fought against her natural instinct to scream or fidget. That's when it happened.

SCRAPE!

Anna screamed out as Jon abruptly left a cut on her areola. He spit out the razor onto the bed then licked the blood from her wound, which was luckily minor. He caressed Anna's face, causing her to shudder.

"Don't be frightened, darling," Jon crooned as he ran his hand over her horrified face. "Perhaps you could use some help loosening up. I have just the thing."

Jon crawled over to the nightstand and grabbed a tiny baggie of cocaine, showing it to Anna and me. Anna's eyes widened. She had never tried cocaine before.

"What do you say, Anna?" Jon asked. "Care to try a wee bit?" He waved the baggie in front of her.

Anna swallowed and trembled slightly. "I'm not sure."

Jon opened the baggie and dipped his forefinger into it, so a slight dusting of the drug covered the tip. He slowly moved his finger up to her nose. "I think you might like it."

Anna hesitated briefly but eventually caved. "Ok, fine."

She snorted the contents off Jon's finger. Jon turned to me and smiled, the look in his eyes sinister.

"My bitch, may I do a line off your luscious bum?" He raised his eyebrows as he caressed my arse.

My nostrils flared but I nodded at his request. I positioned myself so I was lying flat atop Anna, letting myself thrust into her gently a few times before remaining still for Jon.

He wasted no time cutting himself several lines of coke, one of which rested at the top of my arse crack and one on either cheek. He snorted them rapidly. I breathed a sigh of relief, assuming he was done violating me. But that wasn't the case.

Before I could react, he used one of his hands to spread my cheeks apart then used his other hand to shove something up my arsehole. I yelped in surprise and tensed up something terrible, ready to lose my temper.

"Bloody hell, Jon!" I barked. "What did you just shove up my arse?!"

Jon chuckled before answering. "Relax, honey," he crooned as he ran his fingertips up and down my back, giving me chills. "It was only an edible. I'm going to eat it out of you. Now relax and make love to Anna while I toss your salad."

I didn't even have a chance to answer him before he used both hands to spread my arse cheeks and lowered his face to my hole. It felt invasive and pleasurable at the same time. I took several deep breaths and focused my attention on Anna as Jon made love to my arsehole with his long tongue.

Anna kissed me gently on the lips and wrapped her arms around my waist, perhaps sensing that I needed comforting. Her pupils appeared slightly dilated, most likely an affect of the coke. I did my best to relax and avoid flinching as Jon violated my backside with his mouth. I prayed that he would suck the edible out of my arse and stop what he was doing so I could give Anna my full attention, but he seemed to be taking his sweet time.

SMACK!

Jon landed a heavy blow to my right cheek as he ate my arsehole, causing me to tense up once again. I took some deep breaths and did my best to relax, kissing and caressing Anna as I made love to her. After what seemed like forever, Jon was able to suck the edible out of me, and backed away from my violated bum.

He crawled around to my front, a satisfied smirk on his face as he chewed and swallowed the edible. Then he grabbed the two way dildo off the nightstand and waved it in front of Anna, who chuckled.

Jon smiled at us both. "I'm in the mood for an arse-to-arse," he admitted. "I will get on my knees and take one end up my bum and you take the other end up yours, Anna. As for you, Ken," he said, turning to me, "You get to have your dick sucked by yours truly while this is going on. Does that sound like a plan, darlings?"

Anna agreed to it. I breathed a sigh of relief and nodded, glad that he didn't expect me to eat anything out of his arsehole. As for his fellatio skills, they were nothing short of incredible, so I was looking forward to him sucking me off.

I withdrew from Anna, then she and Jon got into position on their hands and knees, facing away from each other. Jon spat on one end of the dildo, then eased it into his bum. I spat on the other end of the toy and gently guided it into Anna's arsehole. She moaned sexily. Once the dildo was secure between them, Jon began moving his hips, and Anna did likewise. Before long, they had a nice rhythm going.

I got up from the bed and stood at the front of it, widening my stance until my cock was level with Jon's mouth. He looked up at me with a huge grin, roughly grabbed my cock, and rapidly took an impressive amount of it into his mouth and down his throat. The bloke had no gag reflex, and I was in absolute heaven as I closed my eyes and succumbed to rapture.

Jon used his teeth a fair bit as he sucked my shaft, and the sensation drove me wild. I moaned as he grabbed my arse cheeks and made love to my manhood with his mouth for a solid fifteen minutes. It took every bit of willpower for me to postpone climax for that long, since Jon was so skilled.

How was I supposed to give up sex with Jon when it felt so good? Part of me felt violated and exploited, but another part of me felt that the sex was just another way to experience pleasure, which, in and of itself, was a natural and healthy concept. Still, what did Jon get out of it? Was he really looking out for my well-being, or was I simply his puppet? Or worse, his "bitch?" I shoved these conflicting thoughts to the corners of my mind and surrendered to a mind-blowing orgasm, unloading a generous amount of cum into Jon's mouth.

I opened my eyes slowly, watching Jon back away from my member, swallowing my load with a smile on his face. He caressed my arse cheeks for a few moments as he gazed up at me lovingly, his pupils dilated and his body covered in a slight film of sweat. He was high as a bloody kite.

Without warning, he reached over and grabbed the razor blade from the edge of the bed and placed it between his lips. My heart raced as he lowered his mouth to my ballsack and began grazing the razor along my balls. What made the razor play all the more nerve wracking was the fact that he was still moving his hips, continuing the arse-to-arse with Anna. He managed to remove some of my ball hair with the razor, and I struggled to stand perfectly still as he made his way to the underside of my sack, which was especially sensitive.

SCRAPE!

I jumped and gasped as Jon nicked the underside of my balls with the razor. He then spat out the razor and licked the blood dribbling from the wound, just as he had done with Anna's breast. I began to shake as he sucked at my balls and I tried to back away, but he bit down hard on my ballsack then used his strong arms and hands to hold me to him, his grip vise-like on my arse cheeks. My eyes filled with tears as he bit and sucked me, and I felt ashamed at how powerless I was to fight a man who was smaller than me. The wound was undoubtedly minor, but I had never experienced a cut on my scrotum before and it felt very uncomfortable. I resisted the urge to flinch and abruptly wiped away my tears as Jon backed away from my balls, looking up at me with a cocky grin. He loosened his grip on my arse cheeks and began rubbing his hands up and down my backside.

"Good boy," he crooned. "Now get underneath me and suck my dick."

I swallowed and positioned myself on the bed so I was lying partly underneath Jon. Then I grabbed a hold of his cock, and placed it in my mouth. He continued his arse-to-arse with Anna as I did this. His shaft still tasted and smelled like Anna's secretions, which turned me on to no end. I fondled myself as I blew Jon, rapidly getting hard again. It didn't take long for him to come, and he moaned and panted as he ejaculated into my mouth.

"Ken, don't swallow it," he said breathlessly. "Feed it to Anna."

With my mouth full of Jon's cum, I got out from underneath Jon's body and crawled over to Anna, who was still moving her hips in time to Jon's. I loved the way the dildo moved in and out of her dainty arsehole. I grabbed the back of her head and landed an aggressive, open mouth kiss on her lips. She eagerly swallowed the cum and kissed me tenderly on the lips after, a sweet smile on her face. I reached down between her legs and fondled her pussy, which was nice and wet. When I pulled my hand back, there was a fair amount of blood on it. Knowing damn well how much Jon loved tasting a girl's menstrual blood, I crawled over to him and held my hand up to his lips.

"Fancy a snack?" I asked with a smirk.

His eyes widened and a huge smile spread across his face. Then he grabbed my hand and began sucking it clean.

"Mmmm," Jon moaned as he licked the blood from my hand. "It tastes so fucking great. I so need to fuck this. Let's wrap up the arse-to-arse session so my manhood can get covered in this sweet nectar."

With those words, he gently removed the dildo from his arse and Anna did the same. I took a moment to help myself to a line of coke then lit myself another cigarette. Jon had me light one for him as well. Anna then situated herself on her back and Jon got up and stood at the front of the bed, ciggy in his mouth.

"Ken, would you use the riding crop on us while we fuck?" He asked with a sexy smile, smoke pouring out of his mouth as he took several deep drags and rapidly finished his cancer stick.

I grinned widely, more than delighted to be in the dominant role once again. My cock hardened even more as Jon stood at the foot of the bed and lined himself up with Anna's bleeding cunt, energetically plowing into her. His body slapped against hers as he held her legs to his front, his thrusts becoming faster and harder as the minutes rolled by. I put out my cigarette then grabbed the riding crop from the nightstand, getting into position behind Jon.

CRACK!

I whaled Jon in the arse with the riding crop. He neither flinched nor broke rhythm, continuing to fuck the shit out of Anna, who was moaning and panting up a storm. Jon's penis and pubic area became covered with menstrual blood, and he reached down with his hand to spread the blood around his lower abdomen as well as Anna's. He turned to look at me as he thrusted.

"Harder, Daddy," he panted with a smile.

The man was crazy. Still, I obliged, drawing my arm back and whipping him in the arse as hard as I could with the heavy leather instrument.

"Mmm...again, Daddy. Jonny's been a bad boy."

I continued to beat him with the riding crop, until his arse cheeks were covered in pink welts. If he was in any pain, he didn't show it. Then, unexpectedly, he grabbed the riding crop from me and stared at me intensely.

He drew his arm back and rapidly struck Anna in the stomach with the riding crop.

CRACK!

Anna screamed and covered her stomach with her arms, clearly in pain. I couldn't help but wince when I'd heard the leather crop slap against her tender flesh. Jon smiled sadistically, the look in his eyes cold as ice as he stared at Anna. His thrusts were merciless, and their bodies made loud slapping sounds as he slammed into her.

"Ken, hold down her arms," he ordered in a low voice. His green eyes glowed once again.

"But Jon-"

"Do it!" He barked, causing me to jump. It was rare for Jon to raise his voice, so when he did, it was quite startling.

I swallowed and reluctantly climbed onto the bed, positioning myself behind Anna. Then I grabbed her arms and held them down. She trembled and her eyes filled with tears. I leaned over to whisper soothing words to her.

"I will take good care of you after this, sweetheart," I whispered with a gentle smile. "You're such a good sport and you're doing a great job. Keep it up, dear."

"Shut up, Ken," Jon ordered coldly as he glared at me. "Otherwise, I will tie you up and burn your dick with the lit end of a cigarette. Don't think I won't do it."

About midway through this hardcore session, I split a blunt with Jon, which helped the hour go by a wee bit faster. I let Anna take a few hits, much to Jon's annoyance. As "punishment" for smoking some of his weed, he forced her to taste her menstrual blood and she complied, afraid of what would happen if she refused. She had done her best to avoid gagging as he shoved his blood-covered fingers deep into her mouth. Her patience and stamina were admirable, but after being tortured for so long, she eventually began to falter.

"Jon, I need a break," Anna panted.

"No." Jon's tone was matter-of-fact. His hard thrusts continued.

"Please, I'm going to pass out. I at least need some water." She sobbed and began to tremble.

SMACK!

Anna screamed as Jon slapped her in the face as hard as he could, his thrusts speeding up once more. Tired of his bullshit and concerned for Anna's safety, I let go of her arms, grabbed a bottled water from the nightstand, and held the bottle to her lips so she could have a drink. She eagerly gulped some of the water, just before Jon slapped the bottle out of my hand and made it fly across the room.

Jon pointed his finger at me, his face a mask of anger.

"Stop interfering, KEN." His jaw was clenched, as was his fist, and he appeared ready to strike me. I was ready to fight back. The bastard was drunk on power, and I was determined to knock him down a few pegs.

"Anna was thirsty, JON," I spat back.

CRACK!

The sick fuck had actually hit me in the face with the riding crop! It stung like a motherfucker, and I was momentarily stunned. He drew his arm back again, ready to strike me a second time, but I grabbed the leather monstrosity from him at the last second.

CRACK!

I whaled him in HIS face with the riding crop. He hadn't even flinched or blinked, and simply stared at me coldly with those piercing green eyes. Then he directed his gaze to Anna.

"Now that I have my cock and balls and torso covered in your delicious blood, I want my fists covered in it, too. Have you ever been fisted, Anna?" He grinned evilly and grinded against her as he waited for her answer.

I felt the blood drain from my face and saw Anna begin to shake. Our experience with fisting had been traumatic for her, and she had told me she didn't want to try it again. Jon hated being told "no." This wasn't going to end well.

"I did it once but it wasn't my thing," Anna admitted in a shaky voice.

Jon smiled gently and caressed Anna's face. "So, are you refusing?" He asked in a soft, sweet voice.

Anna nodded.

Jon's expression turned cold once again and he stopped thrusting, slowly withdrawing his penis from her and leaning in close to her face.

"That's a shame."

The next few moments seemed to happen in slow motion. Jon grabbed Anna by her hair and forced her to a standing position, then began to half-carry her out of the bedroom. She screamed and squirmed, doing her best to fight him, but he easily subdued her. He also managed to grab both a pack of cigarettes AND a sharp knife en route to the bathroom. I followed closely behind.

"Jon, don't do anything stupid!" I shouted as we entered the bathroom. Jon threw Anna to the tile floor, causing her to land on her tailbone. She

"Anna, take some deep breaths and try to calm yourself," I advised in a gentle voice. "I am going to hold you under for about a minute. If you agree to the fisting, we can wrap things up here quickly. But, I promise that whatever you decide to do, I won't let you get hurt. Ok?"

Anna looked at me pleadingly, her eyes full of tears. Eventually she nodded, and began breathing deeply.

"Enough with the hand-holding and Molly-coddling," Jon interjected as he knelt next to me on the floor. "Hold the bitch under." He put the knife to my throat as he took a drag from his cigarette.

I swallowed hard and blinked back tears before I spoke to Anna in as calm a voice as I could muster. "Alright, dear. On the count of three, take a deep breath. One... two... three. And, go."

Anna took a deep breath and I pushed her head down into the toilet, holding it there. I looked at the clock on the wall to keep track of the time. I did my best to ignore the knife being held against my throat, as well as the smoke than Jon kept blowing in my eyes.

"That's a good bitch," Jon growled as he kissed the side of my neck, causing me to squirm. "See how easy it is to follow orders? Hmm?"

I avoided his gaze and kept my eyes trained on the clock, doing my best to stay calm as I took ragged breaths through my nose. The sharp blade teased my Adam's apple, and I knew that if I moved too much, Jon would cut me...on purpose.

Thirty seconds passed. Forty five. Predictably, Anna let go some bubbles after fifty seconds and I began to ease up on the pressure I placed on the back of her head. At fifty five seconds, I let go altogether and allowed her to surface. She immediately began crying and shaking, and I gently placed my hand on her shoulder to comfort her.

SCRAPE!

I gasped as Jon abruptly ran the blade against the side of my neck. The wound was undoubtedly superficial, but I was still nervous because the man was unpredictable and capable of being much more savage. In fact, he had nearly cut off my nipple during a particularly hard core session several years back. I had lost a ton of blood en route to the hospital, and had required stitches. Jon had felt awful about it, and it was one of the few times I had seen him close to tears. We laughed about it later on, referring to the incident as "Nipplegate," but it had been horrifying at the time.

"Jon, what the hell?!" I shouted in a mix of anger and fear, holding my hand to the wound.

He stared at me coldly, green eyes blazing. The knife made its way to my eye and I instinctively closed it.

"That wasn't long enough," Jon stated in a flat voice. He pulled Anna's soaking wet hair until her head snapped back and she was facing him. She gasped and whimpered.

"Jon, I'm sorry," Anna muttered in a shaky voice.

"Hmmm," Jon began as he glared at her, continuing to pull at her hair. "So are you agreeing to let me fist you, then?"

Anna appeared tongue tied, then simply began to cry. I tried to comfort her again by caressing her back but Jon grabbed my hand roughly and shook his head "no."

Jon put down the knife, then got up to grab something off one of the shelves next to the vanity and knelt back down next to me. Upon further scrutiny, I saw that it was a sewing kit. He opened the clear, tiny plastic box and plucked the largest needle out of it before closing it back up. My heart jackhammered. I so despised needles, and he knew it. He was acting like a total madman! Despite my best efforts, I began to tremble.

He held the needle in front of my eyes with a sadistic smirk on his face.

"Ninety seconds for Anna," he growled. "If you let her come up for air before then, you get a free eyebrow piercing." He waved the needle back and forth, taunting me.

I swallowed and did my best to avoid attacking Jon right then and there. This entire situation was becoming too much to handle, for Anna OR me. Still, I grabbed the back of Anna's head and whispered some encouraging words to her before letting her take some breaths. Then, reluctantly, I placed her head back into the toilet, looking at the clock as I did so.

Jon held that damn needle an inch away from my eye. My body shook and I closed my eyes, doing my best to drown out what was happening. Tears formed behind my closed eyes and I was rapidly losing my ability to keep my cool. I had never once broken down in tears during edge play with Jon, but this was about to change.

As I held Anna's head underwater, I began to think of Jon's and my history - all the things we had been through, and all the times he was there for me. Despite his tendency to be a bully and control freak, he was endlessly patient and generous. In fact, Jon had saved my life on at least one occasion.

The week my wife had left me, I had tried to drown myself in the ocean and Jon had risked his life to rescue me. He had also spent countless hours listening to me cry and complain, and had even cuddled with me when I was lonely and needed to be held. He always had great advice for me, and had given me so many books to read over the years. The subjects covered everything from philosophy, to Zen Buddhism, to self-help. I thought of my wife and how much fun we'd had with Jon and his ex Lisa, all the trips we had taken together and the fuckfests that lasted all night. Oh, how I missed my girl. I was so lost without her. I felt the hot tears fall from my eyes, unable to stop the floodgates from opening.

"Hey." Jon's voice whispered in my ear. I opened my wet eyes, neither a needle nor a knife in sight. Jon's expression was soft and kind. It was the expression of a concerned friend. "Are you alright, mate?"

He gently ran his thumb under my eye to wipe away a tear, and I initially flinched and turned away in shame. I hated losing control of my emotions in front of him. But I nodded slowly. I noticed the clock. A minute had passed.

"It's ok, Ken," he whispered as he ran his hand down my back and gave me a gentle hug. "Let her come up for air. We can wrap this up." He smiled gently.

Without hesitation, I let go of Anna's head and let her come up for air. She gasped and coughed as she reached the surface, and I held her gently for a few moments as she cried quietly.

Jon lit another cigarette, then looked at me as he took a deep drag. "That was a dick move on my end," he admitted sheepishly as smoke poured out of his mouth. "I know you're not a fan of needles." He took another drag then handed me the ciggy. I took a much needed drag and held in the smoke. "I deserve to be punished, Ken," he whispered, before grabbing his ballsack. Then he leaned in close to me as he pointed to his left testicle. "Burn me."

My eyes widened. "What?" I asked in disbelief as I exhaled the smoke. "With the cigarette?"

Jon nodded. "I can take it," he assured me in his deep voice.

I sighed and, with a shaky hand, lowered the lit end to his left testicle until it made contact with his skin. The sizzling noise made me cringe. Anna looked on in horror, whimpering as fresh tears spilled down her cheeks. Jon bit his lip and began breathing heavily, remaining incredibly calm as I left a second degree burn on a sensitive part of his anatomy. After perhaps three seconds, I began to lift the cigarette from his skin, but the crazy bastard actually held my hand there for a solid ten seconds, smiling tightly at me with a red face. Clearly he was in pain, but felt that he deserved it for what he'd done to Anna and me.

I finally yanked my hand away, sick of hurting him. I looked at the ugly burn I had left on his testicle, knowing he would need first aid to the wound right away. I grabbed the antiseptic, bandages, and first aid cream from the cabinet under the sink, quickly cleaning and dressing his wound. Then he turned his attention to Anna, who appeared so exhausted and haggard after enduring hours of rough sex and torture, and it wasn't over yet.

Jon looked at her with an expression of pity and sadness. "Anna, dear," he began softly, "I'm a bit... disappointed that you don't want to try the fisting. See, I can tell how strong you are, and I know you're capable of handling so much more than you think. It upsets me that you aren't applying yourself. Don't you want to make me proud?" He looked at her pleadingly, rubbing her leg as he waited for her answer.

She shook slightly, considering what Jon had said. I could tell she was about to give in, and, in a strange way, I wanted her to...if only to prove to Jon how strong she indeed was. I had seen this strength for myself. Anna was fierce.

She cleared her throat and wiped away the tears that had begun to form. "Ok," she said softly. "I will let you fist me."

Jon's face lit up and he gave Anna a warm hug. I joined in. I was impressed by Jon's ability to get the upper hand in an edge play session without yelling or becoming vulgar, which was, admittedly, my default tactic. Being quietly manipulative had its good points.

"That's my girl," Jon crooned as he helped her off the floor. We exited the bathroom, and I took a much needed detour to the kitchen to grab a bottle of water and the fifth of scotch Jon had given me, as well as several shot glasses. This was going to be an intense experience, and some liquid courage was in order!

I had only been in the kitchen for a few moments, but, when I returned to my bedroom, Jon was already setting up the restraints on the bed. Anna was going to be tied down by her ankles and wrists, her legs spread wide. It was for the best, because if she squirmed too much, she risked getting hurt. Also, Jon would find a way to punish her if she didn't cooperate.

I lit a few candles and selected some new music. We drank a good amount of water. Jon considered fisting to be a transcendental experience, so we did a ritual that Jon called the "ceremony of fists:" we all took a shot of scotch and shared a blunt before doing a sort of meditation designed to clear our minds. We sat on the bed in a circle and held hands with our eyes closed for several minutes, breathing deeply. Once the ritual was done, we were relaxed and comfortably buzzed, so we had Anna lie face up and then we fastened the restraints.

Once Anna was tied to the bed, I knelt beside her and kissed her tenderly, caressing her stomach and breasts periodically. Then I spit on my hand multiple times and began prepping her vagina and arsehole with as much natural lubrication as possible. The fact that she had per period would definitely reduce the friction, and therefore pain, of being impaled by Jon's fist.

As I was doing this, Jon helped himself to a few hits from the bong then crawled up onto the bed. He knelt between Anna's spread legs, caressing her inner thighs before leaning down, spreading her pussy lips apart, and blowing a stream of pot smoke into her wet hole. She moaned with pleasure at the sensation.

Jon began covering both his hands with spit and gave me a sinister look. This alarmed me somewhat, and it became clear that he planned on using both fists on Anna, who'd had a hard enough time handling one of my fists in her vagina with a modest sized dildo up her arse. So far, there were only two girls Jon and I had been with who had been able to handle "double fisting" - my wife, and Jon's ex.

"Anna," Jon said softly. "Close your eyes, darling, and start taking some nice deep breaths. I am going to go nice and slow. Just try and relax."

I knelt next to Anna and began caressing her hair and kissing her gently on the lips as she closed her eyes, breathing deeply. Jon positioned one hand at Anna's vagina and the other at her arsehole, placing his fingers closely together as if he were about to pick up a tissue. Then, ever so slowly, he slid his hands, inch by agonizing inch, into both of her holes.

Anna's initial reaction was to cry and hyperventilate, but I spoke calmly to distract her from the pain and discomfort. Before long, Jon's hands had disappeared inside Anna's orifices up to his wrists. She squirmed and cried as she did her best to endure the sensation of being split open. I knew the exact moment that Jon's hands formed fists inside her, because she let out a sharp scream. Jon and I both expected her to yell out the safe word at that point, but, aside from some whimpers and muffled sobs, she remained impressively silent. I placed my hands on either side of her face and began to praise her. Meanwhile, Jon was grinning ear to ear as he panted in ecstasy, appearing ready to orgasm.

"Oh my god, I can't fucking believe it," Jon breathed. "You are something special, Anna."

"It hurts so much!" Anna cried as Jon moved his fists around inside her, testing her limits.

I kissed her face and neck, doing my best to comfort her. "You're so strong, Anna," I assured her. "Go with it. Relax and try to enjoy it."

Anna panted and cried as she lay there, squirming slightly as she fought against the restraints. But she appeared to loosen up as Jon fucked her with his fists.

"That's a good girl," Jon panted as sweat appeared on his brow. He was minutes away from climax now.

I began to stroke myself. Feeling especially bold and knowing damn well how much Jon loved being jerked off, I crawled closer to him and grabbed his manhood, my grip vise-like. He smiled and panted as I pleasured him with my hand.

Anna began bucking her hips, and it appeared as if she were approaching some sort of climax as well. This excited me to no end, since I had yet to witness a girl have an orgasm through fisting.

"Jon, can you believe this?" I panted as I jerked us off. "She's about to cum with your fists in her!"

Jon laughed in ecstasy as he breathed heavily and continued moving his fists inside her. "This is a first! I fucking love this girl!" He looked at Anna admiringly, who was moaning with pleasure as opposed to pain. He moved his hands faster, and her moans intensified. Meanwhile, I gripped Jon's and my cocks even harder. Before long, the three of us were approaching an earth-shattering orgasm, our moans and grunts drowning out the music coming from the stereo.

I ejaculated on top of Anna's stomach. Jon was still a few seconds away from orgasm, so he slowly removed his fists from Anna's holes, reveling in the amount of blood that covered both his hands. The one that had been inside her pussy was particularly caked in crimson delight.

"This is so...beautiful!" Jon gasped as he admired the state his hands were in. He giggled with glee, letting go a generous load of cum on Anna's breasts.

Jon wasted no time rubbing his hands together and smearing the entire front of his body with the blood, including his face and hair. I watched in wide-eyed amazement as Jon transformed from a metrosexual pretty boy to a blood soaked madman who looked like he belonged in a horror movie. Blood covered his face and hair like war paint. He licked some of it off his fingers, only to eagerly reach down to Anna's pussy for a second helping of the red stuff. Then he slathered the contents over her front, mixing it with the puddle of cum that sat atop her stomach and breasts. It quickly became a runny mess and Anna couldn't help but chuckle at the messiness.

Jon smiled and reached over to me, smearing my stomach and chest with the mixture. Before long, the three of us were covered in a mess of blood, semen, sweat, and vaginal secretions. A shower was in order!

We all made our way to the bathroom, our bodies sticky and red. I was about to take a piss before running the shower while Jon knelt in the bathtub and spoke.

"Don't piss in the toilet," Jon objected. "Piss on ME." His green eyes were dead serious. "Come on. Piss on me, Daddy."

I stifled a chuckle but walked into the tub and stood above him, giving him a golden shower.

He smiled and closed his eyes as he knelt before me, letting the stream of my urine cascade over his blood caked hair, face, and body. He even opened his mouth and drank some of my piss, appearing to enjoy the taste as well. A fair amount of the blood washed off as I emptied the contents of my bladder onto him. Anna simply stood outside the tub with an amused grin, her eyebrows raised. This must have been a strange scene for her to witness, and undoubtedly kinky!

The mixture of yellow and red liquid swirled down the drain as Jon looked up at me with a sexy grin, slowly rising to his feet and kissing me on the lips. His breath tasted like an unsavory concoction of blood, semen, and urine and I nearly gagged.

"Thank you, Daddy," he whispered. "I feel so delightfully dirty. But I know it's time for us to get clean."

I nodded and turned on the water, motioning for Anna to join us.

The three of us lathered each other up in the hot shower, occasionally fondling and kissing each other. Unlike the first experience with fisting, Anna had experienced very little trauma to her nether regions, requiring little more than gentle cleansing and a wee bit of antibiotic cream on her vagina and anus. Jon and I both had minor cuts and scrapes that needed tending to, but we were otherwise in good shape. We took the time to pamper Anna, massaging her scalp in the shower then lovingly applying lotion to her body. After we had finished in the bathroom, we dressed her in a comfortable robe and began cooking a late night meal for her.

Like me, Jon was a wizard in the kitchen and, with my help, made an impressive feast. Per Anna's request, we made grilled salmon with mixed vegetables and baked potatoes. We partook of some of the incredible food, of course. Jon ate an impressive amount of the salmon, and I had joked about where he was able to put all that food since he was so thin. He had laughed at my comment.

After eating, we chatted for a while, then fell into a bit of a food coma on the living room couch. Sometime around 4am, I awoke to change the bedsheets and grab some water from the kitchen before retreating to bed. I quickly noticed that Jon wasn't on the couch. Then I heard some strange sounds emanating from the bathroom. I tiptoed to the door and put my ear to it.

Jon was throwing up. I was ready to knock to ask if he was ok but decided against it, figuring it would be wise to give him privacy. He must have had too much to drink, I thought. But I hadn't seen him drink all that much.

I shrugged and walked to the refrigerator to get a bottled water. Just then, Jon came out of the bathroom. He saw me and appeared startled, then quickly covered up his alarmed expression with his usual confident smile.

"Having a little late night water, mate?" He asked as he helped himself to a water as well. "Wise idea." He opened the bottle and gulped half the contents, then smiled.

I cleared my throat. "Jon, I, um, heard you throwing up in the bathroom. You ok?"

Jon's eyes widened and he actually appeared scared, like a deer in headlights. I had only seen that look on his face once or twice before, most notably when he had gotten into a fight in school and the principal had told him he was calling his dad to tell him about the incident. Jon has always had a turbulent relationship with his father, who was very strict with him from day one. He had appeared panicked during that conversation with the principal. I saw that look in Jon's eyes again.

Jon swallowed and quickly reverted back to his cocky stance, his eyes going back to normal and his mouth forming what I called his "resting smirk." His lips naturally turned upward at the corners ever so slightly. As a kid, Daryl liked to joke that Jon always looked like a llama about to spit. When he told Jon this, he had reacted by holding him down and repeatedly spitting in his eyes, until he was screaming and crying hysterically, begging Jon to let him go. Daryl had been 9 at the time, and Jon, 14. That was the last time Daryl had made that joke, at least to his brother's face.

"Oh yes," Jon assured in his velvety timbre. "I must have eaten something that didn't agree with me. But I'm fine now." He nodded and appeared eager to get out of the kitchen. "Thanks for your concern, mate. See you in bed, yes?" I nodded, then he smiled shyly and gave the thumbs up before heading to the bedroom.

Something was off about him but I shrugged it off and woke Anna, encouraging her to get off the couch and come to bed with us. She happily accepted.

I got very little sleep that night, awakening several times from nightmares, one of which involved Jon trying to kill me with a knife. My eyes had snapped open from that dream, and the first thing I saw was Jon facing me in bed, looking at me with a love-struck grin on his face. Anna lay between us, and Jon reached past her to run his hands through my hair, giving me chills. Then he got up from his side of the bed and came around to my side, spooning me. He wrapped his arm tightly around my waist, his erection pressing uncomfortably against my arse crack. I tried several times to free myself from his grip on me but he wouldn't budge. I eventually fell into a restless sleep, continuing to have nightmares..

I loved Jon, but I did not trust him 100 percent. I had a hunch he was hiding something - if not from me, then perhaps from the world. I was determined to find out what.

Chapter 2:: Poison, Incorporated

"You will feel a slight pinch," she told me.

I sat atop the doctor's exam table, my body covered in a fine film of sweat as my heart jackhammered in my chest. Jon sat in a chair across from the exam table, holding my hand for moral support. Dr. Patel was Jon's favorite plastic surgeon on the east coast, and had done a number of procedures on my best mate, including dermal fillers for his face and micro-lipo for his midsection. I was there for the former, to help with what Jon referred to as my "expression lines," which he insisted were becoming too prominent on me. I had never considered my expression lines to be an issue before Jon oh-so-helpfully pointed it out to me. Also, since I despised needles to the point that I avoided getting the flu shot, this particular procedure was nothing I would have done on my own. Yet, like so many other things, Jon had talked me into it, insisting I would "look and feel like a new man."

When I had asked Jon why he felt the need to get cosmetic procedures done, his reply was simple. "Well, Ken," he had begun in his sultry voice, "I'm a sun-worshipper who smokes like a chimney and parties like a rock star. But I can't afford to look like it, because I'm an actor and a model. Staying young takes work, mate." Then he had winked, before lighting himself a cigarette.

I closed my eyes and winced as the pretty, Indian doctor made the first of several painful injections. None of them were "slight pinches." She did my forehead first, then a few other spots on my face, including what John called my "puppet lines." Once I was fully traumatized and about to cry in front of a woman I had never met, I jumped off the exam table and slumped down on the nearby chair, feeling utterly defeated and ready to throw up. Jon smiled and squeezed my hand as I did my best to avoid losing my lunch.

Dr. Patel gave me some advice on aftercare (I reckon, it was not the kind of aftercare following my edge play sessions, which were much more fun). She also gave recommendations on frequency of visits to maintain the results. Then she changed the covering on the exam table, washed her hands, and replaced the gloves on her hands in preparation for her next patient.

Jon leaped up from his chair with glee and plopped himself onto the exam table like a little boy ready to meet Santa Claus. After having been turned into a human pin cushion at his expense, I wanted to punch him in his smug face. But I simply sat there fuming as we sat in the exam room.

We had arrived in New York City early that morning, and I'd had the pleasure of riding on the back of Jon's pimped out motorcycle for the duration of the ride. The purpose of the trip was a photo shoot that Jon had, and he had insisted that I accompany him. It felt great riding on the back of such a luxurious ride, and Jon got tons of compliments en route - from both drivers and pedestrians alike. We had both scored a girl's phone number. Of course, he went insanely fast for the majority of the trip, and I would be lying if I said I didn't white-knuckle the sissy bar for the better part of the journey.

Jon did not flinch or blink once as Dr. Patel made multiple injections into his face. Even when she got close to his eyes, his face was a mask of total calm. The bloke could handle anything, it seemed.

My best mate and I had been inseparable over the past few weeks, doing everything from browsing locations for opening a second gym, to taking a trip to our favorite amusement park in Massachusetts, to running several races together. We had even gone on a yoga retreat for a weekend. I was there when he bought himself a Tesla (with cash) as well as a second boat, which he insisted he needed for "entertaining." He'd told me he felt that he deserved some "toys," as a way to console himself after Lisa had unexpectedly broken up with him, and I hadn't disagreed. And the sex? Nothing short of incredible. We had no shortage of threesomes, and had visited Rhode Island's largest S & M club, for what Jon called "Grade A, top choice, Providence pussy." Our unspoken motto was, "Work hard by day, fuck hard by night."

Once Jon was pumped full of dermal fillers, he got off the exam table and flirted with Dr. Patel, who blushed and smiled, giving him similar advice on maintenance and frequency of visits. Then we thanked her and shook hands before opening the door. Jon took my hand and guided me out of the exam room to pay at the reception area. Needless to say, the appointment had cost a pretty penny but Jon insisted on treating.

Part of me was pissed at Jon for guilting me into having such a silly procedure, but another part of me was grateful that he had once again pushed me outside of my comfort zone. While Jon paid for our appointments, I gazed in the mirror on the wall of the waiting room. My skin did indeed appear smoother, although some of it could have been minor swelling from the injections. I looked over at Jon and smiled gently at him, and he smiled back. The receptionist grinned flirtatiously at Jon as she gave him his receipt, then we put on our backpacks and headed out into the busy streets of midtown New York, stopping at a nearby cafe for breakfast.

Jon barely ate and merely picked at his food, and when I asked him about it, he said he wasn't very hungry. I hadn't seen him eat very much for several days prior to the trip, either... but I shrugged it off. The man had always had bizarre eating habits, sometimes stuffing himself and other times barely eating anything.

The studio where Jon was having his photo shoot was walking distance from the cafe, so we didn't bother taking a cab. Jon and I both got a lot of looks and smiles from both ladies and gentlemen alike as we strolled down Broadway, smoking cigarettes. Several weeks prior, he had made a joke to someone that we were a "power couple," and I had laughed in a good-natured way to appease him, but I had cringed inwardly at what appeared to be his growing romantic attraction to me.

We arrived at the studio within twenty or so minutes, and Jon introduced me to several dozen people - most of them drop-dead gorgeous. Even the middle-aged, female photographer was easy on the eyes, sporting a full head of long, wavy black hair. The models and makeup artists, like Jon himself, were stunning and possessed a natural beauty that didn't require makeup.

There was an unnaturally skinny blonde with high cheekbones who, despite being around six feet tall, couldn't have weighed more than 130 pounds. Her name was Noelle. Then there was Andre, a handsome, muscular black man in his late 30's, with a shaved head and an easy smile. He nearly crushed my hand as he shook it, then winked at me and made a kissy face. I simply smiled politely. Jon later revealed to me that Andre was gay and had a thing for young white men, including Jon himself. In fact, Jon had slept with Andre a number of times, and had participated in edgeplay sessions with him. According to Jon, Andre was the dominant one. I had a hard time picturing Jon in a submissive role but, after Amy had dominated ME, I knew that anything was possible.

The aforementioned photographer, whose name was Jeannie, took an interest in me and told Jon as much. She loved what she referred to as my "sharp" features. According to her, the intensity of my eyes contrasted nicely with my full, sensual lips. She asked if it was ok to take some pictures of me and I nodded, more than flattered. Jon reluctantly agreed, appearing jealous that I was the center of attention.

"Remember Ken," Jon began, "If you ever get tired of that unsightly ski-bump on your nose, Dr. Patel can fix you right up. Now you and Jeannie have fun!" He winked and turned towards the makeup artists and hair stylists, who were ready to prep him for the photo shoot.

My face turned red and I clenched my teeth after digesting what Jon had just said about my nose. I admit that I had a bit of a beak, but it fit my face and I didn't dislike my nose enough to get it "fixed." Jeannie, sensing my annoyance, put her hand on my shoulder and smiled warmly.

"There is absolutely NOTHING wrong with your nose, Ken," she assured me in a motherly tone. "Don't listen to your surgically enhanced friend." We both shared a hearty laugh. "Don't get me wrong, I love Jon. He has a good heart, but his ego is kinda big. And he's a little too...pretty. He looks like a mannequin come to life. YOU, on the other hand? You're the real deal." She smiled again.

I didn't have the heart to tell her that I had just gotten dermal fillers with Jon so I simply smiled and thanked her.

Jeannie took a fair amount of pictures, having me pose with and without a shirt. Eventually I stripped down to my boxer briefs. She was very impressed with my physique, particularly my abs, which she said "look like you could grate cheese on them." I had laughed. She also complimented my leg muscles, at one time leaning in close to me between picture-taking.

"Between you and me, you have better leg muscles than Jon. If he wants you to get 'work' done on your nose, then he needs to stop skipping leg day. His lower body is TOO SKINNY!" We both howled at the private joke, which, I hated to say, I agreed with.

I loved Jeannie's outspokenness. We bonded as she took dozens of pictures. I had asked at the beginning of the shoot if she wanted me to get my hair and makeup done first, and she had shaken her head, saying that she missed photographing people in their "unvarnished" state, and that I had a natural handsomeness.

Before long, Jon and the other models emerged from the other room, their hair and makeup complete. They wore short robes, since it was an underwear photo shoot. The three of them looked breathtakingly beautiful, almost too perfect to be human. Jon took off his robe first, standing in the bright light of the set. His skin had a bronze sheen to it that made his muscles pop even more. His hair was styled to perfection and his complexion was similarly flawless. He was definitely the most attractive of the three.

One of the makeup artists scurried over to Jon to do what appeared to be a last minute touch up.

"I can still see the scar on your arm," she muttered as she took out her makeup kit and added what appeared to be concealer and powder to the inside of Jon's arm, just below his elbow. It was where he had gotten his new snake tattoo, presumably to cover it up. Jon bit his lip and appeared embarrassed but quickly covered it up with a confident smile. I hadn't noticed the scar up until that point, and asked how he got it.

That deer-in-headlights expression crossed his face again for the briefest of seconds, before reverting back to the usual cocky stance. "Drunken antics, mate," he explained with a smirk. "Last year, I was in my kitchen and dropped a glass full of vodka. It smashed to pieces, then I slipped and fell on the goddamn floor, cutting my arm on one of the shards. Gave me an excuse to get new ink, anyway."

I chuckled at the story, not surprised that liquor was involved. The makeup artist backed away from Jon, satisfied with the job she did. The other models removed their robes and the photo shoot began.

Jon simply glowed as the camera flashed repeatedly. He was truly in his element, and I loved being able to see him do what he enjoyed. It was easy to see that he had good chemistry with the other models as well, and there was plenty of laughter on set. I couldn't help but get aroused seeing the three of them get photographed in their undergarments. Even with his boxer briefs on, it was obvious that Andre was well-endowed. As for Noelle, her B-cup breasts spilled sexily over the tops of her black lace bra. Her matching high-cut bikini bottom showed off her long legs and tight arse cheeks. I fantasized what it would be like to have a four-way with them. I envisioned Noelle sitting on Jon's face and her sucking my dick at the same time, and Andre arse-fucking Jon as this was going on. I got an erection as the fantasy played out in my head.

Jon occasionally got into some eye-catching poses while in his underwear, doing everything from backflips to one-arm handstands. Jeannie smiled and laughed with delight as she took pictures of him in what she called "acrobat mode." He definitely enjoyed being acrobatic, and every morning, he did what he called "pot yoga." This consisted of him smoking several blunts over the course of an hour, while doing advanced yoga poses. His strength, flexibility, stamina, and balance were impressive. His mum had signed him up for gymnastics as a young boy and he quickly developed an affinity for a number of sports. By the time he was in his teens, he was super athletic, and his activities included parkour, cross country running, swimming, skateboarding, diving, rock climbing, wrestling, mixed martial arts, weightlifting, surfing, skiing, and bicycling.

Between the sports, the sex, and the drugs, it became clear from an early age that Jon loved pushing his body to the limit. Some things never changed.

Sometime around 2pm, the photo shoot was finished, and Jon and I once again grabbed our backpacks and began heading out. We stood outside for a little while, smoking ciggies and making small talk. Then we hailed a cab, which drove us through the congested streets of Manhattan. Our next stop was the Palace Hotel, where Jon had reserved a suite for us. On the ride there, Jon revealed that he had made plans for us to meet up with Andre, Noelle, and Jeannie for drinks and dancing later that evening, at a fancy club. This excited me, and I smiled as I pictured us grinding against each other on the dance floor. I was looking forward to the fuckfest that would inevitably follow the partying.

We arrived at the fancy hotel, and I did my best to avoid looking like an awestruck tourist. I had done a fair amount of traveling and had seen some nice places, but there was something especially impressive about this hotel. The decor combined old-school with modern, which I liked.

Jon had scored a suite on the top floor, and the view was stunning. There was a giant jacuzzi tub situated next to the bed, which was a California king with a super soft bedspread. There was an honor bar with a huge array of liquor and wine, as well as snacks. The bathroom was marble and very spacious. The door clicked behind us. Jon wasted no time in "expressing his affection" for me, rapidly dropping his bag and planting a feverish kiss on my lips. He took my bag off my shoulder and threw it to the ground, his kisses growing in intensity. I began to breathe heavily as he shoved his tongue to the back of my throat and pushed me backwards onto the bed. Before I could protest, he unbuttoned and pulled down my pants and underwear, before pulling down his own.

"Jon, wait-" I gasped between kisses.

He put his finger to my lips. "Shhh, darling." Then he tore his shirt off in a frenzy, then removed mine with equal enthusiasm. He snuck in passionate kisses as he undressed us. Our shoes and socks were the last items to come off. Then Jon unexpectedly rolled over onto his back.

"I want you on top, Daddy," he panted with a smile.

I swallowed, hesitating before climbing on top of him. This would be my first time doing the missionary position with Jon. It made me nervous, because the doggie-style position allowed me to pretend he was a woman. This was also our first time having sex one-on-one, and not as part of a threesome. As a result of this, it took longer than usual for me to get an erection. Jon noticed and got off the bed to grab some liquor from the honor bar. He handed me two tiny bottles of scotch, downing a nip of vodka himself.

"Here you go, honey," he said, as he wiped his mouth dry. "This should help."

I knocked back the two bottles of the strong liquor, feeling the effects quickly. Jon grinned sexily and lay back down onto his back, stroking his cock. I climbed back on top of him and he began to stroke me. He ran his hand through my hair. I closed my eyes and smiled, thinking of Anna. Within seconds, I was hard as a rock.

Jon slathered my dick with saliva and guided the head of it to his tight hole. He moaned quietly as I entered him. I bucked my hips and got a nice rhythm going, my eyes remaining closed as I focused less on who I was fucking and more on the pleasurable sensations going through me.

"I want to look at those beautiful, brown puppy dog eyes of yours," Jon breathed. "So open them up."

I reluctantly opened my eyes, initially having a hard time looking at Jon. When I did make eye contact, I had to look away every few seconds to keep from going limp. Jon lifted his legs high, allowing me to slam deeper into his arse. He smiled as he took every inch of me, caressing my face lovingly.

"You're so sexy, Ken," he whispered as he ran his hand over my forehead and cheeks, grazing my stubble. "You look so young now. I love it. But I still like calling you 'Daddy.'"

I smiled shyly as I thrusted into him, doing my best to think of other things, and other people. Despite the mixed feelings I had regarding our sexual relationship, I much preferred being his "Daddy" to being his "Bitch." At least as the former, I could be dominant. I decided to take advantage of this.

"Son," I began in a low voice as I glared at him, "You've been a bad boy again."

Jon smiled broadly, more than happy to participate in the role play. "I agree, Daddy," he replied in a voice that was higher than his usual low-pitched rasp. "I need discipline. Hit me."

I thrusted harder into his arsehole and drew my hand back, slapping him in the face as hard as I could. His eyes remained open and a tiny smile remained on his face.

Had he not felt any pain? Sometimes I questioned whether Jon was human. Perhaps Lawrence was right about him being an alien or a robot. I felt shivers travel down my spine as I fucked him.

"Again, Daddy." A broad smile crossed his face again.

I took a breath, then backhanded him with all my might. He gasped slightly, just before his nose began to bleed. He stuck out his tongue and ran it over his upper lip, reveling in the taste of his blood. A grin spread across his face again.

"Thank you, Daddy."

I nodded and continued to fuck the hell out of him. The man scared me. I closed my eyes, and visions of Anna began crossing my mind once again. Before long, I was on the brink of orgasm, as was Jon. He moved his hips in time with my hard thrusts, occasionally running his hands over my stomach and gripping my arse.

Within minutes, we were moaning and grunting our way to an intense climax, our bodies covered in a film of sweat. Despite my ambivalent attitude towards our sexual encounters, I couldn't help but love the way it felt physically. He knew just how to move and how to touch me, and his back door was so incredibly tight. So, despite wanting a break from the sex, I gave in over and over, on account of it feeling so bloody good!

"Oh, fuck!" Jon called out as he gripped my arse. "Don't stop fucking me, Daddy! I'm gonna cum!"

He gripped his cock and began to fondle himself vigorously. True to his word, he orgasmed within a minute or so, ejaculating all over his stomach. He rubbed his hand all over the slippery substance, licking for a few seconds before putting his hand to my mouth. I grabbed his hand and sucked it clean, ejaculating into his arsehole a few moments after. He howled in delight at the sensation of my hot cum filling his bowels.

"Eat it out of me and feed it to me, Daddy!" He cried out breathlessly. "Jonny needs a little snack before din-din!"

I couldn't help but chuckle at his words. Slowly, I withdrew my cock, knelt down to his arsehole and put my mouth to it, sucking the semen out of him. He moaned sensually. Then I crawled up to his face and planted an aggressive, open mouth kiss on his lips with my mouth full of spunk.

Jon swallowed the contents with a smile on his face, rubbing his hands up and down my toned chest. "Jonny needs a bath, Daddy." He nodded at the jacuzzi. "I'm a dirty little boy."

I nodded enthusiastically and got up from the bed to start running the water. Suddenly, I realized how hungry I was and, once the faucet was running, I walked over to the honor bar and grabbed a canister full of cashews. I offered some to Jon, and he grabbed a handful from the large glass container.

"By the way," Jon said with a mouthful of cashews as he sat at the end of the bed, "I made dinner reservations at this really great Asian restaurant uptown. Five stars. Amazing service and incredible menu. You will love it."

Excited for Asian cuisine, I grinned and thanked him. Jon knew how much I loved that kind of food. He was too generous, having spent insane amounts of money on me over the years. Part of me wished he wouldn't spoil me so much, but another was flattered that he enjoyed treating me.

I know some of Jon's generosity stemmed from the fact that he had a twin brother who had died after a few short months of life, and, despite us becoming friends, he grew up feeling like he was still missing a part of himself. Daryl was born five years after Jon, but they never had an easy relationship. So Jon compensated by developing a closer bond with me, treating me as if I were a "brother from another mother." By puberty, however, Jon began to develop romantic feelings for me. Since then, I had been trying to reestablish more of a brotherly bond with him, but was largely unsuccessful in my efforts. Jon's heart was in the right place, though. So I tolerated his advances and his occasional bullying, seeing them as the price I had to pay for an otherwise amazing friendship.

The jacuzzi was soon full of hot water and we both entered the tub. I leaned against the pristine porcelain, closing my eyes. The jets felt so good against my back. I felt Jon's body grind against mine within seconds, and he was kissing me before I had a chance to back away. I opened my eyes to see a closeup of his cocky facial expression. His green eyes glowed as he spoke.

"Take a nice deep breath, Ken," he advised in his sensual voice.

I began breathing slowly and deeply for a few moments, then took in as much air into my lungs as I could. Jon was going to hold me underwater, whether I liked it or not. And who knew how long it would be before he allowed me to take a breath again?

He forced me underneath the surface, his strong hands and arms pushing on my shoulders as he kissed me aggressively on my mouth. Water entered my nose as I struggled to avoid drowning, nervous and somewhat unprepared for his advances. My head grinded against the bottom of the tub, the sound of the jets deafening. I let go some bubbles as he continued to devour my mouth with his teeth, biting my lips and tongue hard enough to draw blood. I tried to fight him and push myself to the surface, but he was too strong. It destroyed my ego to fight a man who weighed at least twenty pounds less than me and have him win. I felt like such a wimp.

Jon savagely shoved one of his fingers up my arsehole as he kissed me underwater, making me lose a good amount of my breath. It hurt so much and I found myself becoming incredibly pissed off. My anger must have given me strength, because I was able to push him off of me and rise to the surface for a much needed breath. I couldn't have been underwater for more than three minutes, which was a fairly short time for me, but, given the nerve wracking nature of the circumstances, it felt much longer. When I shoved him off of me, he fell backwards and landed against the opposite end of the tub. He gasped upon impact.

"For Christ's sake, Jon!" I barked. "You know I fucking hate when you shove things up my bum and that includes your finger! DO NOT do it again. Ok?" My nostrils flared as I stared at him intensely.

Jon's expression softened and he appeared guilty. He slowly crawled closer to me and I inched away, still not ready to have him touch me. "I'm sorry, Ken." His voice was sincere, and his eyes were a soft, calm shade of green. "I got carried away. You know I care about you. I mean, Christ, I LOVE you, mate." He smiled and reached his hand out, touching my shoulder gently. "Please accept my apology."

I glared at him for a few more moments. He kept looking at me, his guilty expression morphing into a silly grin. Within moments, I began to smile back at him until I was laughing. He began to laugh as well, and we exchanged a warm hug as the water percolated around us. It was impossible to stay mad at Jon Moore. He was just too bloody charming.

"You're a dick, you know that?" I said with a chuckle as we embraced in the tub.

He chuckled. "I am what I eat, mate!"

We both laughed heartily at his comment. I reached over the side of the tub to grab my backpack, taking a fresh pack of cigarettes and my lighter out of the front pouch. Jon's eyes lit up and he asked to bum one off me. I nodded, lighting two of them and handing him one. He was a bad influence on my smoking habit. Since he had arrived back in town, I was going through at least two packs a day. Drinking and fucking always made me crave cigarettes, and with Jon around, I did plenty of both.

After chain smoking around ten ciggies apiece while making small talk in the jacuzzi, we retreated to the bathroom for a quick shower. Jon had a huge assortment of products that he used on his hair as well as his body, and I looked on in amazement as he grabbed no fewer than a dozen assorted products from his backpack.

He insisted on using his own hair products, soap, and washcloth in the shower, stating "quality concerns" as a reason. When he asked if it was ok to lather me up and shampoo my hair, I obliged, on the grounds that I loved being pampered in the shower. Anna was especially skilled at massaging my scalp and body in AND out of the shower, but Jon managed to one-up her. His strong hands provided consistent pressure, and the speed of his strokes were neither too slow nor too fast. I closed my eyes and smiled, allowing Jon's hands to linger around my cock, balls, and arse crack, once again pretending I was with Anna.

When we exited the shower stall, I did a double take. Everything from cologne, to shaving cream, to body oil, to assorted facial products and hair styling aids covered the spacious vanity. He had even brought his curling iron and electric razor. When I questioned him on why he had to travel with so much stuff, he smirked and said, "Packing light is for pussies. I travel in STYLE, mate." Then he took a tube of hair gel and squirted me in the chest with a ribbon of product. I laughed and wiped the wee amount from my chest and ran it through my hair.

We primped for a while, and, as usual, Jon took at least a half hour longer than me. He had even applied foundation and powder to even out what he thought was less than perfect skin. I had helped myself to a bit of his foundation to cover up the bite mark he had left on my lower lip, and he assisted with the blending. Jon was a highly skilled makeup artist, having dabbled in cosmetics since he was a young boy (much to his strait-laced father's horror). Years ago, he had helped me cover up a black eye he had given me during a particularly rough session of fucking.

We both dressed in silk shirts, black dress pants and Italian loafers. Jon had an affinity for clothes with classic patterns, and he looked sharp in his black, button-down shirt with classy white stripes. I was partial to solid colors, and sported a deep burgundy colored top. He leaned in for a final kiss before we got ready to head out for dinner.

"You look so yummy," Jon commented with a tiny smirk on his poreless face as he lit a cigarette. His beard was neatly trimmed and there wasn't a hair on his head that was out of place. He abruptly grabbed my arse and smacked it, taking me by surprise. "Time for me to take my bitch out to eat," he growled as smoke billowed out of his mouth and nose in thick bursts. His eyes once again got that ominous look. It seemed I had been demoted from the role of "Daddy," and had no choice but to settle for being his submissive once again.

I swallowed and took a deep breath, knowing that, for the rest of the night, I would most likely be at the mercy of Jon's whims. I was determined to get the upper hand, if only temporarily.

He insisted that we hold hands as we walked down the hallway to the elevators "just for shites and giggles, mate. It's fun to fuck with people's heads." Especially MY head, I thought bitterly.

By the time we had reached the hotel lobby, Jon wasn't just holding my hand but groping me and nuzzling the side of my neck, much to the delight of several people. An elderly woman smiled at us as we walked past her.

"You boys make a BEAUTIFUL couple!" She remarked with a twinkle in her eye. "I think it's great that same-sex marriages are legal now. Love is love, dammit!" She winked and smiled. I felt my face turn beet red and chuckled nervously.

Jon smiled and waved at the lady, then looked at me with a megawatt grin on his face and stars in his eyes. "Did you hear that, Ken?" he asked as he ran his hands down my front and grabbed my arse. "We make a beautiful couple."

I forced a smile and laughed uneasily as I backed away from him slightly. "You're so silly, Jon," I said, trying to keep the mood light.

Jon and I walked hand-in-hand through the revolving door of the hotel and into the streets of New York. Despite the fact that it was rush hour, he had no trouble hailing a cab, and we were on our way to the fancy restaurant.

The establishment was impressive, to say the least, and the menu was as upscale as the decor. Jon, as always, insisted on treating.

"Order whatever you want, mate," Jon said as he placed his hand on mine and squeezed it. "This is our night. Now that my photo shoot is done, we are on vacation. Enjoy."

I promptly ordered a martini, as did Jon, and we toasted to friendship. As I perused the menu, I found something that, for the longest time, I considered the ultimate "bucket list" item. In fact, there were only a select few places in the U.S that served the dish, and several of them were in New York City. We happened to be at one of those places. The item in question? Fugu.

A type of blowfish, fugu demanded a certain level of expertise from the chef, who required a special license to prepare it. When made correctly, it was relatively harmless. When not, it was deadly, due to the fish being highly poisonous. Emboldened by my martini, I decided to chance it, figuring that if the chef was less than skilled, I would at least die happy while on vacation with my best mate.

The pretty Asian waitress came by to take our orders. Jon's eyes grew to the size of pie plates when I placed my order. For all his adventurousness, he was notoriously picky when it came to food. In addition to insisting that nearly everything he ate be organic or at least super healthy, he had a habit of sending dishes back if something appeared even remotely "off." He was obsessed with avoiding contamination, and had a knack for finding "flaws" in his meals. A supposed bug in his soup or a piece of brown lettuce in his salad was enough to kill his appetite for the rest of the day. His charming personality made up for his exacting standards, however, as did his generous tipping. But, at this moment, his charm appeared to vanish and he looked scared.

"Ken, it's poisonous," he warned with a tremble in his voice that I hadn't heard before. "Surely you would prefer the shrimp or the tuna?" He smiled tightly and did his best to sound calm as he spoke.

"Jon, I will be fine," I insisted. "I'm sure the fugu is very good. Why don't you order the same thing, along with another round of martinis? This way, in case it's a bad batch, we can both die drunk and happy in the best city in the world?" I smirked at him as I awaited his reply. Tired of his attempts at controlling me, my sadistic side was in full swing, and I enjoyed giving him a taste of his own medicine.

Jon squirmed slightly before knocking back the rest of his martini, then he sighed, trying so hard to stay in control. "Fine," Jon said in a resigned tone. "I will have the fugu as well. AND another round of martinis." He smiled and winked at the waitress, who giggled and took our menus.

Jon and I both had to sign waivers, agreeing to avoid suing the restaurant in the event we got sick as a result of eating the fugu. I could tell my best mate was pissed at me, the way he kept sneaking icy looks my way.

"You're always encouraging me to take risks, Jon," I pointed out. "So I'm doing just that." I smiled and winked as I took a sip of my second martini.

Jon simply looked at me with a blank facial expression. This was his favorite way of gaining control of a situation, by remaining silent for a long time and staring a person down with his reptilian eyes. After a while, he would raise an eyebrow and throw in his trademark smirk, his arms folded across his chest. The other person would become uneasy and feel pressured to talk, spinning their wheels as they looked for a distraction from his penetrating gaze and judgmental stance. I had lost count of how many times Jon wound up getting his way by using this passive aggressive tactic. The man could be such a manipulative prick.

It didn't take long for the food to arrive. Jon continued to glare at me with his arms folded across his chest. He briefly looked up to thank the waitress with a flirtatious smile, before resuming the stare-down.

I simply ignored him and prepared myself for the first taste of fugu. Using chopsticks, I picked up a tiny piece of the fish and placed it in my mouth. As I expected, I did feel a subtle tingle on my tongue, a result of the chef keeping a trace amount of the toxin in the fish. This tingle was commonly referred to as the "taste of death," because, if too much of the toxin was left in the fish, the consumer would be unlikely to survive the meal!

Jon watched me eat, refusing to touch his own food. Perhaps he was waiting for me to keel over? I thought of all the times Jon had messed with my head, as well as Daryl's, with practical "jokes."

There was one especially harrowing moment at age 16, where Jon pretended to have drowned to death in his parents' pool. Daryl and I had been frantic, pulling his limp body out of the water and discovering that he wasn't breathing. I was ready to call 911 when Jon's eyes had snapped open and he began to laugh at us. I had chuckled in relief and called him a jerk. Daryl, however, had started yelling at him and socked him in the arm. This had only made Jon torture his brother even more, berating him verbally while smacking him upside the head and pulling his hair. This had continued for ten minutes, by which time Daryl was hyperventilating and crying hysterically, and wound up having an asthma attack that was severe enough to land him in the hospital. I had thought Jon was unnecessarily mean to Daryl that day, and had told him as much. So that night, I decided to fuck with Jon in an especially cruel way.

With my mouth full of fish, I pretended to choke, gripping my throat and making some wretching noises. Wide-eyed and close to panic, Jon sprang up from his seat and rushed over to me.

"Ken! Oh my god, are you ok, mate?!" He placed his hand on my shoulder and was about to either whack me in the back or do the Heimlich maneuver, and a few of the other patrons noticed what was going on. Suddenly, I put an end to my cruel joke and stopped my fake choking. I looked at Jon's concerned expression, a big grin forming on my face.

"Gotcha!" I said in a song-song tone before sticking my tongue out at Jon, who now appeared ready to punch me. I smirked at him as I chewed and swallowed what was in my mouth.

"That's not fucking funny, mate," he hissed at me as he returned to his seat. "That's a sick thing to do. You can take that fish and shove it up your arse. Take MINE while your at it, too. I'm not fucking eating it. I lost my appetite." He shook his head and took a hearty swig of his martini before he resumed glaring at me. "Bastard," he spat.

I sighed as I continued to eat my fugu, allowing several minutes to go by before speaking. "I'm sorry, Jon," I finally said. "That was rude of me.

But you should seriously try the fish. It has a bit of a tingle to it and I think you will like it."

"I will eat it when and if I feel like eating it." He downed the rest of his martini and signaled for the waitress to bring him another. Despite his annoyance, he was beginning to appear more relaxed, and perhaps a bit tipsy. His phone buzzed and he glanced at it. A sexy smile spread across his face as he read a text.

"Who is it?" I asked Jon as I helped myself to more of the fish.

He looked at me with a star struck expression. "It's Andre," he said. "He's bringing his boyfriend, Todd to the club tonight. This young bloke is an adorable white boy, and at least fifteen years younger than Andre. He's delightfully submissive and baby-faced, and I so want to fuck him." He grinned.

I smiled and felt more relaxed, since Jon was no longer pissed. "Well, that's good news. Are you going to try your fish now?"

Just then, his third martini arrived and he took a few sips. "In a few moments, mate," he assured. "I just want to have a little bit more of my drink first. You know me, I like to take my time at meals."

I nodded and drank some of my own martini, thinking of the fun we would have at the club later that night. New York had no shortage of good clubs, and I was excited. I envisioned dancing with Noelle, feeling her up and slipping my finger inside her wet womanhood as bright lights shone all around us, the loud music booming. My cock hardened at the thought.

Jon quickly finished his third martini, then tentatively picked up his chopsticks and helped himself to a modest amount of the fish. He studied it for a few moments before putting it in his mouth. As he chewed, I noticed his somewhat alarmed facial expression.

"I feel that tingle," Jon noted. "I hope it's a normal amount, mate." He winked and smiled, helping himself to some more of the fish.

"Well, Jon, I'm still breathing," I assured him with a chuckle. I was almost done with my fish by that point. "Shall we order another round of drinks?"

Jon nodded as he ate his fish at a very slow pace. I could tell he was apprehensive about the "poison" factor, given his preoccupation with contamination.

"Ken, promise me that if I keel over from eating this crap, you will blow me, so that way I can die with a smile on my face." Jon smiled wolfishly as he shoveled a decent amount of fish into his mouth.

I laughed and shook my head. "You're sick, Jon."

The fourth round of martinis arrived just then. Jon greedily slurped at it, appearing rather intoxicated but at least happy. I chuckled as he ate the rest of his fish at a comically rapid pace, making silly faces as he did so.

"I guess you're not afraid of dropping dead from poisoning after all, seeing how you devoured that fugu?" I winked at Jon, who smirked back at me.

"Perhaps not, but my stomach is gurgling. I believe I need to take a massive shit. Be right back, mate."

I laughed at Jon's crude revelation and he headed to the men's room. As I sat at the table, I quietly sipped my martini and fantasized about how the rest of the night was going to go. Visions of half-naked, dancing women flooded my mind. I knew there would be no shortage of pussy and tits that evening, both on and off the dance floor, and my manhood stool full attention at the notion.

After a while, I glanced at my watch and noticed that Jon had been gone for twenty minutes. Just as I was about to get up and check on him, he emerged from around the corner, staggering ever so slightly as he approached the table with his usual self assured smile. He sat down and took a few hearty sips from his martini.

"I thought you fell in," I chided. "Was ready to check on you."

Jon sighed. "Yes, well, whatever I ate just went right through me." There was an edge to his voice. "For a high end establishment, their bathroom is disgusting. I hated sitting on that filthy toilet. If only you had let me order the shrimp instead of pressuring me into getting the poison fish, maybe I wouldn't have crapped my brains out." He sneered at me.

My jaw dropped and I felt my face turn red. His accusation pissed me off. "Jon, I'm sorry your stomach was bothering you, but I did NOT pressure you into getting the fugu. I merely suggested it. If anything, YOU'RE always pressuring ME to do things I'm not comfortable with, and I wind up doing them because I want to avoid the huge guilt trips you put on me when I refuse."

Jon continued to glare at me, then he took a sip from his glass of water and held it in his mouth. Without warning, he leaned over and spat the contents right in my face!

I was livid and backed away in my chair, wiping my face down with a napkin as I cursed him out as quietly as I could manage.

"Bloody hell, Jon!" I hissed. "Are you fucking three years old? Spitting water in my face like a demented toddler? I can tell you're drunk right now and I know how obnoxious you can get when you've had a lot to drink, but still. We are in a public place - a NICE public place - and the least you could do is show some respect and not resort to childish antics when I tell you something you don't want to hear."

Jon sat there with his arms once again folded across his chest, glaring at me defiantly like a little boy sent to time-out by his mum. He sipped at his martini several times. After a few minutes of silence, his expression softened. He sighed before speaking.

"I was a dick, mate," he admitted. "I shouldn't have spit on you, or accused you of pressuring me. My apologies. And I don't mean to pressure YOU, either. It's just that I love seeing you step out of your comfort zone so you can really experience life. Daryl won't do anything fun with me...well, nothing that I consider fun anyway. And most of my other friends are just as lame. I've had more fun with you than with anyone else in my life, Ken." He took another sip of his drink. "Have we not had some amazing times together?" He placed his hand on mine and smiled gently as he awaited my response.

Once again, Jon's charm had won me over, making it impossible for me to stay angry with him. I took a sip of my martini and slowly nodded. "Yes, we have," I replied, resignedly as a tiny smile formed on my face.

Jon squeezed my hand and flashed his megawatt smile at me. "Thought so. And tonight is going to be epic. We are going to party ALL fucking night."

I smiled broadly, taking the last few sips of my fourth martini. Jon did likewise. After what Jon had told me about how much fun he had with me, I couldn't help but think of how different Daryl was from Jon. I thought of the last time the three of us hung out, which was about two weeks prior to our New York trip. We had met up at one of our favorite local dive bars for dinner and drinks, and all Jon had done was complain.

He had even sent back a salad that appeared "wilted." Afterwards, Daryl had done a hilarious impression of Jon. Needless to say, it had just been Daryl and me by that point in the evening.

"This table is sticky," Daryl had said in a low, raspy voice intended to sound like Jon as he picked up a cigarette and pretended to smoke it. "They have nicer places on Sunset Boulevard, and the waitresses were born after World War Two. I bet the salad here has E. coli. Good thing I brought my fancy green smoothie mix." Then Daryl had sniffed a few times, which Jon tended to do when displeased, or, as Daryl put it, in "snob mode." We had both laughed hysterically.

I admit, despite all the incredible times Jon and I had experienced together, sometimes I preferred hanging out with Daryl because he was lower maintenance, and didn't put me down or try to control me the way Jon sometimes did. Daryl had a guy-next-door vibe about him that Jon lacked. I loved them equally, but our relationships were as different as the men themselves.

After dinner, we decided to go back to the hotel for a while to freshen up and do some "pre-gaming." Jon had some weed and pills that he wanted us to get high on, as well as some psychedelics that I was a bit frightened to try.

When I stood up from my seat in the restaurant, my head spun and I nearly fell over. Luckily Jon had decent reflexes and kept me from collapsing to the floor. He appeared less intoxicated than I, most likely because he had gone to the bathroom earlier. I, on the other hand, felt no such urges and only wanted to get to the hotel room in one piece.

"I reckon my tolerance for martinis is a bit for shit," I slurred as Jon quickly paid the bill and half carried me outside for fresh air and cigarettes while we waited for a cab. He chuckled and kissed me on the cheek as he held onto me.

"It's ok, mate," he assured with a grin. "I'm happy to take care of you."

Luckily a cab showed up within a minute or two and we arrived at the hotel quickly.

Once we were in the room, Jon lit himself another cigarette and took out several bottles of pills as well as a small bong that he used for travel. He packed the bowl full of what he called "the good stuff" and used single malt scotch from the honor bar in place of bong water. Then he helped himself to a few nips of vodka, encouraging me to do likewise. I shook my head, insisting that I was drunk enough for the time being.

"Then take one of these," Jon suggested, holding out a white pill. "It's ecstasy. You've had it before and I recall you liked it. I just took one."

Reluctantly, I plucked the pill from his hand and washed it down with some water. No sooner had I gulped down the ecstasy when Jon was busy cutting himself several lines of coke on the marble nightstand, his cigarette dangling from his mouth. My eyes widened.

"Jon, how many drugs are you doing at once?" I asked with concern in my voice. "Be careful."

Jon placed his ciggy in the ashtray and smiled at me as he held a straw in one hand and razor in the other. "I can handle it, mate. And so can you. Do a line with me. A wee one."

I swallowed and took the straw from Jon, doing a tiny line. Jon made a face that let me know he thought I was "lame" for doing such a small amount but I didn't care. I much preferred the weed, so I took a big hit off the bong, the smoke made all the more potent by the scotch. Within seconds, I felt three times as drunk and twice as high. I had to sit for a few moments, afraid I would fall over if I did not. I held the smoke in my lungs for several minutes, exhaling gently through my nose. My legs barely had any feeling and my eyes were heavy.

Jon laughed as he saw me sitting on the bed, fucked up and borderline paralyzed. He had finished the lines of coke and went straight to the bong, taking a bigger hit than I did. He sat next to me on the bed and held in the strong smoke for a solid ten minutes as he fondled and kissed me. The man had lungs of steel.

The ecstasy was soon kicking in, competing with the weed and alcohol for center stage. I liked the combined feeling of the substances, my limbs feeling light and heavy by turns as my head tingled. Jon smiled and winked.

"I have one other thing for us to try later when we are at the club," Jon revealed with a smirk. "DMT. It's like shrooms, but better. And there's this stuff you take with it that makes the high last for hours. I've done it once before while camping in the woods with Lisa, and it's fucking amazing. Sex is incredible while on this stuff, as in otherworldly." He winked.

I nodded. "I will try it, but only if you do it with me," I warned. My first experience with hallucinogens had been scary, but Jon had taken good care of me. The subsequent "trips" had been pleasant, and, even though psychedelic drugs weren't really my thing, I hadn't ruled them out. So I was curious about DMT.

"Of course, mate," Jon assured me.

We chain-smoked five more cigarettes apiece and touched up our appearances briefly before heading back out, ready to go to the dance club. The others were going to meet us there. My head was swimming with drugs, but I was feeling good. So when Jon had insisted on licking my face and exposing my cock in the hotel lobby, while loudly informing everyone that I was his "fuck boy," I hadn't cared less and laughed my arse off. Similarly, when he had given me a blow job in the back of the cab, I let him do it, and had even bragged to the driver about how talented Jon was with his mouth. The cab driver was thankfully a good sport and chuckled, thanking me for the tip.

Noelle, Jeannie, Andre, and a young man who I rightly assumed was Todd, were already outside the club and waiting for us by the time we pulled up. They all looked incredible, their hair and clothes perfect.

Noelle wore a short black dress that showed off her legs, and her platinum pixie cut was styled to perfection. Jeannie wore a low cut red top with a black mini skirt, with sexy stiletto heels. Andre wore a dark blue silk shirt with black pants, and Todd, who looked all of eighteen, wore black from head to toe. Todd was tall and slim, and very attractive. He was unsurprisingly a model himself. He resembled Daryl somewhat, with his porcelain skin, crystal blue eyes and cleft in his chin. His hair was light brown and he had a dimpled smile. Despite my preference for girls, I could see why Jon was smitten with him.

Always the subtle one, Jon greeted Todd, who he had met only once before, by kissing his hand and grabbing his bum. Then he leaned in close to his face.

"I'm gonna FUCK you tonight," Jon growled at Todd, who turned beet red and chuckled. He was the shy type, unlike Jon.

After everyone had hugged and greeted each other, we made our way inside the club. The bouncer had double checked Todd's ID, having a hard time believing he was 22. Jeannie commented with a laugh at how nice it must be to look so young, adding that, at age 48, she couldn't remember the last time she was carded.

"You look incredible," I assured Jeannie with a smile, putting my arm around her.

She broke into a huge grin, revealing her perfect teeth. "Thank you, Ken! I think I'm dancing with you first!"

I laughed as we all made our way out onto the dance floor. Half-naked women danced in cages, and dry ice filled the air as lights of all colors shone throughout the club. Even the dance floor lit up in places. Women and men alike were dressed scantily, many of them electing to dance with their shirts completely unbuttoned. I followed suit, as did Jon, Andre, and Todd. It was New York City in the summer, and it was a dance club where nearly everyone was drunk or high, so who really gave a fuck?

We quickly ordered a round of shots at the bar before making it out onto the crowded dance floor. Jeannie grabbed my hand and wasted no time dry humping me and running her hand down my bare front. I decided to be bold right back and let my hand travel up her skirt. Surprise, surprise: she wore no knickers! Granted, she was old enough to be my mum but she was gorgeous, so I went with it.

Jon laughed and gave the thumbs up as he danced with Noelle, who wasted no time lifting up her dress and exposing her sexy thong underwear. Jon came in close to her and spanked her arse multiple times as they "twerked" on the dance floor. Sweat covered Jon's body as he moved sexily to the music, his fingers traveling to Noelle's crotch. Her head tilted back in pleasure as he fingered her clit. He kissed her feverishly on the mouth before asking her a question, to which she nodded excitedly.

Jon took off his shirt and handed it to Noelle. His muscles popped even more than usual, thanks to the bright lighting and the sheen of his sweat. Suddenly, he did an air split, rapidly followed by a spinning handstand. He appeared to defy gravity as he did an impromptu breakdancing routine, and, before long, a crowd had gathered around Jon. He spun around on his head and did several backflips, and the club-goers roared. I watched in amazement and cheered him on as he flipped, spun, and leaped through the air with impressive speed and grace. Before long, Noelle joined him and he wasted no time in lifting her up and spinning her around, much to the delight of the crowd. As a grand finale, he lifted up Noelle's dress, exposing her thong as well as her bra, and knelt before her. He roughly yanked down her panties and began eating her pussy. Everyone was going crazy now, cheering and clapping at the little sex show. I looked around me and saw that Andre had pulled down Todd's pants and was indiscreetly fondling his surprisingly huge cock, before getting on his knees to suck him off. Jeannie suddenly knelt before me and unbuttoned my pants, pulling down my boxer briefs with a devious smile.

"You know we old ladies have a lot of experience," she assured as she gripped my erect penis.

Before I could react, she lowered her mouth onto me and began giving me one of the best blowjobs I'd ever had in my life.

Bright lights shone all around us as music reverberated through the air and the dance floor itself. I closed my eyes and placed my hands on Jeannie's head as she deep-throated me. The high from the ecstasy pill was in full swing, and I felt so euphoric as she sucked me off. Nothing mattered but the sheer joy of that moment. I orgasmed within five minutes or so, moaning and grunting as I did so. Jeannie pulled up my underwear and zipped my pants, then rose to her feet and kissed me aggressively, feeding me my own cum. I pulled her hair as I continued to kiss her, then moved my hand down to her wet pussy, finger fucking her. She moaned and began to move to the music as I pumped my fingers in and out of her, our lips locked. It didn't take long for her to climax either, and I withdrew my fingers ever so slowly from her ladybits, sucking my fingers clean before kissing her once more. Suddenly, I felt a tap on my shoulder. It was Noelle.

"I want to dance with you," she said suggestively as she grabbed my crotch. The night was only getting better!

I nodded excitedly and danced sexily, grabbing Noelle's bum and tits as my body gyrated against hers. Jeannie kissed me on the cheek, then went to sit at the bar for a while to take a breather and sip some wine. Out of the corner of my eye, I saw Jon dancing in a sort of circle with Andre and Todd, who all took turns kissing and rubbing each other's torsos. The three of them were shirtless by that point. I knew it was only a matter of time before those horny blokes started fucking on the dance floor. But in the meantime, Noelle was keeping me entertained with her hands as well as her mouth.

She unzipped my fly, pulled down my underpants, and grabbed my cock. Her hands were strong and I loved the way she stroked me. It didn't take long for me to get hard again. As she did this, she kissed me deeply on the mouth. Her lips were super soft and her breath tasted like tequila. I moved my hand down to her crotch and moved the material of her thong to the side, fingering her. She panted in ecstasy and backed away from my face to talk to me.

"Fuck me."

My eyes widened and a huge smile spread across my face. "Have you ever been 'wheelbarrowed?'" I asked her as I grabbed her exposed cunt.

Noelle laughed and nodded. "Just last week!"

With those words, she turned around and bent over, placing her hands on the ground. I wasted no time in slamming my dick into her sopping wet snatch, then immediately grabbed her legs and lifted them until they were level with my waist. She had no trouble holding herself up with her arms, on account of being so slim. Others in the club quickly noticed what we were doing, including Jon, who immediately pulled his pants down and got into a handstand position. With Andre's encouragement, Todd pulled down his own pants, spit on his hand to wet his cock, then abruptly entered Jon's tight arsehole before holding onto his legs. Todd's head tilted back and a huge smile spread across his face as he fucked my best mate, who laughed ecstatically as he remained inverted.

Similar to our experience at the club in Providence on Tracy's birthday, other club goers began fucking and, before long, it was a full-on orgy, complete with partner swapping and blatant drug use. One woman snorted coke off a man's exposed arse, and a few other patrons swallowed pills. I made out the faint scent of marijuana. Within moments, the dance floor had transformed into a chemical-addled buffet of exposed tits, wet pussies, and erect cocks. It was beautiful and erotic, and best of all, there didn't appear to be any security guards to put an end to the fuckfest.

I pounded the shit out of Noelle as I held onto her legs. Feeling especially bold, I spun her around a few times as my manhood remained burrowed inside her, leaning back so her arms broke contact with the floor. She squealed with delight. It was my first time going "airborne" with the wheelbarrow position and I didn't want it to be my last, seeing how much of a thrill it was.

I looked over at Todd and Jon and noticed them switch places. Jon was much stronger than Todd, so he had no problem picking up Todd's legs or spinning him around as I had with Noelle. Just when I thought the situation couldn't get any edgier, Andre came up behind Jon as he was wheelbarrowing Todd, bent him over slightly, and slammed his cock into my best mate. It was the most creative take on three-way sex that I had seen up to that point, and I loved it.

Still holding onto Noelle's legs and remaining inside her, I moved closer to the boys, intent on lengthening the "sex chain" by at least two more people. I slowly let go of Noelle's legs and withdrew from her. She turned around to face me with a sexy smile, her face flushed.

"What's next?" Noelle asked breathlessly.

I raised my eyebrow and smiled suggestively, speaking loudly enough for Todd and the other men to hear. "Todd's going to toss my salad while you suck me off!" I leaned in closer to Todd, who was still inverted in the wheelbarrow position. "Isn't that right, dear friend?"

Todd turned his head to look at me, his face red from being nearly upside down for so long. He wore a huge smile. Jon laughed heartily and let go of Todd's legs, remaining inside of him as he leaned over to talk to his new young friend.

"Go for it, Todd!" Jon encouraged. Andre smiled as he continued fucking Jon, loving every moment.

I smiled broadly and turned my back to Todd, who wasted no time spreading my arse cheeks and devouring my arsehole. If not for the inordinate amount of drugs and alcohol in my system, I never would have wanted Todd eating my arse. Besides Jon and our mutual friend Nick, I had never let another man touch me. But Todd seemed kind and gentle, as well as feminine, so I decided to be adventurous.

Noelle got on her knees and grabbed my cock, sucking me off with reckless abandon. I was in heaven and moaned sensually, as the music pulsed through the floor and my entire body. It was a spiritual experience.

Jeannie approached us with a huge smile on her face, taking turns kissing and fondling each of us. Others on the dance floor began forming their own sex chains and before long, practically all of the club goers were forming X-rated conga lines. I felt as if I were surrounded by miniature centipedes, the segments of which were held together by interlocking pussies and cocks. The thought fascinated and aroused me, and I soon felt myself climax again.

Noelle enthusiastically swallowed my cum and rose to her feet with a smile on her pretty face. She leaned in close to me.

"Let's get high," she suggested in a sexy voice. "I brought a bong and I know Jon brought DMT. It's an amazing buzz. A little intense but I think you will like it."

I nodded and broke away from Todd, turning around to talk to the three guys. Todd smiled and rose to his feet, kissing me gently on the lips before going up to Andre and putting his arm around him. Andre pounded Jon in the arse a few more times before withdrawing from him.

"Noelle wants to get high," I said to Jon. "I think I'm ready to try the DMT." I smiled.

Jon clapped and grinned ear to ear. "That's great news, mate! Let's all head outside for a smoke. Follow me, guys."

Jeannie elected to stay inside and relax at the bar, since she didn't smoke or get high. She smiled and blew kisses at us, and we agreed to meet up with her after we were done outside.

We all put our shirts back on then followed Jon outside, and he led us down the sidewalk to a somewhat private, dimly lit alley to get fucked up. Jon handed each of us a cigarette and we smoked for a while, making small talk. Noelle quickly finished her cigarette and filled the bong with some bottled water that she had in her purse. Then she added some other stuff to it that I assumed was DMT, as well as another substance intended to make the high last longer.

Jon lit himself another cigarette then fished a baggie of coke, two straws, and razor out of his pocket. He placed the ciggy in his mouth then looked at Andre with a smirk.

"Take off your shirt, Andre," he said. "I'm going to do a line off your back, and so is Todd." He smiled suggestively at the young lad, who blushed and smiled shyly.

"I don't know," Todd mumbled. "I already had a lot of coke tonight."

Andre nodded as he removed his shirt. "Yeah, he sure did!" He said with a chuckle. "But do whatever you want, honey. It's our night out." He kissed Todd on the lips then got on his knees, hunching over.

Jon knelt next to Andre, then cut himself two hearty lines on his back. Todd reluctantly followed suit, kneeling across from Jon.

"I'll race you," Jon challenged. "Whoever finishes their line first receives a blowjob, and the loser has to give it." He raised his eyebrow and smirked again.

Todd laughed. "Ok, fair enough!"

Jon took a huge drag off his cigarette then handed Todd one of the straws. "On my count," Jon began. "Ready, set, and...go!"

Noelle and I looked on and cheered as Jon and Todd leaned over Andre's back, using their respective straws to snort the twin lines of coke as quickly as possible. It was a close "race," but Todd actually won, rising to his feet with a triumphant grin on his face. We clapped and congratulated him. Andre got up from his hunched position and patted Todd on the back, a big smile on his face.

Never a gracious loser, Jon rose to his feet with a slight scowl on his face, which morphed into a tight smile. He shook Todd's hand and kissed him on the cheek.

"Good job, mate," Jon said. "I owe you a hummer." He took another drag off his ciggy before putting it out. "But first? Let's get fucked up on this DMT." He turned to me. "Ken, do you want first dibs on this?" He raised his eyebrows.

I swallowed. Noelle stood there with the bong in her hand, ready to pass it to me. I was nervous but decided to go for broke.

"Ok," I said. "Fuck it. Let me have the bong. Just keep me safe!" I reminded with a chuckle. Jon nodded assuringly.

Noelle handed me the glass piece as well as her butane lighter. I took a deep breath then took a modest hit. After a few moments, I exhaled the smoke, then helped myself to more. This time I inhaled more deeply and held in the smoke for longer.

"I think that's good, mate," Jon said with a grin as he gently took the bong from me. "This shit is strong. You don't want to wind up on the bloody moon!" Everyone laughed.

Jon took a relatively wimpy hit before passing to Andre, whose hit was even less ambitious. I gulped, wondering if I had taken too big a hit and would wind up "on the moon," like Jon said.

Todd followed, inhaling only briefly before letting out the smoke, then handed it to Noelle, who did the same and immediately lit a cigarette.

We all stood in a circle, sort of watching each other to see who felt what, trying to sense changes in ourselves as well as one another. Jon lit yet another cigarette, as did Todd. Those boys were both chimneys, unlike Andre, who was a relatively light smoker.

I lit up as well, mainly for a distraction from the inevitable chemical storm that I sensed was brewing inside me, one that would turn my sense of reality inside out. I studied my cigarette as I smoked it, noticing the lit end change color. The smoke appeared to form the shape of a dragon. I stared at it, mesmerized by the combination light-and-dragon show. Everyone seemed quiet. I looked around me and noticed how they were all watching me. Todd giggled. Then Andre, Noelle, and Jon followed suit. Before long they were cackling nonstop. It honestly freaked me out but I forced a laugh, determined to avoid letting on how fucked up I was beginning to feel.

"I told you that you could wind up on the moon, Ken!" Jon chided with a grin as he put his arm around me.

I forced a smile as I looked at him. His face had changed. His eyes appeared dark and evil, the green irises replaced by black and the whites replaced by red. Had I not been under the influence of this crazy drug, I would have attributed the appearance of his eyes to the fact that he was high on the coke and the pot, thus causing his eyes to be bloodshot and his pupils to be dilated. But in my altered state, I only saw a demon.

"You're evil," I slurred, having a hard time forming words. My mouth felt so uncomfortably dry and I felt like I was melting into the ground. I held onto Jon's hand a little tighter, discreetly trying to steady myself.

Jon laughed as cigarette smoke escaped his mouth and nose in heavy bursts. I remembered I still had my cigarette in my hand and took a drag, muttering something about three dragons as I exhaled through my mouth and nose.

Andre and Todd began kissing and groping each other, before suggesting we go back into the club to dance. Noelle nodded numbly in agreement, appearing in her own little world as she stared at her fingernails. Perhaps she was seeing colors change as well?

Jon took my hand and walked with me to the club. Walking felt strange, almost as if the ground were in the wrong place, but I pressed on.

It felt like we had been walking for twenty minutes despite the fact that it was only a two minute walk.

"How you feeling, mate?" Jon asked in a voice that sounded low and slowed down, like a record playing at the wrong speed. His eyes still appeared evil and his teeth appeared pointy.

"Your teeth are sharp," I remarked as I put my finger in his mouth. He laughed and began to suck on my finger.

"I'm a vampire," Jon said jokingly. "But I prefer sucking your dick to sucking your blood!" He laughed heartily at his own joke.

I fucking lost it, laughing so hard that my legs gave out from under me. "Bloody hell, Jon!" I said in a high pitched voice as I laughed hysterically. "You're so fucking funny! Oh, Jesus! Sucking dick instead of sucking blood! I love it!" While still on the ground, I pointed to Jon and announced loudly, "My best mate is a cocksucking Dracula!" My voice echoed through the night, as did my uncontrollable laughter, and several others on the street laughed along with me.

Jon cackled in amusement as he helped me up off the ground and half-carried me through the entrance of the club.

Jon pulled me out onto the dance floor, where he began dry-humping me. The lights appeared painfully bright and the music was uncomfortably loud. The temperature also felt unbearably hot. I felt as if I were burning up, so I hastily unbuttoned my shirt. Jon did the same, a broad grin on his face.

Jeannie approached us, smiling sexily as she danced alongside us, until we were forming a sort of triangle. My head was pounding and I felt like I was about to faint but I forced myself to dance. I looked around me at the sea of bodies gyrating to the music, feeling a sense of doom.

Flashes of light flooded my vision, and I wondered if anyone else noticed it. The bright light reminded me of a cross between a flash of lightning and the electromagnetic pulse effect that occurred before a nuclear attack, like those depicted in world war three movies. I gulped and tried to tell Jon and Jeannie what I saw.

"Did you see the light?" I asked them, my speech slurred.

Jon leaned in closer to me. "It's just a strobe light, mate," he assured me with a smile as he grinded his hips against mine.

I saw the light again, then saw the club go dark. Panic set in.

Just then, the entire club glowed radioactively, then turned an eerie yellow, which darkened to a fiery orange. They had dropped a nuclear warhead on us!

"No, Jon," I argued. "It's a bomb!" My voice shook.

I looked at the clubgoers and noticed that most of them had turned to skeletons, and some others appeared to be on fire. I looked at Jon and saw that he was engulfed in flames. I screamed.

"Jon! We gotta get out of here! The place is on fire! YOU'RE on fire! There was a bomb, I saw it!" I began to cry and shake.

Jon turned to Jeannie, who appeared burned to a crisp. "Excuse us, dear," he said to her as fire shot out of his mouth. His skin appeared to melt off as he took my hand and walked me to the men's room, which was luckily empty, and strangely not engulfed in flames.

He rested his forehead against mine and held onto my shoulders. I had a hard time understanding how his head and hands felt so cool when he was on fire. Nothing made sense to me at that point, but I at least felt calmer in the men's room than out on the burning dance floor.

"Ken, close your eyes," Jon said in a soothing voice.

I continued to quietly cry as I closed my eyes. "Jon, everyone is dead. The world is gone. You're probably dead, too, or at least about to die. You were just on fire." I sobbed.

"Shh," he soothed as he kept his hands on my shoulders and his forehead to mine. "Just breathe, and listen to me, ok? It's just the drug. You're having a scary hallucination. Everyone is safe. I'm safe. You're safe. We are in Club 88 in New York City. There is no fire. There is no bomb. I'm your best mate and I'm going to take good care of you. Ok?"

I stood there crying as he held me, digesting what he had told me in his soft voice. Slowly, I opened my eyes and looked at him.

His features had returned to normal, aside from his eyes appearing bloodshot. He smiled gently.

"We're safe?" I asked. "There's no fire? We aren't at war?"

Jon nodded and hugged me gently. "That's right, mate. We are all ok. Now, I am going to get us a cab soon, and we will go back to the hotel for some much needed rest. But first, drink some water, ok? Maybe splash some on your face so you feel cooler." He walked me over to one of the sinks and turned on the faucet.

I bent over and splashed some of the cold water on my face then gulped some of it down. It tasted delicious so I guzzled as much of it as I could.

We both took a much needed piss. When we were done washing and drying our hands, I turned and smiled at him.

"I feel better now," I said. "I'm in Club 88. With my best mate. Sounds like a rap song. DJ Ken is in the house!" I laughed hard at my silly joke.

Jon shook his head and laughed. "You crack me up! C'mon, let's go back out there for one more dance!"

He took my hand, leading me out onto the dance floor where Andre, Todd, Noelle, and Jeannie were all dancing up a storm. The lights were still too bright and the music too loud, but the fire appeared to be out and there wasn't a skeleton in sight. Perhaps the club owners had removed them, stuck them in the closets? I chuckled at the notion. Jon looked at me with a smirk and asked what was funny.

"Oh nothing, just thinking about skeletons in the closet! We all have them!" I laughed goofily.

Jon's expression turned serious. "Very true."

I continued to laugh as we all danced together one last time before calling it a night.

Todd appeared high as a kite, his body covered in sweat as he jumped and spun around with Andre and Jon in a sexy triangle. I danced as best

I could on unsteady legs, occasionally holding onto Jon's shoulder or hip for support. This arrangement continued for a while. The drug affected my perception of time, so an hour could have been five minutes, or vice versa. My other senses reacted as well. The lights had distinct aromas, as did the music. Blue strobe lights smelled like raspberries, and the sound of drums evoked the scent of burning wood. I felt like I was in another dimension.

An extended remix of a popular 1980's song began playing from the speakers and the crowd went wild. Jon began hopping up and down like a coked-up rabbit as he got behind Todd and held onto his hips. In turn, Todd got behind Andre and did the same thing. Jeannie and Noelle followed suit, as did the other clubbers. Before long, there was a conga line of dancers stoned and drunk beyond belief. My legs were still not working well, so I stood transfixed as I watched half the crowd form a hyperactive, technicolor snake that slid and hopped across the dance floor. That was when I noticed something disturbing.

Todd's nose had begun to bleed and he didn't even seem to notice. Then Jon's nose started bleeding as well, but he kept dancing and jumping with an oblivious smile on his face as the music blared from the speakers. The song lyrics mentioned "poison," or more specifically, a poison arrow. I thought of how much coke Jon and Todd had both snorted earlier. Granted, I was fucked up on hallucinogens but I was coherent enough to notice how high those two blokes were. If they had any more coke, they would surely succumb to the "poisoning" referenced in the song. I walked up to them as they danced, my legs feeling rubbery. By that point, the conga line had begun to break up.

"Your noses are bleeding," I said to Jon and Todd.

Their hands immediately went to their faces and they stopped dancing. Todd's nosebleed appeared to be especially heavy and he looked frightened by the amount of blood on his hand. Andre appeared upset and began walking Todd to the men's room, muttering something about how badly his boyfriend needed to cut back on the coke if he wanted to live to 23.

Jon walked up to the bar and asked the bartender for a stack of napkins, which he used to wipe his nose clean. He smirked.

"I guess we all have our moments, mate!" he said with a laugh.

I smiled and nodded. Within a few minutes, Andre and Todd emerged from the men's room, smiling as they approached us. Jeannie and Noelle joined in, ordering drinks for themselves. They asked the rest of us if we wanted anything. Andre and Todd agreed and ordered some beers. Jon politely refused, explaining that he was bringing me back to the hotel to take care of me, but assured them we would hang out the following evening.

Jon and I hugged everyone goodbye then made our way out of the club. I was still a bit unsteady on my feet so Jon held onto my hand as we stood out on the sidewalk and waited for a cab. He lit two cigarettes and handed one to me, then handed me half of a pill. It was ecstasy.

"It will help take the edge off," Jon assured with a grin. "Trust me."

I took several drags off my ciggy then eagerly downed the ecstasy, glad to have something to "dilute" the DMT. The scary hallucinations had luckily subsided, but my senses were still uncomfortably distorted.

It seems like an hour before a cab pulled up to us, and my legs were about to give way. Jon held onto my hand as he walked me to the taxi and helped me inside. Once we were situated in the back seat, he put his arm around me. I began to feel an overwhelming sense of warmth and love. Perhaps it was the ecstasy talking, but I suddenly felt great. I smiled at Jon, placed my hand on his thigh, then kissed him tenderly on the lips. A look of pleasant surprise crossed his handsome face. This was my first time initiating a kiss with Jon.

"Well, well, well! Look who just made the first move for a change?" Jon remarked with a huge smile on his face and stars in his eyes.

I moved my hand up to his crotch and began to feel him up through his pants, then unzipped his fly so I could fondle him through his underwear. He now appeared absolutely giddy, and quickly pulled down his pants and boxer briefs, freeing his fully erect cock. I wrapped my hand around it as I gazed into his beautiful green eyes.

"I love you, Jon." I smiled broadly at him before lowering my mouth to his penis.

He placed his hands on the back of my head as I sucked him off. What would ordinarily feel like a bit of a chore suddenly felt so natural. He was my best mate and I wanted to make him feel good.

The cab rolled through the busy streets at a steady pace as I blew Jon, who began panting and moaning with pleasure.

"Oh, god," he breathed. "Ken, this is fucking amazing. I fucking love you so much. Oh, sweet Jesus. Oh, fuck. I gotta take this stuff more often! Ahhhh!"

Jon let loose with an intense orgasm, filling my mouth with his semen as he groaned and yelled out in rapture. The cab driver played it cool, neither reacting to the noises nor turning around to see what was going on. Perhaps he was used to people fucking in the back seat. I chuckled as I swallowed Jon's cum and sat back up, thinking of all the blokes who had received blow jobs in the back of that cab.

Jon grabbed me by the back of my neck and kissed me hard on the mouth, pulling my hair and grabbing my crotch as he did so. He was about ready to unzip my pants, when the cab driver stopped the car. I looked outside the window, and saw that we were at the hotel.

Jon backed away from me, breathless. "To be continued in the hotel room," he said with a smirk as he paid the driver and pulled up his pants.

I got out of the cab and found that my legs were utterly useless. Jon luckily caught me before I fell, then he looked at me.

"Fancy a piggy-back ride?" He asked with a smile.

I laughed and agreed, hopping onto Jon's back like a giddy little boy. He carried me through the near empty lobby and down the hallway to the elevator. I giggled as he made airplane noises and other various sound effects.

"Jon, aren't I heavy?" I asked as he continued to carry me during the short elevator ride.

"Nope. You're light as a feather, mate."

We quickly reached the top floor and Jon carried me down the hall, breaking into a bit of a run as he did so. The man was so silly. I loved it.

"Wheee!" I called out in a high pitched voice as he carried me down the hallway at a rapid pace to our suite. Once we reached the door, he set me down and used the key to get in. The lighting in the suite was suitably dim.

He walked me to the edge of the bed, where I began undressing, feeling somewhat warm. Jon lit a cigarette then grabbed a bottle of champagne from the honor bar as well as two glasses. He popped the cork and poured us each a glass full of bubbly, handing me one.

"Cheers, mate." He clinked his glass to mine and we both drank. He devoured his cigarette within moments, smiling seductively at me as smoke poured out of his nostrils.

I resumed undressing and Jon did likewise, as he continued to gaze at me with stars in his eyes. The champagne intensified the effects of the ecstasy, and I was once again overwhelmed with feelings of love. I looked at Jon, and saw him for what he was: my protector. Unlike in the past, I no longer cared that he was a man or my best mate. Gender suddenly didn't matter. He was a beautiful being, and I wanted to be inside of him. I wanted to make love to him. I rose from the bed and wrapped my arms around his naked torso. By that point, we were both completely undressed. I looked into his stunning green eyes.

"Let's make love." I kissed him feverishly on the lips, my arms tightening around his lithe waist.

He returned my embrace with equal passion, his body rubbing against mine as we stood at the foot of the bed. Suddenly, he picked me up and gently lowered me down onto the bed. He lay on top of me, his breathing heavy. He backed away from my face to talk. Tears of joy filled his eyes as he smiled at me.

"You have no idea how happy you just made me," he whispered, planting a gentle kiss on my lips. "I have waited so long for you to tell me you wanted to make love." He caressed my face.

"You are a beautiful soul, Jon," I said in a soft voice as I glided my hand down his front until I reached his hardening manhood. My eyes remained locked with his and I smiled gently. He lowered his face to my shaft and sucked on it for a few moments, covering it in spit as he did so. Then he left a trail of kisses up the front of my body until his face was level with mine. Our eyes locked once again, and there was so much love and kindness in his gaze that I thought I would die of happiness right then and there.

I grabbed my shaft and guided it to his opening, lifting my hips until the head was burrowed inside of him. He held onto my hand, then ever-so-slowly lowered himself onto me, until every inch of me had disappeared into him. The sensations were so intense and so pleasurable, it was as if we had become one with each other. My body felt translucent, and my mind was pleasantly heavy with feelings of unbridled joy and love. In that moment, we were no longer separate entities but the same person - joined not just in body, but in spirit.

We panted as we held onto each other, our lips locked and our bodies intimately tangled together. Our hearts beated in sync. Tiny beads of sweat emanated from our pores. Nothing else existed but us. There was no hotel room, no city, no world outside our cocoon of carnal pleasure. My manhood pulsated with life as it glided in and out of Jon's beautiful body. He appeared to glow as he grinded against me, kissing me passionately. I felt so invigorated by our union. In that chemical influenced moment, I truly believed I could be Jon's boyfriend one day. The notion, once disturbing, felt completely natural.

"Mmmm," I moaned as I ran my hands through his soft mane of hair. "This is paradise." My eyes filled with happy tears.

He smiled and held me tighter as his hips undulated against mine. My shaft hardened all the more.

"Every day can be like this, you know," he whispered with a grin before he kissed me deeply, running his hand over my stubble.

"Every day..." I repeated drowsily, mulling over the idea.

Jon nodded, and he began gently pushing on the backs of my legs until my knees were almost on either side of my head. I moaned with pleasure as my cock went even deeper inside of him.

"You're not just my best mate," he breathed. "You're my SOUL mate."

"Your soul mate..." I panted as we made passionate love. I ran my hands all over his front, sucking at his pierced nipples and fondling his enormous penis, which sported a new "earring." He moaned as I touched his manhood, so I tightened my grip and began to move my hand up and down its impressive length.

"Oh...," Jon panted. "Oh my fucking god, Ken. This is so great. Don't stop. Please don't fucking stop..."

Jon's head tilted back and a huge grin spread across his face as I pleasured him with my strong hands. He got into a bit of a squatting position and began to bounce up and down on me like a giddy young lad, allowing himself to be impaled repeatedly by my maleness. I loved the way he kept falling onto my body, jolting me into a new sphere of pleasure.

Since the clock wasn't visible from the bed, it was impossible to tell how long our lovemaking session was, not that it mattered. I will say, however, that I didn't want it to end. If making passionate love under the influence of that magic, otherworldly substance was all I did for the rest of my life, I would be completely happy. My body vibrated with pleasure, every cell screaming in rapture at what would be my most intense orgasm to date. I held Jon tightly as he made love to me. Our movements gradually quickened, as did our breathing and our heartbeats. It was like music, a sort of erotic symphony where our bodies were the instruments.

My manhood and balls drummed against Jon's sexy body as he repeatedly crashed onto me. Our breathing became increasingly labored and smiles spread across our faces as our eyes locked. His gaze was hypnotic, and I felt as if I were looking into a green abyss - one that was both mysterious and sensual. Jon had me under his spell, and he knew it.

"Faster!" Jon gasped as he squatted up and down at a more rapid pace.

I moved my hips quickly, meeting his thrusts. The slapping sound of our bodies echoes off the hotel room's walls, creating another layer of percussion to the sexual symphony that was our lovemaking. Jon took my hands and placed them on his arse, and I began to grab and slap at his cheeks. He moaned with pleasure, and reached down to fondle himself.

Time seemed to slow down as we made feverish love to each other. Sweat poured from our bodies and our moans grew in volume. My manhood began to spasm and I began to experience the beginning of the most intense orgasm I'd ever experienced. Jon started to climax himself and he touched his throbbing member with increased feverishness, moaning and grunting loudly as he did so.

"Ohhhh!" Jon cried out as he pleasured himself, still maintaining the rhythm of his energetic thrusts. "Oh, Ken! Oh fuck! I love you!"

With those words, he ejaculated all over my stomach. His warm semen felt so good against my skin, I couldn't help but place my hand in the puddle and rub it all over my front. I let go a moan as I moved my hips even faster. Jon smiled.

"That's it," Jon encouraged breathlessly as he caressed my face. "Come for me, Ken." He leaned over and kissed me passionately. That did it for me.

I grabbed the back of Jon's head so I could kiss him more deeply, reveling in the taste and the smell of him. The aroma of tobacco intermingled with the scent of cologne and champagne, and the combination drove me wild. My toes curled up and my entire body tingled. My manhood spasmed once more and before long, I was letting go several generous loads of cum into Jon's body. I wailed in ecstasy as I came, as did Jon.

Our sweaty bodies remained joined for a while, and he lay atop me, holding and kissing me. I could feel his heart beat as he rested on me. He loved the way his semen covered my abdomen and chest and he enjoyed sliding his own stomach against mine, so he could be covered in it. As he lay on me, I grabbed his arse and gently withdrew my penis then slid my finger into his bum, loving the way my cum seeped out of his opening and covered my finger. Then I removed my finger and placed it in my mouth, so I could taste our combined secretions. Before I had time to swallow, Jon kissed me on the mouth, sucking and swallowing as much of the semen as he could. He looked at me intensely and ran his fingers through my hair.

"That was so fucking beautiful," he whispered with a sexy smile on his face. His hypnotic green eyes glowed with passion.

"I love your eyes, Jon," I remarked.

He chuckled. "I love YOU, mate."

"Likewise."

We lay there holding each other for an indeterminate period of time. I felt so incredibly relaxed and peaceful. My eyes grew heavy, as did my body, and I felt sleep beckoning me. I twitched a few times, startling myself awake. Jon kissed and held me, eventually climbing off of me and lying next to me with his arm around my waist. I felt so safe with him in that moment, so cared for.

"You're my protector," I mumbled sleepily. "Thank you for keeping me so safe, and for loving me so much."

Jon chuckled gently. "Well, um, I have a confession, mate."

I opened my eyes and turned onto my side to face him. "What's that?"

"I don't just love you," he began. "I'm IN LOVE with you. I have been for quite some time. Now, I know that you prefer girls, and that you're probably not ready for a relationship yet, with anyone. But if that changes and you ever find yourself wanting to...broaden your horizons, just know that I'm here. I know how to take care of you, and I think we would make a great couple. But like I said, I respect whatever decision you make and I'm still your best mate no matter what. I just wanted to share my feelings with you."

I smiled gently at him, not at all surprised at his confession. "Thank you for telling me, Jon. I love you so much. But you're right, I'm still not ready for a relationship with anyone - male, female, or anything in between!" I chuckled, as did Jon. "And I do prefer girls. BUT, if I were to, as you put it, 'broaden my horizons,' you're the only man I would want to be with." I kissed him gently on the lips.

Jon sighed with relief. "That's good to hear. To be honest, I wasn't sure if you would be creeped out by what I had to say. I didn't want you to think I was trying to 'convert' you."

I laughed. "Jon, I just had the most amazing sex of my life, with YOU. A MAN. If anyone could 'convert' me to bisexuality, it's Mr. Jon Moore!"

We both broke into raucous laughter at my comment.

"You're too much, Ken!" Jon said with a laugh as he sat up slowly. "Well I must take a piss and perhaps sit in the jacuzzi for a while before bed. Care to join me?"

I nodded.

Jon lit himself a cigarette then grabbed a bag of coke, straw and razor from the nightstand. "I think I need a little 'nightcap,'" Jon said with a smirk before going into the bathroom.

I got up from the bed and went over to the jacuzzi to turn on the water. As I waited for the tub to fill up, I poured myself another glass of champagne, then sat at the edge of the tub. The warm water felt so good on my feet, and the champagne tasted amazing. This was the life!

Jon emerged from the bathroom looking slightly crazed, as if he had seen a ghost. A cigarette dangled from his mouth, and he intermittently took drags from it, letting the ash fall onto the carpet. It was obvious that he was high as hell. He lowered himself into the jacuzzi on shaky legs, placing the ciggy in the ashtray that sat at the edge of the tub. His eyes darted around the room. As soon as he looked at me and noticed my concerned facial expression, he did his best to appear more relaxed, flashing me his trademark smirk.

I lowered myself into the tub, turning off the faucet and turning on the jets in one smooth movement.

"Jon, how much coke did you do?"

He stared at me blankly, his pupils huge. "Enough." He sniffed.

I raised my eyebrows. "Did you finish the entire bag?"

His face contorted into a frown. "What are you, my mum? Inquiring about a bag of crisps? That's something she would ask when I was a young boy. She would put her hand on her hips and ask, 'Jonathan, did you finish the whole bag?'" He made his voice very high-pitched and nasal when quoting his mother, imitating her. I couldn't help but chuckle. "That shit was annoying. Now YOU'RE annoying. Mind your business, mate." He sniffed again and scratched at his arm. "Bloody mosquitoes."

I had experienced the effects of too much coke firsthand, and I knew that Jon was dealing with the same thing. The irritability and agitation, and the sensation of being itchy or of being bitten by insects, were all things I dealt with after snorting one too many lines.

"Sorry," I said quietly, not wanting to agitate him further. I closed my eyes and tried to relax in the jacuzzi.

Sleep overcame me momentarily as I lay there in the warm water of the hot tub, so I got out and toweled off then headed to the bathroom. Jon was still sitting in the tub, chain-smoking and fidgeting.

Surely enough, I saw the empty baggie of coke on the marble vanity, as well as a blood-covered tissue in the wastebasket. Jon must have suffered another nosebleed. I shook my head sadly. He really needed to be careful with the cocaine, especially since he was mixing it with so many other things. I sensed that my best mate was struggling more than he let on, since his breakup with Lisa. The hard partying was a way to cope with the loss. I would know, since that's what I did when I lost my wife. Those first few weeks, I'd spent endless hours and days in a drug and alcohol induced stupor.

After relieving myself and brushing my teeth, I was more than ready for bed. I left the bathroom and noticed the jacuzzi was empty. I popped my head into the living area adjacent to the bedroom. Unsurprisingly,

Jon was still up. He was sitting on the couch, smoking and watching tv. The clock revealed that it was 3am.

"Good night, Jon," I said with a smile.

"Good night," he replied, without taking his eyes off the telly.

I got comfortable under the covers, falling asleep within minutes.

That night, my dreams were vivid and my sleep was fitful. One dream involved the hotel's room service knocking on the door at some ungodly hour, and Jon tripping and falling on his face on his way to the door. Then I dreamed that Jon was frantically opening and slamming cabinets and drawers, and cursing under his breath with a cigarette in his mouth, complaining about a "poisoned sandwich." Dream number three involved Jon standing by the window for a long time. He was scratching at his back, wiping his nose with a blood soaked tissue, and chain-smoking as he looked up at the sky with a panicked expression. As was typical in my dreams, I tried to speak but my mouth wouldn't form words. Random images of food popped into my head, as did the faces of Todd and Andre. Admittedly, my thought process was muddied by the combination of drugs I had taken, so my dreams felt like wakefulness and vice versa.

After what seemed like endless hours of bizarre imagery as well as plenty of tossing and turning, I awoke feeling relatively alert and coherent. However, my head throbbed something terrible. When I turned my head, I felt dizzy, so I avoided excess movement. Slowly, I looked to my left, noticing Jon lying next to me. His eyes were closed but they opened a crack when I turned on my side to face him.

"Good morning, Ken," he whispered with a gentle smile as he put his arm around me. Then he grabbed my penis and began stroking me.

He wrapped his leg around mine and started to move his hips, dry-humping me. Then the kissing started. I did my best to avoid refusing sex with Jon, mostly because I wanted to avoid the guilt trips he would put on me when I said no. But that morning I was battling a terrible hangover and simply couldn't handle any extra motion. I decided to take a chance.

"Um, Jon?" I began sheepishly.

"Yes, love?" He asked between kisses.

"I just want to rest this morning. I'm not feeling so hot. Perhaps later we can do stuff but I need to relax for now." My heart sped up as I awaited his answer.

Jon sighed. "I understand," he said softly. "Could I at least cuddle with you?"

"Of course," I said, beyond relieved that he hadn't given me a hard time.

Jon wrapped his arm around me a little tighter and stopped fondling me. I placed my arm around him as well, and we stayed in that position for about a half hour before deciding to get up and order some breakfast before heading to Central Park for a run.

As we got dressed, I told Jon about my weird dreams. For the briefest of moments, he looked startled, but then his expression returned to normal and he laughed.

"Yeah, those are some fucked up dreams, mate." He winked.

I sat on the edge of the bed as I laced up my running shoes. Then I reached over and grabbed the room service menu from the nightstand near the window, looking at the breakfast section. That's when I saw the trash can under the nightstand.

It was overflowing with cigarette butts, empty cigarette packs, tissues soaked with blood, and a half-eaten sandwich, presumably from a room service order.

Just then, Jon walked up to me, startling me. He had his shorts on, but was still shirtless and shoeless. I sat up a bit straighter, pretending not to have noticed the garbage.

"Let's order some breakfast," he said with a smile as he lit a blunt and sat next to me, looking over the menu. That's when I saw the scratch marks on his back.

I nodded and gulped, doing my best to stay calm. Those "dreams" of Jon weren't really dreams after all. They were completely real. He had most likely been suffering from cocaine-induced psychosis. My heart sank.

This marked the beginning of Jon's slow descent into madness...

Chapter 3: "Hanging On By a Thread"

I ran through Central Park like someone was chasing me, despite the fact that Jon was ahead of me by about an eighth of a mile. It was his idea to run an impromptu marathon through the park, and I was happy to oblige since it was a beautiful morning in mid-June. As with most things, Jon insisted on making it a competition, and the loser would buy the winner lunch. Jon was an incredibly fast runner, so I was prepared to pay up when our little race was over.

My feet struck the soft pavement at regular intervals, creating a hypnotic rhythm. Despite the hard partying the night before, I felt renewed and perhaps even reborn. Nature has always had a restorative effect on me.

Prior to breakfast, Jon and I had smoked two blunts apiece while doing yoga in the hotel room. I had never combined a "wake and bake" with yoga, so I was curious to see how it would feel. It was an interesting sensation, doing forearm handstands and downward dogs while stoned.

My joints had felt so light, and my body so limber. As for the breakfast? Those scrambled eggs and French toast had tasted so bloody good!

The lightness in my limbs had long disappeared by mile 21, replaced by an incessant burning that was made worse by a desire to catch up with my best mate. Jon's willpower was nothing short of legendary, as was his physical endurance. I pressed on, closing in on him as I passed countless trees and people. My cell phone's running app revealed a speed of 15 miles per hour as I forced my legs to run as fast as they could. Before long, I was sprinting alongside Jon, who was panting and sweating up a storm. He glanced over at me with a smirk.

"You still trying to beat me, mate?" He asked breathlessly, speeding up ever so slightly.

"Always!" I gasped as I struggled to keep up with him.

We ran side by side for about a mile or so, breathing heavily. Then Jon looked over at me again.

"Eat my dust!" he bellowed, before darting ahead of me.

I groaned as I tried and failed to catch up, my calves feeling as if they were on fire. The mid-morning sun was beginning to burn my scalp, and I prayed for a cool breeze as I huffed and puffed my way through the last few miles. By mile 25, Jon was ahead of me by a solid quarter of a mile. This pissed me off. I decided to channel my anger into my run and began to speed up until I was once again running alongside him. He turned to me and looked at me with raised eyebrows. He glanced at his smart watch to check the distance.

"Half a mile to go, mate!" He gasped. "Let's go all out! Remember, loser buys lunch!"

Jon broke into a sprint once again, as did I. We remained tied until the last minute or so, and Jon inched ahead of me ever so gradually. My lungs burned as I dragged myself forward, wanting so badly to beat him for a change. Just when I thought I had a chance of pulling ahead of him, our devices beeped and Jon threw up his arms in victory as he crossed the imaginary finish line. When he had lifted his arms, I was able to see the finish time on his watch. I glanced at my device, which revealed my time to be two hours, twenty five minutes and fourteen seconds for the 26.2 miles. He had beat me by one second!

The little bastard turned to me and smiled, breathless and drenched in sweat from head to toe. He put his hands behind his head to slow his heart rate, taking deep breaths as he did so. I grudgingly held out my hand to shake his.

"Congrats, Jon," I grumbled as he took my sweaty hand in his and shook it. "You won again, and now you get free lunch. Fleet-footed bastard!" I chuckled and pretend-punched him in the arm.

"Hey, it was a close race," Jon said with a chuckle. "Remember you're five months older than me, so I have a slight age advantage!" He stuck out his tongue.

I tilted my head back and laughed. "Wow, five whole months!" I teased. I grabbed a water bottle from my waistpack and took a hearty swig, and Jon did likewise.

We decided to walk and stretch a bit before getting a taxi back to the hotel to shower. We moved at a leisurely pace, since we had over two hours before our lunch date with Todd. Andre got out of work around 2:30, so he was going to join the three of us for an early Broadway show. After that, Noelle was going to hang out with all four of us at the hotel for drinks, dinner, and other "activities." According to Jon, Noelle was a VERY kinky girl, and no stranger to edge play. I was beyond excited to push her to the limit. Jeannie unfortunately had other plans, but promised to join us the next time we hung out. I got semi-hard as I imagined that foxy older lady spread eagle on my bed, naked and blindfolded.

"This was a good idea, Jon," I remarked with a smile as I walked alongside him in the park, breathing in the fresh air.

He smiled then slowed his walking pace until he was standing completely still, an alarmed expression forming on his face. He put his hand to his chest and appeared unsteady for a moment. My eyes widened and I placed my hand on his back.

"Jon, are you ok?" I asked shakily.

He slowly looked over at me and nodded. "Yeah. I just felt a little dizzy for a moment there."

"Perhaps we should call a cab sooner and do the stretching in the hotel room instead?" I offered, as we resumed walking at a slow pace.

Jon agreed, and took a sip of his water. A few more seconds went by and Jon appeared even more unsteady, this time dropping to his knees on what was luckily soft grass. I immediately knelt down to help him up, walking him over to a nearby bench for him to sit. He looked dazed as well as frightened.

"Let's rest a bit," I said. "Perhaps you need some sugar? You didn't have much of a breakfast." He had only eaten a tiny portion of scrambled eggs and home fries that morning. I reached into my waistpack and pulled out a packet of dried fruit, which was my go-to snack while on long runs. I opened the pouch and handed it to Jon, who began eating it without hesitation.

"Yes, I think that's it," Jon agreed in a shaky voice. "All the partying last night didn't help, either. I reckon we aren't in our twenties any more, mate," he said with a nervous chuckle and a wink.

I laughed and patted him on the back, still concerned. We sat on the bench in silence for about five minutes while he ate the fruit and sipped from his water bottle.

"Has this sort of dizzy spell happened to you before?" I asked.

Jon shook his head. "Nope," he said with his mouth full of raisins. "I didn't get a lot of sleep last night and I drank more than I usually do. I'm sure that's it. But I'm feeling better now, so I think we can start walking again. Thank you for the snack, mate." He winked.

I nodded. "Of course."

I knew firsthand how unsettling it felt to have a dizzy spell after a hard workout, and was certain that the drug and alcohol consumption played a part. The partying was affecting us more now than it had in the past. Jon was right: We WEREN'T in our twenties anymore.

After a few more moments, we both slowly got up from the bench and made our way out of the park, getting a cab ride back to the hotel.

While riding in the cab, I fantasized about Noelle, Todd, and Andre. It didn't take long for my cock to stand attention in my running shorts, and Jon noticed. A huge grin spread across his face as he looked at my crotch and then at me.

"Hmmm," Jon said as he uncrossed his legs, revealing his own erection. "Fancy a little shower sex when we get to the room?"

I chuckled. "Actually," I began, determined to be the dominant one as much as possible for our second day in the Big Apple, "I wanted to save my energy for Noelle and the two blokes. It's bloody time we have ourselves a full-on orgy. Todd and Andre will be our appetizer, then Noelle can be our main course. And perhaps New York style cheesecake for dessert. What better place to get New York cheesecake than New York City, right?" I winked.

Jon laughed and shook his head. "Correction: Todd for an appetizer, Todd AND Andre for the main course, then Todd, Andre, and Noelle for dessert! YOU can eat your cheesecake, and I will eat three dicks and a pussy."

I snorted as I laughed at Jon's proposal. "You sure have a Todd-heavy menu!"

"Indeed I do!" Jon agreed gleefully as he grabbed his crotch. "That Todd chap is so young and fresh, I bet his junk tastes like breast milk!"

We both cackled with delight as the taxi pulled up to the hotel. I was so looking forward to a hot shower and a cigarette.

"I'm curious to see how long Todd can hold his breath," I said as I tore off my sweaty underwear and socks, then bent over to touch my toes. It felt so good to be nude.

"Well, Todd's a chain smoker like me," Jon said as he took off his undergarments and lit a cigarette, taking a deep drag. "We're talking 'crazy chimney' here. Andre told me that Todd goes through five packs a day. But as you know, some of us chimneys are regular Houdinis, mate." He took a really long drag, finishing the entire cigarette. Then he inhaled deeply, holding his breath for at least ten minutes as he sat naked, doing gentle stretches. When he finally exhaled, he smirked at me and winked before lighting himself another ciggy.

I laughed and shook my head, lighting myself a cigarette as well. My manhood hardened as I envisioned Todd getting sucked off in the pool by Jon. My mind then traveled to Noelle. She would undoubtedly love sex in the jacuzzi. I finished my cigarette quickly before retreating to the shower, where I masturbated to climax. Jon joined me soon after, lathering me up from head to toe with one hand while pleasuring himself with the other. He avoided climaxing because he wanted to save his load for later, claiming that the orgasm would be more intense when he did finally cum.

We toweled off, chainsmoked around eight cigarettes apiece while watching the telly, got dressed, then made our way down to the lobby to meet Todd. Jon had told him to dress casual and bring a bathing suit.

Todd showed up within seconds, walking through the hotel's revolving door with a shy smile on his face. He wore a backpack and was dressed in a dark blue polo shirt, khaki shorts, and boat shoes. His face lit up when he saw us.

Jon ran up to Todd and lifted him up in the air, twirling him around. Todd simply giggled and blushed.

"You look so adorable," Jon remarked in his sexy voice as he set Todd back down and ran his fingers through his hair. "Good enough to eat. You smell good too." He buried his face in Todd's hair and inhaled deeply, then licked the side of his neck. Once again, Todd blushed and chuckled shyly, then looked over at me with a gentle smile.

"Hi, Ken," Todd said in his quiet voice. Jon graciously let go of his new "bitch" so I could greet him.

I smiled at Todd and gave him a warm hug. "Glad you were able to hang out today, Todd," I said with a wink. "Did you want to go to the pool and order lunch while we are there?"

Todd nodded. "I'm down for whatever," he mumbled bashfully.

Jon smiled broadly and put his arm around him. "I will keep that in mind," he growled. Todd turned beet red.

I bit my tongue to stifle a laugh. Todd reminded me of Eugene in terms of personality, or perhaps even Amy. He was completely submissive. Jon was clearly in heaven, since he was a sucker for young subs, or what he referred to as "twinks." As much as he enjoyed fooling around with me, I was often too dominant for his tastes.

"Let's head to the pool," I suggested.

Todd and Jon nodded in agreement and we walked down the hallway to the hotel's impressive indoor pool. We were pleased to discover that we had the entire place to ourselves. There was a bar adjacent to the pool area where customers could order drinks as well as food. There was a gym across the hall. The place was decorated with palm trees and spotted a high ceiling that was colored blue, and reggae music played softly over the sound system. It felt like we were on holiday in some tropical place rather than in New York City.

The three of us went to the locker room to change into our bathing suits. That's when Jon dropped a delightfully naughty bomb on me.

"I brought zip ties," Jon whispered with a huge grin on his face as we undressed and put on our swim trunks.

My eyes widened and I grinned. "You packed them?" I asked in amusement.

Jon nodded. "Mmm-hmm. Oh and the gym has ankle weights, which we can 'borrow.' I spotted them when we walked past the gym to the pool."

"Holy shit. That's brilliant." I was so excited for our little watery adventure. Todd was in for an unforgettable experience.

Before long, we were all wearing our swimsuits and headed back to the pool area. Jon wore flattering burgundy-colored cargo swimshorts that went to mid thigh, showing off his quad muscles. Todd looked adorable in dark olive colored swim trunks with a light green Hawaiian flower print. He was very thin but was muscular, and had great definition in his abs. I wore my classic black shorts.

"Boys, I will be back in a moment," Jon said to Todd and me. "I have to grab some 'supplies.'" He winked at me and I smiled back. He was going to grab the ankle weights from the gym.

I lay on my recliner, and Todd did likewise. I cleared my throat and looked over at him, deciding to ask him some questions.

"Todd, have you ever had sex in the water?"

Todd blushed. "Um. Does the shower and bath tub count?"

I smiled. "Sure. I personally love the water. I've fucked in the tub and shower hundreds of times but I've also fucked in the ocean, freshwater lakes, several waterfalls, and countless swimming pools. And not just IN the water, but underwater. See, Jon and I are experienced swimmers and freedivers, and we have a breathplay fetish. Do you know what breathplay is?" I raised my eyebrows at the young bloke.

Todd nodded. "That's like erotic asphyxiation and stuff, right? Andre likes to choke me sometimes, and I think it's pretty cool. Like I get dizzy but it feels good at the same time. Or he will hold me underwater when we take a bath together, and I will get excited by it. I don't know. Maybe I'm weird." He chuckled and blushed again.

My cock hardened. "No, Todd," I insisted as I placed my hand on his thigh. He tensed up for a moment. "It's not weird. It's perfectly natural."

Just then, Jon showed up with the ankle weights. Todd looked up at him with a quizzical expression.

"What are those for?" Todd asked sheepishly.

"I'm so glad you asked," Jon said with a smirk as he placed the ankle weights on his lounge chair. "They're for our little water adventure." He began placing the weights on his own ankles, then handed me a pair to put on. Finally he handed a pair to Todd.

"Are we doing some kind of workout in the water?" Todd asked naively as he fastened the weights around his dainty ankles.

Jon broke into a hearty laugh, as did I. "Something like that. Come on, let's go in the pool."

With our ankle weights strapped on, we walked over to the shallow end, gradually descending the steps into the heated pool. The water temperature was perfect, neither too warm nor too cold.

"Todd, I owe you a blowjob from last night," Jon began as he fished something out of his swimsuit pocket. "From when you won the 'cocaine race?'" He smiled.

Todd nodded as he walked deeper into the water. "I remember," he said with a coy smile.

"And I will give it to you. But," Jon said as he dangled the zip ties in front of Todd's face, "there's a string attached. Or in this case, a zip tie."

Before Todd could react, Jon got behind him, roughly grabbed both his hands and placed them behind his back, securing the zip ties tightly around his wrists. Todd giggled.

"Oh, wow," Todd mumbled with a tiny smile. "Sometimes Andre likes to put me in handcuffs. These feel more comfortable, though."

"Hmm," Jon commented as he walked around to face Todd again. He began running his hand up and down Todd's chest, giving him goosebumps. I decided to run my hand over Todd's bum, making him jump slightly. "Has Andre ever sucked you off underwater?" Jon whispered in Todd's ear, his hand traveling lower until his hand was on his crotch. He blushed once again.

"N-no, Andre hasn't done that."

I piped up. "Todd and I had a little conversation while you were getting the ankle weights," I explained to Jon. "He's never had sex in a pool. Only the bath tub and shower. Barely counts, if you ask me," I teased as I grabbed Todd's arse harder. Todd moaned.

Jon's eyes widened as he smiled. "We will have to broaden Todd's horizons today," He crooned.

Todd trembled slightly, his face turning pink. Jon walked in front of Todd, then began running his hands through his hair. Without warning, he began kissing him hard on the mouth, his lips grinding against Todd's. Jon pulled violently at Todd's hair, making him gasp. I decided to tag team by pulling down Todd's swim shorts, exposing his lovely round arse. Jon wasted no time grabbing his cock, making him moan even more as he kissed him passionately. My own dick got hard as I rubbed Todd's arse, occasionally teasing his crack with my finger. Suddenly, Jon backed away from Todd's lips to talk to me.

"Hey, bitch," he growled. "Pull down my swim trunks and give me a rusty trombone while I jerk him off. Stay underwater as long as you can. When you resurface, we can go for round 2 in the deep end, where you can fuck me while I suck him silly. For the grand finale, I will pound the shit out of Todd's back door while you face-fuck him." Jon turned to Todd. "If you need air while I'm sucking you off, signal by blinking twice. If you need air when I'm fucking you from behind, signal by blowing a stream of bubbles. Sound good, boys?" Jon asked as he looked at Todd and then at me.

Todd and I nodded. I began slowing down my breathing as I got behind Jon, pulling down his swim shorts. Jon continued to kiss Todd, while grabbing the young man's erect penis. Todd moaned as my best mate jerked him off with his strong right hand, intermittently pulling his hair with his left.

I grabbed Jon's arse and ran my finger along his crack, gently sticking my fingertip inside his hole. The water made his opening even more tight. I kissed the back of his neck as I breathed deeply, then began to lower myself slowly into the water. I inhaled as much air into my lungs as I could then knelt down until I was completely submerged and my face was level with Jon's arse. I glanced at my watch to keep track of the time.

With one hand, I spread his arse cheeks and began to devour his tight hole with my mouth. My other hand reached around to grip his cock, which was already rock hard.

I enjoyed being submerged, and loved the way Jon's flesh felt with the added friction of the water. My dick hardened as I thought of how nervous Todd must have felt, with his hands being tied behind his back as Jon groped and kissed him. He was truly helpless, and in the hands of two hardcore sadists who he barely knew. Jon and I were aggressive as hell, and Todd was so incredibly shy. Still, timid personality aside, the fact that he was willing to hang out with Jon and me ALONE was proof that he had an adventurous side. I found this to be incredibly arousing.

Jon leaned back slightly, grinding his bum against my face as I ate his arsehole. Despite the fact that I was underwater, I could make out the sound of Todd's moans. Jon's cock spasmed several times, but he didn't climax.

I looked at my watch and saw that six minutes had passed. I spread Jon's arse cheeks farther apart and blew several bubbles into his hole. He moaned and giggled at the sensation. My tongue went deeper into his bum and I knew it was becoming more challenging for him to avoid having an orgasm. He grinded against me some more and wrapped his hand around mine as I jerked him off, so as to tighten my grip. As the minutes rolled by, it was becoming more painful for me to continue to hold my breath.

Before long, ten minutes had passed and I really needed to breathe. I backed away from Jon's bum and let go of his penis, beginning my ascent to the surface.

Jon abruptly twisted around and pushed on the tops of my shoulders to keep me from surfacing for air. My heart rate sped up as I began to fight him, doing my best to swim away from him but he was too quick as well as strong. My ankle weights didn't help matters, either. He managed to drag me several feet over to the wall and slam me against the tile surface, holding me down as he did so. I felt dazed by the sheer impact of being thrown against the wall of the pool, and subsequently let go of most of my breath. Adrenaline coursed through my veins and I knew I had to step up my game if I didn't want to drown in that hotel pool. With great effort, I used my legs to push myself to the surface, choking and gasping for breath. Jon's green eyes glowed ominously as he glared at me.

"Where's my orgasm, bitch?" Jon growled as he placed his hand around my throat. "You were supposed to make me climax." Todd stood behind him, trembling slightly and appeared close to tears. The young lad was scared shitless.

I got in Jon's face, prepared to fight back. Despite what he thought and said, I wasn't his "bitch."

"I needed to BREATHE, Jon," I spat. "I was down there for over ten minutes."

"Hmm," Jon cooed as he let go of my throat. "It's ok. I will simply double the amount of time my little friend Todd here will spend underwater." He smirked and turned to Todd, wrapping his arms around his tiny waist. "I hope you can hold your breath for a while, mate. I'm about to suck you off underwater and I won't let you come up for air until you cum." He ran his hands through his hair and kissed him gently on the lips.

Todd shook and swallowed, appearing about ready to piss himself. I reached down to my penis and began stroking myself, getting ready to fuck Jon. We were moments away from round 2 of our adventure, and despite my annoyance at Jon's bullshit and power games, I was excited for my first underwater threesome.

"You boys ought to start taking slow, deep breaths because it might be a while before you breathe again," Jon advised as he began walking Todd to the deep end. I walked alongside them and glanced over at Todd, who shook something awful. His face was beet red.

"J-Jon?" Todd mumbled as his eyes filled with tears.

Jon stopped walking and turned to him. "Yes, my little twink?" He asked in a soft voice.

"I'm scared," Todd said as his voice cracked and his lower lip trembled. "I don't know if I can stay underwater for longer than two minutes, and it usually takes me at least five minutes to climax. I don't want to drown." He looked so horrified, it was heartbreaking.

I was so tempted to give Todd a hug and offer some soothing words. But I knew better than to interfere with Jon, who would only make things worse for the young bloke. So I simply smiled gently at Todd when he made eye contact with me.

Jon caressed Todd's face and kissed him tenderly on the forehead. "I promise I won't let you drown," he assured in a soft voice. "You just signal with your eyes by blinking twice, like we discussed earlier, and I will remove your ankle weights right away so you can resurface. Then once you're ready to go back under, I will make love to that beautiful bum of yours and you get to suck Ken's delicious cock." Todd giggled. "And after we are done in the pool, we will all get high together, then treat you to a nice lunch. Alright, honey?" Jon asked sweetly as he ran his hand through Todd's hair.

Todd nodded and smiled shyly. "Alright," he murmured.

Jon smiled. "Ok. Now focus on slowing down your breathing," he advised in a soothing voice as he walked Todd into deeper water. I did likewise, knowing that Jon might challenge me again. I began to fondle myself again as we walked deeper and deeper, until the water was up to our necks. Jon stopped.

"Ok, boys," Jon began. "Just a few more steps and the water will be over our heads. Todd, I'm going to have you stand with your back against the wall while I suck you, and Ken fucks me from behind. Before we go under, let's take a minute to breathe deeply and relax. In through the nose and out through the mouth. Nice and slow..."

Jon closed his eyes and began breathing, inhaling through his nose and exhaling through his mouth. I followed suit, as did Todd, who looked very shaky and pale. My eyes met his and I gave him a sympathetic smile to let him know he was safe. He smiled back, his eyes filling with tears once again. I gave him the thumbs up and winked, then closed my eyes and waited for Jon's directions. Within a minute or so, he spoke.

"On my count, we will walk a few more steps until we are submerged. Three...take some deep breaths...Two...deeper breaths now...and...One. Inhale as much air into your lungs and GO."

The three of us took as deep a breath as we could and we took several more steps, submerging ourselves beneath the surface. Jon positioned Todd against the wall and pulled down his swim shorts. I pulled down my own shorts and positioned myself behind Jon, who bent forward at the waist and began sucking Todd's penis. My dick was hard as a rock and I wasted no time lining myself up with Jon's arsehole. Then I slowly entered his incredibly tight back door. I glanced at Todd, who looked like he was in heaven as Jon sucked his cock and played with his balls. I fondled Jon as I fucked him, which resulted in him letting go some bubbles.

Two minutes quickly passed. I watched Todd for signs of distress but saw none. I pounded Jon as hard as I could as he blew his new fuck toy. I so loved the friction of the water, and it was so difficult for me to delay orgasm. Still, I pressed on, grabbing Jon's arse cheeks as I thrusted.

Two minutes turned into four. Todd was still going strong and began moving his hips slightly, perhaps in an effort to climax faster. I saw Jon begin to back away occasionally from Todd's penis, taunting him, prolonging the amount of time it would take for the poor guy to cum. I was about to withdraw from Jon out of sheer protest, but he quickly resumed pleasuring Todd, moving his head up and down at a faster pace. Todd let go some bubbles as he moved his hips, and within another thirty seconds or so, he climaxed. His head tilted back, and his cheeks puffed out as he began to struggle to hold his breath.

Jon backed away from Todd's cock, then tilted his head way back until he was looking straight up. He then opened his mouth and allowed Todd's semen to come out and mix into the water in a giant plume. It looked like smoke. Jon smiled and kissed Todd on the cheek. That's when Todd blinked twice.

While I was still inside Jon, he bent down to remove Todd's ankle weights. Once they were removed, Todd floated up to the surface for much needed oxygen. I glanced at my watch. Six minutes and twelve seconds had passed.

I withdrew from Jon, giving his arse a playful pat as I did so. He gently grabbed Todd's arm and held him up so he wouldn't sink, since he was still restrained and staying afloat was more difficult. Then, still holding onto Todd, he began walking to the shallow end. I followed suit and within a few moments, our heads were above water and we could breathe again. That first full breath felt so good!

Todd was breathing heavily but smiling, appearing much more relaxed than before. Jon and I gave him a big hug.

"You did remarkably well, my dear friend," Jon said with a warm smile. I nodded in agreement. "Six minutes is impressive. How do you feel?"

Todd blushed. "I feel good. A nice head rush. I admit the last minute was scary but I pushed myself to stay underwater until I came. I...." Todd's voice trailed off and he swallowed, looking away shyly.

Todd put his arm on his shoulder. "Yes, love?" He encouraged in a soothing voice.

"I-I wanted to... make you proud of me." Todd blushed again and bit his lip.

Jon smiled broadly at Todd, appearing flattered. Then he gave him a warm, prolonged hug. "You made me VERY proud," he assured. Then he backed away to look into Todd's crystal blue eyes. "Andre is a very lucky man."

Todd's eyes filled with tears and he smiled sweetly. "You think so?" He asked sheepishly. "I think I'M the lucky one." He chuckled.

I piped up. "You and Andre make a beautiful couple," I commented as I ran my hand down Todd's back. "And we're all going to have a lot of fun together this evening."

Jon nodded. "That's right. This is only the pre-game!"

We all laughed at Jon's comment. Then Todd cleared his throat.

"I think I'm ready for round three now," Todd mumbled with a bashful grin on his face as he looked at Jon and then at me.

Jon's face lit up. "Well, well, well! Look who's asserting himself!" He patted Todd on the back, as did I.

"I-I'm sorry," Todd stammered. "Should I not have done that?"

Jon tilted his head back and laughed heartily. "No, silly boy! I love how you spoke up. Confidence is sexy." He kissed Todd passionately on the mouth for several moments, grabbing his arse cheeks as he did so. Todd let go a moan.

My cock hardened once more as I envisioned Noelle in the bathtub with her legs spread. As sexy and kinky as it was to see Jon and Todd go at it in the pool, I couldn't help thinking about that blonde waif and all the fucked up shit that Jon and I would do to her when she was in our suite. In the meantime, I was curious to see how good Todd was with his mouth. In my experience, submissives gave better head than dominants, because of their natural desire to please. The only exception was Jon, who could probably suck a watermelon through a garden hose!

Jon took a breath and went underwater to re-fasten Todd's ankle weights, resurfacing quickly. Then the three of us once again began breathing deeply and inching slowly into deeper water.

"Remember, Todd," Jon crooned. "Blow a stream of bubbles when you need to come up for air."

Todd nodded as he took some deep breaths in preparation for round three. I looked at Jon, who returned my gaze. He had the slightest bit of a smirk on his face, and his emerald green eyes sported an all-too-familiar sinister look. I swallowed as I breathed deeply, knowing my best mate was plotting something, and I was prepared to intervene.

"On my count," Jon said. "Three...two...one. Deep, deep breath."

We once again took as much air into our lungs as possible before stepping back into the deep end.

Jon wasted no time positioning himself behind Todd and lining up his fully erect penis with Todd's tight arsehole. As this was happening, Todd bent over at the waist and leaned over to suck my dick. I held onto my manhood and thrusted my hips forward, forcing every inch into Todd's mouth as Jon slammed into his back door. The young lad let go some bubbles, seemingly unprepared for the experience of being fucked in both holes while underwater. Jon wrapped his arms tightly around Todd's waist and flashed me a sinister grin as he plowed harder into his little fuck slave.

Feeling somewhat sadistic myself, I pushed onto the back of Todd's head and began to face fuck him with considerable force, or at least as much force as I could for being submerged underwater. Once again, Todd let go some bubbles. I reckoned this was going to be a long couple of minutes for the frail bloke.

One minute turned into two, which turned into four. Jon fucked Todd's back door with reckless abandon as I violated his pretty face. I waited for the telltale stream of bubbles to escape Todd's mouth. Around the five minute mark, Jon looked at me intensely, then reached around Todd's front, roughly grabbing his balls. That did it.

Obviously startled, Todd quickly let go a stream of bubbles, and I was able to make out the sound of a moan emanating from his mouth. Jon continued to fuck him, despite his promise to let him come up for air, so I mercifully backed away from him and bent down to unfasten his ankle weights. But once the weights were off, Todd's feet remained anchored to the bottom of the pool. That's when I noticed that Jon had a cast iron grip on him, and was refusing to let go so he could get air.

I glared at Jon and began to attempt to pry his arms off Todd's torso, but he wouldn't let up. Todd appeared in agony, most likely from the combination of being crushed and having to hold his breath for an uncomfortably long time. I dug my fingernails into Jon's skin, but he simply sneered at me as he kept his arms wrapped around Todd's waist. I became livid at that point and used my forefinger and middle finger to poke Jon in the eyes, using more pressure than I needed to.

Perhaps instinctively, Jon let go of Todd and rubbed his eyes, grimacing in discomfort. I didn't want to hurt him, but it seemed that he was going to let Todd drown, or at least swallow and inhale some water, if I didn't act quickly. I knew he would get back at me later for what I did, but I didn't care.

I grabbed Todd's arm and walked him back to shallower water, where he immediately gasped and choked for air. My watch revealed he had been forced to hold his breath for over seven minutes. He looked at me, shaking and close to tears as he breathed heavily.

"I thought Jon was gonna drown me," he said in a shaky voice.

I wrapped my arms around him in a warm embrace, doing my best to help him calm down.

"No, Todd," I assured. "He just gets carried away sometimes. That's why we make a good team, him and me. He knows I will intervene when necessary, and make sure everyone is safe."

It was a bit of a lie, because I honestly couldn't be sure of Jon's intentions - or even his sanity - at that point. His behavior was so unpredictable and hard to decipher. I wanted so badly to believe what I told Todd, but part of me was convinced that Jon was a madman, and saw me as his pawn...or, more specifically, his "bitch." I looked behind me and noticed Jon was still underwater, and he was walking over to the wall. As tempted as I was to check on him, I decided against it. Todd needed me more.

"Is Jon ok?" Todd asked. "He hasn't come up for air yet."

I once again looked over at the deep end and noticed a ton of bubbles forming at the surface, just above where Jon was standing. My heart raced. I promptly removed my ankle weights and dove down to make sure Jon wasn't in trouble.

When I reached Jon, I noticed his eyes were closed and his head was lolling to one side. It appeared he was unconscious. I prayed he was just playing one of his sick jokes, but I refused to take chances. So I removed his ankle weights then wrapped my arm around him, carrying him to the shallow end.

When we got to the surface, I propped him against the wall off the pool and, while holding onto his limp body, checked to see if he was breathing. It appeared he was not. I also checked his pulse, which felt weak. A panicked Todd waded over to us.

"Is he ok?" Todd asked, appearing ready to lose his shit.

"I'm not sure," I replied as calmly as I could, ready to pull him out of the pool and do CPR. "Damn it Jon," I whispered as my eyes filled with tears. "Breathe."

Todd piped up again. "Let's get him out of the water," he suggested in a quivering voice. "I know CPR. I was a lifeguard in college."

I nodded. "I was a lifeguard in college too. Wise idea. Let's do this." I was still holding out hope that Jon was fucking with us and would open his eyes any second. In the meantime, I had Todd get on Jon's left side to help me get him out of the pool.

Just then, I heard quiet laughter. I looked at Jon, whose mouth was turned upward into a shit eating grin as he opened his reptilian green eyes. His chuckles grew in volume. Just like the incident many years ago when he had pretended to have drowned in his parents' pool, the little bastard had once again faked me out. Only this time, I wasn't laughing.

I let go of his shoulder, then leaned over close to his snickering face and glared at him.

"Fuck you, Jon," I growled. "FUCK YOU."

He abruptly stopped laughing and looked like he was about to speak but I didn't care what he had to say. In that moment, whatever relief I felt regarding his safety was overshadowed by my anger. I wasn't just mildly annoyed, either; I was fuming!

I turned my back to my cocky, obnoxious, manipulative dick of a friend and focused my attention on Todd. I put my arm around his shoulders and smiled gently.

"Let's go to the locker room and get dressed," I suggested as I carried the three sets of ankle weights and began walking with him to the pool steps.

"Ken, wait," Jon called out as he began crawling out of the pool.

"Save your breath, Jon. You're a sick bastard!" I barked as Todd and I walked out of the pool and grabbed our towels, then headed to the locker room to change.

I unzipped the front pouch of my bag and fished my cuticle scissors out of it, using them to cut Todd's zip ties. He thanked me, then shook out his arms and smiled in relief, happy to be free of the restraints. Once we toweled off and began changing out of our bathing suits, he looked at me with a curious expression.

"That thing that just happened with Jon, what was that about?" Todd asked as he pulled off his swim trunks and began putting his regular clothes on.

I sighed. "Years ago, Jon pretended to have drowned in his parents' swimming pool. His younger brother, Daryl, who happens to be my other best mate, helped me carry his seemingly dead body out of the pool. Once I was about to call 911, Jon's eyes opened and he began laughing, having faked us out. I thought it was funny, since I was an immature 16 year old and was relieved that he was ok. Daryl, on the other hand, was furious at his elder brother and called him a jerk, then threatened to tell his parents on him. Mind you, Daryl was a frail 11 year old boy at the time - asthmatic, underweight, and not in good general health. Jon, on the other hand, despite being a heavy smoker and a druggie, was super healthy and an elite athlete, and strong as hell. He began pulling his little brother's hair and abusing him verbally, calling him a 'stupid little shit' and a 'pussy,' as well as throwing all sorts of threats his way to keep him from snitching to his mum. Poor Daryl got so upset that he had a horrible asthma attack. Jon had me stay with

Daryl while he went into the house to grab his brother's inhaler. He returned empty handed several moments later and in a panic. It turned out he couldn't find his inhaler anywhere. Meanwhile, Daryl was turning blue and losing consciousness. I was crying as I held him. Jon called the paramedics, who showed up quickly, thank god. Of course, he felt terrible that his little brother nearly died because of his antics, but that situation is an example of what happens when you carry a joke too far. Now, seventeen years later, he's up to the same old shit? AND he nearly makes us drown? It's too much. He's out of control."

Todd nodded sympathetically. "I was like Daryl when I was younger, before I got into modeling. I was an only child so I never got picked on by an older sibling, but I got bullied a lot in school. Between being skinny, sickly, and homosexual, I got my ass kicked all the time. But then I learned martial arts and began fighting back. Started lifting weights, too. I was still skinny but I at least had muscle. By my senior year of high school, I had a third degree black belt in karate and nobody bothered me. Around that same time, I met Andre. He was, and still is, my first boyfriend." He smiled shyly.

"Good for you, Todd," I said with a warm smile. We were both dressed by that point. "I might also mention that Daryl got into fitness once he entered high school. He developed an affinity for weightlifting and running. He even joined the track team his sophomore year and did remarkably well. Over time, he continued to get healthier and was eventually able to ditch his inhaler. These days, he's a personal trainer and teaches CrossFit, like me. In fact, Daryl and I are business partners."

Todd smiled and nodded. "That's a great success story," he said, then looked past me. I turned around to see Jon, who was still wearing his swim trunks. His face was full of guilt. He cleared his throat.

"I reckon I'm on your shit list, mate?" he asked me quietly as he began to disrobe and change into his normal clothes.

My nostrils flared as I gave him a dirty look. "For now, yes," I said matter-of-factly.

Jon sighed. "I suppose I deserve it," he grumbled as he put on his shirt. "But, there's more to the swimming pool story. For instance, you left out the part about how I'd cried the entire time I rode in the ambulance with Daryl, holding his hand and apologizing for nearly killing him. I had stayed with him for hours at the hospital, to make sure he was ok. Let's not forget the part where my father had yelled at me for not looking after him, and accused me of misplacing his inhaler. But then he'd actually apologized to me later, when he'd found Daryl's inhaler in the trunk of the car. It had fallen out of the grocery bag after he and mum had gone shopping and had the prescription filled at the store. I'd made an effort to be much kinder to Daryl after the incident, and treated him to the movies, a shopping trip, and dinner the next day. Also," Jon added as he put on his shorts, "let's not forget who encouraged my little brother to get into fitness." He paused for a few moments as he put on his socks and shoes. "It's not like I'm a heartless monster. I loved my little brother and I still do. I just got carried away that day. Just like I got carried away today. I'm sorry for pretending to have drowned, Ken." Jon turned to face Todd. "And I'm sorry for nearly making you drown, Todd." He placed his hand on Todd's shoulder.

Todd smiled and gave Jon a prolonged hug. "It's ok, Jon," Todd said meekly as he wrapped his arms around my best mate. "You're a good brother, and you have a good heart." He eventually backed away from Jon and kissed him tenderly on the lips.

Jon's smiled broadly at Todd. "I'm SO glad we met," he said softly as he ran his hand through Todd's hair. "You're such a kind and loving person. And fierce! I had no idea you had a black belt. I'm a martial artist myself."

Todd's eyes lit up. "Really?"

Jon nodded. "Like you, I was picked on when I was a boy, for playing with dolls and wearing eyeliner. Then when word got out in junior high that I was bisexual, all hell broke loose. Nobody touched me, but there was a group of boys who loved to taunt me and threaten to beat me up, and I knew it was only a matter of time before they made good on their threats. By freshman year in high school, I knew mixed martial arts but didn't tell anyone. One day, the ringleader of the tormentors, a football player wanker by the name of Scott Foley, decided to shove me against a row of lockers and call me a 'fag.' I went completely nuts and beat the crap out of him in front of all his friends. The wrestling coach witnessed the fight and convinced me to try out for the wrestling team. So I tried out, and made the team. By the end of the school year, I was a star athlete and won countless wrestling matches. That Scott bastard never bothered me after that fight. He had gotten his arse handed to him something terrible that day. Of course, I had to face my father's wrath after that stunt." Jon turned to me. "Remember that, Ken? Dad was not happy when he had to show up at school to meet with the principal!"

I nodded slowly, still pissed at Jon for his mind fuck games. "Yes, I recall. Shall we retreat to our suite for some ciggies before going out to lunch?"

Todd nodded. "I could use a cigarette. Or maybe even five!" He chuckled.

Jon agreed, putting his arm around Todd's shoulder. "Yes, let's go."

We exited the pool area and started down the hallway, and I made sure to stop in the gym to put the ankle weights back. Jon occasionally kissed Todd's cheek or grabbed his arse as we walked, and didn't pay too much attention to me, or I to him. I felt it wise to avoid engaging with him too much, at least not until I had cooled down a bit more.

As soon as we reached the suite, Todd placed two cigarettes in his mouth and lit them, taking deep drags. Jon chuckled, as did I.

"Bloody hell," Jon commented with a laugh as he took out his own pack of ciggies and lit one. "Someone who actually one-ups me in the chimney department!"

I lit up myself, still feeling on edge from the pool incident.

With both cigarettes in his mouth, Todd unzipped the front compartment of his backpack and pulled out a small sandwich bag. It contained a baggie of cocaine, a straw, and a razor. No sooner were the items out of the sandwich bag that Todd emptied the baggie's contents onto the coffee table in the living area and cut himself several lines with the razor. He looked up at Jon and me, taking a huge drag off his cigarettes as he did so.

"Either of you want some coke?" Todd asked as smoke billowed out of his mouth.

Jon and I shook our heads. "No, thank you," Jon said. "But I would love a bong hit right about now."

With those words, Jon retreated to the bathroom and returned within seconds with his bong, which was already packed with his favorite strain of weed.

Todd snorted several lines of coke as Jon took a big hit from his bong. I decided I wanted in on the high, so when Jon offered me a hit, I graciously accepted. I passed the bong to Todd, who also took a hit.

Within minutes, the three of us were comfortably stoned and sitting near the window of the living area, chainsmoking cigarettes. The smoke looked so pretty, swirling around the rays of bright sunshine coming from the window. Todd perused the room service menu as Jon and I looked at our phones, trying to decide on a place to eat. While researching restaurants online, Jon had discreetly sent me a text, admitting that he wanted to eat off of Todd's naked body. I had a hard time objecting to that, especially since food play was one of my favorite fetishes. So, we decided on room service.

We all looked at the room service menu, quickly deciding on what to order. Jon placed the call.

One hour later...

"We are so proud of you, Todd."

Jon smiled and kissed him on the lips before wiping tears from the young man's eyes with a tissue. I ran my hands through Todd's soft hair as he lay on the bed, offering my own words of praise before going to the bathroom to grab the first aid kit.

Todd had suffered minor burns from having hot pasta and marinara sauce piled on his lower abdomen and penis but, like a typical submissive, he was a trooper. Jon and I gently massaged burn cream into his damaged skin before applying bandages, discussing what had just happened.

"What part of the food play was the most difficult for you to get through, Todd?" I asked in a soft voice as I lovingly applied the soothing cream to his stomach.

Todd sniffled as he thought about my question for a moment. He had finally stopped crying.

"Um. When Jon entered me really roughly and force-fed me a piece of Italian bread at the same time, that was a lot to process."

Jon nodded sympathetically, as he gently rubbed the cream onto his penis and scrotum.

"Also, when he shoved his fingers down my throat and almost made me throw up, that was intense."

I lightly bandaged Todd's abdomen and smiled gently. "You showed tremendous patience and grace, Todd," I said with utmost sincerity.

"Yes," Jon agreed as he picked up Todd's underwear off the floor and gently put them on the young bloke. "You have such strength."

Todd blushed as he slowly sat up in bed, clad in his grey boxer briefs. "You really think so?" He asked meekly.

We both nodded, reassuring the shy lad that he was indeed a force of nature.

The lunch had started out perfectly normal, with room service arriving around a half hour after we placed the order. We had told Todd to order whatever he wanted, so he decided on pasta with marinara sauce, meatballs, and Italian bread. Jon and I both loved pasta so we got the same thing. When the food arrived, Jon opened a bottle of white wine from the honor bar and poured each of us a glass. We toasted to friendship, then sat around the coffee table and began eating.

Todd was so incredibly thin and had admitted to skipping meals frequently, so it made me happy to see how much he enjoyed eating his lunch. He ate so quickly, as if he hadn't eaten in days. Jon and I stifled a chuckle as he shoveled forkful after forkful of pasta into his mouth. As the minutes rolled by, I began to get aroused, as I envisioned piles of hot food on Todd's body. Jon appeared to get an erection as well. He raised his eyebrow and leaned over to whisper to me.

"Todd is so obedient," Jon noted with a smirk. "I think it's time for us to turn him into a serving tray." He took a bite of his bread.

My eyes lit up. "I agree," I whispered back. "Let's undress him."

Todd looked over at us, appearing to be in heaven with his mouth full of pasta. He smiled broadly as he chewed. "This is really great, guys," he said, helping himself to a piece of bread. "I'm so careful about how much I eat because of the modeling, and I can't remember the last time I had pasta or bread. This is so nice of you." He blushed.

Jon got up from his seat and placed his arm around him. "Anything for you, my dear friend," he said, bending down to kiss his cheek.

"I feel like I should do something nice for YOU guys," Todd said.

"You CAN," Jon emphasized with a sinister grin, caressing Todd's face. "Take off your clothes."

Todd blushed again. "Um. Ok."

He immediately took off his shirt and, before he was able to react, Jon roughly pulled down his shorts and underwear, then nodded at me. I lept up from my seat and picked up Todd, carrying him into the bedroom and throwing him onto the bed. Jon and I rapidly got undressed, grabbed our pasta plates, then walked back over to the bed. Todd lay there, naked and shaking as he looked at Jon and me. We stood at the side of the bed, holding our plates of food.

"Um. What are you doing with the plates?" Todd asked in a timid voice.

Jon tilted his head back and laughed evilly, then looked over at me. "Ken, why don't you demonstrate to Todd here what we are doing with the plates?"

I smirked. "I would be happy to," I said in a low voice, my eyes locking with Todd's.

"I warned you, didn't I? You whiny little bitch." Jon snarled. Then he bent down and lowered his mouth to Todd's cock, sucking him clean. I continued to eat pasta off Todd's stomach as this was going on. Despite the discomfort of the burns, Todd began moaning and moving his hips as Jon sucked his cock and fondled his balls.

"Mmmm," Jon moaned as he blew Todd, a ring of marinara sauce around his mouth. "Your dick tastes even better with the sauce on it." He gave him an evil look, then bit down hard on the poor lad's member.

Todd panted and winced. "Ow!" He yelped.

SMACK!

Jon had abruptly stopped sucking Todd's cock and slapped him in the face, making him whimper in pain. By that point, I had finished the pasta on his stomach and helped myself to a few more sips of wine.

Jon leaned over and got in Todd's horrified face.

"You need silencing, dear friend," Jon growled before straddling him. Then he shoved his fingers deep into Todd's mouth and down his throat, until he was gagging and wretching. I was surprised he didn't throw up. After a few minutes of that, Jon roughly took his fingers out of his mouth, grabbed a piece of Italian bread, and wiped it along the young man's dainty arsehole, making him moan. Then he lined up his erect penis with his opening and dangled the piece of bread in front of his scared face.

"Open wide, Todd! It's time for the second course!"

With those words, Jon shoved the piece of bread into Todd's mouth and slammed his manhood into his buttered arsehole at the same time. Todd let out a muffled cry as fresh tears formed in his eyes, doing his best to avoid choking on the bread. Jon pounded the hell out of him, a sadistic grin on his face.

"Take it all!" Jon ordered. "Take every inch of bread and every inch of cock! You're too frail. You need to be FILLED. You need to be pushed. You need toughening up. You're a PUSSY!" A vein popped out of his forehead as he shouted in Todd's tear streaked face, his hard thrusts continuing.

Todd struggled to chew and swallow the bread that Jon was force-feeding him as his body jolted from the thrusts. I decided to pour a glass of wine and give some to Todd, who I reckoned could use something to wash down the bread, as well as something to help him feel more relaxed.

"Here you go, Todd," I said, holding the glass of wine near his mouth as he finished the last bit of bread. "Drink up."

Todd lifted his head and I put the glass to his lips. He took a few modest sips before lowering his head back down on the pillow. Jon's hard thrusts continued and he looked over at me.

"May I have some of that wine, too?" Jon asked in a tone that was a bit too sweet to be genuine.

I warily handed him the glass. He snatched it out of my hand, took a swig, then leaned over and spit the contents in Todd's face.

Todd jumped and squealed as his eyes filled with fresh tears. Jon put down the empty glass, then leaned down and proceeded to lick the wine off Todd's forehead, cheeks, and chin, ending at his lips. He kissed him passionately for several minutes, speeding up his thrusts. As he did this, I grabbed Todd's erect penis and began jerking him off. Jon, in turn, grabbed my hard cock and did the same. Within perhaps two minutes, the three of us approached an intense orgasm, our loud moans echoing off the walls.

Todd's semen exploded all over my hand, which I licked clean. Similarly, my dick exploded all over Jon's hand, but he licked only a wee bit off his hand before sharing my jizz with Todd, who smiled as he sucked Jon's hand clean.

It has always amazed me how quickly an edgeplay scene can go from intensely painful to pleasurable, often within minutes and sometimes within seconds.

Todd's rapture was short lived, however. He was still panting from his orgasm when Jon got up from the bed, grabbed his plate, and dumped the remainder of hot pasta, meatballs, and sauce all over Todd's stomach and groin.

"Ahhhhh!" Todd cried out in agony, his skin already sensitive from the initial ambush.

Jon handed me a fork. "Let's make this a buffet, shall we?"

I nodded and knelt next to Jon at the side of the bed, quickly devouring the remainder of our lunch off Todd's stomach.

He was crying quietly as we ate the food off of his body, sniffling on occasion and wiping his eyes. Within a few moments the food was gone, and I caressed Todd's wet face.

"Well done, Todd," I said warmly.

And at that point, Jon and I hugged him, then tended to his wounds as we offered our praise to the young twink.

Once we finished putting bandages on Todd's stomach and had put his underwear back on, his phone rang.

Jon grabbed Todd's phone from the coffee table in the living area and glanced at the phone's screen before handing it to Todd.

"It's Andre," Jon said.

Todd smiled broadly as he took the phone and answered it. "Hi, Daddy!" He said in a high pitched voice.

"Hello, Junior," Andre said in his low, authoritative voice. "Have you been a good boy?"

"Yes, Daddy, I've been a good boy."

"You sure? I don't want to find out that you misbehaved. I will have to spank you and take away your toys again."

Jon and I giggled, amused with the ageplay. Jon also enjoyed pretending to be a little boy, so it was refreshing to see someone else engage in that sort of role playing.

"Noooo!" Todd whined as he began to suck his thumb. "I've been good, Daddy. I swear."

"Ok, Junior, I trust you. I'm coming up to the hotel room right now. I got you a present."

"Ooooh! Is it a matchbox car?" Todd asked excitedly. Jon and I couldn't help but chuckle.

"No, son. But you will like it. See you in a few minutes."

"Ok, Daddy! I love you! Mwah!" They ended the call.

A few seconds later, there was a knock on the door. Still sucking his thumb, Todd sprang up from the bed and ran to the door, clad only in his underwear.

"DADDY!!!"

Todd jumped up into Andre's open arms, covering his face in kisses. Andre hugged and kissed him back, chuckling at the enthusiasm with which his boyfriend greeted him. Andre then lifted him up and began twirling him around. Todd squealed with joy. After Andre set him back down on the ground, he set down his backpack and took a chocolate bar out of his pocket, handing it to Todd.

"Thank you, Daddy!" Todd exclaimed as he tore open the wrapper and began eating. "This is my favorite!"

Andre nodded with a smile. "I TOLD you that you would like the present I got you." That's when he noticed the bandages on Todd's stomach.

"What happened?" Andre asked with raised eyebrows as he pointed to his boyfriend's torso.

"I got a boo-boo," Todd replied with his mouth full of chocolate, still in "baby" mode.

Andre looked over at us with a smile. "Were y'all playing rough with Junior?"

Jon and I chuckled and nodded. "Guilty as charged," Jon said with a laugh. "But it was all in good fun. Isn't that right, Todd?"

Jon's eyes glowed hotly and his lips formed a sneer as he waited for Todd to answer. He would make Todd sorry if he made it sound like we abused him, which, in a sense, we had. Unlike the pool session, there were no safety parameters during the food play - no eye signals or safe word, no option for Todd to refuse what we did to him. It had been, for all intents and purposes, a free-for-all.

Unsurprisingly, Todd played along and nodded. "Yes, it was fun. We ordered room service. I had spaghetti and meatballs, Daddy!" He smiled broadly at Andre.

Andre nodded with a grin and ran his hands through Todd's hair. "Did you clean your plate like a good boy?"

Todd nodded. "Yep!"

Andre turned to Jon and me. "The boy seriously doesn't eat enough," he said with a sad smile.

"We were happy to treat him," Jon said as he began to get dressed. I did the same. The Broadway show doesn't start for about two hours, but we wanted to take our time getting ready, and allow for traffic delays.

"That was so nice of you guys," Andre remarked with a smile. "Now let's get ready for the show. I'm so excited. I've been wanting to see this play for a while."

Todd smiled and started to get dressed as well. He had brought another outfit to wear to the show, which consisted of a royal blue button down shirt, black pants, and black loafers.

Like Todd, Jon and I dressed nicely, opting for outfits that were similar to what we had worn the night before. As usual, my best mate took forever in the bathroom, taking the time to consume several lines of coke as well as a full blunt. As for the cigarette consumption? Jon and Todd easily smoked a pack apiece by the time we left the hotel.

On the cab ride, Jon leaned over to whisper to me.

"Remember when we were racing each other in the park, and I told you that the loser pays for lunch?"

I rolled my eyes and nodded, preparing to take out my wallet.

Jon put his hand on mine and shook his head. "I was the loser, mate. I might have won the race, but that stunt I pulled in the pool was a loser's move. I'm happy to treat, and I'm sorry again for acting like a jerk." He smiled and winked, then planted a kiss on my cheek.

I smiled appreciatively. "Thank you, Jon. Apology accepted." I kissed him on his cheek, then rested my head on his shoulder. I couldn't stay mad at Jon if my life depended on it, charming bastard that he was.

Andre and Todd looked over at us and smiled, excited for the evening's plans.

Three hours later...

Noelle was already waiting outside the theater, looking ravishing in a sexy black dress and matching stilettos. She gave each of us a big hug, then we made small talk and smoked several cigarettes apiece before hailing a cab back to the hotel.

The show had been terrific, with great music and impressive acting. We'd all had a great time. The only thing that had been a touch disturbing was Todd's nosebleed, which caused him to retreat to the men's room and miss a solid twenty minutes of the show. Andre had accompanied him, concerned boyfriend that he was. When they had finally returned, Todd's eyes were bloodshot and swollen from crying. Andre had leaned over to me and Jon, a sad look on his face.

"He really needs to slow down with the coke," Andre had whispered to us. "This is the fourth nosebleed he's had in two days, and they're getting worse."

Jon had patted Andre on the thigh, smiling sympathetically. "It's going to be ok," he assured in a soft voice.

Even though I was worried about Todd, I was even more worried about Jon, whose own drug use had increased significantly over a few short weeks.

By the time we arrived at the hotel, I was deep in thought. I wanted so badly to voice my concerns to Jon about his drug use, but had no idea how to go about it. My brow furrowed as I went over different approaches in my head. My thoughts preoccupied me so much that it took a few seconds for me to notice Jon waving his hand in front of my eyes, trying to get my attention.

"Yoo-hoo!" Jon called out with a chuckle. "We are at the hotel! It's time to party, bitch!" He smiled broadly as he shook a tiny baggie of coke in front of my face.

I forced a smile as I got out of the cab. "Did Noelle give you that baggie?" I asked.

Jon nodded. "Indeed! Turns out the little whore is good for more than just giving blow jobs!" He stuck his tongue out at Noelle, who laughed.

"Hey, fuck you, Jon!" she chided.

"Later," he quipped, winking at her.

Noelle laughed again and shook her head. "Did you know, Andre brought a black light lamp, as well as bondage rope that glows in it?" she revealed to me and Jon as we walked through the lobby to the elevator. Todd and Andre followed several feet behind us, lost in their own conversation.

Jon and I both smiled and laughed at the revelation. "Andre is a true 'dom,'" Jon said. "It takes one to know one!"

I nodded. "I can't wait to experiment with that rope and the lamp," I said excitedly. "The question is, who do we tie up first?"

Noelle raised her hand. "Meeee!"

I smirked seductively at Noelle, picturing what she would look like tied up and completely at my mercy, as well as Jon's. Unbeknownst to Jon and the others, there were several items of torture that remained tucked away in my overnight bag, and I was intent on using them.

The second we reached the room, the cigarettes, booze, and drugs came out and the clothes came off. Wild sex was an inevitability, but, in order for us to enjoy ourselves to the fullest, a pre-game was in order. So for the next half hour, the five of us partook in a veritable buffet of psychotropic delights. Piles of weed, heaps of coke, handfuls of pills, and assorted bottles of top-shelf liquor adorned the top of the coffee table, just begging to be consumed.

Andre reached into his bag and unpacked an enema kit. He then proceeded to make Todd a "cocaine enema," so the young bloke could get high without having to worry about a nosebleed. Jon, Noelle, and I sat and watched in wide eyed wonder as Andre mixed bottled water with a generous amount of the drug, making sure the solution was well mixed before having Todd lie face down over his knee. Then, after applying some lube to his arsehole, he spread his cheeks and eased the tip of the bulb into his bum, squeezing the bulb gently. Within moments of holding the mixture in his bowels, Todd was high as a bloody kite. He excused himself to the restroom to relieve himself, and we all decided to continue partying a little more.

Jon filled his bong with fresh weed and helped himself to a few more lines of coke. Noelle took some ecstasy and Andre lit a blunt. I fancied some hard liquor so I knocked back a few shots of vodka before taking a hit off Jon's bong. By the time Todd returned from the loo, the living area was thick with pot smoke and we were all good and fucked up.

Covered in a fine film of sweat, Todd ran up to Andre and jumped onto his lap, nearly knocking him backward as he straddled him. Then he wrapped his arms around him and began kissing him passionately. Andre chuckled as he returned his embrace and kisses.

"I love you, Daddy," Todd cooed between kisses. "Wanna tell me a bedtime story?"

"I have one!" Jon blurted drunkenly, before Andre had time to reply. He got up and walked over to Todd and Andre, running his hands up and down Todd's back as he sat on Andre's lap. Goosebumps formed on Todd's skin within seconds.

"Yaaay!" Todd replied, clapping with glee. "Jonny has a story!"

Jon nodded and continued, running one hand over Todd's back and stroking himself with the other. "Once upon a time, there was a sexy young lad by the name of TODD. And he got fucked up the arse by a horny, older bloke by the name of ANDRE. While this was going on, another chap by the name of JON sucked Todd's yummy dick. Then a third gentleman by the name of KEN joined in and face-fucked Todd, ejaculating inside his pretty mouth. And best of all? A nice young lady by the name of NOELLE recorded the entire thing on video, for everyone to wank off to at a later time! For the grand finale, the four boys stood around Noelle in a circle, jerking off. They eventually ejaculated all over Noelle's naked body. And they all lived hornily ever after!"

We were all dying with laughter at Jon's little "story." He could be quite entertaining when he wanted to be.

I piped up. "I say we make that story a work of non-fiction!" A smile spread across my face as my cock hardened.

Jon's eyes widened and he grinned at me. "I couldn't agree more, mate. It's bloody time for a four-way. Or perhaps even a five-way, if Noelle wants to do more than take a video." He looked over at Noelle, raising his eyebrows. "What do you say, doll? Would you rather be a spectator or a participant?"

Noelle scoffed. "What do YOU think? Of course I want to participate!"

In preparation for the fuck-fest, we all spent the next few minutes knocking back shots of hard liquor and smoking some more weed. Noelle let me do a body shot off her perky tits, much to my delight. She had such incredibly soft skin, and it made sucking vodka off her breasts that much more pleasurable. Then, within perhaps a minute's time, I saw Jon consume four shots of whiskey, snort three lines of coke, and swallow an ecstasy pill, rapidly smoking a cigarette as he did so. I cringed inwardly, knowing it was only a matter of time before his substance abuse caught up with him. Still, I swallowed hard and did my best to keep my mind on the fun, kinky sex we were all about to have. I used an app on my phone to play some music, opting for heavy metal. Thanks to the drugs and alcohol, we were all so bloody horny that we decided to skip the foreplay and get right down to fucking.

Andre walked to the bedroom and got on the bed, lying on his back and stroking himself. Then Jon positioned himself so his back was to Andre, in a reverse cowgirl position. Andre spat on his dick several times before entering Jon's bum. Jon then straightened his legs and leaned back as Andre thrusted repeatedly upward, making my best mate moan with pleasure. Todd joined in, spitting on Jon's cock before straddling him. Jon eased his engorged member into Todd's bum, at which time Todd began to ride him. I crawled onto the bed and began to kiss Jon. Noelle finally joined in, grabbing my arse and nuzzling my neck.

"Noelle, get on my right side," Jon panted as he lay on his back, appearing to be in heaven as Andre pounded him and Todd rode him. "Ken, get on my left. I want to pleasure you both with my hands." He smiled sexily.

Noelle and I obliged, getting on either side of Jon, who wasted no time shoving the fingers of his right hand inside Noelle's bald pussy and his left hand around my cock. Noelle and I leaned across Todd, locking lips passionately as we panted with pleasure at Jon's touch. The alcohol and drugs were in full effect, and my heart pounded with a mix of arousal that was just as much chemical as it was sexual. Within perhaps ten minutes, Noelle and I orgasmed and the three blokes followed shortly after, their moans and grunts echoing off the walls of the bedroom. Sweat poured from their bodies.

Andre chuckled as Todd and Jon kissed. "Oh, man!" He panted, as sweat dripped down his face and chest. "I feel like I need a shower, or at least a bath. Hey, I have an idea! How about we all get in the jacuzzi?"

We all agreed enthusiastically, getting off the bed and making a beeline for the oversized tub. I turned on the water, making the temperature more warm than hot. Andre and Todd jumped right in the tub, giggling and cuddling as they sat and watched the water level rise. I turned to Noelle.

"You ever fuck in a hot tub, sweetheart?" I asked her.

She shook her head. "Nope. I've done it in the shower, the swimming pool, and the beach, but never a hot tub. I like sex in the water, it's different and it's fun."

Jon piped up, putting her arm around her shoulder as we stepped into the tub. "If you think fucking one-on-one in the water is fun, just think of how much more fun a threesome will be," he said with a sexy smirk. "I can fuck you in your tight pussy while Ken fucks your pretty mouth, then he and I can switch places. Maybe you would be willing to take a finger or two up your bum for good measure, and get violated in all three holes. And when it's all done, I can tie you up and whip the shit out of you. What do you say, my little virgin?"

Noelle chuckled. "I love how you still call me your 'little virgin.'"

Jon smiled warmly as he kissed her cheek. "Well, you have always had an innocent, childlike way about you. Even after I popped your cherry on your eighteenth birthday, I still thought of you as a virgin, someone who needed protecting and nurturing. In fact, no matter how many times you have had sex, whether with me or someone else, I have always seen you as the sweet teenage girl I met seven years ago. I don't think that will ever change." He ran his hand through her short platinum hair and smiled sweetly.

Noelle's eyes filled with tears and she smiled. "You're so sweet," she murmured, then kissed him tenderly on the lips.

Jon smiled sexily then leaned over to turn on the jacuzzi jets. Within seconds of pushing the button, the water began to percolate. Satisfied with the water level, I turned off the faucet then leaned back in the tub and closed my eyes, fondling myself as I did so. I found it endearing how close Jon and Noelle were, and their chemistry reminded me of the relationship I had with Tracy. I came close to nodding off as I thought of my Baby Girl while wanking off in the tub, but I got startled awake when something hit me in the face.

SMACK!

My eyes snapped open and I was greeted with a close-up of Jon's erect penis. He tried to whack me in the face with his dick once again, but I ducked my head just in time before looking up at him and giving him a dirty look. He smirked down at me, licking his lips.

"What the hell was that for?" I barked.

He leaned down to talk to me. "You're going to suck me off before I fuck Noelle," he growled. "I want to be nice and hard for her. Now, go on and eat my dick, bitch."

Before I could react, he positioned himself so his dick was level with my mouth and thrusted his hips forward, forcing me to suck him. I opened my mouth wide and did my best to take as much of his manhood into my mouth and down my throat as possible - no easy feat, considering his penis was at least ten inches long and sported a large head. It took great effort to avoid gagging on his member, so I did my best to avoid breathing altogether and, out of sheer desperation, gave what I believed to be the best blow job I had given him up to that point.

"That's a good little bitch," Jon panted as he held the back of my head and face fucked me with his huge penis. "Choke on it."

With those words, he pinched my nose closed, making it impossible for me to sneak a breath. I closed my eyes and willed myself not to puke or pass out as I deep throated him for what must have been close to ten minutes, desperately needing to breathe and swallow. Whenever I attempted to back away from his penis to try and catch a breath, he simply pushed harder on the back of my head and thrusted his hips harder against my face. I suddenly felt something hot land on my face and I jumped, opening my eyes. Jon was smoking a blunt and letting the ash fall onto my face. He smiled sadistically as smoke trailed out of his nose, flicking more ash onto me. Between being unable to breathe or move away, and having hot ash burn my face and head as I was forced to suck a huge cock, I felt like I was in hell. My so-called best mate didn't seem to care that I was in agony. In that moment, I fucking wanted to kill Jon. Tears of anger filled my eyes.

I reached out with my hand and grabbed Jon's ballsack. He moaned in pleasure, which morphed into moans of discomfort as I used more and more pressure. Before long, I was squeezing his balls as hard as I could, then twisted them savagely before letting go. He grunted and instinctively backed away from my mouth, grabbing his scrotum. I immediately gasped for breath and choked for a few moments. Andre, Todd, and Noelle sat in the tub, looking at me with concern. They had seen what I'd just endured with the madman, who was busy cursing under his breath while examining his balls for signs of trauma.

"You ok, man?" Andre asked.

I nodded and swallowed, still pissed off at Jon for his increasingly sadistic ways. The jacuzzi jets felt good on my back and I took some deep breaths as I recovered from the ambush.

Jon stood and glared at me for a few moments as he rubbed his ballsack, grabbing himself a cigarette from the edge of the tub and lighting it. Smoke poured out of his nose in a thick stream as he stared me down with his intense green eyes.

"You're lucky you didn't hurt me, mate," he said in a low voice, taking a long drag off his ciggy. "I would have cut your dick with a razor. You would have lost a ton of blood. Remember 'nipplegate?'" He smiled evilly as a cloud of smoke escaped his mouth.

I shuddered as I recalled that incident, with the incredible amount of blood loss and the trip to the ER. "How could I forget?" I said bitterly as I glared back at him. "It's not every day someone nearly gets their nipple cut off with a knife and almost bleeds to death."

Andre, Todd, and Noelle exchanged horrified glances in the tub. They were only mildly acquainted with the extremes that Jon was capable of going to, when it came to edge play. Severe cuts and bites requiring stitches, broken bones, near drowning, electric shocks, genital piercings, and second degree burns were among the indignities that Jon's submissives have had to endure over the years. At one point, he even had a pet snake that he incorporated into his sexual encounters - a boa constrictor named Samantha, who he credits for his love of erotic asphyxiation, and the inspiration for the snake tattoo encircling his arm.

Jon sneered. "I SAID I was sorry. Anyway, incidents like that build character," he crooned, running his hand through my hair. I turned away, not wanting him to touch me. "I made you the strong man that you are today. You were a mousy little shit before I ADOPTED you, and made you my 'bitch.'"

I felt my face turn beet red as my nostrils flared. "I'm sorry you feel that way," I growled.

"Hmm," Jon said with a smirk. "Deep down, you know it's true." He sat down in the tub, looking over at Noelle with a sexy grin as he began to fondle himself. "Come over here, little virgin. I want you to ride my dick."

Noelle turned pale, her movements hesitant as she crawled over to Jon, who abruptly put out his cigarette and ran his hands through her short platinum hair. She straddled him and began to kiss him, and he wrapped his arms around her in a tight embrace. A few moments later, she grabbed his erect cock and guided it to her opening before lowering herself onto him. He moaned sensually and began bucking his hips. I couldn't help but get hard at the sight of Noelle's frail body essentially being split open by Jon's enormous manhood. She grimaced as he dug his fingernails into her arse cheeks, his thrusts becoming harder. The friction of the water made it a struggle for her to tolerate his deep thrusting, and he clearly reveled in her discomfort. Andre and Todd watched in awe from the opposite end of the tub, touching each other sensually as they did so.

"Take every inch," Jon whispered in Noelle's ear as he thrusted upwards into her, making her wince as she did her best to ride him. "After so many years of rough, hard fucking, I would have thought your cunt could handle my huge cock by now."

Noelle whimpered. "It's the water," she murmured in a shaky voice. "There's more friction so it hurts."

SMACK!

She screamed as Jon whaled her in the arse. "Just for that, you get to choke on Ken's dick as I fuck you. And you better do a good job." He looked over at me. "Fuck this little whore's face," he growled.

I grudgingly stood up and walked over to Noelle, grabbing her face and turning her head until her mouth was level with my cock.

"Open wide, sweetheart," I said in a low voice.

Noelle groaned as I forced my manhood into her pretty mouth, holding her head to me as I thrusted. As this was happening, Jon was lifting his hips higher, slamming into her as the jacuzzi water splashed around. This went on for several minutes, then Jon looked over at Andre, who was kissing Todd.

"Andre, would you like to plug in the lamp and get the restraints?" He raised his eyebrows.

Andre smiled broadly. "Noelle told you what I brought?" He asked, to which Jon nodded. "I'd be happy to!"

He kissed Todd on the cheek, then got out of the tub and retrieved the black light lamp and coordinating restraints from his overnight bag. He placed the lamp on the nightstand next to the bed, then plugged the cord into the spare outlet. The lamp immediately turned on. Then he turned off the other lights, and a sensual purple glow took over the bedroom. The restraints sat atop the bed, and they glowed bright orange. I couldn't wait to restrain Noelle!

Jon stopped thrusting and I let go of her head. Then the three of us exited the tub and headed over to the bed. Andre and Todd elected to stay in the tub and watch us.

"Climb onto the bed width-wise and get on your back," Jon ordered. I'm going to tie your wrists to your ankles."

Noelle's eyes grew wide. "What are you going to do to me when I'm tied up?"

Jon began laughing evilly. "First, I'm going to fuck you in the arse while Ken fucks your face. We will do that until we both cum. Then you get the shit whipped out of you with a heavy belt. I might even use the paddle if I'm feeling especially savage."

Noelle trembled as she lay on the bed width-wise, tentatively rolling onto her back. "What's my safe word?" She asked shyly.

"Why would I give you one?" Jon taunted as he began fastening her wrists to her ankles.

"It's only fair," Noelle said pleadingly as she looked close to tears. "If it gets too intense, I need to have the option of stopping. Please?" She begged.

Jon sighed, then leaned over and whispered the safe word into her ear and she nodded. Once the ties were in place, Jon had her roll over onto her left side. Then he crawled onto the bed and positioned himself behind her, spitting on his dick several times before slamming into her bum. She yelped in pain as he pounded her from behind. I stood at the foot of the bed and crouched down until my cock was level with her face then began to face fuck her. Todd and Andre had a perfect view of the sex show, and began to fondle each other in the tub as they watched us.

The room was awash with violet, and the orange restraints contrasted nicely with the light. Noelle struggled against the restraints as we fucked her, and it turned me on to see her fight against the strong material. Jon noticed as well and smirked.

"What's the matter, love?" Jon asked as he pounded her bum. "Are the restraints uncomfortable? Do you need me to loosen them?"

Noelle panted and backed away from my cock to answer. "Would you?" She asked before resuming the blow job.

"No." Jon smacked her arse several times as he sodomized her, making her scream. I began to pull her hair as I fucked her face, moving my hips faster as I did so.

Andre and Todd lit cigarettes as they sat in the tub, and the smoke filled the room within moments, creating a sultry glow when combined with the black light.

"Ken, would you fetch me a cigarette?" Jon asked with a smirk.

I backed away from Noelle and grabbed one of Jon's cigarettes from the pack, lighting it and taking a drag before handing it to him. I brought the ashtray over to the bed as well, placing it at the edge.

Jon took a huge drag off his ciggy and inhaled deeply as he continued to fuck Noelle in the arse. I lined up my dick with her mouth once again.

"Noelle, darling," Jon began as he placed the ciggy in his mouth. "Do you have any more underwear or swimwear photo shoots coming up?"

I backed away from her mouth so she could talk. "No, I have a fall preview shoot coming up in about a week," she panted. "So jackets, flannel shirts, and boots. That kind of stuff."

Jon chuckled evilly. "That means I can do that thing."

"Do what thing?" Noelle asked nervously.

Jon ashed his cigarette then held it close to her right shoulder blade. "This."

Noelle screamed as Jon held the lit end of his cigarette to her skin, burning her. She thrashed around and began crying. I couldn't help but look at her sympathetically, wanting so badly to comfort her. I looked over at the boys and, surely enough, Todd looked ready to cry and Andre was consoling him, assuring him that Noelle was safe and would be pampered when the edge play was over.

Jon glared at me, finishing his cigarette and putting it out in the ashtray before resuming the hard thrusts. "Keep fucking her face," he ordered in a low voice. "We aren't done here yet."

I shook my head and reluctantly slid my dick back into Noelle's mouth. Tears fell from her eyes as she struggled to suck me off.

"Noelle, you have a choice," Jon began. "You can get whipped and paddled for five minutes or you can have your head held underwater for two minutes. If you want the first choice, moan once. If you want the second choice, moan twice. Do NOT stop sucking Ken's cock to answer my question. You've done enough TALKING already."

Despite Jon's warning, Noelle unwisely backed away from my penis to negotiate. "Can't I just get whipped for two minutes?"

SMACK!

Jon slapped Noelle hard in the arse, making her cry out. "Just for that, you get a minute of being held underwater in addition to SIX minutes with the belt and paddle."

"But Jon-"

SMACK! SMACK! SMACK!

He delivered three more hard blows to her arse cheeks, making her scream in pain one again. "THAT'S what I think of your back talk!" He shouted. "Now shut up and eat Ken's dick!"

Noelle whimpered and cried but did as she was told, occasionally sniffling.

After a few moments of fucking in silence, Jon looked over at Andre and Todd. "Boys? Why don't you come over here and join us in a circle jerk? I'm in the mood for a bukkake. Our little whore here deserves to be covered in jizz...and the more, the merrier."

Andre and Todd slowly rose from the tub and stepped out, making their way over to the bed with their hands on their dicks. Jon smiled at them and slowly withdrew from Noelle's bum, then got up from the bed and stood next to the two blokes. I backed away from Noelle's mouth and joined them. We formed a semi circle at the corner of the bed, and began jerking off over Noelle's trembling body.

"Hey, doll, get closer to the edge of the bed and get on your back," Jon ordered. "This way, we can cover you more thoroughly with our cum."

She wriggled closer to the edge of the bed and rolled onto her back, her atomic orange restraints as tight as ever. The four of us panted and moaned as we approached climax, and within minutes, we orgasmed in unison, showering Noelle in our semen. She flinched and squealed as her stomach and chest became covered in our spunk. Jon, always the overachiever, aimed for her eyes and successfully came all over her tightly closed lids, chuckling as he did so.

"Bull's eye!" Jon quipped with a huge smile as he shook his penis, making sure every last drop of cum landed on her.

Noelle sniffled as she struggled to keep her eyes tightly closed. "It burns my eyes!" She cried.

Jon picked her up off the bed and carried her over to the jacuzzi, entering carefully. "It's ok, darling," he said cheerfully as he lowered her into the water. "You get to rinse off! Start taking some deep breaths, Noelle. I'm about to hold you under."

"But just for a minute, right?" Noelle asked shakily as she lay with her back against Jon's stomach, her restraints still on.

Jon smirked up at the three of us as we sat and watched from the edge of the bed, taking a smoke break.

"Of course, dear," he said in a low voice, his facial expression making it clear that he was up to no good. I shook my head and glared at him as I smoked, wishing he would stick to his word for a change.

Noelle began breathing deeply, doing her best to relax before Jon's "attack." I felt for that poor girl, who was completely defenseless against my loose cannon of a best mate. With any luck, Jon would be kind to her. However, given his track record, he would most likely push her to a breaking point.

"On my count," Jon began in his sultry voice as he backed away from Noelle's head, which he had been holding in his lap. Her nose barely cleared the water's surface. "Five...four...three...two...one."

Noelle took a deep breath before Jon took his hands and used them to hold her head underwater. He looked at the clock on the wall to keep track of the time.

I could only imagine what must have been going through Noelle's head, aside from the deafening sound of the jacuzzi jets. Perhaps she trusted Jon to let her come up for air within sixty seconds, like he had promised. Or maybe, like the rest of us in that room, she was apprehensive and not entirely sure what Jon's motives were. It seemed we were simply playthings to him, existing for his amusement. It was hard to tell when his persona as a "dominant" ended and his true personality began... or was it one and the same? He did possess a soft side, but it seemed to show up less and less frequently. My brow furrowed as I attempted to dissect Jon's complicated personality.

Before long, a minute had passed and Jon's hands remained on Noelle's submerged head, a sinister smirk forming on his face. I rose from the bed and walked over to the hot tub, until I was just a few feet away from Jon. Andre and Todd looked on in a combination of horror and curiosity.

"Time's up," I barked, prepared to attack Jon if it meant saving Noelle's life.

Jon raised his eyebrows as he stared at me. "So?"

My face reddened and I stepped into the tub. "'So?!' Let Noelle come up for air! NOW!" I pointed my finger in his face.

Like some kind of wild animal, Jon rapidly leaned forward and bit down hard on my finger, refusing to let go. The bite was hard enough to break the skin and the more I pulled away or fought him, the harder he bit down. I yelped in pain and started to shout for him to let go. Blood began to drip steadily from the wound. Noelle let go a stream of bubbles at this time, and Jon let go of her head so she could resurface. She gasped and choked, then quickly noticed Jon stubbornly clamping down on my finger, her eyes widening in horror. Andre and Todd approached the tub and started to protest.

"Let go of his finger!" Andre bellowed at Jon.

My eyes filled with tears as I futilely tried to pull my finger away, which was bleeding pretty badly by that point. Noelle began to shake and cry and moved away from Jon as much as she could.

"Jon, please!" I yelled. "You're hurting me! I'm fucking bleeding!"

He glared up at me but reluctantly let go of my finger, his mouth full of my blood, which also dripped down his chin and settled into his beard. I examined my finger and saw two ugly bite marks that bled a good deal, and I knew I would need to clean and dress the wound. But first, I had to have some words with Jon, whose behavior was beyond crazy. In the meantime, I wrapped a nearby tissue around my finger and applied steady pressure. I stared at Jon angrily.

"You're out of your fucking mind, Jon!" I shouted through tears. "Why would you do that? You sick fuck!"

Jon sneered as he rose to his feet, licking my blood from his lips and wiping his chin. His eyes glowed once again.

"Remember this one thing," Jon growled. "I am NOT your submissive right now. You don't fucking tell me what to do, and you CERTAINLY don't call me names. Understood?"

I shook my head. "Noelle was about to DROWN. You told her a minute, and it was closer to a minute and a half. She was obviously very uncomfortable. What happened to safety? Hmm? I know the point of edge play is to push limits, but all you have done these past few days is ignore visible signs of distress. I mean, I love you, mate. But it's not fair to keep pushing limits to the point that others nearly get killed."

Jon stood in front of me, digesting what I had just said. Noelle sat cowering in the tub, worried about how Jon would react. Andre stood behind me, tightening his fist and ready to back me up if Jon got violent. Then there was Todd, who stood by Andre and nervously held onto his arm. My finger throbbed something terrible. Jon cleared his throat.

"You're right, Ken," he said softly. "It isn't fair. It's important to honor safe words and other signs of distress. I know I tend to get carried away. It's just...I get in this 'zone,' you know? Like nothing else exists but that moment and I sort of enter this...trance. I can't explain it. I would compare it to being on a runaway train. It's like, you know it's a wise idea to stop, but the brakes don't work and the only thing that will put an end to it is a big...crash." He shrugged.

I understood his mentality all too well, having been guilty of similar thought processes and behaviors myself. Being a dominant and being in control were two different things.

"I'm sorry, mate," Jon said as he undid Noelle's restraints, praising her quietly for doing such a good job. Then he stepped out of the tub and put his hand on my shoulder. "I was out of line. Let's retreat to the bathroom to clean and dress that wound, hmm?"

I swallowed and nodded slowly. "Yes, let's." I got out of the jacuzzi and began walking to the bathroom, grabbing a much needed cigarette from the edge of the tub as I did so.

Jon smiled and turned around to address Noelle and the boys before opening the bathroom door. "Why don't you all help yourselves to some refreshments from the honor bar while we freshen up in the loo? My treat."

Noelle smiled and nodded as she got up from the tub, joining Todd and Andre on the way to the honor bar in the living area.

Jon and I entered the bathroom and he wasted no time snorting another line of coke off the vanity, then lighting a cigarette. The disinfectant sat atop the sink, as did the bandages. We all knew at the beginning of the night that it was only a matter of time before someone had an injury that needed tending to. Little did Jon or the others know, my pride was injured more than my finger. Adding insult to injury was the fact that I didn't trust Jon farther than I could throw him. Much as I loved him, the man was unpredictable, and therefore dangerous.

I winced as Jon flushed the wounds with saline and disinfectant. Luckily, the ointment had a pain relief ingredient that helped get rid of the sting.

Lastly, he secured a bandage on my finger. The entire process couldn't have taken more than two minutes. Now that the wound cleaning was complete, I was able to focus on the next scene of our adventure: whipping and paddling.

We made our way back out into the bedroom, where Todd, Andre, and Noelle were sitting on the bed and eating from a jar of nuts and sipping from a bottle of wine. Andre offered some to us and we gratefully accepted, suddenly realizing we were hungry as well as thirsty.

"I will order us some room service a bit later," Jon assured with his mouth full of food. "But first? It's whipping time!" His eyes glowed as a huge smile spread across his face. He turned to Noelle, who looked scared. "Remember, dear. Six minutes." A sadistic grin spread across his face.

Noelle's eyes filled with tears. "Please try not to make me bleed," she mumbled shyly.

Jon's expression softened. He reached out and ran his hand through her hair, sitting next to her on the bed. "There might be some scratches," he admitted. "But I promise to take care of you after, and I will make sure you don't develop any scars. Wouldn't want to ruin that beautiful, porcelain skin." He kissed her bare shoulder.

She smiled appreciatively. Then Jon got up from the bed and got some supplies out of his overnight bag, which included a wooden paddle and a heavy leather belt with a large buckle. I went through my own bag, quickly locating the clothespins and a remote control vibrating egg. I then selected some appropriate music from the app on my phone, in order to set the mood. It was showtime.

"Andre? Todd?" Jon began with a smile. "I love you boys, but I need you to get off the bed for now. But, you're welcome to watch the show." They nodded and decided to get back in the jacuzzi, which had fresh water. Jon turned to Noelle. "Get on your stomach, darling. And spread your legs."

Noelle nodded, doing her best to hide her fear. "Y-you're not going to tie me up?" She asked sheepishly.

"Nope, you're a big girl and I expect you to lie still," Jon warned as he stood at the foot of the bed, holding the belt. He looked over at me, looked down at the vibrating egg I held in my hand, and nodded at me.

I winked and crawled up onto the bed, positioning myself between Noelle's legs. I spat on the egg several times then eased the object into Noelle's opening. She flinched slightly as I inserted the egg deeper until it was burrowed into her vagina.

"What is that?" Noelle asked shakily.

I got off the bed and grabbed the remote to the egg, my finger hovering over the "power" button. "It's a surprise," I said simply.

Meanwhile, Jon was taking some deep breaths and psyching himself up to whip Noelle with the heavy belt. I knew he enjoyed the suspense, and wanted Noelle to get more nervous as she lay there. Thirty seconds turned into a minute, which turned into two minutes. The tension in the air was so thick, you could cut it with a knife. Noelle began to tremble and whimper, tempted to peek at Jon but knowing better than to move. Finally, Jon drew his arm back.

WHACK!

The hard leather strap slapped against Noelle's tender flesh, leaving a welt on her porcelain-toned buttock. She squealed in pain. Jon gave her a mere five seconds to recover from the initial blow before drawing his arm back again.

WHACK!

She cried out this time, struggling to remain still. This would be a long six minutes for her. I pushed the button on the remote, resulting in the vibrating egg buzzing inside her pussy. She jumped, then began panting and moaning with pleasure.

"Be quiet!" Jon barked, and she abruptly fell silent. He walked over the nightstand to grab the paddle, then drew his arm back again, deciding to beat her with the heavy wooden instrument.

WHACK!

He walloped her very hard in the arse with that paddle, making her howl in pain. The egg continued to vibrate inside her vagina, and I decided to intensify the level of vibration. I used the remote to adjust the egg to "level two." She did her best to avoid moaning, knowing Jon would torture her worse if she did.

WHACK! WHACK! WHACK! WHACK!

Jon paddled her once on each arse cheek, then did the same thing with the belt. Noelle screamed this time, and red welts as well as scratches quickly appeared on her backside.

"Did that hurt, doll?" Jon asked sarcastically.

Noelle sniffled. "Yes," she whimpered. "It hurt a lot."

"Hmmm," Jon cooed, rubbing his beard. "Well you only have five minutes left. Suck it up and you will be rewarded."

Noelle sobbed quietly as Jon pummeled her repeatedly with the belt and the paddle, occasionally striking the backs of her legs. Once three minutes had passed, she was hyperventilating and her arse cheeks were raw, as were her hamstrings. Jon paused.

"Turn over on you back."

Noelle hesitated for a moment, wiping tears from her eyes as she flipped over. The egg continued to vibrate inside her vagina, and I adjusted the vibration strength to level three. She jumped as she lay on her back with her legs spread, her eyes swollen from crying.

Jon turned to me. "Put the clothespins on her nipples," he whispered with a smirk.

I smiled sadistically and nodded, grabbing the clothespins off the nightstand and walking over to Noelle, whose eyes were the size of pie plates.

"You're going to feel a pinch," I warned her in a low voice, placing the clothespins on her tender nipples. She yelped in pain and bit her lower lip, doing her best to keep calm.

Jon drew his arm back. "This may burn a bit, darling," he crooned.

WHACK!

The leather belt slammed against the delicate flesh of her vagina, making her scream loudly. I winced, and I heard Andre and Todd gasp in horror and surprise. I could only imagine how much that must have hurt.

"Shall I use the metal buckle?" Jon taunted. "You think THIS is painful, just wait until you feel the cold, sharp metal slicing the flesh of your womanhood. You will bleed. A LOT. It would be like getting your period early. Would you like that? Hmm? An early visit from Aunt Flo, in a room full of men?" He ran his hand up and down the length of the belt as he waited for her to answer.

Noelle shook her head as she brought her legs closer together, her eyes filling with tears. "No, please don't do that," she whimpered.

Jon then leaped onto the bed, straddling Noelle, who began shaking. He tossed the belt and paddle onto the floor. "Who needs those tools, right?" Jon asked with a chuckle. "Especially when my hands work just fine."

SMACK!

Jon slapped Noelle hard on her vagina, which still had the vibrating egg inside. She squealed and cried, her breathing heavy.

"Take the pain," Jon growled, slapping her womanhood again. "Take it. You're a big girl."

SMACK! SMACK! SMACK!

He slapped her in the face several times, making her head roll. She put up her hands to protect herself from further blows and began to sob and shake uncontrollably.

"Fugu!" She blurted, her hands covering her sore face.

I stifled a laugh, amused at the safe word Jon had picked. Then, just like that, his expression softened.

He gently removed the clothespins from her nipples and the vibrating egg from her vagina. I hit the "off" button on the remote. Play time was over for Noelle, who desperately needed to be pampered and nurtured. I sat down on the other side of her on the bed and gave her a gentle smile.

Jon repositioned himself so he was sitting alongside her, then held out his arms. "Great job again, Noelle," he said warmly. "You're such a dear friend. Would you let me hold you? No funny business, I promise." He smiled gently.

Noelle let go a laugh and sniffled, then sat up so Jon could comfort her. He wrapped his arms around her in a sweet embrace. He looked over at me.

"Care to join us in a group hug?" Jon asked.

I smiled and obliged, wrapping my arms around Jon and Noelle. Todd and Andre sat in the hot tub, smiling at the scene as they smoked cigarettes.

"How cute!" Andre commented with a smile.

"Well, don't get too comfortable," Jon said with a chuckle as he held Noelle and me. "Your little boyfriend is next."

Todd swallowed before breaking into a nervous smile. I had a hunch that Jon would be very rough for the "final round" of the evening, as was often the case after so much drinking and drugging. But at that moment, tenderness was the name of the game.

"Noelle, darling," Jon began in a soft voice as he held her, "As it relates to what just happened, what was the hardest part for you, and why?"

Noelle sniffled and cleared her throat, backing away to talk to him and me. Her answer surprised me. "Being slapped in the face," she said timidly.

Jon's eyebrows raised. "Really? Of all things?" She nodded. "Including when I held you underwater?"

"Yes. Remember Jay? That guy I was with last year?"

Jon's nostrils flared. "Oh yes, how can I forget a man who always yelled at you, then got you pregnant and deserted you, but not before demanding that you get an abortion?"

My eyes widened as I backed away from Noelle and Jon in shock. "Bloody hell," I mumbled. "What a bastard."

Noelle nodded and cleared her throat. "Well, he used to hit me. In the face. And not as part of rough sex, either. He would just get so angry over the stupidest shit. A few times he gave me a black eye and I had to go to work looking like I got into a boxing match." She laughed bitterly. "Luckily the makeup artist was skilled enough to cover it up."

By this point, Andre and Todd had joined us on the bed, comforting Noelle and apologizing. Jon swallowed, his eyes misting over with emotion.

"I can't say I'm surprised by this information," Jon said softly. "Jay always gave me a bad vibe. And I'm so sorry you had to deal with that abuse. I wish you had told me. I would have protected you. And I certainly would have been gentler with you tonight." He kissed her hand. "But I'm glad I was able to go with you to the doctor when you had your abortion. You needed emotional support."

"I so appreciated that," Noelle said softly. "And I loved how you took care of me in my apartment afterwards and cooked for me. You even did my laundry and gave me a bath, and cuddled with me for hours. It meant so much. And I remember how much Jeannie changed towards you when she found out what you did for me. She hated you for a while there, was convinced you were messing with my head when she first found out we were sleeping together."

Jon chuckled. "Ah well, Jeannie is a protective mother hen, and old-school," he said with a smile. "She doesn't understand the whole polyamory thing. For her, sex is strictly about love and romance. But for people like us," he gestured broadly with his harm to include everyone in the room, "It's about... friendship. Physical expression. Release. Fun. Adventure. And...TICKLES!" He began to tickle Noelle, who howled with laughter.

Todd, Andre, and I joined in on the tickle fest, laughing and having a great time before Noelle and Jon retreated to the bathroom to dress her wounds. While they were in the loo, I digested what I had just learned about Noelle, and her friendship with Jon. For all his sadistic behavior, he was capable of being very supportive and kind, especially in a crisis. I loved him for that. In fact, seeing how tender he was with Noelle reminded me why he was my best mate. Perhaps he wasn't a madman after all?

One hour later...

"Bark for your master, Tiffany!" Jon demanded with a red face, wiping at his nose which had just stopped bleeding after snorting too much cocaine. Despite having gone through 120 cigarettes that day, he lit up once more, blowing the smoke downwards at his new "dog."

Todd walked on all fours throughout the hotel suite, a collar around his neck and a leash attached to it, which Jon used to walk what he called his "pet bitch." Todd had lost his "human" privileges about a half hour earlier, having been demoted from a young, lipstick-wearing girl to a female dog after failing to give Jon an orgasm. According to Jon, Todd's fellatio skills were inadequate, and, to quote Jon, he could "get off faster with a bloody vacuum cleaner." Todd's lipstick had long since worn off, as had any trace of dignity he might have had at the beginning of the scene.

"Woof!" Todd uttered shakily.

Jon kicked him in the ribs, making him gasp in pain. "Louder, Tiffany!"

Todd sniffled as tears of humiliation formed in his eyes. "WOOF!" This time, his voice projected.

"That's better."

Andre, Noelle, and I sat naked on the couch, drunk and high, our attention divided between a movie on the telly and the live action drama happening right in front of us. Andre leaned forward and cleared his throat to talk to Jon. His expression was serious.

"Hey, man," Andre slurred, "Don't you think he's had enough? This is getting to be too much."

Jon stood before Andre, glaring at him with his glowing eyes as he held the leash in his hand, his "dog" obediently beside him.

"That's what the safe word is for, ANDRE," he spat. "The bitch will tell me when it's too much." He took a drag off his ciggy then leaned down to talk to Todd. "Isn't that right, Tiffany?" He asked as smoke trailed out of his mouth in heavy bursts.

"WOOF!"

Jon ran his hands through Todd's hair, scratching behind his ear. "Good boy," he cooed. Then he turned to me. "Hey, bitch, can you set up the restraints on the bed? And grab the blindfold from the front pouch of my backpack as well?" He smirked.

I nodded and slowly rose from the couch to grab the gear from his bag, setting up the restraints on the bed within moments. When I was finished, I walked back into the living area and saw that Todd's leash and collar were off and he was rising to his feet. Jon stood behind him and whacked him upside the head, startling the poor bloke.

"Walk to the bed," Jon ordered and Todd complied. "Now, lie down on your back. Ken is going to restrain and blindfold you."

I began fastening his wrist and ankles to the restraints, making them tighter than necessary. Todd winced. Then I tied the blindfold around his head. Once I was done, Jon gave me the thumbs up then turned around and addressed Andre and Noelle, who were sitting on the couch and smoking weed.

"Why don't you two join us?" He suggested. "The boy deserves an audience, and will most likely need moral support when I'm through with him." He grinned evilly, then reached into his backpack for one more item: a big, sharp knife.

Andre's eyes widened at the sight of the knife, which, frankly, looked scary with its razor sharp, serrated edges and heavy handle. Clearly, it was designed to kill. Andre put down the bong and got up from the couch. He cleared his throat.

"Jon, this is REALLY too much now," he whispered. "He's gonna freak out. The boy has been through some shit and I can't get into it, but please. I wish you wouldn't use that on him."

Jon's face appeared defiant, his glowing eyes getting a look that screamed, "How dare you question me?" Then his expression softened, and he placed his hand on Andre's shoulder. "It will be ok, Andre," he assured. "I promise to stop if he becomes distressed. And, I will even let you tie me up after, and let you and Todd do whatever you want to me.

This would be a first for me, being restrained and dominated by two people. You know me, I love control, so being tied up is not my favorite thing. But I trust you guys."

Andre swallowed then nodded. "Alright. But please, if he goes bananas, y'all have to stop right away. He's a fragile little dude." He chuckled and winked.

"You have my word."

Andre smiled and nodded appreciatively and joined Noelle and me in the bedroom. We all decided to sit in the jacuzzi and sip champagne so we could watch the little show in style. While holding onto the knife, Jon slowly climbed onto the bed and straddled a nervous Todd, whose stomach was rising and falling with his rapid breathing.

"Try your best not to move," Jon advised, to which Todd nodded. Then he began moving the knife ever so slowly over Todd's tender flesh, starting with his neck and moving downward. The blade barely grazed his skin, and goosebumps rapidly formed on his body as he resisted the urge to squirm. At one point, he giggled slightly. I glanced over at Andre, who was appearing more and more scared. Perhaps he had a feeling that something bad was about to happen.

Jon eventually made it down to Todd's feet, then began gliding the knife upwards to his neck, eventually holding the tip of the blade to his Adam's apple. His movements were so steady and calm. We all sat motionless and wide eyed, waiting for something to occur, something awful or injurious. Everything went quiet. Finally, Jon spoke.

"I'm going to remove the blindfold so you can see what I have been using on you," Jon said, as he continued to hold the knife to Todd's neck. With his opposite hand, he lifted up the black satin material, allowing him to see what was happening. "Open your eyes."

Todd slowly opened his baby blues and looked at Jon. He unsurprisingly broke into a full blown panic the second he saw the sharp knife that the sadistic bastard now held in front of his face. His entire body trembled as his wide eyes filled with horrified tears.

"AAAAAAAAAHHHH! Please stop! I can't do this anymore! Don't hurt me! FUGU!"

His scream had been deafeningly loud, and his sobs and accompanying pleas were relatable in their desperation. He began to hyperventilate and cry uncontrollably, his limbs straining against the leather straps.

The three of us jumped out of the jacuzzi and ran to the bed to comfort him. Jon quickly put down the knife and began to soothe Todd, undoing the restraints as he did so. Andre wasted no time putting his arms around his boyfriend, who began crying into his shoulder while curled up in the fetal position. Noelle and I sat at the edge of the bed, offering water and tissues to the young bloke, who refused, wanting nothing more than to be held by his partner.

Jon tentatively placed his hand on Todd's shoulder as Andre held him in a gentle embrace. Initially he jumped at Jon's touch but relaxed after a few moments.

"You're safe," Jon assured in a kind and soft voice. "It's ok. We all care about you. We are very proud of you. Everyone in this room is your friend. You are loved, Todd."

The young man continued to cry as Andre held him, and we all murmured in agreement at Jon's words. He sniffled a few times before speaking, his voice thick with emotion.

"My friend was stabbed to death with a knife a few months ago, and I saw it happen," Todd sobbed.

Noelle and I put our hands to our mouths in shock and our eyes filled with tears. Jon swallowed and squeezed Todd's shoulder. Andre looked at Jon with an "I told you so" look on his face.

"I'm so sorry," Jon said in a soft voice.

"I couldn't stop it, it happened so fast," he cried. "When I saw your knife, it brought me back to that moment and I just lost it." He wiped his eyes.

Andre held him tighter, rocking him back and forth. "You're ok, honey," he assured in a whisper. "Nobody's gonna hurt you. Remember, I will always make sure you are safe. I love you." He bent down and locked lips with Todd for several minutes as he caressed his face and body, his movements slow and gentle.

There was so much love between Todd and Andre that I couldn't help but get choked up. I locked eyes with Noelle, whose eyes had tears in them as she smiled warmly at the scene. Jon looked over at Noelle with a wink and a flirty grin, then locked eyes with me. He reached over and squeezed my hand, then leaned over and planted a gentle kiss on my lips.

Andre took a break from kissing Todd and looked over at Jon with a serious expression. "Thank you for stopping right away," he said sincerely. "That was so intense for him. He's been through a lot the past year, between watching his friend die and having to deal with his father disowning him because of his homosexuality."

Jon nodded sympathetically, knowing all too well how painful it felt to have a father who was cold and critical. "I can only imagine how hard that must be. And I know I pushed him - and everyone else - to a breaking point tonight. But now you get your revenge," he said with an amused smile. "After all the torture I have put everyone through, I deserve it. What do you say? Care to tie me up after we order room service?" He raised his eyebrows.

Andre ran his hand through Todd's hair and nodded. "With pleasure," he said with a wink. "I'm starving!"

Jon chuckled. "Great. I'm hungry, too. Let's all have something to eat, then you all get to beat the shite out of me."

Jon treated all of us to a decadent feast of seafood, steak, caviar, assorted hors d'oeuvres, cheesecake, and multiple cocktails but barely ate anything himself, saying that the food tasted like metal. The rest of us shrugged as we chowed down, unable to notice a metallic taste to anything. Once we were done eating, Jon positioned himself face up on the bed, and Andre began restraining him. Todd and I assisted while Noelle watched in awe, smoking a cigarette as she did so.

It was strange seeing my incredibly dominant best mate being restrained. True to his nature, he did his best to remain "in charge," giving instructions on how to tighten the restraints as well as requesting an extra pillow to be placed under his head. In the BDSM world, some people referred to this practice of giving pointers and making requests as "topping from the bottom," and was a way for dominants to feel more in control while in a submissive role.

Once the restraints were secure and the pillow was in place, Andre grabbed a bottle of vodka from the honor bar and took a hearty swig before passing it around, taking the time to share some with Jon as well. According to him, this hardcore session called for some "liquid courage." Todd became especially drunk, and his sweet personality became noticeably more aggressive after downing several shots of the strong booze. Despite his cocky smirk, I picked up on the slightest bit of fear in Jon's eyes as he lay there, watching Todd become intoxicated. Perhaps Jon had a feeling that Todd harbored some built up rage over the things he had been forced to endure, a feeling that was about to prove true. However, nobody, including myself, was prepared for the intensity of that rage.

Half an hour later...

"WHO'S THE FUCKING 'BITCH' NOW, PRETTY BOY?!" Todd shouted as he sodomized Jon, whose nose had begun to bleed after being punched in the face several times. Despite his small size, Todd had one hell of a right hook, and I couldn't help but flinch when I saw him strike my best mate in the face.

Jon looked up at Todd with a mixture of apprehension and awe, clearly impressed with his assertiveness.

"That's it, Todd," Jon panted with a smirk on his face. "Let out all that anger."

Within seconds, Andre approached the bed, holding a ball gag. Jon's eyes widened. I knew for a fact that he didn't like having his speech restricted.

"Andre, my friend," Jon began as he did his best to stay calm, "Perhaps we could do without the gag? I will remain quiet." His smile was confident but his eyes were full of fear.

Andre shook his head. "You had your chance to call the shots and now it's OUR turn, pretty boy. Open that pretty mouth of yours."

Jon glared at Andre and Todd but tentatively opened his mouth. Andre abruptly shoved the breathable ball in his mouth and locked it in place with the attached straps. A pained expression formed on Jon's face, and it was clear that he was out of his comfort zone.

Todd continued to fuck Jon with reckless abandon, his thrusts quickening. Within a few minutes, he abruptly pulled out and ejaculated onto his stomach. He then licked off the semen and swallowed it, reveling in the taste. When he got off the bed for some water and a cigarette, he nodded to me.

"Want sloppy seconds, Ken?" Todd asked with a ciggy in his mouth.

For the briefest of moments, I hesitated. Then I thought of all the disrespectful things Jon had done to me over the past two days. While I loved the bloke dearly, I couldn't stand how controlling he could be and how often he disregarded others' feelings, including my own. Within less than 48 hours, he had pressured me into getting a cosmetic procedure, nearly drowned me in the jacuzzi as well as the pool, bit my finger until it bled, accused me of forcing him to eat food he didn't like, referred to me as his "bitch" multiple times, embarrassed me in front of Jeannie by reminding me that his plastic surgeon could "fix" my nose, exposed my dick in the hotel lobby, and spat water in my face while at a restaurant. When I thought of these things, I was ready to give him a taste of his own medicine... if only for a short while.

I took a sip of water and straddled Jon on the bed. Then I spit the contents in his face, getting it in his eyes. He squinted and turned his head, his gag muffling the moans of protest emanating from his mouth. Then I lined up my cock with his arsehole.

"I love you, Jon," I began, as I wiped down his face with my hand. "But sometimes, you can be a real DICK!"

I slammed into him, the force of my thrusts making him grunt. His eyes appeared frightened. I nearly felt sorry for him, but once again forced myself to think of all the shit he had done to me, as well as others. Once again my anger surged through me. The others watched in awe from the jacuzzi, drinking and smoking.

"You are such a cocky bastard," I growled as I pounded him. "Always making everyone do things for you, making them your 'bitch.' Well, now YOU get to be the bitch! YOU get to see how much fun it is to be at the mercy of someone else. Take what I'm giving you!"

SMACK!

I slapped Jon hard in the face. His eyes filled with tears, and he moaned several times, as if he were trying to talk to me. I felt regret over having hit him, and decided to temporarily remove the gag so he could speak.

"What is it, Jon?" I asked, continuing to thrust.

He panted as he smiled sweetly up at me. "Ken, you're my best mate," he said in a soft voice. "And I love you. You don't want to hurt me. Let's all just go to bed, hmm? We can talk in the morning? I can treat to breakfast." His voice shook slightly.

Before I could answer, Andre was marching up to the bed and wasted no time shoving the gag back into Jon's mouth.

"Shut up!" Andre shouted in Jon's face. "You've said enough!" He turned to me. "Ken, mind if I step in? I want to pound him for a while."

I nodded, feeling ready for another drink and cigarette. I slowly withdrew from him and got off the bed, pouring myself a stiff drink and lighting a cancer stick before sitting in the jacuzzi. Noelle smiled sympathetically and put her arm around me, perhaps sensing my guilt. Todd, by contrast, appeared ready for round two as his face formed a scowl.

"I think I'm in the mood for a bath," Todd said, a sinister grin on his face. He got up and retreated to the bathroom, running the water. Meanwhile, Andre was fucking the hell out of Jon while giving him a hand job. Jon's moans intensified and he bucked his hips, approaching climax. Andre heard the water running and saw Todd in the bathroom, hunched over the tub as he waited for the water to fill.

"Guess who's about to get dunked in the bathroom while getting fisted up the ass?!" Andre growled at Jon, before putting the blindfold on him. Jon began moaning loudly and thrashing around, clearly in distress. I swallowed, knowing that Jon was now completely at Andre's mercy, and, with the blindfold on, he was now unable to signal with his eyes. In fact, he didn't even have a safe word or signal of any kind. This was a free-for-all, and things could get dangerous very quickly without safety precautions. I got up from the jacuzzi and made my way over to the bed.

"Hey, Andre," I began, "perhaps it's wise for us to give Jon a way to signal to us when he's had enough?"

Andre glared at me as he fucked Jon. "Oh you mean, like Jon did when he nearly drowned my boyfriend? Or when he ate boiling hot pasta off his stomach? Nah, man. I'm good! He didn't give Todd respect when he did those things so I'm gonna hold off on giving HIM any. Karma's a bitch!" He turned to Jon, who was panting and thrashing around. "Right, bitch?"

Just then, Todd appeared at my side and got on the bed with Andre. "Let's undo the restraints and carry him into the bathroom for the grand finale," Todd growled, a wee bit of cocaine lining his left nostril.

Andre agreed, and they undid his restraints. As much as I hated to admit it, Andre had a point. Jon had either ignored signals of distress or refrained from providing any safety parameters for the majority of the day. He needed a lesson in humility.

Once the restraints were off, Andre and Todd lifted Jon off the bed and carried him to the bathroom. Once there, they threw him onto the floor, where he landed on his arse and grunted loudly. I thought I was able to make out the sound of something cracking when he fell, and I got very concerned that he might have hurt himself. I ran up to him and removed his blindfold. His eyes were wild looking and bloodshot. He grimaced in discomfort as he shifted his weight.

"Jon, are you ok, mate?" I asked.

With the gag still in his mouth, he nodded and winked. Just then, I felt a nudge.

"Step aside, Ken," Todd growled with a crazed look on his face. Noelle appeared in the doorway just then, looking concerned. I walked up to her and held her hand, more for my own comfort than for hers. These men were starting to really scare me.

"Yeah, we have business to take care of!" Andre spat as he got into the tub, then bent down to yell at Jon. "Kneel at the edge of the tub, pretty boy!"

Todd pulled Jon by the hair, then Andre grabbed and pulled his arms until he was kneeling before the tub. Andre knelt down in the tub and smacked Jon in the face.

"Take some deep breaths," Andre instructed. "You're about to get dunked."

Gag in place, Jon began taking ragged breaths through his nose. Todd spat on his finger and began playing with Jon's bum, distracting him. A minute or two later, Andre grabbed the back of Jon's head and forced him underwater. He remained silent for a solid five minutes before speaking. The tension in the air was so thick, I could have cut it with a knife.

"How does it feel to be ambushed?" Andre yelled as he held Jon's head under the surface. "I hope you can stay submerged for a good long time, pretty boy. I heard you made Ken stay under for ten minutes and Todd for over six. And that you even pretended to drown! It seems you like fucking with people's heads!"

Andre pushed down harder on Jon's head, then Todd began fondling him, occasionally teasing his arse crack with his fingers. After a while, Jon let go some bubbles.

I looked down at my watch and saw that ten minutes had passed. Noelle looked frightened, concerned that Andre was going to drown Jon. To be honest, I was convinced that he WOULD try to drown my best mate, and I was prepared to intervene if he did.

Suddenly, Andre looked up at Todd. "Fist him."

Todd swallowed but agreed, spitting on his fist multiple times. I prayed he would be gentle with Jon, but given his level of intoxication and the extreme nature of the sex act, gentleness was not likely. I noticed that Todd began to play with Jon's genital piercing, tugging at the delicate ring until Jon let go a few more bubbles. I gulped, knowing that he must have been in some pain.

Todd began to graze his fist along Jon's arse crack until he was at the precipice of his hole. "Get ready, Jonny boy!" He shouted.

With those words, he quickly forced his entire fist into Jon's bum, using his other hand to yank violently at his piercing. Immediately, Jon screamed from beneath the surface, bubbles forming in a heavy stream. Todd quickly removed his fist from his arse, which immediately began seeping blood. I marched right over to Andre and grabbed his arm.

"Let him come up right now!" I barked. "He's injured!"

Andre nodded, and let go of Jon's head. He sprang up for air immediately, and it was clear he was choking. I removed the gag from his mouth, so he could catch a breath.

Blood trailed from his bum as well as his penis as he choked and gasped for air, vomiting up some of the water he had managed to swallow and inhale while submerged. I looked down at his member and my jaw dropped. Todd had managed to completely rip his piercing out of his penis, leaving a sizable tear that began to bleed heavily.

Noelle began to sob as she saw what happened, and Todd and Andre appeared frightened as well. I decided to take charge, and knelt before my injured friend.

"Jon, I'm going to get you some ice for your penis and bum to slow the bleeding, and some water to drink, ok?"

Still somewhat in shock, Jon nodded slowly as he began to tremble. "Ok," He panted. "Can you also get me a blanket, as well as my cigarettes and bong?"

I nodded. Once I got up, Todd, Noelle, and Andre knelt before Jon to comfort him, giving him a prolonged hug. Todd began to cry and apologize, but Jon assured him it was alright.

I came back into the bathroom within seconds, armed with a soft blanket, ice, and water, as well as Jon's smokes. He sat at an angle with his back against the wall, appearing to be in pain when he shifted his weight. Still, I managed to apply ice and direct pressure to his injuries, and the three of us helped disinfect and bandage his wounds. Since his hands were shaking badly, I held the water glass to his lips when he needed a drink, then also lit his cigarette for him. Then we all took hits from his bong, and I draped the blanket over him. After a while, Jon's eyes began to appear heavy.

"You know I love you all," Jon said groggily. "But I need to be alone for a while, just to chill out and get my bearings. I'm in 'subspace,' so I need some quiet in order to process everything." He smiled and winked.

We all agreed to leave him be in the bathroom, giving him a hug before exiting. I turned around once more to look at him.

"You sure you're going to be ok? You're comfortable sitting there on the floor?"

He nodded eagerly. "Oh yeah, and then we can all have breakfast together in the morning." He flashed me his self assured grin.

I smiled and nodded before saying goodnight, then closed the door behind me.

We were all exhausted by that point and decided to go to sleep. Noelle collapsed on the recliner opposite the couch, where Todd and Andre quickly fell asleep. I had the bed to myself, and fell asleep within perhaps ten minutes.

Some time after 2am, I awakened to the sound of a loud yelp followed by groans. They were coming from the bathroom. I got up and knocked on the door to check on Jon.

"You ok?" I asked through the door.

More grunts. "Yeah," Jon gasped. "I just got startled by a bad dream, that's all. Gonna head to bed soon, mate."

"Alright, Jon. Love you." Then I retreated back to bed.

Perhaps an hour later, I awakened once more, this time to the sound of Todd crying.

"It won't stop," he sobbed. "It just won't stop."

Andre whispered something I couldn't make out. Then a few minutes later, I heard the door close and everything went quiet. I shrugged and went right back to sleep, still exhausted.

The next time I opened my eyes, it was early morning and the room was just starting to fill with light. I sat up, put on my robe, and went to the loo. I expected Jon to be there but the bathroom was empty. When I came out and popped into the living area, I saw that nobody was there either. That's when I saw a note on the coffee table. I picked it up and read it.

"Dear Ken and Jon, thank you guys for a great time. I had to bring Todd to the hospital because he had a nosebleed that wouldn't stop. Noelle came along for moral support. We will talk to you boys soon. Best, Andre."

Just then, the door to the hotel room opened. It was Jon. He walked with a limp and avoided my gaze altogether as he silently made his way through the door and began packing our stuff. I immediately knew there was something very wrong with him.

After many hours of silent treatment brought on by post traumatic stress, Jon revealed that he had gone to the ER. When Andre and Todd had thrown him to the floor, he had broken his coccyx, which, according to the doctor, had suffered such a severe fracture that the bone was "hanging on by a thread." Only time would heal it, and pain meds would help with the discomfort. He had also required stitches for his penis, which he had managed to do himself in the hotel bathroom using his sewing kit, and cocaine for a local anesthetic. Jon said the hospital staff was shocked and impressed that he did his own stitches, as well as the fact that he was able to walk at all.

I learned some other disturbing details regarding the incident with Todd and Andre. In short, the edge play scene started out consensual but did not end that way, which meant that what they did to Jon was, in the strictest sense, considered assault. I was none the wiser and had assumed that, since eye signals were not an option, Jon would have fought back or revealed to me that he wasn't ok and needed me to help him. It turned out that his level of intoxication made it virtually impossible to fight off the two men, and that his pride had gotten in the way of asking me for help. My heart broke when he revealed this information to me.

As for the painkillers? After seeing what they had done to my wife, I was a bit skeptical when Jon told me the doctor prescribed them but decided it was alright, because it was a pain medication that wasn't as likely to cause dependency. Little did I know that what started out as a comfort measure for my best mate would turn into a full-blown addiction to opiates, and his behavior over the next few weeks would completely spiral out of control.

Chapter 4: The Green-Eyed Monster, Part 1 - Fireworks and Waterworks

"Why? Why? WHY?!"

I sobbed to myself as I lay in the fetal position, letting the water rain down on me as I bled. I had been in the shower for almost an hour, trying in vain to cleanse myself of what had just happened to me. But all the water and soap in the world couldn't erase my humiliation and shame. The fact that it occurred in my own home, and at the hands of my supposed best mate, made it all the more horrific.

My mind went over the events of the past few weeks, searching for anything resembling a sign, a hint that Jon was going to lose his mind enough to do what he did.

The incident with Andre and Todd had shaken Jon to his core. His broken coccyx made anal intercourse - and a number of other activities - prohibitively painful, and his injured penis made regular intercourse and masturbation uncomfortable. As a result, his sexual activity was mostly limited to giving blowjobs, and he became increasingly impatient over time. The combination of the trauma of an assault (however unintentional), the inconvenience of having his cock and bum out of commission at the same time, a growing addiction to pain meds, and the grief associated with the end of a decades-long relationship with Lisa, all contributed to Jon's deteriorating mental state.

The trip home from New York City had been a turbulent one. Jon was completely silent for several hours after he had returned from the hospital. There were times in the past when he had gone "offline," appearing to enter his own world and seemingly unable to speak. I had noticed these quiet spells as early as middle school, not long after he saw his neighbor attacked whilst we lived in London. He had never spoken in detail about the incident with the neighbor, and was always eager to change the subject when I brought it up. It was clear that he was very traumatized by the event but was evasive whenever I pressed for details. "It was a long time ago, mate," he would simply say with his trademark smirk.

I knew better than to pressure Jon into conversation when he entered "quiet mode," so I simply gave him space. When we checked out of the hotel, I assisted with the process so he didn't have to interact with the front desk clerk. Then when it was time to hail a cab, I took care of it and made small talk with the driver.

Once we got to the parking garage and rode off on his motorcycle, I experienced a sense of dread, and his driving habits only added to that feeling. It was a vague feeling of doom, an "unraveling" of sorts that I could sense was occurring in Jon's psyche. In addition to speeding like a maniac, he popped several "wheelies" on the highway, causing me to white-knuckle the sissy bar and beg him to knock it off. I said a silent prayer that we would arrive home in one piece.

We took a much needed break at a rest stop on route 15 in Fairfield, Connecticut, which happened to be when Jon finally broke the silence, and spoke of his ordeal.

I ordered breakfast inside the shop while Jon got gasoline, then he drove his bike over to a parking spot so we could sit at the picnic bench for a quick nibble and a smoke before resuming our trip home.

We ate egg and cheese sandwiches in silence for a few moments when I decided to talk to Jon, who barely looked at me and appeared a million miles away.

"It's so nice out today," I commented, deciding to start out with small talk.

He looked down and didn't respond, chewing silently. I tried again.

"You don't have to talk about what happened last night, but I'm here for you. I can tell you're in pain by how you're limping, and by how you're sitting on the bike."

He still averted his gaze, taking a sip of his drink. I decided on a new tactic. Jon had always loved when I imitated his father, so I lowered my voice to sound like Jon, Sr. and began mimicking his body language.

"Jonathan," I said in a low voice and a British accent that was thicker than my usual one, "It's not very becoming to ignore people when they're talking. You best get your life in ORR-DER," I trilled, exaggerating the pronunciation of the last word. I could see the corners of Jon's mouth turn up. I continued on. "When I was your age, I respected my friends and my teachers. Son, why can't YOU be more like that instead of a discipline case? Jonathan, I'm TALKING to you!"

By this time, Jon was laughing heartily and shaking his head. I smiled broadly and reached across the table to pat him on the arm. "There he is," I said warmly. "My best mate is back online."

He smiled warmly and winked. "Getting there," he mumbled as he took another bite of his sandwich.

I sighed and took a sip of my tea, deciding to ask a serious question. "Andre and Todd really hurt you badly, didn't they?" My voice was soft and my tone sympathetic.

He swallowed and looked at me for a moment before nodding slowly. "Yeah." His voice was barely above a whisper.

I got up and sat next to him on the bench and gave him a gentle hug, which he returned. "I'm sorry."

He shrugged. "I will be fine, mate."

"May I ask what happened?"

That's when he told me everything. He took a deep breath and cleared his throat.

"Last night was all one big miscommunication," he said with a sigh, looking down as he spoke.

I rubbed his back. "Go on," I encouraged gently.

"After Andre blindfolded me, I no longer wanted to continue," he confessed. "Between having my speech restricted by the gag, my sight gone due to the blindfold, and lack of coordination and strength in my limbs due to extreme drunkenness, I felt it unwise to keep going. But my protests appeared to be part of the act. So, like any well-meaning dominant, Andre continued, as did Todd. They had no way of knowing that the assault went from a simulation to the real deal. They figured it was fake. But it felt bloody real to ME." He took another bite of his sandwich before continuing. I patted him on the thigh.

"When Andre held me underwater, I nearly drowned. The ball gag had filled with water and it was so hard to avoid swallowing or breathing it in, especially after being forced to hold my breath for so long. I felt like karma was biting me in the arse for all the times I did similar shit. Also, when Todd shoved his entire fist in my bum with my newly fractured tailbone, it was the worst pain I had ever experienced," Jon revealed. "I knew my coccyx was broken, because I've broken it twice before from skateboarding mishaps so I know how it feels. So I dragged myself to the ER."

My eyes widened. "Bloody hell," I mumbled in shock. "You shouldn't have suffered alone. I would have helped. I did hear you grunt and and yelp a few times, and I had believed you when you told me you had awakened from a bad dream. I had no idea that you were that severely hurt."

Jon nodded, taking another sip of tea. "It was unbelievably painful, getting into a standing position with a broken coccyx after sitting on the bathroom floor for several hours, and walking was even worse. But I did it. Unsurprisingly, this was, by far, the worst of the three tailbone fractures. The bone was, to quote the doctor, 'hanging on by a thread.' And only time will heal it. Twelve weeks is a rough estimate. Good thing I got a prescription for painkillers." He took another sip of his tea before continuing. "I know I should have asked you for help, but my pride got in the way, mate."

I nodded and patted him on the arm. "I understand. I can be rather prideful myself." I thought of Anna, and how she had reacted after that hardcore session at my house several months prior. Sometimes it was just easier to be alone, even when we needed help.

I listened sympathetically as he continued on about his ER experience, telling me about how kind and caring the doctors and nurses were, and how impressed they were at his ability to walk at all. They had treated him very delicately, as if he'd been raped...which he technically had been. I winced when he told me about the stitches he did on his own penis after Todd had ripped out his piercing.

"I rubbed some of Todd's leftover coke on the hole in my dick for local anesthetic, then I used a sewing kit that I'd nearly forgotten to pack. You have no idea how challenging it was to thread that needle when my hands were shaking so badly. But I did a pretty respectable job for a non-surgeon. Would you like to see my handiwork, mate?" He offered with raised eyebrows and a smirk as he pointed to his crotch.

Despite my initial horror, I laughed at his proposal. "Perhaps after a few drinks!" I quipped. We both roared with laughter.

"On a more serious note, I am so sorry you had to go through all that," I said as I placed my arm around him. He returned my embrace and smiled.

"That which doesn't kill me gives me blue balls," he quipped. I laughed. "That's the worst part, having two 'pleasure pieces' out of order at the same time. But perhaps with my pain pills, it should be manageable." He lit a cigarette, and I did likewise.

I swallowed and tried not to think of my wife. "May I ask what they prescribed?" I tried to sound casual, taking a drag off my cigarette.

Jon smiled sympathetically, perhaps knowing that I was thinking of my best girl. He reached into his pocket and took out the prescription bottle, handing it to me. I took it and saw it was a different type of pill than what my wife had taken, one that wasn't as likely to cause addiction. I breathed a sigh of relief and handed the bottle back to him.

"Don't worry," Jon assured in a soft voice as smoke escaped his mouth and nose. "I will be careful with these meds, I promise."

I nodded and swallowed, having heard the same exact words from my wife years ago, just before she developed a severe addiction to pain pills and intravenous drugs. Jon was similar to her, in that he had an addictive personality. He was a man of his word, except when it came to his two vices: sex and drugs. When it came to those things, he got completely carried away.

We smoked one more cigarette apiece before continuing on our ride home, my mind temporarily at ease.

Later that evening...

"Jon? Jon?! You ok?"

I knocked on the bathroom door, concerned for my best mate. He had decided to take a bath after getting drunk on shots of tequila and washing down a double dose of his pain meds with two large glasses of red wine. As for his cocaine use, I had lost track many hours prior. He had been in the loo for over an hour, and wasn't answering me. To make matters worse, the door was locked.

"JON!" I barked, thumping on the door even harder.

My heart jackhammered in my chest and I made the decision to break down the door. One swift kick with my strong right leg was all it took for the door to fly open.

I walked over to the bathtub and saw Jon submerged beneath the surface of the water, with his eyes closed. After waiting a few moments, I decided to poke him. Clearly startled, he sprang up from the water, gasping for breath as he looked at the clock, then at me. His pupils were dilated and his eyes bloodshot, and his lips turned upward into a smirk.

"Twelve minutes, mate," he slurred. "A new breath holding record! Not bad for a drunken pillhead, I reckon!" Then he began cackling.

Far from amused, I glared at him. "Did you not hear me knocking? I was fucking scared! Then you had the stones to lock the door, while drunk and high off your arse, AND take a bath? You could have easily slipped and fallen, OR drowned. I KNOW you took extra pain pills. I understand you have had a rough day but for God's SAKES, mate, could you at least try to be more careful? Please?"

Jon looked up at me, smiling sweetly and rubbing his hand over my chin. "Aw, Ken," he cooed. "You're such a protective papa bear. No wonder you got the nickname 'UNCLE Kenny.' You're adorable." He landed a sloppy kiss on my lips.

I was getting more pissed off by this point and backed away from his face. "I'm fucking serious, Jon. You need to slow down. You know what happened to my wife and I do not want to go through that with you. Can you even stand up on your own, or do you need me to help you?"

Jon sat up straight and placed his hands on either side of the tub, slowly pushing himself up to a standing position. His knees buckled slightly and he nearly fell down, but I held onto him to keep him steady. He looked over at me and smiled, wobbling back and forth slightly.

"See? I'm standing." He winked.

"Yeah with my help," I pointed out. "Now step out of the tub carefully." I continued to hold onto him.

"Yes, Uncle," he slurred, lifting his right leg up until it cleared the edge of the tub, then doing the same with his left leg. His knees still buckled slightly. "I'm just tired, mate," he insisted, sounding incredibly drunk.

"Mmhmm," I said sarcastically, holding onto his arm a little more tightly as I dried him off a bit with a towel then wrapped it around him. "You're 'just' tired. And I'm the queen of England."

"Hey, I'M the 'queen,' you little bitch!" He protested with a chuckle. "I'M the one who's fucked three hundred men! Or is it four hundred? I lost count of all the dicks, they just keep coming at me so bloody FAST!" He howled with laughter at his comment.

I bit my lip, ready to burst out laughing at his ridiculous words, but managed to keep it together. "Let's take a walk to the couch, shall we?"

"Aye, aye, SIR!" He said, holding onto me as I half carried him to the living room sofa and sat him down.

I handed him a bottle of water that had been sitting on the end table. "Suck some of this down," I said, holding the bottle to his lips.

"Can I suck your COCK after?" He asked as he drank some water.

I chuckled softly. "If you're good."

"I'm a good boy," Jon insisted in a baby voice as he drank from the water bottle. "I'm cooold, though."

"Would you like your footed pajamas?" I asked. "You're literally the only man alive who can manage to make fleece onesies look sexy."

Jon chuckled and nodded. "I would love those pajamas right about now. Thank you."

I nodded and went to the bedroom to grab his black onesie, and I even helped him get dressed in it. That was when he shared a memory, one involving Lisa and himself.

"Lisa and I used to play a game," he said in a wistful tone as he placed his feet into the built in slippers, the slightest smile on his face. "I would come home from work and she would greet me with a kiss. Then I would sit down on the couch and she would slowly undress me. But, she would keep my underwear on and tease my package until I was hard as a rock. Then she would look into my eyes and ask me, 'Would you be my baby?' And I would say in a high pitched voice, 'Yes, Mommy.' Then she would pour me a baby bottle full of scotch and soda and feed it to me. After that, she would dress me in these same pajamas. The first time we did the age play, I thought it was silly but after a while, I liked being her 'baby.'

"Sometimes we got creative. I would start out talking like a little boy and ask for her booby, and she would give it to me so I could 'nurse,' but then halfway through sucking, I would turn into an adult again, would start talking dirty while biting her tits roughly and feeling her up. She would then ask me, 'Who ARE you? Where's my sweet little boy? Where's my little Jonny?' And I would growl back at her, saying, 'Little Jonny is dead. I'm Jon. But you will call me 'Master.' Then I would dominate her. I would start off by licking and sucking her pussy, saying things like, 'Little Jonny came out of your pussy, but Master is about to go IN.' Then after completely devouring her cunny, I would rip off my pajamas and undies and pound the shit out of her for a solid hour, making her squirt multiple times and tremble with pleasure. Ultimately, we would fall asleep in each other's arms, and I would wake up feeling so secure. So...loved. Like a baby in his mama's arms. Hmm..."

He let go a sigh as he reclined on the couch and cuddled up to me, his faraway gaze revealing the extent to which he was reliving the fond memory. I was glad that he shared that story with me. I felt sad that he and Lisa were no longer together, but happy for all the good times they shared. Jon and I may have both lost the loves of our lives, but we still had each other, and the thought gave me comfort. We both fell asleep on the couch within minutes, our arms around each other.

One week later...

"I'm only trying to help, Daryl."

Jon's voice was devoid of emotion as he sat in our office at the gym, making suggestions for boosting sales and overall improvements. I found his ideas useful, but Daryl wasn't having it and began to shout at his elder brother.

"Why don't you just mind your own fucking business and start your own gym instead? Fuck this partnership idea! I don't want it! We do our thing and you do yours! You're a goddamn tyrant and a dictator! And don't fucking touch my filing cabinet either!"

Daryl slammed the top of our desk with his fist before storming out of the office. I had never seen him so angry. I turned to Jon, who was sitting calmly at the desk, slowly shaking his head.

"I just don't understand why he must behave so stubbornly," he said calmly. "I am simply trying to help the business become more successful."

I shrugged, doing my best to be a referee and avoid taking sides. "Daryl is just stubborn by nature," I said. "I think once you open the second gym location and it does well, he will be more receptive."

"I hope so. The man is impossible."

I swallowed, thinking to myself that Jon was the impossible one. He had a nasty habit of talking down to Daryl, causing him to get defensive. As for his behavior over the past week? It had been nothing short of obnoxious, and he had gotten very drunk several times after unwisely mixing pain pills with huge amounts of alcohol. I found myself becoming a caretaker of sorts, making sure he was safe while intoxicated. One night, I had to follow closely behind him as he walked around my kitchen on wobbly legs, making sure he didn't fall over while cooking dinner. When he asked me why I kept following behind him, I told a white lie, saying I just liked being close to him. He had reacted by kissing me hard on the mouth and fondling my dick, calling me his "lover boy." I preferred that title to "bitch."

The day after we returned home from New York, Jon had taken me, Anna, Tracy, Eugene, Amy, and Daryl sailing on his new boat. Everything was great until Jon decided to get drunk and high while at the helm, realizing a little too late that he wasn't very good at boating under the influence after we nearly crashed into a yacht. Luckily nobody was hurt, and the girls had even found it rather funny, but Daryl and I had been livid. Rather than apologize and show concern for our feelings, he had laughed in Daryl's and my faces, then told us to "lighten the fuck up and stop being such cunts."

In an effort to take my mind off all the drama, I decided to plan a Fourth of July party at my house. When I mentioned the idea of inviting Todd and Andre, Jon shook his head, insisting that he needed more time to pass before he spoke to them again. I understood, but I felt the need to let them know the situation. Unbeknownst to Jon, I had contacted the two blokes myself, to fill them in on what had happened and to assure them that Jon was alright but just needed time to heal, and work through some past trauma. They were very understanding as well as apologetic, and agreed to give him space. Per my conversation with Andre, Todd's hospital visit revealed that he had managed to burn a hole through his septum due to his coke use, and was going to outpatient rehab to try to get clean. I had refrained from discussing Jon's addiction issues, believing it was only fair to allow my best mate some privacy when it came to certain matters.

Jon acted as my self-appointed consultant for the party, making suggestions on what kind of food and drinks to serve, who to invite, what music to play, and what themes to incorporate. With the amount of energy he put into planning MY party, one would have thought it was a royal fucking wedding. I found myself getting increasingly irritated with his attempts at "helping," which were morphing into something closer to sabotage. In order to have some breathing room, I found excuses to send him on little errands that I could have done myself, like purchasing decorations and random supplies. Thanks to his still-healing coccyx, he was driving his Tesla more than his motorcycle. Either way, Jon traveled in style, turning heads in parking lots whether he showed up in his Fatboy or his high-end, cherry red sedan.

About two days before the party, Jon showed up from one of these errand runs high as a kite, sniffling nonstop and sweating profusely despite the relatively cool temperature. He was talking a mile a minute as he dumped a bunch of bags on the kitchen counter. After a few minutes of rambling, he must have noticed how I was looking at him and abruptly stopped talking, holding up his hands in confusion.

"What is it, mate?" He asked with raised eyebrows.

"Are you high?" I asked stupidly, knowing the answer already.

Jon's nostrils flared as he stared me down with those glowing eyes and a flushed complexion. Then he pointed his finger at my chest.

"Listen," he began in a hostile tone as he got in my face, looking ready to hit me. I backed away slightly. "I just went out and bought supplies for your little soirée. My tailbone is FUCKING killing me. It hurts when I WALK. It hurts when I SIT. It hurts when I FUCK. It hurts when I SHIT. If you had a fractured coccyx and an extra hole in your dick, you would get high, too. Now, sod off. Mind your business."

I was shocked to silence, unaccustomed to seeing Jon so angry. I was about ready to walk out of the kitchen and leave him be until his high wore off, but his nose began to bleed heavily. He didn't even notice, since he was busy putting away his purchases.

"Jon, your nose is bleeding a ton," I said softy, grabbing a box of tissues from the end table and placing it in front of him. Just then, some of the blood dripped down his chin and got onto the kitchen floor. He looked at me with alarm, then wiped his face. He appeared even more apprehensive when he saw the amount of blood on his hand as well as the floor.

"Oh, Christ," he muttered as he rushed to the bathroom, his hand covered in blood.

I followed behind him and watched from the doorway as he frantically splashed cold water on his face then pinched his nose closed in an effort to stop the bleeding. He looked up at me after a few moments, flashing me his self-assured smirk.

"It's all under control, mate," he said in a calm voice. "Just a little blood. Happens sometimes."

I shook my head and walked up to him. "Jon, unpinch your nose. Let's see if the bleeding stopped. These nosebleeds of yours are getting worse and more frequent."

He sighed and let go of his nose. Sure enough, blood dribbled from his nostrils within seconds. He sniffled and ran the water again to splash his face. "It's no big deal," he insisted as he resumed pinching his nose. "Go on, let me have some privacy, please. I appreciate your concern, but I'm fine, mate." He winked and smiled gently.

I reluctantly left the bathroom, since it was clear he didn't want my input, and he wasn't ready for the tough love talk I had rehearsed in my head for several weeks regarding his drug use. To be honest, I wasn't ready for it, either. Sooner or later, I would have to face the music and tell Jon how I felt, but decided at that moment that I would devote my attention to the upcoming party, and confront him afterwards.

For the next 48 hours, I busied myself with work and house cleaning. The gym was busy, and it seemed everyone wanted to get in a good workout before the holiday. The day before the party, Jon insisted on accompanying Daryl and me to the gym, helping with answering phones and office work as well as cleaning. He had decided on a location for the second gym and was planning to sign the lease on the space the following week. This particular space had already been a gym, but the owner had retired and the rent was reasonable. To top it all off, it was located on a main road in a high traffic area, so would most likely be very successful. Daryl and I tolerated Jon's overbearing attitude and tendency to micromanage, knowing it was only a matter of time before he had his own space and was out of our hair.

Before I knew it, the day of the party had arrived. It was a picture perfect July afternoon, and the air held just enough humidity to make it tempting to go for a refreshing swim in the ocean. Jon had gone all out with the alcohol, insisting on purchasing an array of top shelf liquor, as well as a number of different types of wine and beer. Several of our neighbors were coming, as well as some friends that Jon and I hadn't seen in a while. Jon had suggested we all go on his sailboat to view the local fireworks show, and I had agreed, as long as he allowed me to help him with the sailing if he got too impaired. Surprisingly, he said yes.

By 4pm, all the guests had arrived, and the air was saturated with the aroma of charcoal from the grill intermingled with ocean air. There was a total of sixteen people, including myself. The usual gang had shown up, including elder brother Lawrence and his wife Diana. Lawrence and Jon had words with each other very early on, with my best mate unsurprisingly being the instigator.

"I see you're back to wearing a shirt again," Jon commented with a smirk as he sat on my deck, lounging in a beach chair.

"Yes well, last time I was here, some idiot squirted ketchup on it. So I had no choice but to go shirtless," Lawrence fired back.

Jon chuckled as he lit a cigarette. "You're cute when you're mad."

Lawrence scoffed. "Don't you have some place to be? Perhaps a pedicure, or a butthole bleaching appointment?"

Jon tilted his head back and roared with laughter, and I couldn't help but giggle at Lawrence's comment. "A 'BUTTHOLE bleaching' appointment!" Jon cackled. "That's classic, Lawrence. Did you come up with that all by yourself?"

Lawrence rolled his eyes and shook his head in frustration. "You're ridiculous, Jon."

"Hmm," Jon commented. "Speaking of appointments, I know a great plastic surgeon who can help you with your-"

"NEVERMIND!" Lawrence barked before storming off into the house, most likely to get a drink.

I walked up to Jon and placed my hand on his shoulder. "Hey, let's go in the water," I suggested with a wink, knowing damn well how badly he wanted to splash some of the girls and watch their nipples get hard through their bathing suits.

Jon nodded excitedly as he took several drags off his cigarette, finishing it quickly. "Brilliant idea." He got up from his beach chair and ambled his way towards the ocean.

I followed several paces behind him, encouraging the other guests to follow suit. Anna, Tracy, and Amy ran right up to me, giggling with delight at the prospect of going in the water. Daryl, Eugene, and Diana followed, then a few of the other guests. Even Lawrence came out to join us, still wearing his shirt, of course.

Jon quickly began splashing and groping some of the ladies, who giggled with glee at his playful ways. He was especially aggressive with a neighbor by the name of Brittany, who was clearly smitten with my best mate. She was a petite and cheerful brunette, and 23 years of age. Jon eyed her like she was a medium-rare filet mignon, and I knew it was only a matter of time before he seduced her.

"Do you like to get wet, Brittany?" Jon asked suggestively, as he splashed water at her chest. Her nipples rapidly hardened, as did my manhood.

She squealed and laughed. "Of course!"

Jon got in close to her and ran his hands up and down her arms, his face merely inches from hers. "I want to get you wet," He crooned, licking his lips. "Soaked, even. Completely, utterly...DRENCHED."

Brittany began panting as Jon touched her, giggling nervously as she gazed into his vivid green eyes.

"Why don't you get a room?" Daryl joked, as he splashed Tracy and Amy in the water, making the girls giggle and jump.

Jon raised his eyebrows and smiled broadly at Daryl, then looked back at Brittany with a sexy little grin on his face. "What do you say, Brittany? Care to get better acquainted indoors before we go sailing? Hmm?"

Brittany stammered for a few moments before answering, appearing completely stunned. "Um, sure," she said nervously.

With those words, Jon smiled then picked her up and carried her as he walked out of the water and onto the sandy beach, gazing at her lovingly. They disappeared into the house.

The rest of us laughed at what we had just witnessed, commenting on what a horny bastard Jon was. I was annoyed, knowing I had just lost a bet, but also excited by the chance to have a ménage-a-trois with my sexy next door neighbor. I splashed Anna a few times before excusing myself, making a beeline for the house.

Earlier in the afternoon, he had encouraged me to join him once he "sealed the deal" with Brittany. I had asked him what made him so confident that she would sleep with him, much less agree to a threesome. He had gazed at me with his cocky smirk and blazing emerald eyes. "I can catch fresh pussy blindfolded with both arms tied behind my back. In fact, one hundred bucks says that she and I will fuck before sunset tonight, and that she will let you join us." Then he had laid a crisp hundred dollar bill on the dining table. I had swiftly put down five twenties, feeling especially bold after having consumed several strong drinks.

Once I reached the bedroom, Jon and Brittany were already naked and standing at the foot of the bed, their bodies tangled in a feverish embrace. He was kissing her passionately as he ran his hands all over her. She hadn't even heard me open the door, but Jon had. He took a break from kissing and turned to look at me.

"Welcome, Ken," he said warmly. "Why don't you get comfortable."

Brittany momentarily froze when she saw me, then began giggling drunkenly. A half empty bottle of vodka sat atop the dresser, and it was clear that Jon had given her a few drinks to relax her. I took the bottle and drank from it, guzzling several shots worth of booze before pulling down my swim trunks. My cock was already hard, as was Jon's. I could make out the faint scent of Brittany's wet pussy. It was party time.

I came in close to Brittany and began kissing her as Jon positioned himself behind her, teasing her arse crack with his cock. Then he fingered her for a few moments, increasing her level of wetness and making her moan sensually.

"Do you like fireworks, Brittany?" Jon asked in a low voice, as he held something behind his back.

Brittany backed away from my lips to answer. "Uh-huh," she panted, continuing to kiss me. I looked at Jon as I locked lips with her, curious what he was up to.

He picked up a lighter and another object I couldn't make out. There was sinister look on his face. He leaned in close to me, his green eyes aflame.

"Hold her down on the bed and have her spread her legs," he growled in my ear.

I swallowed and did what he said, picking her up and throwing her onto the bed. I knelt behind her head and held her arms down. She began to giggle.

"Ooh, I like it rough," she slurred, as she opened her legs wider.

"Good," Jon purred. "I hope you like it HOT, too!"

With those words, he took a sparkler and used one of his hands to spread her pussy lips apart. Then he used his other hand to abruptly shove the end of the sparkler inside her, tilting it upward. Before either of us could react or intervene, he took the lighter and lit the sparkler.

Brittany let go several screams as the firecracker sputtered and sparked between her legs, knowing better than to struggle. Her futile protests grew in volume and desperation as an evil grin spread across Jon's face. I held down her arms tighter, intrigued as well as horrified by the sight of the lit sparkler getting closer and closer to her labia, threatening to burn the delicate flesh of her inner thighs and vagina.

Just when I thought the sparkler would burn her, Jon bent down and spit on it, extinguishing the spark. Tendrils of smoke emanated from the end of the sparkler, which he gently plucked from her opening. She was shaking and whimpering, a film of sweat covering her front and tears forming in her eyes. Jon leaned in close to her, smiling gently as he caressed her face.

"I didn't let you get hurt," he cooed. "See?" He bent down and kissed her mound. I let go of her trembling arms.

"That was so scary," she panted. "I can't believe you did that."

I ran my hands through her hair. "How do you feel now, sweetheart?"

Brittany swallowed. "A little shocked but...relieved? Maybe a little bit high, actually? Is that crazy?" She chuckled.

Jon smiled and crawled onto the bed, his erect penis grazing her womanhood. "Not crazy at all, Brittany." He cupped her chin then leaned over to kiss her, the tip of his manhood grinding against her ladybits. This went on for several minutes. Her breathing got heavy as she grabbed fistfuls of his hair. It was clear she was horny as hell.

"Fuck the shit out of me," she panted.

Jon let go a laugh. "Listen to this little whore!" He said to me, then kissed her a few more times. "Don't worry, love. We are BOTH going to fuck your brains out. In fact, Ken is going to fuck you in the arse while I pound your pussy." He resumed kissing her as I began jerking off, making sure I was nice and hard.

yours for good measure?" Jon pinched her tiny nipples several times until she flinched and whimpered in pain.

Brittany trembled as her body jolted backwards and upwards from our well-timed thrusts. "No, please don't do that," she begged in a voice that was on the verge of tears.

SMACK!

Jon backhanded her in the face then began pulling her hair with one hand and choking her with the other. She screamed and wailed and began squirming, unprepared for the ambush. Within minutes she began to shake uncontrollably and hyperventilate, before begging Jon and me to stop.

"Please, no more!" She cried breathlessly as Jon gripped her dainty throat in his hand and yanked at her chestnut tresses. Her body jolted continually from our intense thrusts. "It hurts! I can't continue!"

Jon glared at her for a few moments before removing his hand from her throat and letting go of her hair. His thrusting speed slowed down from vigorous fucking to a tempo better suited for gentle lovemaking. Then he smiled and leaned over to kiss her lips.

"Great job, Brittany," he whispered as he wrapped his arms around her. She eagerly returned his embrace, giggling shyly.

Still positioned underneath her, I wrapped my arm around her waist, gently squeezing her breasts and nuzzling her neck before slowly withdrawing from her bum. Similarly, Jon withdrew from her vagina, wincing as he did so. He clutched his still-healing member. He would later reveal that his stitches had begun to unravel and some of Brittany's juices had entered the wound, causing a level of discomfort I could only imagine.

The three of us discussed the session as we cleaned up in the bathroom. It turned out that Brittany had just broken up with her boyfriend, who had turned her on to BDSM during their two year relationship. He had enjoyed putting objects inside her various holes - bananas in her vagina, gags in her mouth, and even jelly beans up her arse which he enjoyed eating out of her. This explained why she had been so tolerant when Jon had shoved a sparkler up her pussy. As adventurous as I was with Anna, I had yet to engage in such risky fire play with her, my experiences having been limited to pouring candle wax on her and using her body as a serving tray for a hot breakfast. I decided to bring along a package of sparklers for the sailing excursion, intent on setting Anna's pussy ablaze.

After freshening up, we retreated to my bedroom once more, smoking cigarettes as well as a tiny bit of weed from my bong. I cringed inwardly as I saw Jon wash down two more pain pills with vodka but knew better than to bring up his substance use at that moment. Once we had finished our cigarettes, we got dressed and joined the others, who were gathered on my deck and in my living room, talking over food and cocktails. Their faces lit up when they saw us.

"Hey, are we going sailing soon?" Tracy asked excitedly.

Jon nodded. "Yes, indeed. In about five or so minutes we are going to walk to the marina and go for a sail before the fireworks show starts. The view will be spectacular from the water."

After a few moments, we all began to walk down to the marina, which was perhaps a quarter mile down the road from my house. I had a package of sparklers in my pocket, and a satisfied smirk on my face. Jon held Brittany's hand as they walked, and I held Anna's. The girl looked so radiant in the glow of dusk, with her long red hair blowing in the gentle breeze and her navy blue dress hugging her curves. Little did she know that I was going to turn her into my very own fireworks show.

As soon as we reached the marina, we got onto Jon's boat. It was a beautiful evening, and the sun was about to set. Anna looked breathtakingly beautiful at dusk, her auburn locks appearing even more intense by the diminishing daylight. I stood on the boat, my arm wrapped around her as I breathed in the sea air. Then I leaned in close to her, inhaling HER scent.

"This boat has a bedroom below deck," I crooned. "I say we go down there and make our OWN fireworks, after the show."

Anna giggled. "Sounds like a plan."

I smiled and kissed her on the lips, as Jon began sailing the boat. My best mate appeared in heaven as he stood at the helm, with Brittany at his side. After his ordeal, he deserved some happiness. Somehow sensing that I was looking at him, he turned his head and met my gaze. He grinned ear to ear.

"This is the life, isn't it, mate?" He said with a wink.

I nodded. "It sure is, Jon."

Everyone loved being on the boat, enjoying the sights of the shore and the smell of the ocean air. Fireworks gradually began going off, punctuating the darkening sky with streaks of bright color. Our eyes remained fixed on the horizon, and before long, the big fireworks show began. As impressive as it was to see the fireworks from the beach itself, it was even more breathtaking from the water. I wrapped my arm around Anna more tightly as we enjoyed the show. In that moment, nobody else existed but us. It was as if we had the entire boat to ourselves. I did my best to focus on the show, but found myself becoming ravenously horny as the minutes ticked by.

"Why don't we go below deck?" I whispered.

Anna raised her eyebrows. "Now? During the show?"

I nodded, taking her hand and walking her to the bedroom located below deck.

Jon took notice and smiled wolfishly at Anna and me as Brittany fondled him. "Going downstairs to create your own 'fireworks,' are you?"

I laughed. "You got it!"

Anna and I descended the stairs and retreated to the bedroom, which, despite being small, was just as luxurious as the rest of the boat. A king sized bed took up most of the room, and sported black satin sheets with a matching bedspread. The lighting was suitably dim, and a vase full of roses sat atop the nightstand. It was the perfect bedroom for an impromptu fuck. I wasted no time ripping off her blue dress as I covered her face and lips in feverish kisses. Then I quickly took off my own clothes and shoved Anna onto the bed, straddling her. The package of sparklers remained nestled in my shorts pocket. It would be the perfect finale to our tryst.

I yanked at her hair then wrapped my hand around her throat, while using my other hand to line up my cock with her pussy, which was suitably wet as hell. Then I violently thrusted my hips forward, making her scream and moan in pain. Even after several months of hard fucking, she still had a hard time taking all of me.

"What's the matter, my little firecrotch?" I growled as I raped her, my grip tightening around her throat. "Still having difficulty taking my enormous cock? That's unacceptable. You're my trained whore! STOP WHIMPERING!" My face nearly touched hers as I screamed.

She sniffled, doing her best to keep quiet as I pounded her vigorously. We fucked in relative silence for several minutes before she spoke. When I wasn't choking her, I was pulling her hair or smacking her face. She struggled to keep quiet, still letting go an occasional yelp or gasp. Finally, she cleared her throat.

"Why can't you ever just make gentle love to me?" She asked shakily as a red mark formed under her right eye from when I slapped her. "Just once, I wish you would be tender and loving. It's always an assault."

I tilted my head back and laughed evilly. "That's because you're my PLAY THING," I explained in a low voice as I grabbed and squeezed her breasts, my fingernails digging into her flesh. "I play rough. That's the deal. Suck it up or I will find a new toy."

Anna's eyes filled with tears, and for the briefest of moments, I felt bad for her. It was as if I knew how she felt, wanting to be nurtured and loved, desiring more than just a friends-with-benefits situation with rough sex. I felt more than a little guilty that I wasn't ready to let myself appear vulnerable with her, and had to resort to rough play as a way of camouflaging my sensitivities. I also admired her ability to be open with me, wishing I had the nerve to do the same. But all I could manage was a smirk.

"Oh, Ken," she panted, perhaps more out of resignation than rapture.

"'Oh, Ken,'" I parroted back. "That's what I thought!" I growled as I pounded her even harder. My thrusts sped up and my body slapped against hers. The sound of the fireworks provided a nice soundtrack to our fucking. Within minutes, she was squirting and howling with pleasure as she orgasmed. It was the first time she had ever squirted, and I was beyond happy. I quickly ejaculated inside her, moaning sensually as I did so.

We lay on the bed for a few moments, holding each other as we savored the afterglow. The fireworks finale was audible from the bedroom, and we could make out the sound of clapping and cheering. That was when I decided to grab the package of sparklers.

I bent down and fetched my lighter and the sparklers from my shorts pocket, and plucked one of them out of the package. I turned to Anna.

"Close your eyes and spread your legs," I said in a low voice. "Then lie still."

She hesitantly did as I asked, then I spread her dripping labia apart and inserted the sparkler into her, angling it upwards like Jon had done with Brittany. Her chest rose and fell at a quickening rate as she lay on the bed, revealing her level of apprehension. I lit the sparkler.

The crackling sound and bright light forced Anna's eyes open and she immediately screamed in horror. I put my hand over her mouth.

"Shut up," I ordered. "Unless you want me to shove more of them inside you."

She trembled and cried as the firecracker got closer to the lips of her vagina. With seconds to spare, I spit on the end of the sparkler and removed it from her pussy. Then I leaned over and caressed her still-terrified face.

"Amazing job, Anna," I said softly with a grin. I grabbed a mini bottle of vodka that sat atop the nightstand next to the flower vase and handed it to her. "I assume you could use this?" I said with a smirk.

She shook for a moment, still in shock. Then she broke into a smile and laugh. "Yes, I could!" She agreed as she downed the contents.

I felt the boat come to a stop. I could hear some commotion upstairs, and it was hard to tell if it was an altercation so I decided to get dressed and investigate. Anna followed suit.

When we got upstairs, the boat was back in the marina and the engine was turned off. Daryl quickly approached me.

"Jon and Brittany just jumped off the boat," Daryl said with an amused laugh. "That crazy brother of mine took off his shirt then stepped up onto the ledge and encouraged her to do the same. Then he did a backflip into the water. She jumped off right after, and now they're splashing around down there. Guess they were drunker than I thought!" He laughed.

I chuckled and joined the other guests in watching Jon and Brittany horsing around in the water. At least my best mate appeared happy and was relatively safe. Still, his impulsivity was legendary. I leaned over the side of the boat to talk to him.

"Jon, isn't the water a wee bit cold?" I asked with a smile.

Jon shook his head as he splashed at Brittany and grabbed her breasts, making her squeal. "Nope, I have her to keep me warm!"

Everyone laughed and continued to watch them in the water, encouraging them to come out so we could party some more at my house. Jon wasn't having it, however, and continued to make out with Brittany. He appeared to whisper something to her before disappearing beneath the surface of the water, presumably to go down on her. My cock hardened and I decided to walk back to the house, figuring Jon would join us once he was done servicing Brittany. I took Anna's hand and walked off the boat.

Anna and I were walking down the street and were about fifty meters away from the marina when we heard Brittany's voice shout out.

"Please, someone help me!" She called out. "Jon is in trouble! I think he's drowning!"

I turned around and broke into a sprint, Anna following behind me. My adrenaline was pumping as I approached the marina, and I hoped that

Jon was simply playing one of his sick jokes again. When I reached the marina, Lawrence and Daryl were already pulling Jon's limp body out of the water and onto the dock as Brittany swam her way out. The party guests, and countless others, hovered around the dock to see what was going on and to check in. I walked to the edge of the dock and knelt beside my brother, who announced that he wasn't breathing and began doing CPR. I could tell by Jon's pale color that this was no joke. Daryl knelt next to me, and began to cry. I put my arm around him to comfort him. Then I turned to Brittany, who was also in tears.

"What happened, Brittany?" I asked as Lawrence began giving Jon mouth-to-mouth.

"We were making out and he told me he felt dizzy, then had a hard time staying above water," she explained in a scared voice. "He must have passed out or something. I tried to pull him above the surface to breathe but I couldn't. He was too heavy." She began to sob.

I placed my hand on her hand. "It's not your fault," I assured her, as I did my best to avoid breaking down in tears myself.

Sixty horrifying seconds and multiple chest compressions later, Jon began to puke up some water, then started coughing and gasping for breath. Everyone cheered and expressed relief that he was ok. Jon looked up and appeared dazed.

Lawrence patted him on the shoulder. "You're ok, Jon," my brother said breathlessly with a smile. "I did CPR. Almost lost you for a minute there."

Jon blinked in shock. "Lawrence?" He breathed. "You saved me. You saved my life. Why did you do that? I've been such a dick to you." His eyes were wide.

Lawrence chuckled. "Maybe because you would do the same for me? Besides, drowning is a terrible way to go. Anyway, are you ok? You need an ambulance or anything?"

Jon shook his head. "I'm fine. That was pretty frightening, though."

Lawrence put his hand on his shoulder. "I can imagine. Just take it easy when you stand up."

Jon nodded. "I will. Um..." His voice trailed off before he continued. "Thank you, Lawrence," he said sincerely. "Thank you for saving me. You're a great person, and a hero to boot. Sorry for being so rude to you all these years."

With those words, Jon sat up and gave my brother a huge hug, startling him. Surprisingly, Lawrence returned his embrace and assured him it was fine, accepting his apology.

A moment or so later, Jon noticed everyone else surrounding him and congratulating him on his recovery. Brittany gave him a kiss, which he returned as he thanked her for intervening so quickly. Then Daryl hugged him, expressing relief that his elder brother was ok after all.

"I helped Lawrence pull you out of the water," Daryl said as he held Jon in a tight embrace. "It was the least I could do."

"Thank you, little brother," Jon said softly. "You're a hero, too. And you're also my favorite pain in the arse." They both laughed.

After hugging Daryl, Jon's eyes settled on me. His expression turned cold. It seemed he was disappointed that I hadn't been the one to save him. Still, I leaned over and gave him a hug. His body completely tensed up and he kept his arms at his sides.

"I'm SO glad you're ok, mate," I assured. "I love you so much."

Jon avoided my gaze as I let go of him and abruptly stood up, turning his back to me as he began to walk down the street towards my house. Brittany walked alongside him, as did Lawrence. Diana followed behind my brother and walked alongside me, perhaps noticing that I was upset by Jon's icy reception.

"I wish I had gotten there sooner, so I could have rescued him," I said to Diana as I walked with Anna, who squeezed my hand, smiling sympathetically. "I should have been the one to pull him out of the water and give him CPR. I'm his best mate. Besides, he has saved my life once before. Since then, I have felt like I owe him one."

"Don't worry, Ken," Diana soothed. "Lawrence just happened to be there and wanted to help. I'm sure Jon understands. He's just in shock."

I swallowed, then nodded. "Yeah, I suppose."

Just then, Jon turned around and gave me a dirty look, one that made it clear that I was in trouble. My eyes filled with tears. It SHOULD have been me. I should have been the one to save him. Just then, I overheard my brother's conversation with Jon.

"What do you think happened when you were in the water?" Lawrence asked as he walked with him.

"I just got dizzy all of a sudden and lost consciousness," Jon explained as he lit a cigarette. "Too much booze and not enough food, I think. I'm definitely going to eat something as soon as we reach the house."

Also too many drugs, I thought to myself as I walked. Once we arrived at my house, I grabbed some towels that had been sitting on my deck and handed them to Lawrence, Jon, Daryl, and Brittany so they could dry off. Then I retreated inside and poured myself a much needed drink. If my best mate wanted to hold a grudge against me for "failing" to save his life, then so be it. I was so tired of walking on eggshells with that man, whose behavior had become so volatile over the past few weeks.

Eugene came up to me in the kitchen, looking upset. He poured himself a stiff drink as well.

"What's the matter, Eugene?" I asked. "You alright?"

Eugene shook his head as he sat o the bar stool. "Tracy broke up with me yesterday. It's been a long time coming. She complains that I always want to stay home and play video games when she wants to go out. I wanted to come to your party anyway, and so did she. But the situation sucks." He took a sip of his drink.

I put my arm around him, noticing Amy in the background. "I'm sorry," I said in a gentle voice. "Time is a healer, though. It will get easier."

Eugene nodded slowly. "Tracy and I have been friends for years so I know that we will most likely STAY friends. But it still hurts. I lost my virginity to her." His eyes filled with tears. I gave him a gentle hug, knowing the pain of heartbreak all too well.

Amy approached us, having overheard the conversation. She looked beautiful in a light blue dress and cute white sandals. She looked at Eugene sympathetically and placed her hand on his shoulder. He blushed slightly.

"I'm sorry, too, Eugene," she said in her soft voice, then gave him a warm hug. He then turned beet red, returning her embrace. Despite the fact that I was rather jealous of the chemistry between Amy and Eugene, I was moved by her kindness and empathy. Just then, Jon came into the kitchen to pour himself a drink. He didn't acknowledge me but wasted no time talking to Eugene and Amy.

"What's going on, guys?" Jon asked.

"Tracy just broke up with Eugene and he is upset," Amy replied.

Jon smiled gently and placed his hand on Eugene's shoulder. "That's too bad. I'm sorry. I have some advice for you, as well as some book recommendations. But first? Let me fix you a drink, mate."

Then he turned back to the kitchen counter and began fixing a stiff cocktail for the heartbroken bloke, adding tequila, his green smoothie mix, and a host of other liquors together in a tall glass full of ice. He poured himself one as well, and offered one to Amy, who refused politely. I waited for him to offer me one, but he did not. It was as if I wasn't even in the room.

The two men toasted. I could tell from Eugene's facial expression that the drink was very strong. Jon laughed and patted him on the back, and began giving him relationship advice as well as a little philosophy lesson, quoting everyone from Buddha, to Ghandi, to Confucius. He even offered to let Eugene borrow a first edition book that I had given him for Christmas one year, a collector's item that had been signed by the author, and had cost me an entire paycheck. Amy occasionally chimed in, reassuring Eugene that he was a good catch and that sometimes people are just better off being friends.

Tired of feeling invisible as well as betrayed, I excused myself and went out onto the deck for some fresh air and a smoke.

The moment Anna saw me, she put her arm around me and kissed me on the lips. I knew it was almost time for her to leave. She had wanted to spend the night but couldn't because she had to go to work early the next morning. Being a school teacher, she usually picked up a summer job to make ends meet. Of all nights, I wished that she had stayed with me, to keep my mind off of Jon's growing insanity. Sensing my insecurity and sadness, she whispered words of comfort in my ear as she held me.

"It's going to be ok," she soothed.

I swallowed and nodded. "I know."

We chatted for a few more minutes then I walked her to her car. Tracy was in the parking lot, smoking a cigarette and appearing deep in thought. I walked up to her.

"Tracy, I heard about you and Eugene," I began. "I'm sorry."

Tracy nodded. "It's ok. I'm going to head home in a few and chill out. Amy is going to join me later for a sleepover. I need some girl time to go with my alone time." She chuckled.

"I understand, Baby Girl," I said as I hugged her. "Goodnight, sweetheart. Thanks for coming."

Tracy and Anna also exchanged hugs and goodbyes before I walked Anna to her car and kissed her goodnight, making her promise to text me when she got home.

I walked back to the house with my tail between my legs, once again feeling a vague sense of dread.

When I approached the deck, Jon, Brittany, Amy, Eugene, Diana and Lawrence were dancing to music playing from my sound system. Several other guests joined in as well. Amy noticed me first.

"Come join us!" Amy said excitedly, as she grabbed Eugene and began dry humping him, much to his delight.

I danced in a triangle with Amy and Eugene, and the others danced in pairs - Jon with Brittany, and Lawrence with Diana. Similarly, the other guests danced in pairs, which only made me feel like more of the odd man out. Luckily, Daryl emerged from the house after a few moments, appearing rather intoxicated. I smiled and walked over to him.

"Hey, buddy," I said with a smile. "I know you don't get high too often but I could use a bong hit right about now, especially with your brother giving me the cold shoulder. What do you say? Fancy a smoke in my bedroom?"

Daryl nodded and smiled. "Sure. Let's go inside."

We got to my bedroom and I wasted no time packing the bong full of weed and taking a hit. Then I passed it to Daryl.

"I'm sorry that Jon is being such a wanker," Daryl said before he took a hit off the bong. "He shouldn't be treating you like that just because you weren't the one to give him CPR. He needs to get over himself. It's like, he's become so much more hostile since he's arrived home, and it's gotten even worse since he started taking those pain meds."

I nodded and took the bong from him and helped myself to more weed, taking a bigger hit than last time. "I think I need to stage an intervention of sorts with Jon," I said with a lump in my throat. "Would you be willing to join me? I think he needs to hear it from more than one person. We can just tell him we are concerned about him and want to support him."

"Support WHO?"

Daryl and I spun around and saw Jon standing in the doorway of my bedroom, cigarette in one hand and martini glass in the other. He walked closer to us. His face was a mask of rage.

"I asked you a QUESTION," he growled, looking at his brother and not me.

Daryl began to shake, seemingly tongue tied. So I spoke up.

"Jon," I began in a soft voice as I put down the bong, "Daryl and I care about you very much and we want to make sure you are happy. Since you started taking the pain meds, we noticed a change in you and we are concerned you are taking too much medicine. My wife had issues with pain meds and, with the way you have been acting lately, I feel like I'm reliving the horror of her addiction. I want you to get help, Jon. Maybe some counseling? I can even go with you. We can be in this together. What do you think?" I smiled shyly.

Jon's eyes were glazed over and he hadn't even looked at me when I spoke. He put out his cigarette, finished his martini in a single gulp, and then grabbed the bong from the dresser, taking a huge hit. Then he glared at me for a solid minute before leaning over and blowing a heavy plume of pot smoke in my eyes. Then he smirked and walked out of the bedroom, joining the others outside.

I stood there in shock and after a few moments, began to cry. I couldn't believe how abusive Jon was becoming. Daryl put his arm around me, appearing close to tears himself.

"Your approach was perfect, Ken," he assured me. "He isn't ready to face the music yet. At least now he knows how we feel, and what he does with that information is up to him. We can't make him change. We did our part, and the rest is his responsibility."

Daryl was right. I wiped my eyes and we both took one final hit from the bong before going back outside.

Jon was dancing suggestively with Brittany, groping her multiple times and licking her neck and breasts. Several guests cheered and clapped. Brittany appeared completely wasted, and nearly fell over. Jon luckily caught her before she hit the ground, asking if she was alright.

"I think I need to go home," she slurred. "I'm not feeling so good."

Jon nodded. "Very well. I can carry you home since you live next door."

With those words, Jon scooped up Brittany, who waved goodbye to me and the others.

"Thanks for coming, Brittany," I called out as Jon carried her to the house next door.

"I bet Jon is going to have himself a little 'encore' sex while he's over there," I said to Daryl, who laughed.

"Yes well, whatever gets him out of our hair for a while," Daryl said. "He's acting like a total douche."

I decided to enjoy myself while Jon was fucking his new little toy, so I ate, drank, smoked, and danced to my heart's content. My best mate was acting like an obnoxious prick, but I wasn't going to let it ruin my night.

Amy came up to me and began grinding against me, giggling drunkenly. I picked her up and twirled her around, making her squeal. She was so adorable, my little rag doll.

A few short weeks prior, Jon and I were discussing plans for Amy's 21st birthday, which was about six weeks away. The original plan was for Jon, Daryl, and me to treat Amy to a casino trip, and that Tracy and Eugene would join us. However, since Tracy had broken up with Eugene, and Jon was turning into an abusive addict, it was becoming more likely that it would be just Amy, Tracy, Daryl, and myself taking the trip. Being naturally introverted, I knew Amy would be fine with this arrangement. Part of me wanted Jon to be there, to celebrate a milestone with a girl he had known most of his life. Another part of me wanted to have space from him, to carve out an identity that was separate from him and his overbearing ways.

In less than a month's time, Jon had infiltrated nearly every aspect of my daily life, sabotaging everything from get-togethers, to weekend trips, to my job. Even my choices of food, wardrobe, and physical appearance were matters of debate and subject to criticism. I needed breathing room, plain and simple. As I danced with my sweet little Amy, I decided that I would talk with Jon over breakfast, when we were both sober. I would tell him that, although I appreciated our friendship, I needed him to back off.

BANG!

I jumped, as did several of the guests, at the sound of a loud explosion.

BANG! BANG! BANG!

Bright flashes of light emanated from my driveway and I walked over, as did all of the guests. That's when I saw the source of the noise.

Jon was drunk as hell, and setting off M-80's and Roman candles in my fucking driveway. He began cheering and clapping as the firecrackers went off, and some of the other guests followed suit, hooting and encouraging Jon to set off more. I stood there, horrified and shocked, as Jon lit several more illegal fireworks on my property. Once they were all done, Jon took a bow and several guests clapped and cheered, applauding him for putting on such a nice little surprise show. Needless to say, I wasn't clapping.

Jon staggered onto the deck, deliberately bumping into me as he did so. He bent over and grabbed himself a beer from the cooler, taking a hearty swig from the bottle. Then, for the first time in hours, he actually spoke to me.

"Did you think I was pretending to drown?" He asked me as he came in close to me, eyes aflame with anger and bitterness. "Is that why you didn't pull me out of the water, or do CPR? Because you thought I was fucking around?" He raised his eyebrows as he waited for my reply.

My nostrils flared and I shook my head, my eyes filling with tears of shock and despair. Lawrence intervened, seeing that I was becoming distraught.

"Jon, I was close by so I jumped in to help," Lawrence explained. "Ken was already walking home and didn't see you. But he ran back to make sure things were ok as soon as he heard Brittany call for help. Ken didn't think you were playing around. He WANTED to help. I just happened to be there first, that's all."

Jon guzzled the rest of his beer and threw the empty bottle in the garbage, causing a loud "clank."

"I don't believe it," Jon growled. "I think Ken ignored me."

"No, Jon," I said in desperation. "Lawrence is right. I wanted to help, but he was already there, so he was able to act quickly. I was HOPING you were playing around, but I didn't think you were."

Jon got in even closer to me. His face was mere inches from mine. "Hmm. Well, how about this? Since you were so slow to respond? The next time you try to drown yourself in the ocean, I won't risk my life to rescue you. I almost died myself that day, swimming in that godawful undertow, to pull you out from that choppy water. And what did YOU do tonight when I nearly drowned? You just sat there and watched your brother do CPR. It doesn't seem fair to me."

I hadn't told anyone about that incident, so, up until that moment, Daryl and Jon were the only ones who knew that I had tried to drown myself. Now my brother knew, as did his wife, who put her hand over her mouth in shock at Jon's words. Eugene and Amy sat a bit farther away, as did the other guests, so the chances were small that they had heard Jon mention my suicide attempt. Still, I didn't want anyone knowing, and I felt so exposed and embarrassed. Tears of betrayal spilled down my face at that point. I was so upset with Jon at that moment, for "outing" me and for saying such a cruel thing.

In a rare display of warmth, Lawrence put his hand on my shoulder. "Jon doesn't mean it," he said softly. "He's just drunk. And I'm so sorry that happened. I had no idea you tried to drown yourself. Was it after the wife... you know...?"

I nodded and wiped away my tears. Daryl came up to me then and hugged me, apologizing for Jon's behavior before turning to his brother in a rage.

"You bastard!" Daryl shouted at Jon. "That was a lousy thing to do. Ken did nothing wrong. You didn't have to say all those things and air his dirty laundry. Ugh, bloody hell. I need a drink."

Daryl began to march back into the house to fix himself a cocktail, walking past his brother as he did so. At the last second, Jon stuck out his foot, making Daryl trip and fall on his face.

I ran up to Daryl to help him up, asking if he was ok. His nose was bleeding a bit but he insisted he was fine. He began to lunge at Jon, ready to hit him, but I restrained him, telling him to go inside and get cleaned up. He did as I suggested. The I marched up to Jon until my face was almost touching his.

"You crazy fuck," I growled. "What the hell is wrong with you? You need to leave. I need some space from you. Sleep off your drunken stupor, then I want you out of the house by morning."

"You gonna make me?" Jon sneered before shoving me. I nearly fell backwards but stopped myself. At that moment, I saw red.

Before I could stop myself, I picked up Jon by the collar of his shirt until he was about a foot off the ground and slammed him against the side of my house. Completely unaccustomed to being on the receiving end of my wrath, he looked terrified.

"Don't fuck with me, Jon," I spat, as I held him up. "You need to cut the shit!"

"Ok," Jon gasped. "I'm sorry. Can you let me down now?" His eyes looked so scared, and he began to clutch at my forearms with his hands. "Please?"

I glared at him for a few moments then roughly let go of him, letting him drop to the ground. Unfortunately, he stumbled and fell, landing on his still-healing tailbone. I winced, knowing how much that must have hurt.

Jon gasped and grunted in discomfort, struggling to get up. Lawrence offered to help him, but he insisted he was fine and carefully rose to his feet. Once standing, his face was a mask of pain and he began limping severely, headed towards the sliding door of my house. Several of the guests, including Lawrence, called after him to ask if he was ok.

"Yes," Jon said as he leaned against the door, squinting in pain. "I just need my pills. It's hard to tell, but I might have reinjured my tailbone."

Amy stood up. "I will get you your pills," she said sweetly. "You should just sit down on the chaise and relax. I will get you some water, too."

Jon smiled at Amy as he slowly walked the five or so steps to the chaise lounge on the deck and carefully sat down. "That's awfully nice of you," He said with a sexy grin. "Thank you. You have always been good at serving others. I like that in a woman." He winked.

Amy giggled and blushed before disappearing into the house to get Jon his meds and a drink. Out of the corner of my eye, I noticed Eugene giving Jon a dirty look. I know he was very protective of Amy, and didn't want to see her get taken advantage of. This protectiveness would come in handy later in the evening.

I sat down on a nearby chair and began to feel incredibly guilty that I had reacted so violently to Jon's infantile behavior, which was obviously fueled by drugs and alcohol. Incidentally, I was craving another drink.

Amy emerged from the house just then, carrying a bottle of water and pills for Jon as well as a martini glass. She handed Jon his water and meds before giving me the martini. I smiled broadly at her and touched her hand.

"You always seem to know what I need, and when I need it," I said softly to my little rag doll.

Amy's dimpled smile spread across her face as she leaned down to kiss me sweetly on the lips. "Anything for a friend," she cooed before sitting midway between Jon and myself. I so adored that girl. I eagerly sipped my martini, reveling in the taste of the strong booze. It was one of the few cocktails that had a calming effect on me, and Amy knew this.

Jon took his pills and drank some of the water, then looked over at Amy lustfully.

"Why don't you bring your chair closer?" He asked her in a soft voice.

Amy blushed and moved her chair closer to Jon's chaise. He smiled and reached over, running his hand through her long, black hair, making her giggle.

"Little Dolly Number Two, all grown up," Jon crooned with a chuckle. That was the nickname he had given Amy many years ago, since she was born about four months after Tracy, a.k.a. "Little Dolly Number One."

I couldn't help but laugh, remembering the day that Jon had given the girls those nicknames. Up until that point, I had always referred to the girls collectively as my Little Dollies, but, as with most things, Jon "improved" the names. He had always been the "cooler uncle." I had taught Amy and Tracy how to swim, but Uncle Jonny had taught them how to dive. I taught them how to ride a bike, but Uncle Jonny had taught them how to skateboard and rollerblade. I made sure the girls ate their vegetables at dinner, but Uncle Jonny made sure they saved room for dessert. There was, however, one thing I did better than Jon, with regard to the girls: I had remained involved in their daily lives over the years. As tempting as it was to move out west and begin a new life, my loyalty to my family and friends was stronger than my thirst for adventure. I sensed that my well-traveled, daredevil best mate felt a bit of guilt over having missed out on so many of the girls' milestones, and was trying to make up for lost time.

"Isn't this nice?" Jon asked in a soft, seductive voice as he lit a cigarette and took a deep drag. "We get to spend so much more time together, now that I'm back home. I've missed my sweet little friend." He looked her up and down, licking his lips as he did so. His eyes began to glow again.

Amy smiled shyly and giggled once more. She found Jon even more intimidating than me, perhaps because she had spent more time with me and was used to my personality. Yet I also suspected it was because Jon had a mysterious energy about him, a quiet air of unpredictability that contrasted with my "open-book" persona. There was always this sense that Jon was holding something back, and often possessed an eerie "stillness," not unlike a snake about to zero in on his prey. I finished the rest of my martini and retreated to the kitchen for a refill, keeping my eye on Jon and Amy.

Eugene joined me in the kitchen, fixing himself a cocktail. Daryl lay on the couch in front of the telly, half asleep with a can of beer in his hand. Eugene and I both chuckled at Daryl's level of sleepiness.

"He looks so comfortable," Eugene commented with a smile as he fixed himself a drink. "I think I might crash on the recliner for a while and watch TV, if that's cool?"

I nodded, pouring a bit of extra vodka into my glass before adding an olive. "Of course," I said. "Make yourself at home. I'm staying outside for now." I smiled and winked before going back out onto the deck.

Lawrence and Diana stood next to the sliding door, tired smiles on their faces.

"We are going to head home," Lawrence said. "Thank you for having us."

I smiled and nodded, hugging him and Diana goodbye. "Thanks for coming."

Jon piped up. "Hey, thanks again for saving my life, Larry!" He said drunkenly. "May I call you Larry?"

Lawrence chuckled softly and nodded. "My friends call me Larry."

Jon raised his eyebrows. "Wow. I'm your friend now?" A flattered smile spread across his face.

Lawrence smiled shyly. "Well, um...sure. As long as you keep behaving yourself." He winked. Then he extended his hand to Jon, who eagerly took it.

"I can't promise I won't misbehave, but I will TRY not to," Jon said with a cackle.

Lawrence shook his head and laughed, as did Diana, who exchanged hugs with Jon. Then I waved them goodbye as they walked to their car. I was amazed at how Jon had managed to win over my uptight brother in a single night, going from being his life-long adversary to being his new "friend," just by pouring on the charm.

The other guests left shortly after, until it was just Jon, Amy and myself on the deck. Eugene and Daryl remained inside, asleep in front of the telly. Between the booze consumption and the relative privacy, I had a hunch things were going to get more intense as the evening progressed, and I was right.

Jon leaned over and grabbed another beer from the cooler, then lit a blunt. He smoked and drank in silence for a few moments before offering the blunt to Amy, who took a few hits. Then she offered it to me, after asking Jon's permission. I eagerly took several tokes, loving the combined effects of the weed and the booze.

"Amy, why don't you lie next to me on the chaise?" Jon asked with a sexy smirk. "There's plenty of room."

Amy looked over at me and I nodded to let her know it was ok. Mixing weed and alcohol always resulted in me being ridiculously horny. So despite my jealousy, the thought of my worldly man-whore best mate touching innocent Amy was giving me an erection.

As soon as she lay next to him on the chaise, Jon placed his arm around her and began running his hand up and down her stomach, making her tremble visibly. She moaned quietly, a tiny smile forming across her face.

"Does this feel good, dear?" Jon asked as he caressed her skin through her blue dress. She nodded as she closed her eyes, reveling in his touch. "Nobody else has touched you like this, I'm sure. Except for maybe Ken. Isn't that right, Amy?" He winked at me.

"This is true," Amy said in her soft voice.

"Hmmm," Jon cooed, letting his hands travel farther down until his hand disappeared under her dress, grazing her inner thighs. She moaned some more. "I know I was mostly absent for a number of years. I want us to be closer, Amy. I want to get to know your body, and I want you to get to know mine."

Jon backed away from her and sat up, taking off his shirt. He sat for a moment, looking at Amy with a gentle grin. She smiled coyly as she looked at Jon's shirtless torso, her eyes moving from his defined abdominal muscles to his chiseled pecs. He gently took her hand and moved it up and down his front, until her hand lay atop his still-covered crotch. He sported the beginning of an erection.

"Why don't you get comfortable and take off that dress," Jon suggested in a voice barely above a whisper. "I love seeing you in your cute little bikini."

Amy blushed something terrible but slowly peeled off her cute dress, revealing her navy blue polka dot bikini. Jon wasted no time running his hands lightly over her stomach and chest, caressing her breasts through the swim material for the briefest of moments. Jon looked at her with a loving gaze then caressed her face and leaned in for a kiss, their lips touching ever so gently before building in intensity. The passion of their kisses increased as the seconds rolled by and before long, it was obvious that Jon was shoving his long tongue down the back of Amy's throat. When he wasn't doing that, he was biting Amy's lips hard enough for her to let go several moans that were the product of pleasure mixed with pain. They kissed for several minutes. Goosebumps appeared on her flesh as his hands grazed her tender flesh. A huge smile suddenly spread across his face as he backed away from her.

"I want you to see more of me," he whispered sexily, and he slowly pulled down his swim shorts until his erect penis was in full view. He grabbed his member and fondled himself for a few moments.

Amy swallowed and blushed once again, her breathing becoming more rapid as she took in the sight of Jon's huge cock.

"Do you like it?" Jon asked as he touched himself. "Is it nice to look at? Hmm?"

Amy nodded shyly. "It's really big," she mumbled.

Jon tilted his head back and laughed heartily. "Indeed it is. And it's also very hard, but very smooth. Why don't you touch it?"

Amy hesitated and looked over at me. I once again nodded my approval. She slowly reached her hand out and gently wrapped her dainty fingers around his enormous shaft, making him moan with pleasure.

"Ohh," Jon moaned. "Your soft hand feels so bloody good on my penis. I love it. Don't stop."

Amy tightened her grip on Jon's cock, and began moving her hand up and down his shaft. Jon then reached out and began fondling Amy's breasts through her bathing suit. After a few moments, he removed her swim top and began grabbing and kissing her bare breasts. Kissing turned into licking and sucking, which morphed into biting. Amy moaned intensely as her hand moved faster over Jon's rock hard penis. As for my own cock, it hardened all the more as I watched the foreplay. I reached down underneath my shorts and placed my hand on my cock, stroking myself. My eyes got heavy as I watched them pleasure each other and before long, I fell asleep.

An indeterminate amount of time later...

"No, Jonny, I'm not ready," a frightened female voice said. "No.... Stop....Please. Ouch!"

My eyes snapped open.

Jon was forcing himself onto a terrified Amy, who was trying in vain to fight him off. He straddled her while holding her arms down with one hand and roughly tugging down her swim bottoms, revealing her stubble-covered vagina. She squirmed and squealed, her eyes looking at me pleadingly.

I went from comatose to leaping out of my chair to pull Jon off of her. However, someone else's reflexes were faster than mine.

"She said 'NO,' man!"

Eugene had flown outside and now stood above Jon and Amy, glaring at my best mate. "Get off her. NOW."

He must have been observing the action from inside the house, in order to have reacted as quickly as he did. Jon looked up at him and pointed, beginning to giggle.

"Bloody hell," Jon slurred as he took in the sight of Eugene. "Today must be my lucky day! I caught a leprechaun!" He began laughing drunkenly.

"Call me whatever you want, but leave Amy alone." He grabbed a towel off a nearby chair and handed it to Amy, so she could cover herself.

Jon put his hands up in an act of surrender, rising slowly to his feet. "Ok, ok. I'm sorry, mate." He then pulled up his shorts and turned to Amy, who was shaking and close to tears. "And I'm sorry for getting carried away, Amy. I'm just really tired. In fact, think I need to go inside and get some rest. Goodnight." He headed towards the sliding door and staggered into the house.

I leaned over to give Amy a hug and kiss. "You alright, doll?" I asked.

Amy nodded. "Uh-huh. He's just drunk and stoned so I know he doesn't mean it." She smiled sweetly.

"I am going to have a little chat with him." I turned to Eugene and gave him a hug. "Thank you for coming to her rescue."

Eugene nodded and smiled. "Any time. I'm going to sit out here for a while to keep her company for a while before I call it a night." He sat down on the chaise next to Amy, who had wrapped herself in the towel he had handed her.

"Sounds great. See you guys later."

I walked through the sliding doors and stepped into my house to face Jon, who was in the kitchen fixing himself another drink. Just then, my phone sat atop the coffee table and lit up with a notification. I picked it up and read the message. Daryl had texted me that he was exhausted and went home to sleep, thanking me for a fun night and apologizing for Jon's ridiculousness. I texted him back, telling him not to apologize for his brother, and that I would see him at the gym in two days. Then I put down my phone and walked up to Jon with my heart racing. As tempting as it was to beat the shit out of him after he nearly raped Amy, I was determined to keep my cool.

"Perhaps you should lay off the sauce for the rest of the night," I said sternly.

Jon continued to pour himself a highball glass full of god-knows-what and didn't look at me. When he finally made eye contact, he looked furious.

"First, I can't fuck Amy, and now I can't have a cocktail?" He growled. "On top of that, my bum hurts something awful from falling on it, no thanks to you pinning me against the house and dropping me. Too many bloody rules. I might as well be in prison. Might actually be more fun in the slammer, because at least there I would have an easier time finding a bloke who's willing to take it up the arse. Unlike SOME uptight bastards I know."

My face grew hot with anger. "Well, good news is, if you keep acting the way you do, you just might find yourself incarcerated. Between boating under the influence, assault, and attempted rape in a single night, you're on the right track. It's a good thing you look attractive in orange."

Jon took a hearty sip of his drink and burst out laughing. "Wow! I was just having a little fun, that's all. Why must you exaggerate? You're a criminal yourself! Wasn't Amy still technically 17 when you popped her cherry? She was born at 6 in the evening and you told me that you had fucked her around 3 in the afternoon on the day of her 18th birthday. That makes you a pedophile. Then you've given booze to both her and Tracy when they were still minors, which is also illegal. In fact, Amy is STILL under age. Focus on yourself, mate. You're in NO position to judge."

I swallowed. Jon had a valid point. Still, I felt that I needed to set some boundaries with him. I cleared my throat.

"I suppose nobody is perfect," I said in a calm voice. "But I still don't like how you forced yourself on Amy. She's a sweet girl and sexy as hell, but she's only had sex with me and isn't ready to sleep with anyone else. So when she says no, you have to honor that. This wasn't an edge play session with role playing and a safe word. This was real life. 'No' meant 'no.' Understand?"

Jon knocked back the rest of his drink and nodded. "Yes, I do. I fucked up. Again. And I'm sorry. Now let's just kiss and make up before retreating to the couch for some TV. I don't want to fight." He came up to me and ran his hands up and down my chest, a gentle smile on his face.

Feeling somewhat immune to his charm at that moment, I simply gave him a gentle hug and a quick kiss before grabbing myself a beer and heading to the couch to relax. I still had to talk with him about giving me some space and to follow up with what he planned to do about his drug use, but I decided it could wait until morning.

Before I sat down, I looked outside and saw that Amy and Eugene were still talking. I watched them for at least a full minute. My little rag doll had a huge smile on her face as she chatted with Eugene, and broke into giggles periodically. It warmed my heart to see her so relaxed and happy. She eventually saw me looking at her through the glass door and waved, as did Eugene. I waved back and sat on my couch. Jon sat down on the recliner, placing a bong, a baggie of coke, and several bottles of liquor on top of the coffee table. I raised my eyebrows.

"Aren't you drunk AND high enough?" I asked.

Jon shook his head. "Nope. And neither are you." He poured us each a shot of tequila, and I reluctantly took my shot glass. He made a toast, clinking his glass gently against mine. "Here's to friendship and lots of fucking!" Jon slurred.

I knocked back the shot of tequila and lay back on the couch, my eyes trained partly on the telly and partly on Jon, who cut himself multiple lines of coke on a magazine sitting atop my coffee table, rapidly snorting them. Then came the bong, which he proudly announced contained grain alcohol in place of water. My eyes widened as I saw him take a massive hit, flinching slightly as he inhaled the harsh combination of undiluted alcohol and strong pot smoke. He held the mixture inside his lungs and handed me the glass piece. I took a modest hit and when I tried to inhale, I nearly choked to death. I had no idea how Jon was able to breathe in such a questionable concoction, much less hold it in. In any case, I felt incredibly stoned within minutes, as well as tired. Sleep began to overcome me once again.

"Hey, sleepyhead," Jon slurred. "Want me to read you a bedtime story? I will even carry you to bed."

I opened my eyes a crack, seeing double. "As long as you're able to stand and walk, sure." My own speech sounded slurred.

Jon laughed and hiccuped. "Well let's test out the old sea legs then, shall we?" He rose from the recliner, faltering for a moment before walking over to me. "Hop on my back, mate."

I hesitantly let him give me a piggyback ride to the bedroom. He staggered several times and nearly dropped me at one point but we reached my bed without major incident. He set me down gently and even tucked me in.

"Goodnight, lover," Jon slurred as he grabbed my ass and kissed me sloppily on the lips.

I mumbled something along the lines of "goodnight" then turned over onto my stomach, falling into a deep sleep within seconds.

About an hour later...

BOOM! BOOM! CRASH! BANG!

"FUUUUUUCK!!!!"

In my inebriated condition, I had a difficult time determining if the noises I heard were a result of a vivid dream or the real deal. In any case, I felt scared, and recalled pulling my blanket more tightly around myself. I heard yelling, banging and slamming of doors and cabinets, then breaking glass followed by more yelling and loud cursing. At one point, I thought I heard a man, presumably Jon, yell out, "Traitors!" Curious as I was, I lacked the fortitude to investigate the noises, writing them off as drunken hallucinations. The commotion ended as abruptly as it had started, and I once again drifted into a peaceful dream state.

Some time later...

I lay on my bed, naked and on my stomach, my arms and legs spread out. I was able to make out the feel of cold metal against my wrists and ankles, and when I tried to change positions, I was unable to do so. I opened my eyes.

It appeared that I was wearing restraints. My heartbeat sped up as I fought against them, my struggles fruitless. Just then, I felt someone's body on top of mine, and I could make out the smell of alcohol and weed.

"Surprise!" Jon slurred in my ear.

I struggled to breathe as Jon lay atop me. "Jon," I panted. "What the hell? Why am I wearing the restraints? Let me out of them!" I struggled against the cold metal once again.

"I've come to collect my debt," Jon growled, his erect penis teasing the crack of my bum. "I'm sick of always being on the 'receiving' end of things. Get it?!" He spat.

My blood ran cold and my heart raced even faster.

"Jon, please," I begged in a shaky voice as I squirmed, trying in vain to shake him off of me. "This isn't the time. You're drunk. Don't do this. Not now. Not tonight." My eyes filled with tears.

"Well, when IS it a good time, mate?! Hmm? I've been waiting almost twenty fucking years for you to let me love you the way I want to. REAL love is give and TAKE, understand? It's time for you to be the TAKER. After two decades of one-sided bullshit, YOU...OWE...ME! You think all the trips and meals I have treated you to over the years didn't have a bloody price tag? You think all those high-end gifts had no strings attached? Think again, Bitch! NOTHING is free! Get it? NOTHING! Now you're going to take what I give you. You're going to let me love you." He licked the side of my face as he fingered my arsehole.

Tears poured from my eyes as my body shook at Jon's words, which he had shouted savagely into my ear. It seemed our entire friendship had been conditional - he had intended for me to give in to him, to be his "bitch." All his generosity had been a way for him to "groom" me, to manipulate me into submission, and refusal wasn't an option. He was going to take what he wanted from me, one way or another. Despite my shock and horror, and his insanity, I did my best to reason with him.

"Jon, I love you, and I know you love me," I began in a quivering voice as he licked and nuzzled my neck. "But what you're talking about doing to me isn't about love, it's about violence. You're not a violent person. I want our lovemaking to be special, and if it happens now, it's just going to be painful. I know you don't want to hurt me. Let's wait, Jon. Please?"

Jon grabbed a fistful of hair from top of my head and yanked my head back, nearly snapping my neck. I yelped in discomfort. "If you only relax and let me do what I plan to do, it WON'T hurt. But if you fight me, it will. Either way, it's happening. It's your choice."

"No," I said firmly. "I have the right to say no. This isn't love, Jon!" I began to sob as he teased my arsehole with the head of his erect penis, and I tried in vain to move away. "Please stop!"

"SHUT UP!!!" Jon screamed, as he began to spread my cheeks apart and force the head of his member into my virgin backside.

Tears rained down my face and I clenched up as much as I could. I began to scream, continuing to beg and plead with him.

"This isn't you, Jon!" I cried. "Please don't do this!"

"LET ME LOVE YOU!!!" He shouted as he continued to force himself inside me, going in completely dry.

The pain was excruciating as he managed to force his manhood inside my vise-like back door. I let go a loud scream as I felt my delicate flesh rip apart. In an effort to quiet my screams, Jon shoved my face down into the pillow, nearly smothering me. I became dizzy as my oxygen supply dwindled, and the pain and humiliation of his rape only made me feel more lightheaded. I pulled more violently at the restraints, trying to escape so I could fight him off.

After several more agonizing seconds of struggling, the arm restraints loosened enough for me to break free. He was less than halfway inside me when I twisted around and elbowed him in the face. The force of my elbow resulted in him rolling off of me completely and falling onto the floor. I quickly undid the restraints on my legs and got off the bed, jumping atop him in a blind rage.

"You son of a bitch!" I screamed as I punched him repeatedly in his shocked face, which already sported a bruise and small cut from where I elbowed him. "Get the fuck out of my life!"

I rose to my feet and kicked him in the ribs before staggering to the bathroom to clean myself up, making sure to lock the door behind me. I could feel the blood seep out of my traumatized bum and trail down the backs of my thighs. Tears of betrayal and anger streamed down my face as I stepped into the shower on trembling legs, turning up the water temperature as hot as it would go.

I stood under the steamy water, my sobs growing in volume as I processed what had just happened to me. My legs got weak after a while and I simply lay down in the bathtub as the shower rained over my broken and battered body.

It was official. Jon Moore, my best friend in the entire world, the one who I went to with my problems, the one who I celebrated my victories with, the one who I trusted with my life, had raped me.

Chapter 5: The Green-Eyed Monster Part 2 - Skeletons In The Closet

"Woohoo! WoohooHOO!" Jon hollered as he sped through the pitch-black dirt road on his motorcycle, popping wheelies left and right despite my horrified, white-knuckled protests. We whizzed past trees, which grew in height and quantity as we ventured down the desolate path, the headlights doing little to drown out the blackness of the night.

The farther we rode through the woods, the more treacherous the dirt road became, and I knew we were getting close to the cliffs. Jon's long, dirty blond hair trailed behind him, his man-bun replaced by free-flowing locks that occasionally grazed my frightened face as I held on for dear life. The faint aroma of pot smoke emanated from his designer leather jacket, intermingling with the smell of his expensive cologne and exhaust fumes from the bike.

His crazed laughter and cheering echoed through the woods, competing for center stage with the sound of his chopper. He was only 18 but was already a millionaire, thanks to years of saving up money from modeling and acting gigs that started when he was just a little boy. This motorcycle was one of his many "toys."

"Hold on, Biiiitch! WOOHOOOOO!" Jon called out as he popped a wheelie that nearly knocked me off the bike. Beyond terrified, I closed my eyes and willed myself not to cry. Just then, the bike made a violent turn before coming to an abrupt stop, and I could hear the sound of the ocean below. When I opened my eyes, I saw that the bike was merely inches away from the edge of the cliffs. Had the bike traveled perhaps a foot farther, we would have fallen to our deaths, crushing our skulls on the rocks fifty feet down.

Shaking and close to tears, I jumped off the bike and walked away so I could take a moment to collect myself. Jon jumped off soon after, hooting and cheering as he walked to the edge of the rocks, then sticking one foot out into the open air as if he were about to jump.

"Whoa!" He said mockingly as he pretended to lose his balance.

I stood there fuming, my lower lip trembling as I did my damndest to avoid breaking down. Jon stopped and looked over at me, his cocky expression changing to one of concern as he walked over.

"Aww, honey," he began in a soft voice as he came in close to me. "You alright? I was just having some fun, mate. I didn't mean to upset you."

I began to cry. "Jon, that was so fucking scary," I said in a shaky voice. "You nearly killed us. Can we go home? I just want to go home. Please?" I sniffled and wiped my eyes.

Jon wrapped his arms around me and smiled sympathetically. "Yes, of course, Ken," he crooned. "I'm sorry." He wiped away my tears with his thumb then leaned over and planted a kiss on my lips. His facial hair was soft, despite appearing coarse. I cringed inwardly, feeling weird about being on the receiving end of a man's advances but at the same time finding his touch strangely comforting.

His kisses continued and he wrapped his arms more tightly around my waist. He opened his mouth wide and forced his tongue deep into my mouth, nearly gagging me. I tried to back away, but he firmly held the back of my head so I couldn't move. After a few more moments of struggle, I decided it was easier to give in to his advances so I let his mouth devour mine, silently wishing he were a girl.

His hand traveled down to my crotch, and he unzipped the fly of my jeans. Then he rubbed my bulge. He backed away from my mouth to look at me seductively.

"I know just the thing to make you feel better," he whispered. Then he got on his knees and unbuttoned and pulled down my pants, followed by my underwear. I protested weakly, but the sound of the surf drowned me out and Jon grabbed my semi erect penis. He lowered his mouth onto my cock, deep throating me with unparalleled skill. I closed my eyes and moved my hips slightly as Jon grabbed my arse cheeks and sucked me off. I climaxed within perhaps three minutes.

Jon backed away from my member with a smile on his face, wiping his mouth as he looked up at me.

"You taste so good, mate," he said as he rose to his feet and kissed me aggressively, forcing me to sample some of my own cum.

KNOCK, KNOCK.

My eyes snapped open and I quickly realized that I had managed to drift off in the shower. As unpleasant as that flashback dream had been, I much preferred it to reality.

KNOCK, KNOCK, KNOCK.

"Kennnn..." Jon slurred outside the locked bathroom door. "I can't waaalk, mate. I'm too fucked up, and I fellll. I hit my head. Busted my tailbone alllll over again. Pain pills doing fuck-all. I had to craaaawl to the loo. Can you pleeease lemme innnn?"

Whatever sympathy I had for Jon and his various issues had flown out the fucking window after he had raped me several hours prior. There were two bathrooms in my house and I refused to let him use the one I was in. I didn't give a shit if he was injured. In fact, I wanted to put off seeing his smug, mannequin-like face as long as possible.

"Fuck off, Jon!" I bellowed as I turned off the lukewarm water and grabbed a towel from the edge of the tub. "Use the other toilet!"

Silence followed by sniffing and groaning.

"Uhhh... no neeeed to get a ATTITUDE, ya wanker. Anyway, that's a long way to craaaawl, mate. But maaaaybe if I start now, I can make it there by sunrise. Wishhh me luck. Keep the mop handy in case I piss the floor." He laughed uproariously at his own comment before crawling away.

I began crying again as I lay in the tub, slowly rising up to towel myself off. My bum had stopped bleeding but I still felt sore, and knew I had suffered some tearing after Jon had forced himself inside me without using even the slightest bit of lube. Once I was out of the shower, I applied disinfectant and antibiotic cream to my backside, brushed my teeth, then carefully snuck out of the bathroom and into my bedroom. I locked the door behind me.

My silk robe hung from the back of my closet door and I put it on, then got into bed. The restraints remained at the corners of the bed but I lacked the energy to put them away. I lay awake for a long time, crying and in shock. After a while, perhaps out of sheer exhaustion, I fell back asleep.

My dreams were vivid and disturbing. One particularly upsetting dream involved the time I had tried to drown myself.

My wife had been gone for two weeks. In that time period, I had barely eaten or slept, or changed my clothes. I was unable to work. The tears were constant. Daryl was a great help, staying with me as much as possible when he wasn't running the gym and doing the work of two people.

Jon had flown in from California as soon as he was able to, arriving with bottles of expensive booze as well as a week's worth of groceries. Since he had arrived at my home, he had completely taken care of me, doing everything from providing emotional support, to cooking, to cleaning, to laundry, to stopping at the pharmacy to pick up my antidepressants, which weren't doing shit. He had even bought a round trip plane ticket for me, insisting I take a vacation out to California for a week. The plan was to spend the week at his beach front house in Malibu, joining him and his fiancée Lisa for some much needed rest and relaxation.

Jon, Daryl, Lawrence, and my other friends made countless kind gestures, which I appreciated a great deal. However, I couldn't find relief from my deep sadness. My body ached from grief, and my heart was completely broken. I wanted the pain to stop. One particularly overcast, windy afternoon, I had decided on a way to stop that pain.

The ocean water was appropriately choppy, and it was high tide. After many hours of getting up the courage, I decided it was time. Jon and Daryl had gone to the store to pick up a few things and I had the entire house to myself. I rose from the couch.

I briefly looked around my house, taking in the sight of the place my wife and I had called home for many years. Then I opened the sliding glass door, stepped onto my deck, and walked onto the beach. When I reached the shore, I removed my shirt and began wading out into the turbulent water.

"Ken?" Jon's voice called out.

I turned around and saw Jon and Daryl coming towards me. I looked at my two best mates, giving them a sad smile. Then I turned back around to face the ocean. After taking several deep breaths and wading deeper into the choppy ocean, I dove beneath the surface, having no intention of coming back up for air.

After several minutes underwater, I let go of most of my breath, daring myself to inhale or at least swallow some water. For some reason, I couldn't get myself to do it. So I simply closed my eyes and let myself sink to the bottom of the ocean, deciding to patiently wait for unconsciousness and death to overcome me. Fate or God had other plans, however.

Before I could react, I could feel Jon's strong arms around me, carrying me to the surface. I choked and sputtered as I breathed in the crisp air, my eyes filling with tears of despair mixed with relief. Within moments we reached the shore, and he set me down on the sand, holding me in his arms as I began to cry harder than I had ever cried. Daryl knelt next to us, sobbing and shaking.

"Don't ever do that again," Jon said in a voice thick with emotion. "Your life is valuable, mate. I love you. I will always protect you. You hear me? I know you miss your best girl. We all do. But you will heal from this. I promise." Jon held me tighter and invited Daryl to join in on the embrace, which he did. Jon directed his attention to his brother. "See, Daryl? I TOLD you I would be right back. I wasn't going to let either of us drown," he said with a wink.

Daryl cried nonstop as he nodded at Jon's words, holding onto us a little more tightly. He had nearly lost both of us and was very shaken up.

"Let's all go inside and have some hot tea," Jon suggested as he helped me up and walked me inside, Daryl following behind.

Words could not express how grateful I was to Jon for diving into that water to save me. I recalled how kind his expression was when he held me in his arms after rescuing me, how trustworthy his eyes were. I felt so safe and so loved. His words echoed in my mind. "I will always protect you."

My pillow was soaked with my tears when I awakened from that dream, and the first glimmer of daylight was visible from my window. I couldn't wait any longer. It was time for me to face him, to tell him that I was done having sex with him and that I needed a break from our friendship.

I got up from bed, opened the door and walked out into the living room, getting comfortable on the recliner as I waited for Jon to wake up.

He lay on the couch in a dead sleep, his chest rising and falling steadily with each breath. A bruise was visible above his right eye, from where I had hit him.

My phone sat atop the coffee table, so in order to kill time, I grabbed it and decided to check my social media. The usual barrage of silly memes and boring statuses flooded my newsfeed as I scrolled idly, only half interested in what was happening outside my own world. An occasional blurry picture of fireworks appeared on my feed, and my thumb scrolled faster, eager to find something that piqued my interest enough to distract me from my dismal reality...and new role as a rape victim.

Finally, I saw it. "Free Bird Skydiving Excursions," the Las Vegas-based company that Jon and I had used for our first time jumping out of a plane together, had posted a new picture. It was a photograph of a blond woman in a wedding dress tandem skydiving with a dark haired man dressed in a tuxedo. Although it was hard to make out their faces, the caption made their identities crystal clear: "Congratulations to Lisa McCabe and Nick Trudeau of Los Angeles, for taking the 'plunge' into holy matrimony on this gorgeous 4th of July day! So happy for you two!"

My jaw dropped. Jon's ex Lisa had tied the knot with our long time friend, Nick, the man who Lisa dumped him for, and who I knew made Jon feel like a third wheel quite a bit during their relationship.

Jon and I had met Nick in fifth grade, the year we moved to the states. Like Jon, he was an actor and model. He had quickly become one of our first friends. Besides Jon, he was the only man I'd ever had sex with.

Despite the friendship, there had always been a bit of unspoken rivalry between Jon and Nick, which culminated in our freshman year in high school. Nick had spent ninth grade at a private school, and like Jon, had joined the wrestling team. Jon and Nick wound up fighting each other at an important wrestling meet. Jon had an undefeated record up until that fight, up until that day. I recall how upset and embarrassed Jon had been, losing to Nick, who had a weight advantage over my best mate. Jon had gained ten pounds during the season, which put him at the low end of the next weight class, so this meant he found himself fighting boys who were bigger than him. Nick was the happy-go-lucky sort, and was eager to make sure that his win didn't affect their friendship. Despite this, Jon was pissed, and avoided Nick for a while after that fight. Adding to the jealousy was the fact that Lisa and Nick had great chemistry from day one, despite a mutual agreement to be just friends. Luckily, by sophomore year, the rivalry had died down and Nick attended the same high school as Jon, Lisa, and me, not long after Jon had taken Lisa's virginity and had begun dating her. Nick and Jon became teammates on the wrestling team as well, and their differences seemed to be a thing of the past. In fact, Jon took Nick's virginity sometime during sophomore year, shortly after Nick had revealed to him he was bisexual.

Fast forward almost twenty years, and the rivalry was alive and well. I browsed the picture's comments.

Jon's comment was the first to pop up and was in all capital letters. "THANKS FOR WAITING ALMOST A FULL MONTH AFTER BREAKING UP

WITH ME TO GET MARRIED. AT LEAST NOW I KNOW HOW MUCH OUR TWO DECADES LONG RELATIONSHIP MEANT TO YOU, AS WELL AS OUR THREE YEAR LONG ENGAGEMENT. FUCK YOU, TOO!!! YOU'RE BOTH TRAITORS!!!!!"

There were plenty of "wow" reactions as well as "sad" ones, and plenty of comments. They ranged in tone from empathic to annoyed. I noticed the men were more likely to take Jon's side, saying things like, "What a bitch, you deserve better," and "Sorry, dude." The women tended to be a bit more cutthroat, calling him a jerk, among other things. One girl left a scathing comment, attacking Jon personally despite not knowing him. She said, "Clearly you have anger issues, based on your reaction. The fact that you can't be happy for your ex speaks volumes about your character. You are a selfish prick, and after looking at your profile, your pics and chosen profession suggest that you are very full of yourself. No wonder she dumped you for a newer, HOTTER guy, who, unlike you, has a kind face. I can tell from your eyes that you are cruel and cold-hearted. Have fun being single forever!"

As tempted as I was to reply to that woman, I abstained, deciding it would be best to avoid fanning the flames. Also, if I was being honest with myself, Jon's profile DID suggest a certain level of conceit, with countless selfies and shirtless pictures. His eyes WERE cold. For those who didn't know him and hadn't experienced his charm, intelligence, and generosity, he sometimes gave off a bad vibe.

It turned out that Jon had responded to that girl, and I cringed as I read the comment. "CLEARLY you haven't experienced a man's touch in a very long time, based on your bitter attitude. Might I suggest a night of 'dancing' with yours truly? I can teach you the 'horizontal mambo' and the 'shag.' I assure you that, by night's end, you will find me to be VERY warm, and GIVING." Then he included an "eggplant" emoji, a common symbol for "penis."

Her reply was similarly crude, and revealed disturbing information to boot. "Omg! Jon Moore, did you really just private message me a 'dick pic?' As if seeing a close-up of what you call your 'impressive package' is supposed to make me fall all over you? Get over yourself! You are a pig!"

Others joined in on the "bashing," calling Jon all sorts of names and giving him advice on where to go and what to do with select parts of his anatomy. I had to swallow laughter as I read some of the things these people were saying. My revelry was broken when Jon began to stir. Within a minute or so, he sat up, rubbing his sore head.

My chair was positioned in such a way that Jon would have had to turn around 180 degrees to see me, so when he sat up, he didn't know I was in the room. He rose from the couch and limped over to the kitchen counter, grabbing a cigarette and lighting it en route to the toilet.

My heart rate quickened as I rehearsed in my mind what I planned on saying to Jon. I indulged in a bong hit before he returned from the bathroom, to settle my nerves.

Within moments, he emerged from the bathroom, lighting another cigarette as he approached the couch. That's when he saw me.

His face broke into a cocky smirk. "Good morning, sunshine," he crooned as he took a drag. "Uh... what the hell happened last night? I don't black out much, but I really can't recall much of anything after that near drowning incident."

I raised my eyebrows as I stared at him, at once pissed off but unsurprised at this information. "You really don't remember?"

Jon shook his head and smirked. "Nope. Why? Was it bad, mate? I know I must have fallen because my face and bum are bruised up." He began chuckling. "I require adult supervision."

I wasn't laughing. "Yes, Jon. It was bad. VERY bad. You might want to sit down for this one."

The bastard laughed again, taking another drag. "Ooooh! Sounds juicy! Jonny was a bad boy again. Well, I want to know all about it. But let me make some tea before 'story time.'" He began walking to the kitchen.

"NO!" I barked, making Jon jump. "You will sit down right now and listen to what I have to say!"

He raised his eyebrows. "Look who's cracking the whip now?" I glared at his attempt at humor. "Ok, ok, sorry. I was just joking, mate. God, you're so SERIOUS this morning." He finished his cigarette and sat on the couch, facing me.

"You really don't remember anything after the near drowning incident?" I asked.

Jon's brow furrowed as he tried his best to recall the night before. "Ugh. It's too bloody early for this," he groaned as he rubbed his temples. "Umm, well I know Lawrence did CPR on me, which impressed me. Then I vaguely recall being annoyed at you and Daryl for some unknown reason and having some pointless argument about god-knows-what. I also remember dancing with Brittany and walking her home, and setting off some fireworks in your driveway, then sitting with Amy and making out with her. Sometime during the night, I fell a few times, but I don't recall when. I know I was really drunk and high off my arse, and had a hard time walking by night's end. But all the other details elude me. Guess I should cut back on the chemicals a wee bit!" He chuckled.

I shook my head as I looked at him stone-faced. "Unbelievable," I growled. "Well, I'm happy to fill in the blanks for you."

Jon swallowed. "Uh, alright. You're actually making me nervous, mate. I need to grab my smokes." He got up and grabbed his cigarettes from the kitchen counter then sat back down, lighting himself ciggy number three. "Ok, now spill the details," Jon said as smoke trailed out of his mouth.

I took a deep breath. I filled him in on every awful thing that had happened after Lawrence's rescue. I told him that I had tried to confront him about his drug use and show concern, and that he had reacted by blowing pot smoke in my eyes. I told him he had been mad at me and ignored me for hours because he wrongly assumed that I thought he'd pretended to drown, and had therefore refused to help him. I mentioned how he had said - in mixed company - that the next time I tried to drown myself, he wouldn't save me. I told him how he had purposely tripped Daryl then shoved me, which resulted in my lifting him up and pinning him against the house. I revealed that, after he had stumbled and fallen on his tailbone, he had gotten even more drunk and forced himself on Amy, nearly raping her until Eugene intervened.

Jon's eyes were wide. "Oh, dear me," he gasped. "I'm sorry, mate. I don't recall any of this. I suppose it doesn't get any worse than saying those awful things to you, and getting physical with you and Daryl, then forcing myself onto Amy. I need to call them and apologize."

I laughed bitterly. "Actually, Jon, it DOES get worse. MUCH worse."

Jon blinked and took another drag. His eyes appeared scared. "How?"

I leaned forward in my chair. "After we sat watching tv and you brought me to bed, I fell asleep. When I awakened, I was lying face down, and in restraints. You jumped on top of me, teasing my bum with the head of your penis, telling me that you came to collect a debt. You said that real love was about give and take and that, after almost twenty years, it was my turn to be the taker. You said that I owed you, that nothing was free and all those gifts and trips over the years came with a price tag, and that I had to 'let you love me.' I tried to get you to stop but you did not. Then you forced yourself inside me. You raped me." My voice shook as I said those last few words and my eyes filled with tears.

Jon sat there with his mouth open, completely stunned to silence. Then he began shaking his head, and his eyes filled with tears of shock. "No," he gasped. "No," he said louder. "I wouldn't do that to you," he insisted in a trembling voice, doing his best to keep up his cool demeanor but failing. "You're my best mate. This is a misunderstanding. That's it. B-because you...um, you were drunk, too," he stammered as he did his best to make sense of what I had told him.

"Am I your best mate, Jon?" I asked skeptically as I rose from my chair and walked up to the couch, standing above him. "Or am I your 'BITCH?!'"

Jon's lower lip trembled, his confident and calm facade crumbling even more. I continued. "There was no 'misunderstanding.' I wasn't that far gone. I knew what was happening! YOU RAPED ME!!!" I screamed in his face.

Jon actually began to cry then. In thirty three years, I had never once seen tears fall from that man's eyes. The tears fell quickly, almost spigot-like. It was as if a geyser had exploded inside him, releasing years of repressed emotions. He sat there with his head in his hands, unable to speak for several minutes as his body shook with the force of his sobs.

"I didn't...I didn't know what I was doing," he choked. "I had no conscious thought. It's those pills. I was blacked out and I didn't mean it. Please believe me. I'm so sorry, Ken. Oh, God..."

Jon lay down on the couch and curled up into a ball as he cried his eyes out.

Despite my anger and feelings of betrayal, my heart broke for him. I knew that it must have been agony to have to process so many traumas in a short time, including the loss of the love of his life, his own assault at the hands of Todd and Andre, a broken tailbone resulting in pain pill addiction, Lisa's shotgun marriage to Nick, and now the news that he had raped his best mate while blackout drunk. Still, I had to get out of that room for a while. In fact, I felt a bit nauseous.

"I think I'm going to be sick," I muttered as I walked to the bathroom.

Jon's sobs continued as I went into the loo and closed the door. That's when I saw it.

A bottle of ipecac syrup and a mouth guard sat atop the bathroom sink. I had long suspected that Jon had suffered from an eating disorder. Between his bizarre eating habits, obsession with food contamination, and his ongoing body image issues, it was no surprise that Jon was bulimic.

I took a piss then drank some antacid and splashed some water on my face, bracing myself for part two of my confrontation with Jon. As much as I wanted him to get the hell out of my house and not come back until I said it was ok, he needed to know that it wasn't just the rape I had an issue with. His constant habit of bullying and pressuring me into doing sexual favors had to stop, and he needed to get help for his addiction issues as well as an eating disorder. I also had a gut feeling that there were aspects of his relationship with Lisa that he hadn't shared with anyone, and that it was wearing on him. There had always been a strange dynamic between Jon and Lisa, one that was more conducive to a best friend relationship than a romantic one, and I secretly felt that Nick was a better match for her.

My walk back to the living room was a nerve wracking one. Surely enough, Jon was still curled up in a ball on the couch and crying. He held a box of tissues in his hand and wiped his eyes and nose periodically with a tissue. For medicinal purposes, I grabbed the bong from the coffee table and took a hit, then passed it to Jon.

He slowly sat up and looked at me cautiously before taking the bong and helping himself to a generous hit. Then he spoke to me in a shaky voice.

"Did I... hurt you?" He asked through tears.

I nodded as I sat back down on the recliner. "You went in completely dry, so I experienced some tearing."

Jon covered his mouth in horror, a torrent of tears once again starting up. "I'm so sorry, Ken," he whispered. "You know that wasn't me, right? I would never have done that in my right mind."

"I believe you," I said sincerely. "But if we are to stay friends, I have to lay some ground rules. Ok?"

"Like what?" He asked, sniffling.

I sighed. "Well, as far back as I can remember, you have put me down, making little passive aggressive comments to make me feel bad. I especially didn't like when you started calling me your 'bitch,' and how you have always pressured me to do things - everything from risky activities, to sex, to drugs, and the list goes on. On top of that, everything is a competition. Granted, I found many of these things enjoyable, but heaven forbid I win a competition, or ever try to refuse joining in on something you want me to do. You sulk and give me the silent treatment, or keep pestering me until I finally give in and do what you want, or let you win. It's at the point where I feel like I have no voice, like I'm your puppet and you control me. I love you, Jon. But after what happened last night, I don't want to have sex with you anymore. This goes for any kind of sex, including oral and hand jobs. I feel violated and betrayed. Some day I might change my mind, but for now, I am done. Also, when I say I don't want to do something, I want you to respect that and avoid putting guilt trips on me."

Jon wiped his eyes and looked down as he digested what I said. "Fair enough," he mumbled. "I didn't realize I was doing those things, much less that it bothered you so much. I'm glad you told me. I apologize, mate. You know I mean no harm, I just get carried away. Being the older brother meant being in charge from an early age, so I have gotten used to calling the shots, I suppose. Perhaps I'm a bit of a control freak, or 'strong-willed,' as my mum would say." He winked.

"I accept your apology. Another thing I wanted to touch on is your drinking and drug use. Frankly, it's out of control and I believe you have a problem. I want you to be happy and healthy, and I think it would be a wise idea for you to get professional help for it. I could even go with you."

He shook his head. "Uh-uh," He said. "I agree that I have a problem but I want to cut back on my own first. You know me, I'm the independent sort. If I have trouble cutting back, I will seek help then. I promise."

Jon WAS the independent sort, to a fault. But at least I had gotten him to agree he had a problem and needed to cut back on the drinking and drugs. He was also quite disciplined so I believed him when he told me he would cut back on his own.

"Alright, Jon," I said. "But there's one other thing." I took a deep breath before continuing. "It's not my business but...I saw a bottle of ipecac syrup and a mouth guard sitting atop the bathroom sink. Have you been making yourself sick?" My voice broke.

Jon's eyes grew wide, and the all too familiar deer-in-headlights expression crossed his face. "Oh, bloody hell..." he muttered as he covered his face with his hands. It became clear he was crying again.

I placed my hand on his shoulder. "It's alright, Jon," I soothed. "You can tell me."

He sighed and sniffled. "When I was ten years old, I saw my neighbor attacked, as you know. Well, after that happened, the first thing I did was run to my bathroom and throw up. I recall having felt so much better after doing that. So throwing up became my go-to. If I was having a 'fat day,' I would just make myself puke after eating. If my dad and I had a fight, I would throw up until my insides felt clean and empty, and it would be like the argument never happened. It was like an 'eraser' of sorts. Or when I gained ten pounds and had to wrestle boys bigger than me, throwing up was an easy way for me to lose the weight. The modeling and acting only encouraged it more. I simply couldn't let myself gain weight. Purging became a spiritual experience after a while, a sort of grotesque form of prayer. I've been doing it for 23 years now, and have cut back some. But old habits die hard, mate. I have managed to keep it a secret up until now, and I believe the fact that you found out is a sign that I need to stop."

I smiled gently. "Thank you for opening up to me. I feel like you have held back a lot over the years, not talking about stuff and trying to be strong for everyone. But now it's time for you to be strong for yourself. Don't ever feel like you can't tell me things."

"Lisa always said I was too closed off and didn't talk about my feelings enough," he admitted with a wistful expression. "The day she broke up with me, she had told me that I had been a near perfect partner, except for my habit of shutting down when I was upset about something. She hated how calm I was, and had always wished I would 'lose it' more often. She often said I was like a robot. Between you and me, mate? I felt like I had to be cool for the both of us. She is so incredibly high strung and dramatic."

I chuckled. "Oh, I know!"

"Well, it looks like I'm making up for lost time now," Jon said with a sigh, lighting himself another cigarette. "I think this is the most I've talked about personal stuff in years." He took a drag and his eyes once again filled with tears. "Dear me," he said with a sob. "This is the most crying I've done in front of you, too, mate. The ONLY crying, really. Guess it's all coming out. So many years of being the calm and strong one takes its toll."

I put my hand on his knee and smiled sympathetically. "Just let it out, Jon."

"I can't believe she got married," he whimpered. "So fast. So bloody fast. Like we were nothing."

My own eyes filled with tears. "I know. So sorry. I did see the post on social media, and those awful comments."

Jon sniffled and wiped his eyes, nodding. "Oh, well. It had been at least a year in the making. That's how long they had been in love, according to Lisa. Nick was practically living in our house, when I was away for the better part of six months filming a movie in England. My prolonged absence made her seek comfort in Nick's presence, and I don't blame her. I admit that the last few years we were together, I wasn't winning any awards for partner of the year. I was devoting too much time to my career, and our relationship suffered for it."

"Did something happen that made you throw yourself into your work?" I asked, lighting myself a cigarette. "I know that, at least for me, working has been a way for me to distract myself from other things. That's why I ask."

Jon swallowed and nodded. "Yeah," he whispered. "It's very painful to talk about." Once again, his eyes filled with tears. "The only one who knows is my mum. I so wanted to tell you but every time I tried to talk about it, I would relive the horror of the situation."

He cleared his throat and took a drag off his cigarette before continuing. "About two and a half years ago, not long after our engagement, Lisa got pregnant. She was nervous but excited at the same time. We found out we were having twins, and I was ecstatic because I have always dreamed about being a father to twins, which, as you know, run in my family. Anyway, about a week before we had intended to share the great news, she..."

Jon's voice broke, then he lowered his head and broke down in sobs. I sat next to him on the couch and put my arm around him. "Go on," I said, with a lump in my throat.

"She woke up in a pool of blood," Jon sobbed. "I called an ambulance and we rode to the ER. It turned out that she had miscarried." He broke down again.

I began to cry and held him tighter. "I am so, so sorry, Jon."

"She had cried so hard and had been in so much pain, all I could do was hold her and rock her back and forth, telling her it would be ok. After she had the D & C, we were able to hold the fetuses in our hands, for closure. They were so tiny, so...incomplete. In those few moments we held our dead children, I envisioned all the milestones they would be missing out on - all the toys they would never play with, the friends they would never meet, the schools they would never attend, the sports they would never play, the jobs they would never get, the children they would never have. It was awful!"

Jon sobbed for a few moments with his head in his hands, then took a few deep breaths and a drag off his cigarette before continuing. By this point, I was crying buckets and grabbed several tissues from the box to wipe my eyes and blow my nose. He cleared his throat and resumed talking.

"Lisa and I both had nervous breakdowns after that happened. She began drinking all the time, and I threw myself into my work in order to give her space, but also to cope with my own grief. Remember those twin baby dolls I had when I was a small boy, the ones I used to push in a double stroller?" I nodded. "Well, I took them out of my closet and began taking them with me on my business trips, cuddling with them at night and pretending they were my real babies as I sobbed myself to sleep. One time, those dolls wound up in a piece of luggage that the airport had managed to lose. I had cried so hard to that poor girl working at lost luggage, explaining that I had items of sentimental value in that lost bag. Luckily they found it, and I was so relieved.

"Meanwhile at home, Lisa was going crazy. She started having drunken tantrums, during which she would abuse me verbally as well as physically. She would throw things at me, pull my hair, and slap me. That scar on my arm? That was from her throwing a piece of broken glass at me in a blackout drunken rage. I had needed stitches for the wound, which had bled a ton. She had felt awful and cut back on booze after that, but the incident horrified me and I couldn't look at her the same way. I felt like a battered husband, and a failure for being unable to control her or my situation.

"I pulled back even more, spending as much time away from home as possible. I worked so much that I burned out, and started losing things like my wallet and my phone. One time I overslept and missed my flight, and wound up missing her birthday last year. I had felt terrible. When I finally came home, the house was empty and she had left a note on the counter saying she went out with friends and that she wasn't upset with me. I sat there for hours on the couch after arranging a lovely display on the dining table for her - a giant rose bouquet, a bunch of balloons, a huge box of chocolate, a diamond necklace, and her favorite wine. When she walked through the door at some ungodly hour, Nick was with her. They looked so happy, laughing and joking, looking like a perfect couple. As soon as she saw me, half asleep on the couch, her face fell. I gave her a huge hug and countless apologies, but it wasn't enough. She hadn't wanted all those gifts, she had wanted ME.

"A few months later, she was hospitalized with severe vaginal bleeding, which turned out to be uterine fibroids. But because I couldn't find my phone and was so busy filming that movie in England, I had no idea she had been in hospital until after she had been discharged. I had been unreachable for FIVE DAYS. I felt like a fool. When I finally found my phone, I had all these voicemails - two from the hospital, a tearful one from Lisa, and concerned ones from Nick as well as my mum. When my phone had been missing, I had used another friend's phone to call her and say hello as well as text her, but she hadn't answered because she was in the ER. Once again, Nick had been there for her, not me. She needed me so much, and I wasn't there.

"By the time I returned home from England - after seeing her twice in six months - I walked in on her having sex with Nick, and I decided to join in and have a threesome like we usually did. I felt like I was interfering, they had such a connection. It was as if I were invisible. I cried myself to sleep that night as they held each other in OUR bed. Two weeks later, she dropped the bomb: She was in love with me, but was more in love with Nick. She broke my heart, mate. But I broke hers first. I wasn't there for her when she needed me most, and it's too late to make it up to her."

I held Jon in silence as we cried. As heart wrenching as it was to hear all of this information, it explained a lot. When I had spent a week in California with Jon and Lisa three years prior, there was a vague tension in the air that I couldn't pinpoint. They hadn't argued, but I had this sense that Jon was being extra cautious around Lisa, almost as if he were afraid of her. Jon was not the shy type, but he almost seemed that way around his fiancée.

One night that week, we had gone out to dinner and Nick had joined the three of us. I noticed that Jon seemed very jealous of him, especially when he showed affection for Lisa. For example, when Nick hugged her, Jon glared at him with those glowing eyes and broke their embrace, insisting on "topping" it by hugging and kissing her aggressively for several minutes. She wound up pushing him away, complaining that he was smothering her. Later that night, I watched the three of them fuck, since it was so soon after losing my wife and I still wasn't ready to have sex. Jon had been incredibly rough with Nick during their edge play, punching him in the stomach and kicking him in the balls several times. Things escalated to the point that Nick briefly lost consciousness during an intense choking session, and Lisa and I had to pull Jon off of him. This was no easy feat, because Jon was incredibly strong. Nick had been a good sport as usual, laughing off the incident. Still, chemistry issues aside, I didn't think Jon was to blame for their relationship ending. It took two to tango.

"I'm so sorry for your losses," I whispered. "But don't blame yourself for your relationship not working out. You had many good years together. Trauma has a way of either bringing people closer together or breaking them apart. You were a kind and caring partner, Jon. Of course you weren't perfect, but neither was she. You both tried your best."

Jon nodded. "The irony is that I had told Lisa years ago that if anything happened to me, she should go for Nick. I just never thought the day would come. But over time, their chemistry was undeniable. I mean, Christ, you've seen them. They're practically the same person, they have so much in common. And as much as I want to hate him, I can't. He's too nice a guy. I'm just upset right now because he has Lisa and I don't."

I patted him on the back. "Well, now you get to take care of yourself, Jon. Long overdue, I reckon."

Jon smiled softly. "True. I DID assume a caretaker role pretty much from birth, what with the way my mum said I put my arm around my twin brother while lying next to him in the crib, as if to protect him. It was as if I somehow knew he wasn't well and didn't have long to live. Poor James." He sighed, and my eyes filled with tears once again. "Then Daryl developed leukemia at age three, and for a year, I became a sort of nurse to him. I'm glad he recovered from that. It had been such a stressful time. Jesus, mate! Between the two of us, there's been so much death and trauma. My twin brother James, most of your family, and several pregnancy losses. And now we're both rape victims. I'm hard pressed to find anyone else in our circle who has gone through what you and I have gone through."

I swallowed as I immediately thought of someone. "Well, we might not know anyone who has been through everything you just mentioned, but we DO know someone who lost a child that was conceived by rape."

Jon's eyes widened. "What?! Who?"

My lower lip trembled as I looked at him, my voice barely above a whisper as I choked out her name. "Tracy."

Jon began to tremble as he stared at me in shock, his eyes once again filling with tears. "No way," he muttered. "Oh my god..."

The floodgates opened once more and he was sobbing. I began to cry as well, recalling the day my Baby Girl had come over to tell me about the rape and subsequent pregnancy and infant loss.

"When did this happen?" Jon asked as he wiped his eyes with a tissue.

"She was raped about three years ago and went into labor a little over two years ago. I just found out in March and I had been shocked. It happened during the first semester of her freshman year."

I got into detail about the horrible incident - the fact that there had been five boys (one of whom had a gun), how they had left her there in the basement for hours covered in their filth, and that she had carried the baby almost to full term, only to have it be stillborn when she gave birth.

Jon was beside himself, shaking and crying as he listened to the disturbing story. "Poor Tracy," he sobbed. "I want her to come over here so I can give her a big hug, and tell her how sorry I am. This is one of the saddest things I have heard in my life, mate. My heart is broken."

I patted him on the back as I sniffled and wiped away my own tears. "I know. Well, why don't we invite her over? Surely, she could use some extra love after her breakup with Eugene. Perhaps we could all do lunch?"

Jon nodded. "Yes, I agree."

I picked up my phone and texted Tracy to ask if she could pop by for lunch, letting her know that I had told Jon about the rape. The day she broke the news, she had told me that she was fine with Jon and/or Daryl knowing since they were my best mates, but preferred I didn't tell anyone else. I had kept my word. She replied within seconds and I smiled.

"It's a 'yes,' as long as it's pizza," I said with a wink.

Jon chuckled. "Works for me."

I smiled and looked out the window, admiring the sunny morning. Suddenly, I craved a sweat session. "It's a gorgeous day out there," I said. "Fancy a jog on the beach before breakfast? I figured the sand would be a nice low impact surface, since your tailbone is still healing."

Jon nodded. "Anything to sweat out last night's indiscretions, mate!"

We both laughed at his comment and got dressed, then headed out onto the beach.

"Hey, Ken?" Jon began with raised eyebrows as we walked near the water, warming up before breaking into a slow jog. "Remember how Lawrence used to call me the 'Green-Eyed Monster?' Because he thought I was jealous of you?"

I chuckled and rolled my eyes. "Oh, yes!"

"Well, I have a confession." He stopped jogging and turned to me, his expression serious.

I stopped to look at him, placing my hand on his shoulder. "Go ahead and tell me, Jon," I soothed with a gentle smile.

"I... I WAS jealous of you," He stammered. "I actually still am."

I stared at him in shock. "Why would YOU be jealous of ME? You're a millionaire with a great career, great family, and great friends. You're intelligent, stylish, and charming as hell. You're also an incredible athlete, and you're perfect looking."

He chuckled. "Go on!" He chided. "But nobody's perfect, mate. In fact, I'm lonely. I can't have the one girl I want, a girl who I thought would love me forever. As for my career, I feel like I was pressured into it somewhat. Granted, I love modeling and acting, but my father pushed me to start doing it at such a young age, so I feel like I didn't have much of a childhood."

He began walking and I began doing the same, letting him continue talking. "I wanted to do what you were doing, helping out with babysitting Tracy and Amy, and actually having time to go to dances and football games, instead of pissing away countless weekends going to New York and Toronto for auditions and photo shoots. Little does Dad know, I began doing coke to keep up my energy on these exhausting trips. It's not like I blame him outright for my drug use, but frankly, the pressures he put on me played a huge factor in my decision to start using. As for my 'perfect' looks? I have always hated my skinny legs and tiny bum. No matter how many squats I do, I can never seem to build up my lower body. Your legs and arse are much better than mine."

I blushed and chuckled. "I don't particularly like my thick thighs and chubby calves, OR my big bum, but thanks for the compliment. We can't help genetics," I reminded him. "My father had thicker legs, so I take after him. Just like you take after YOUR father. In looks, not personality!" I clarified with a wink.

Jon laughed and sped up to a slow jog, and I did the same. "I'm sorry for all the times I put you down or pressured you to do things. I decided at an early age that if I couldn't figure out how to be more like you, I would get you to be more like me. I think losing my twin brother made me feel incomplete, and I have always had this urge to find that missing part of myself. But I haven't always gone about it the right way. Anyway, I promise to be kinder and to stop pressuring you so much."

I smiled appreciatively at him as I jogged alongside him. "Thank you, Jon. I so appreciate your honesty and openness."

He smiled back. "Of course, mate. Hey, let's pick up the pace some!"

Jon and I ran at a faster clip, until we were at an all-out sprint. We remained tied for a solid half mile, until, ever so gradually, I inched ahead of him. Whether he was letting me win, I could not be sure, but after so many times of settling for second place and feeling rather cold in his shadow, I was happy for the roles to be reversed.

Soon, I was several yards ahead of him, and couldn't help but look back at him with a smile. He appeared to be doing his best to catch up with me, but managed a labored grin despite his struggle. We decided to finish our little race on pavement, so we continued on for about another mile before we had reached the end of a cul-de-sac, and then went back the way we came.

By the time I was about a hundred yards from my house, I sped up even more. It was as if Jon's revelations had freed me in some way, had made me feel lighter. He had cleared up so many questions for me, many of which I had never mustered up the courage to ask. So much of his behavior made sense now, and for the first time in our lifelong friendship, I felt like I really KNEW him. Better yet, I felt like I could finally trust him.

"Yessss!" My arms shot up in victory as we reached the imaginary finish line that was my driveway. I turned around to look at Jon, who, despite losing, wasn't sulking. In fact, a broad grin crossed his face. He patted me on my sweaty back.

"Congratulations, Ken," he said breathlessly. "Let's celebrate your win with a bong hit and a shower!" He hesitated. "Did you want me to shower in the second bathroom? I wasn't sure if you wanted a break from showering together after... after what happened." He blushed, still ashamed of what he did to me.

I smiled warmly. "No, Jon," I assured. "I don't mind showering with you." I decided to risk making a joke. "I just have to make sure the bar of soap doesn't slip out of my hand." My mouth formed a smirk.

Jon stared at me wide-eyed for a moment before he realized I was kidding, then burst out laughing. "Very funny, you little bastard!" He said with a chuckle.

We went inside the house then took several hits off the bong before undressing and stretching. Then we stepped into the shower.

Unlike the shower I had taken after Jon's attack, I felt renewed and cleansed. A smile spread across my face as I tilted my head back and let the water cascade over my body. It was amazing how much a person's life can change in such a short time, how a single conversation can transform one's outlook. In ten hours' time, I had gone from feeling broken and despondent - as well as completely incapable of trusting Jon - to feeling reborn, and feeling like I had a new best mate.

"This water feels so bloody good," Jon commented with a goofy grin on his face, his eyes slightly bloodshot from the weed. He grabbed a bottle of body wash from the edge of the tub and poured some onto a loofah, then lathered up his body. I did the same, thinking of Tracy. It had been about four months since she and I'd had sex, and I missed the feel of her body. Perhaps it was time to end the dry spell, with some gentle lovemaking. She needed some nurturing, something to cancel out all the torture she had endured, and I was going to encourage Jon to join in. Tracy had always wanted to have sex with Jon, and always considered him to be the ultimate "bad boy." Today, however, she was going to see his softer side.

After a few more minutes, we finished in the shower, then toweled off and got dressed. Jon made scrambled eggs and toast with fresh squeezed orange juice, and we ate in the living room in front of the TV. One of our favorite shows was on, and we watched several episodes. After a while, I noticed Jon had yet to take any pills, and he hadn't purged after breakfast. I smiled to myself, feeling optimistic about the future. My best mate was going to be ok. There would be ups and downs, but at least now, he was honest about his problems and was willing to get better.

"What does Tracy like on her pizza?" Jon suddenly asked, lighting a cigarette.

"She's a margherita girl," I said. "Fresh tomatoes and garlic, with a thin crust." My mouth watered as I thought of pizza. It was, by far, my favorite junk food.

"Do you recall how I like MY pizza?" Jon asked with raised eyebrows.

I furrowed my brow as I tried to remember. "Hmm. Eggplant and spinach, is it?"

Jon smiled broadly. "I'm impressed! And you're a pineapple guy, are you not?"

I nodded. "Guilty."

"You have always had exotic tastes, mate," he said with a smirk. "I like that about you. I suppose I'm the same way...especially when it comes to sexual fetishes, and vacation destinations. I think I want to visit New Zealand. That's one place I haven't been yet. You and I should go together, plan a little vacay for next year. We could find ourselves a sexy little kiwi girl, and could brag to others about how we shagged in a brand new time zone!"

I laughed heartily, delighted by the prospect of taking a trip to New Zealand with Jon and fucking some of the local chicks. Jon was the best travel partner, always knowing exactly where to go, what to do, and who to fuck. Despite how crazy the New York trip had been, it was still an incredible adventure. If not for that trip with Jon, I probably would have never had the chance to eat fugu, try DMT, or get dermal fillers. Admittedly, the cosmetic procedure was not my cup of tea, but being out of my comfort zone enabled me to learn what I liked and what I did not. Because of Jon, I was more confident, and more willing to take risks. If only I could risk being vulnerable with a woman again...

"Anna," I mumbled, startling myself awake. I looked around, realizing I had fallen asleep on the couch. Jon was sitting in the recliner with a cigarette in his hand, smiling at me and giggling.

"Talk in your sleep much, mate?" He teased, taking a drag.

I laughed sleepily. "I guess so. How long was I out?"

"About an hour, believe it or not. Tracy is coming over in about ten minutes."

I nodded and got up to stretch my legs and drink some water, then retreated to the loo to brush my teeth and fix my hair. My Baby Girl was coming over for lunch with Jon and me. It had been years since the three of us had hung out together.

Knock, knock.

Jon got to the door before I did, and opened it for Tracy. She looked adorable in a pink sundress, and her long blond hair was in a cute side ponytail. She smiled at Jon and opened her arms to give him a hug.

Jon smiled, then picked her up and spun her around, making her giggle. Then both their expressions turned serious.

"Tracy, I am SO sorry for what happened to you," Jon said in a soft voice as tears formed in his eyes. He ran his hand through her hair and caressed her face. "I wish I had known sooner. I would have flown out to take care of you. But I know you didn't tell Ken until recently, either. It must have been so hard, love." He kissed her gently on the cheek. "Sorry."

Tracy smiled softly. "It's ok," she assured. "I am doing a lot better these days. I still have my moments of post traumatic stress, but it's getting easier."

Jon nodded sympathetically. "You're a strong girl."

I stepped in and gave Tracy a warm hug. "You look beautiful, sweetheart. Why don't we all hang out on the deck for a while, then order some pizza?"

Tracy nodded excitedly. Jon grabbed his cigarettes as well as a bong and lighter, and I did the same.

The midday weather was beautiful - sunny, and not too humid. The three of us took hits from Jon's bong and made small talk, before moving on to more serious subjects.

"I'm so proud of you," Jon began as he placed his hand on Tracy's shoulder. "You have turned out so well. A lot of people would have been destroyed by what you went through." He lit himself a cigarette.

Tracy smiled and shrugged. "I have great family and friends to help me through. I still have my moments, though. Like whenever the anniversary of the rape comes around, I'm reminded of it. Same goes for the day I gave birth and the baby was born dead."

Jon's eyes filled with tears, as did mine. He squeezed her hand and cleared his throat.

"I know how you feel," he began in a soft voice. "Like Ken, I was close to becoming a father. But Lisa miscarried. It happened a little over two years ago. Twins." His voice broke and a tear fell from his eye.

Tracy began to cry then and got up from her chair to give Jon a hug. "I'm so sorry. I had no idea."

Jon put his arms around Tracy in a warm embrace for a few moments, then wiped his eye. "I have kept so much to myself over the years, trying to be the strong one," he said, taking a drag off his ciggy. "Little did I know that, by trying to be so strong for others, I have been making myself weaker. I'm fighting a lot of personal demons right now, Tracy. But, I'm learning to be more open about the things I have been through so I can move forward, and be happier. I admit, the breakup with Lisa has turned my world upside down, forcing me to face things I'm not quite ready to face."

Tracy nodded. "Yeah, I can relate. Breaking up with Eugene was so hard because we have been friends for so long and he's such a nice guy. And I love him, still. But it's not a romantic kind of love. More of a friendship love, if that makes sense. We are different people. I was never able to deal with the fact that he wanted to stay home all the time when I wanted to go out. Or the fact that he wants kids, and I'm not sure I ever want them at this point."

"It makes perfect sense," Jon said. "What you described sounds like Lisa and me. There WAS romance and plenty of passion, but in retrospect I think we got along best when we were just friends.

"We had begun dating in high school on and off, and she was hesitant to 'make it official' because she liked the way we got along as close friends and didn't want to ruin the friendship. I was the bold one, of course, and insisted we take a risk. And for a long time, it worked. We got along great. But after many years together, things changed.

"Our careers took off, and we spent less time focusing on each other and more time on our separate interests. I believe the straw that broke the camel's back was when she miscarried. That event shook us to the core, as a couple and individually. She didn't really want to try for a baby after that. She also knew how badly I wanted to be a father, and she felt that she would be letting me down by refusing to try again. Despite my reassurance that it wasn't a deal breaker, she insisted otherwise, saying it wasn't fair to string me along, when I deserved to see my dream of fatherhood come true with someone else. It was one of the things we had talked about the day we broke up. Perhaps she was right. I will always love her, just like you will always love Eugene. But when it comes to certain things, you shouldn't settle."

"You're absolutely right," Tracy commented, then turned to me. "I wish YOU would find someone you're serious about," she said with a smile and wink. "What about Anna?" She raised her eyebrows, as did Jon.

I chuckled and felt myself blush. "Oh, Anna and I are just friends," I insisted. "I'm still not ready for a serious relationship."

"I respect that, mate," Jon said as he patted me on the shoulder and took another drag. "You're better off remaining unattached until you're ready. I will probably stay single for ten bloody years after being with Lisa for nearly twenty. Healing takes time." He winked.

I swallowed as I thought of my wife and the unborn children who never got a chance to experience their first breath. "This is true."

Suddenly, Tracy broke down in tears.

Jon and I both put a hand on her back to comfort her. "You alright, Baby Girl?" I asked in a gentle voice.

She sniffled and wiped her eyes, doing her best to put herself together. "I'm just thinking about what happened my freshman year," she choked. "It was so awful!"

For the next ten or so minutes, she filled Jon in on all the horrible details of her rape, and subsequent pregnancy and delivery. It was just as heart-wrenching to hear the second time around. My eyes filled with hot tears that eventually spilled down my face. As for Jon? He was beside himself, crying harder and harder with every passing minute as he listened to Tracy's tale of woe. By the time she was finished, he was sobbing uncontrollably. Tracy and I joined in, pulled into the vortex of misery that was her trip down memory lane.

The three of us joined together in a tearful embrace, remaining silent except for the occasional sob or sniffle. I was the one to break the silence.

"You talked about how you were in the basement for hours," I said to Tracy as I backed away from her and Jon, wiping my nose and eyes. "How did you finally get out?"

Tracy sniffled and wiped her eyes. "Um, well I was afraid to come up the stairs because the five guys who raped me were partying, so I waited as long as I could until I heard the noise die down. But before I had the chance to go upstairs, two guys came down, probably to get more beer. They were really nice, a gay couple from New York. One of them was a light skinned black guy in his 30's named Andre, and the younger one was named...Tom, I think? He was around my age and white, very cute but very thin, and super shy. Tom was a student at the school, and didn't live far from the dormitory where the party took place. He was friends with one of the fraternity brothers, who was acquaintances with one of the guys who attacked me. They saw me and must have known what happened, even though I didn't want to talk about it. They were so sweet and helped me sneak out of that house, then made sure I got to my dorm safely so I could clean up. Afterwards, they took me to a diner and treated me to a late night meal. I was so grateful for their help, and if I ever see them again, I will give them big hugs. They saved my life that day."

Jon's eyes were the size of saucers. He grabbed his phone and pulled up a picture, then held it up to her face. "Are these the two guys you are talking about?"

Tracy nodded and smiled excitedly. "Yes! You know them?"

Jon nodded. "Indeed I do. They're Andre and Todd. I have worked with Andre many times, doing photo shoots in New York and Toronto. Ken and I got to spend quite a bit of time with the two of them when we were in New York. Crazy times." He winked.

Tracy's eyes widened. "Oh my god, it's a small world! That's nuts!"

"Indeed it is," Jon said. "And now it turns out that they're heroes. They saved 'Little Dolly Number One!'" He chuckled and rubbed Tracy's leg.

Tracy giggled. "Oh my god, I can't believe you just called me that! You're too funny! Hey, I'm hungry. Can we order the pizza now?"

I nodded. "Of course," I said with a grin. "So, shall I order a small margherita, small eggplant and spinach, and a small pineapple?"

Tracy and Jon nodded. "And French fries," Tracy blurted with a wink.

I laughed. "Sure thing!"

I placed the order, which arrived in about twenty minutes, and we ate outside on the deck, making small talk and enjoying the sunny day.

One hour later...

"Are you sure you want to do this?" Jon asked Tracy softly as the three of us stood naked at the front of my bed, his hands gently kneading her shoulders as he awaited her reply. I ran my fingertips up and down her back, gently kissing her neck.

The kissing had started shortly after we had finished lunch. Tracy had suddenly gotten up from her chair, leaned over, and planted a sweet kiss on Jon's lips.

"What was that for?" Jon had asked with a sexy smirk on his face.

"For being such a good friend," she had replied in a soft voice. "And for opening up to me so much."

Jon had stood up and wrapped his arms around her waist. "You have grown up to be such a beautiful young lady, Tracy." He then began to run his hands through her long blond hair. "Such a beautiful...strong woman."

With those words, he had lifted her up and carried her inside the house, nuzzling her neck and kissing her passionately on the lips. I had followed closely behind, taking off my shirt and rubbing against Tracy's back and bum. She had leaned back, letting me graze her neck with my lips. Jon let go of her to take off his own shirt and shorts then slowly lifted Tracy's dress over her head. I unhooked her bra as Jon gently pulled down her panties, testing her wetness with one of his fingers. He kissed and sucked her ample breasts and I caressed her round arse, kissing her shoulders as I did so. She shyly grabbed Jon's erect penis and stroked him slowly for a few moments, making him moan sensually.

"Shall we indulge in a little...refreshment before retreating to the bedroom?" I had suggested as I nibbled on Tracy's ear. They had both agreed.

After taking several hits of weed and drinking two shots of vodka apiece, Jon and I had lifted her up and carried her over to the bedroom, setting her down at the foot of the bed. The sexual tension was thick enough to cut with a knife, so when Jon asked Tracy if she was sure, her answer came as no surprise.

"Shut up and make love to me," Tracy panted as she grabbed his erect member and began jerking him off.

Jon chuckled and began kissing her passionately once again, gently touching her ladybits with his fingers. Then he leaned forward until she fell backwards onto the bed. I lit a candle and turned on some soft music before joining them on the soft bed, wasting no time in sucking and licking Tracy's beautiful breasts.

Jon slowly crawled down Tracy's front, leaving a gentle trail of kisses as he did so. Soon, his face was level with her womanhood and he looked up seductively at her. She opened her legs wider. He began kissing her mound, his hands gently massaging her inner thighs. As he did this, I sucked and bit at her breasts, squeezing occasionally. She moaned with pleasure.

"I've been fantasizing about this for years," Jon crooned as he gently kissed the lips of her womanhood.

Goosebumps formed on her flesh as Jon made love to her with his mouth. "Same here," she panted as she ran her fingers through his soft, golden brown hair. "Don't stop, guys. This feels so good."

I bit and sucked her nipples as Jon devoured her cunny. After a few more moments of gently nibbling at her labia, he went for broke, burying his face in her hole. She orgasmed within minutes, squirting all over his beard. He backed away from her vagina with a broad smile.

"Shall I make you cum again, Baby Girl?" He asked in a sexy voice.

Tracy panted with a huge smile on her face. "Oh god, yes!" She said in a breathless voice.

This time, Jon used his long, quick tongue to pleasure her, going to town on her clitoris. Her moans echoed off the walls as he flicked the hell out of her sensitive knob of flesh, his tongue moving rapidly and expertly over the structure. He then slid several fingers into her vagina, making her squeal. As he did this, I squeezed her breasts harder than before and kissed her passionately, slipping my tongue into her delicate mouth. She cooed and backed away from my face.

"I have missed this so much," Tracy gasped between kisses.

"So have I, Baby Girl." I lowered my face back down to her breasts and sucked at them some more, occasionally pinching her nipples.

"Ohhhh, GOD!" She exclaimed as Jon made her orgasm a second time, making her squirt all over his face.

Jon laughed sexily as he wiped her juices off his face and licked his hand. "Mmmmm," he moaned. "You taste so sweet." He climbed up from her womanhood and I backed away from her breasts, kissing her face and head. He straddled her, looking at her intensely. His erect manhood grazed her tender ladybits. She trembled with desire as he gazed into her blue eyes.

"I want to be inside you, Tracy," he whispered, caressing her face gently. "I want to un-rape you, to undo those tragic things that happened to you, with gentle lovemaking. We both do. Right, Ken?" He looked over at me with a gentle smile on his face.

I nodded. "You deserve love and kindness." I kissed her sweet lips and caressed her breasts.

Jon reached down between his legs and guided his erect member to the opening of her womanhood. She ran his hand up and down his chiseled abs and began breathing heavily. Ever so slowly, he entered her. His movements were gentle and sweet. Tears of joy filled Jon's eyes as he penetrated her more deeply, until every inch of him had disappeared inside her. She moaned with pleasure as her walls strained against the length and girth of his shaft. He held inside her for several moments, his body remaining still as he savored the feel of her anatomy.

"Oh, Tracy," Jon whispered. "This is beautiful. It feels so perfect. Your body is just...incredible." He wrapped his arms around her and began moving his hips in slow, sensual circles.

Tracy held him tightly and began moving her hips in time to his, then lifted her legs up so he could penetrate her even more deeply. She turned her head so she could kiss me, which I eagerly did. I used one hand to fondle myself and used the other hand to caress the backs of her legs as Jon rode her. A soft sheen of sweat soon appeared on both of their bodies as they made sweet love to each other.

"Jonny..." Tracy sighed as she ran her fingers through his hair and kissed him tenderly on the lips. Then she ran her hand down my front and began fondling me gently.

Jon smiled at her before lowering his head to suck at her breasts, making her moan with pleasure. I began to pant as her grip tightened around my shaft, and because I planned on having sloppy seconds with her, I tried my best not to climax. Meanwhile, Jon's thrusts quickened, and within minutes, Tracy was experiencing her third orgasm.

"Oh sweet Jesus!" Tracy cried out as she held tightly onto Jon's shoulders. He laughed and continued to make love to her, grinding his hips against hers.

Over the next twenty minutes, Tracy experienced three more orgasms, and by that time, she was covered in sweat and breathing heavily. Jon leaned down and kissed her feverishly, then backed away from her face to ask a question.

"Would you like to make love to Ken?" He asked in a slightly breathless voice. "I know it's been a while since you two have been intimate."

Tracy nodded. "Ok. But I have one request." She smiled sexily.

"What's that, love?" Jon asked.

"Would you let me suck you while Ken makes love to me?" She reached down to his penis, which was still mostly inside her.

Jon tilted his head back and laughed heartily, and I joined in. "Of course, dear! I would never turn down such a thing." He winked and withdrew from her gently.

Tracy turned to me and kissed me sweetly on the lips. I gently lifted her to a kneeling position and rested my forehead against hers.

"I have missed doing this with you, Baby Girl," I whispered. "Would you like to get on your knees, so I can love you from behind while you pleasure Jon?"

Tracy nodded and got on her knees. My manhood was already hard as a rock so I wasted no time in positioning myself behind her and entering her moist ladybits. My thrusts were slow and gentle, and I cupped her breasts as I made love to her from behind. It felt so good to be inside her again, after so many months.

Jon knelt before her and guided his shaft to her mouth, and she began kissing, licking, and sucking. He placed his hands on the back of her head and closed his eyes, reveling in the feel of her mouth on him.

This continued for a solid half hour, the rhythm of our bodies perfectly synchronized, like an erotic dance. It felt so incredible, our bodies joined in complete harmony. I loved being able to give Tracy the love and gentleness that she deserved... even if it was several years too late.

At some point during the lovemaking, Jon's eyes locked with mine. We held each other's gaze for several moments, and a smile gradually spread across his face. I smiled as well. There was an unspoken message of love and understanding, as well as gratitude. Things were going to be ok between Jon and me.

I sped up my thrusts, and Jon began fucking Tracy's face. The three of us began to moan with pleasure, and within minutes, we were approaching climax. Sweat poured from our bodies as we panted and moaned our way to rapture. We reached orgasm at exactly the same time, laughing in ecstasy as we did so.

We collapsed onto the bed in a sweaty, satisfied heap, holding each other. Tired smiles spread across our faces as we took the time to catch our breaths.

"That was incredible," Tracy panted. "I love you boys."

I kissed her on the lips and brushed her hair away from her flushed face. "We love you, too, sweetheart."

Jon nodded. "Yes we do. Now let's smoke!"

Tracy and I laughed as Jon leaned over and grabbed a pack of cigarettes from the nightstand, lighting one for himself before offering the pack to Tracy and me. Needless to say, we both craved a smoke, so we lit up as well.

As we lay there smoking and talking, I couldn't help but feel completely at peace, like my world was perfect. I had my Baby Girl and my best mate lying in bed with me, and we were naked and carefree. It was like heaven.

After the smoke break, the three of us made love again, and the second time was even better than the first. Tracy gave me the best blow job she had ever given me, while letting Jon have anal sex with her, which she actually enjoyed. As for Jon and me? We exchanged a kiss in front of Tracy, which she said was "totally hot." For the grand finale, Jon and I took turns fucking her while standing and holding her up in mid air, our arms locked under her bum and her legs wrapped around our waists. Much to Jon's delight, Tracy's period arrived near the end of the fuck fest. She had never experienced oral sex during that time of the month, so Jon and I gave her the best - and messiest - cunnilingus she had ever experienced to date.

Once we were completely spent after hours of sensual delight, we took a bubble bath together, complete with glasses of champagne and gourmet chocolates, which we fed to Tracy.

"You deserve the royal treatment," Jon commented with a smile, as he popped a chocolate truffle into her mouth.

I grabbed a bottle of shampoo and squirted some into my hand before lathering up Tracy's hair. She so loved the way I massaged her scalp, and began to moan with pleasure as I moved my fingertips firmly over the surface of her pretty head. Jon smiled and cleared his throat, and began to rise from the tub.

"I think we need some more bubbly," Jon said as he got out of the tub and wrapped a towel around his wet body. "I'm going to grab another bottle of champagne. Be right back."

Tracy giggled as I continued to run her scalp and work the shampoo through her luxurious hair. "This is the life!" She said with a chuckle. "Mind blowing sex, followed by a bubble bath with my two favorite guys, and champagne, AND chocolate? I feel like I've died and gone to heaven."

I laughed with amusement. "This has turned out to be a great day. I'm glad you're here, doll." My lips grazed her neck as my hands made their way down to her breasts. The slippery soap made her skin all the more touchable, and I reveled in the feel of her firm flesh. Slowly, I let my fingers travel farther south, until I was fondling her ladybits from beneath the water. She moaned some more. Just then, Jon came through the door, holding an open bottle of champagne. He smiled, dropped his towel, and reentered the tub, filling our glasses with more bubbly. Despite his cheerful appearance, something seemed "off" about him.

"I would like to make a toast," he said, before he sniffed and rubbed his nose. Then, with a shaky hand, he grabbed his champagne flute, prompting Tracy and me to do the same. "To love."

Tracy smiled and picked up her champagne glass, and I did the same. The three of us toasted and took a drink.

Jon sniffled a few more times as Tracy dunked the back of her head beneath the water to rinse out the shampoo. His pupils were dilated and he avoided looking at me. Then he filled his champagne glass again, draining the contents quickly. His movements were sped up, and he had a hard time sitting still in the tub. I knew better than to ask if he was high on coke, because, aside from wanting to keep the peace, I already knew the answer.

"Is there a problem, Ken?" Jon asked with his eyebrows raised. His voice had an accusatory edge to it. He had caught me staring at him.

I rubbed Tracy's breasts, as the back of her head remained submerged. She smiled up at me, unaware of the dialogue between me and Jon.

I took a deep breath and shook my head. "No problem," I assured him in as calm a voice as I could muster. I knew it wasn't realistic to expect him to quit all drugs cold turkey, but the idea of him accidentally overdosing worried me regardless.

He leaned forward in the tub, his gaze made all the more intense by his dilated and bloodshot eyes. "Keep it that way," he growled.

I was determined to keep the mood light, knowing damn well how short tempered he could get while high on cocaine. After a few minutes of silence, I reached out and grabbed his hand, squeezing it gently as I smiled at him. "I love you, Jon."

Jon sniffled then grinned from ear to ear, squeezing my hand back.. "Aww. I love you too, mate."

Tracy sat up again and took more sips of champagne. "I don't know about you guys," she began in a suggestive tone, "but I'm in the mood for round three."

Jon and I smiled excitedly at each other in the tub, thrilled at the prospect of an encore fucking session with Tracy.

"Let's get down to it!" Jon said with enthusiasm, just before his nose began to bleed profusely.

Chapter 6: Slump Buster

"Jon, answer me!" I demanded, as I stood next to him in the bathroom. "How long have you been vomiting blood?"

Jon had just risen from the toilet, where I had caught him kneeling and throwing up copious amounts of bright red bile. As he walked over to the sink, he appeared unsteady on his feet, which only added to my sense of alarm.

He splashed some water on his face and gargled with mouthwash, before turning to me with a tiny smirk on his face.

"Don't worry, mate," he assured in a soft voice. "This was a tiny slip up."

I shook his head and grabbed his shoulders. "Jon, you didn't answer my question. For the third time, how long have you been throwing up blood?" My eyes filled with tears.

He bit his lip, then gave an irritated sigh. "It's been happening on and off for about two months. Ok? Not a big deal."

"TWO MONTHS?!" I cried. "Jon, this is fucking serious! Please, promise me you won't purge anymore and that you will get medical help? Throwing up blood is not normal. I'm scared for you. This is not a joke."

Jon wrapped his arms around me in a gentle hug and smiled confidently. "I promise, ok?" He kisses me on the forehead. "This was a minor relapse. It happens. I'm FINE. Anyway, I'm headed to New York for a last minute photo shoot. I will be back by tomorrow morning. I would have invited you to come with me, but I know you have to work."

I nodded. "That's fine. Do me a favor and text me when you get to the city? So I know you're safe?"

Jon smirked. "Yes, Papa Bear." That was his new nickname for me, which I found endearing.

"And see a doctor, too."

He rolled his eyes and lit a cigarette. "You sound like my mum."

"Tough shit," I fired back, handing him a protein bar and a bottle of his favorite sports drink, which he grudgingly accepted. "Stay hydrated and fed."

He scoffed, taking a defiant drag off his ciggy. "What's next, mate? You going to tell me not to talk to strangers? Look both ways before crossing the street?"

My nostrils flared. I was not in the mood for jokes.

Jon put his hand on my arm. "I'm kidding. Sorry. I appreciate you caring so much, really. I just feel weird being fussed over is all. I love you, mate. See you tomorrow."

We exchanged goodbyes and bear hugs, then he grabbed his backpack and the keys to his motorcycle, and walked out the door.

After a few moments of pacing around my house and smoking, I decided to discreetly follow behind him on the highway for a while, to make sure he was safe. His unsteadiness made me nervous, and I had a feeling that something bad was about to happen. Besides, it was several hours before I had to go into work. I grabbed my keys, a bottled water, and a set of gym clothes then headed out.

Since the eventful 4th of July weekend two weeks prior, Jon had cleaned up his act considerably. He was devoting most of his time to getting our second gym ready for the grand opening, which was scheduled for the weekend before Labor Day. He had cut back on his drinking and was taking his pain meds as prescribed. The cocaine use was less frequent, and he was eating normally. Despite the improvements, however, he was experiencing more frequent dizzy spells and nosebleeds, and often complained about food tasting "off," almost metallic. His ankles also appeared somewhat swollen, which he attributed to overtraining. Since his tailbone was healing well, he was revamping his workout routine, doing more weight training and running, as well as rock climbing and CrossFit. I urged him several times to see a doctor about his symptoms but he dismissed my suggestions, insisting he was "fine," and that he was most likely experiencing some withdrawal from the drugs. It seemed like a reasonable enough explanation, so I didn't bring it up again.

The nosebleed he had experienced when Tracy was over had been especially alarming, and it had taken over an hour for the bleeding to stop. This incident had been enough to scare Jon into cutting back on the coke. I had been minutes away from demanding that he visit the emergency room, but the bleeding eventually slowed down and stopped. Needless to say, "round three" sex with Tracy didn't happen that afternoon.

About three days after Tracy had come over, Jon and I had bumped into Brittany at the grocery store. She had been so excited to see Jon, whose attitude was rather cold and distant. He was still adjusting to the reduced level of drugs in his system, and was a touch grumpy and queasy as a result. Brittany had asked him out to dinner that evening, but he had insisted with a sexy smirk that they "stay in," and agreed to bring dinner. She had agreed.

That evening, Jon had brought over sandwiches from her favorite diner, but made her suck his cock for an hour, then endure a half hour of rough anal sex while bent over her dining room table before letting her touch the food. He had also choked her a number of times, hard enough to leave bruises on her neck. Afterwards, he had cleaned up in the loo, and when he had come back out, Brittany had set the dining table and lit some candles, ready to have dinner with Jon. He had simply hugged and kissed her, saying that he had eaten already and was heading home. She had been disappointed, but was understanding, and had asked when they would meet up again. Jon had smiled enigmatically, before giving a simple reply. "Soon." Then he had walked out the door, leaving her to eat alone.

That same evening, Jon had told me what happened, revealing that he had left so abruptly because he'd felt very nauseous after their encounter, and had been too embarrassed to throw up in her toilet. Still, I couldn't help but feel bad for Brittany, and, unbeknownst to Jon, had visited her later that night to apologize for his behavior, explaining that he had a lot of stuff happening in his personal life. When I had arrived, she was in "subspace," feeling traumatized and deserted after Jon had left. We had wound up getting drunk and having wild sex on her kitchen floor. She had convinced me to lick nacho cheese sauce off her nipples and eat a jalapeño pepper out of her pussy, which were firsts for me. Afterwards, I had given her the pampering she deserved, taking a bubble bath with her and making her favorite tea.

My emotions ranged from contemplative to worried as I drove through the quiet, early morning streets of my town. Eventually, I merged onto the highway. Within a few minutes, I spotted Jon's motorcycle in the center lane. I stayed a good distance behind him, so he wouldn't notice me following him. As usual, he drove very quickly, reaching a speed of over 90 miles per hour. He wasn't wearing his helmet either, insisting it made him feel too hot and claustrophobic.

I turned on the radio, turning the dial to a classic rock station. Music always put my mind at ease. The sun was still low in the sky and, with the exception of an occasional truck and Jon's motorcycle, I had the road to myself. I sang along with the radio for a while, letting the music transport me back to the more carefree days of my youth. A smile spread across my face as I pictured Jon and me as young boys, riding our bikes through our old neighborhood in London, laughing and joking around. Even as a wee lad, Jon was a cocky bastard, showing off his biking and skateboarding skills to the girls, most of whom had a crush on him.

"Oh, shit!!!" I slammed on my brakes.

My trip down memory came to a screeching halt - literally and figuratively - when I saw Jon's motorcycle abruptly drive off the road and crash into a guardrail, forcing him to fly backwards off his bike and land on his back. It appeared to have happened in slow motion. My brain went numb as I pulled over and parked next to Jon's wrecked bike, and wrecked body.

I stepped out of the car on wobbly legs and walked over to Jon, who was lying on the pavement in agony. His left leg appeared mangled and blood spurted from his rib cage. He moaned in pain. I knelt next to him and called for an ambulance, holding his hand while applying pressure to the bleeding wound and doing my best to comfort him.

Once I had hung up with 911, I talked to Jon. My voice shook horribly as I did my best to avoid breaking down in tears.

"Jon, what happened? You just lost control of the bike."

Blood trailed from his mouth as he spoke. At the very least, he had some broken ribs and a broken leg. He gasped for breath as he struggled to talk.

"I-I got dizzy," he gasped, clutching his ribs and wincing in pain. He lifted his head to assess the damage to his body, and his eyes widened in horror. "Oh, my god, I'm a dead man!" He whimpered, as he began to sob.

I held his hand tighter, and began to cry. "No, Jon, you're a fighter. You will be ok. Stay with me. The paramedics are on the way."

Jon nodded as he lay on the ground, the color disappearing from his face as he continued to bleed. "Will you stay with me?"

"Of course!" I assured, as I placed my hand on his shoulder. Tears continued to fall from my eyes.

"I don't want to die, mate," he sobbed. "I'm scared. I'm not ready!" His body shook so badly.

I leaned down and held his body to mine, not caring about the blood. "You won't die," I sobbed, not entirely convinced of my words.

"In case I don't make it," he began shakily, "I have some things I want you to tell some people."

I shook my head and began crying even harder. "Don't talk like that!"

"Listen," he insisted as his body trembled harder. "T-tell Daryl I'm proud of him, and that I'm sorry for all the times I was a dick to him. And..." he began to cough up blood.

I gently turned his head so he wouldn't choke on the blood. My eyes were swollen from crying and I did my best to keep calm as I waited for the ambulance to come.

He began talking again, appearing in even more pain. "Ugh," he moaned. "And tell my dad that I forgive him, and that I understand why he was so tough on me. He wanted me to succeed. And tell..."

More coughing. I held onto him tighter, my sobs uncontrollably intense.

"Tell Lisa and Nick that I am happy for them, and that I love them both. And I..."

He stopped to catch his breath, then appeared to drift off. His eyes began to close.

"Yes, Jon?" I urged. "Stay with me, mate! Keep your eyes open!" I shook his shoulder gently.

His eyes opened a bit as he struggled to get the words out. "I love you, Ken Smith," he gasped as he looked at me, his mouth forming the slightest bit of a smirk. "You're the best friend anyone could ever hope for."

I began to cry even harder. "I love you, too, Jon," I choked. "You're going to be alright."

He looked up at the sky for a few moments as he lay on the ground, then closed his eyes once more.

"I want my mum," he said in a voice barely above a whisper. "Is she coming?" His eyes remained closed.

"Yes," I gasped. I cried even harder as I held him, running my hand through his hair. Just then, the sound of sirens emanated through the air, and within seconds, the ambulance was pulling up to us.

The paramedics rushed over to my semi-conscious best mate, asking me a number of questions about what happened before taking his vitals and moving him onto a gurney. He began to seize as the EMT's loaded him into the ambulance. I started to panic, but they assured me it wasn't uncommon for this to happen and were able to stabilize him. I climbed into the ambulance truck and leaned over Jon to talk to him.

"I will meet you at the hospital," I said to him. Then I kissed him on the forehead.

Even with an oxygen mask over his face, I could tell he was smiling. He gave a weak thumbs up.

I thanked the ambulance drivers then stepped off the truck, grabbed Jon's backpack from the side of the road, and got back into my car. My next stop: the emergency room.

Three hours later...

It was surreal, imagining Jon's incredibly fit body reduced to a lifeless bundle of cells, kept alive with a system of tubes and wires. Not long after arriving at the hospital, his heart had stopped, and he had needed a defibrillator on at least three occasions. Then, his lungs had collapsed and he was unable to breathe on his own, so he needed to be hooked up to a ventilator. Jonathan Roger Moore, a man who, despite his bad vices, had never been seriously ill in his entire life, had started his day riding to New York on his luxury motorcycle and had ended it in a coma. His future, once full of hope, was completely uncertain.

Jon's father, Jonathan Sr., had arrived at the hospital not long after I had, accompanied by his wife Martha, who was Jon's mum. They sat next to each other in the waiting room, along with Daryl, who was beside himself with worry. We all anxiously waited for another update from a doctor or nurse, to get an idea of what to expect, and to see him. So far, things didn't look good for my poor friend.

I had used Jon's phone to call and text some of his friends and colleagues, including his agent from the modeling company, who had left a concerned voicemail when he had failed to appear for his photo shoot. Next, I had contacted his ex Lisa, then Andre, and a few other friends who I knew would want to stay updated, and visit him. As difficult as it was, I tried my best not to think of what was going to happen next. I put down the magazine that I had been absentmindedly looking at and turned to Daryl.

"Fancy some fresh air?" I asked, which was my way of saying I needed a cigarette.

Daryl nodded and we walked outside into the warm July day. I wasted no time lighting a cigarette and taking a deep drag. Suddenly, Daryl began to cry.

I placed my arm around him. "Hey, it's ok," I soothed. "Jon is tough. He will power through this."

Daryl sniffled and nodded. "I hope so."

I took a drag off my ciggy and patted his shoulder. "I think that you and I need a night out, just the two of us. Since Jon has been back home, we haven't had much one on one 'bro time.' We can take a cab into Providence, get completely drunk and stoned, and fuck the shit out of some horny bitches."

Daryl burst into laughter as he wiped the tears from his eyes. "That actually sounds great right about now."

I nodded and smiled, taking another drag off my cigarette. "Jon has mentioned several times how badly his younger brother needs a 'slump buster.' Admit it, you want to get laid. You NEED it, mate!" I winked.

Daryl laughed again and shook his head. "True. But I would rather hear it from you than from my own brother. You know how he gets."

I rolled my eyes. "Do I ever! But don't worry, Daryl. He's going to be okay. It might take a while but he will get through this. We ALL will."

"Hey, boys."

Daryl and I turned around. It was Jon's father, looking more nervous than I had ever seen him.

"Hi, Dad," Daryl said. "What's going on?"

"The doctor has an urgent update for us, so you might want to come inside."

I put out my cigarette and nodded, then we headed back in. A lump formed in my throat and my heart began to race, as I prepared myself mentally for what might be disturbing news.

One hour later...

Jonathan Sr. sat beside his elder son's hospital bed, holding his lifeless hand as he cried nonstop. Normally formal, uptight, and unemotional, he was beside himself with grief and despair. His wife, Martha, sat beside him and cried quietly as she draped her arm around her husband of thirty-five years, watching Jon's chest rise and fall with artificial breaths.

Jon Sr. and Martha had already lost a child to Sudden Infant Death Syndrome thirty-three years prior, and the idea of losing another one was simply too much to bear. Unlike his late twin brother James, Jon had been the strong one, and continued to be the strong one after his younger brother Daryl was born. Daryl was frequently sick growing up, developing leukemia at age 3 then developing asthma and multiple allergies, neither of which would improve until he was in his teens. Now, the tables had turned, and Jon lay comatose on a hospital bed, hooked up to a ventilator.

An hour prior, the doctor had dropped multiple bombs on us, filling us in on the severity of the situation. Jon's kidneys were failing, partly due to the injuries sustained from the accident but also from decades of binging and purging. Additionally, he had three broken ribs and a compound fracture in his left leg. He was also severely anemic and had a heart arrhythmia, both effects of his eating disorder. Suddenly, all his symptoms made sense - the dizziness, nausea, his complaints of food taking on a "metallic" taste, and the leg swelling were all due to his kidneys malfunctioning. Of course, Jon's parents were so upset when they learned of his bulimia, but were glad that Jon had trusted me enough to come clean.

The prognosis appeared uncertain, and only time would tell how - or if - he would recover. The doctor had recommended that Mr. and Mrs. Moore prepare for his final expenses, an idea that horrified them both and reduced them to tears for hours.

Daryl and I had sobbed uncontrollably when we heard the update, and we prepared ourselves mentally for the worst case scenario as best we could. We joined Jon Sr. and Martha in the hospital room, sitting at the other side of the bed. Jon's body looked so frail lying in that bed, hooked up to machines and wires. His face was partially bruised and he had a breathing tube in his mouth. A heart monitor beeped continuously as the ventilator made hissing sounds, acting as his "lungs." I reached out and held his hand, which was surprisingly warm. I cleared my throat.

"Hey, mate," I choked in between sobs. "I hope you're resting well. Can you squeeze my hand if you can hear me?"

The nurse had mentioned that it might be possible for Jon to hear us despite his comatose state, so I decided to test that theory. I waited a few moments to see what would happen, expecting nothing. Then, ever so slightly, I felt Jon's fingers squeeze back. His parents and Daryl witnessed this, smiling as they cried tears of relief. I continued to speak.

"There you are," I said through fresh tears. "Glad you can hear me. I hope you're comfortable and not in too much pain. Daryl is here, and so are your mum and dad. We all love you and hope you wake up soon..." My voice cracked as I spoke and the tears fell down my face once more.

Daryl was crying hard next to me, to the point that I put my arm around him and let go of Jon's hand, holding onto his. I looked across the bed at Jon Sr. and Martha, who were also sobbing. Suddenly, Daryl reached out and grabbed Jon's hand. He sniffled and cleared his throat.

"Hey, brother," he began in a voice thick with tears. "Can you hear me?"

Surely enough, Jon squeezed Daryl's hand. I smiled and winked at Daryl, who continued talking to his brother.

"I know things haven't always been easy between us," he began in a quivering voice. "But I wanted you to know that I appreciate all you have done for me. I loved how you helped take care of me when I was sick with leukemia as a little boy. And I loved how you kept me company when I had my scary asthma attacks, and how you got me into fitness. Then you encouraged me to start a business, so I could make money doing what I love. You have changed my life so much." He wiped his eyes. "Thank you, Jon. I love you."

Just then, Jon's thumb rubbed gently against his brother's hand, as if to soothe him. Daryl smiled and cried happy tears, knowing for certain that his brother had heard him. He looked up at his parents.

"Do you see this?" Daryl asked as he held onto Jon's hand. "He's rubbing my hand."

They nodded. Then Jon Sr. once again took a hold of Jon's other hand. He cleared his throat, tears falling from his eyes before he spoke.

"Jonathan," he began in his deep voice. "It's your father. I don't know if I have ever told you this, but I'm so proud of the man you have become. I know I was very hard on you when you were younger, didn't give you a chance to have a real childhood. And I'm sorry that I wasn't kinder to you. But you have turned out to be such a bright and successful young man. I want you to wake up, son. I want to make up for lost time, and..." He paused as more tears fell from his eyes. "I love you," he said in a voice barely above a whisper. "I want us to be closer."

Jon squeezed his father's hand several times and a tear actually fell from one of his closed eyes, causing his father to cry even harder. Martha wept continually, moved by the tender scene between Jon and his father. Similarly, Daryl and I began bawling, holding onto each other as we witnessed all this.

Martha was the last to speak. Her husband let go of Jon's hand so she could hold onto it, and talk to her beloved son.

"Jonathan, it's mum," she began in a shaky, but soft, voice. "I'm so sorry this has happened to you. You're my baby, my firstborn. I recall how scared I was when we arrived home from the hospital with you and James. After all, I was a mum to twins at the tender age of 19. But you were so calm and confident, even as a tiny baby. You barely cried and took such good care of James during his short life, putting your arm around him in the crib.

"Then you were a great brother to Daryl. I recall how you had held him after he was born, the way you had cried, talking about how beautiful he was, and how much you loved him. You helped me change his nappies, and you read stories to him at bedtime. Then when he got sick with cancer, you were a little nurse - helping with meal time, keeping him company when he was sick from chemo, and giving him little pep talks. When he developed asthma, you were there for him during his attacks and made sure he was safe and calm, and you always knew where his inhaler was. You encouraged him to get into sports, and he got healthier as a result and even opened up his own business, which you helped him with.

"And you were a great partner to Lisa. I saw it. Even though things didn't work out, you were so kind to her. You're also a great friend to Ken, and to Nick, and Noelle, and a number of other people whose names I can't recall right now. But most importantly? You're a great son. I love you, J.R. Even though I'm your mum, I consider you one of my best friends. Please, please wake up soon, my beautiful son."

The tears continued, and Jon began rubbing Martha's hand, just as he had done with Daryl. He had always been close with his mum, and despite his relative lack of emotion, he tended to let his guard down more frequently with her, confiding in her more than anyone else in his life.

We sat there in silence for a few moments, crying and holding each other, the heart monitor and ventilator providing the soundtrack to our grief.

One week later...

Despite our optimism and hope that things would improve, Jon remained in a coma, requiring a machine to breathe. I decided it was time to call some of Jon's friends and family, and encourage them to visit him before taking him off life support, a decision that Jon Sr. and Martha wanted to put off as long as possible.

Lisa and Nick were the first to arrive in town, flying out from Los Angeles less than 24 hours after I had called them. Then Noelle, Andre, Todd, and Jeannie came the day after, arriving together in Jeannie's SUV. Next were Jon's aunt, uncle, and cousins, who flew in from London. Finally, Jon's friend Chris arrived. A quiet, shy, guitar-playing hippie type with long, blond hair, Chris was a model from Los Angeles and had worked in the business with Jon multiple times, appearing in print ads as well as commercials. He had slept with Jon, Lisa, and Nick many times as well, becoming good friends with them over the years. He had a thing for fireplay. In fact, one of his hobbies was fire-breathing.

Once everyone was in town, I hosted a little get-together at my house, inviting Lawrence, Diana, Anna, Tracy, Eugene, and Amy as well. It was so nice being able to visit with so many friends and family at the same time. We spent a lot of time reminiscing about some of our memories with Jon, taking the time to laugh and cry, as well as eat and drink. I knew Jon would approve. We all needed some good food and company, in order to prepare for the heart wrenching event that awaited us.

That particular visit to the hospital was one of the most depressing events of my life. We entered Jon's room four at a time, each of us taking turns holding his hand and talking to him. The tears were nonstop, and the mood suitably miserable, as everyone said what appeared to be inevitable goodbyes to a man whose lives had touched many.

Daryl had an especially rough time talking to Jon and had to leave the room, crying harder than I had ever seen him cry. Martha got up and followed after Daryl to comfort him. Jon Sr. sat across from me, appearing like a shell of his usual self with his slumped posture, bloodshot eyes, and unshaven face. I smiled sympathetically at him and noticed Lisa and Nick standing in the doorway, asking if it was ok to come in. I nodded.

Nick took a seat next to Jon Sr. and Lisa sat next to me. They both had tears in their eyes. Lisa looked at Nick and smiled.

"You can go first," she said.

Nick nodded and held Jon's hand, studying his dear friend's face as his light green eyes filled with fresh tears. Nick's lion's mane of dark brown, chin-length hair hung in his face, and he hastily tucked a few strands behind his ear. He bore a striking resemblance to Daryl, and people often mistook them for brothers. Unlike Jon, however, Nick got along very well with Daryl, jokingly calling him his "bro."

"Hey, buddy," Nick began in a quivering voice. He had always called Jon "buddy," a term that Jon initially disliked but found endearing over time. "I, uh, I know things have been weird between us recently, and

I've been ashamed to face you after Lisa and I got together. I felt like a bad friend and a traitor, like I had stolen the love of your life from you. And I'm so sorry that things happened the way they did. I never wanted to hurt you. I still consider you a dear friend...one of my best friends, really. I hope you can forgive me, and want you to know how much you have influenced me over the years.

"I will never forget the time you took me shopping for clothes before we started high school, treating me to a designer wardrobe and giving me a makeover. Then there was the time I was struggling with Spanish class, and you patiently tutored me until I went up two letter grades. Then you encouraged me to stick with modeling and acting. I loved working those gigs with you. You got me to do so many wild and crazy things. You even convinced me to go skydiving!"

Nick chuckled and shook his head, before his expression turned serious. "Jon, you have always been my idol. I love you, buddy..." his voice broke and he broke down in tears again.

Jon's thumb began rubbing against Nick's hand, as if to comfort him.

Lisa wiped a tear from her own eye as she witnessed Jon's hand move, and she spoke to Nick.

"He forgives you, Nick," she assured.

I nodded. "She's right," I said. "In fact, right after the accident, before he lost consciousness, he told me to tell you he loves and forgives you both, and wants you to be happy."

Nick smiled through his tears. "Really?"

I nodded, then turned to Lisa. "Would you like to talk to Jon now?"

Lisa sniffled and nodded, then gently grabbed Jon's hand. Almost immediately, Jon's thumb began massaging Lisa's hand. He knew who it was, without having to open his eyes or hear her speak. Even though they were no longer together, Lisa was still the love of his life.

"Jon, it's me, Lisa," she said through sobs. "I need a minute, sorry..."

Without letting go of Jon's hand, Lisa reached over and grabbed a box of tissues from a nearby chair and wiped her nose and eyes. Then she took some deep breaths and cleared her throat.

"Ever since I first met you, I knew I wanted to be close to you. Even as an awkward ten year old with frizzy blonde hair and beady green eyes, I was determined to be one of your closest friends. I felt like you were out of my league, the way you were so smooth and confident, and I was always a tomboy and a spazz. I remember the first day I saw you at school. It was fifth grade. I had poked you in the arm and said, 'you're it.' And you had chased me around the playground, eventually lifting me up and spinning me around until I was laughing and squealing with delight.

"We became close friends, and after three years of friendship, you asked me out on a date. I had said no because I was too nervous to date anyone. But you didn't give up, and I started to date you and slowly fall in love with you. By our senior year in high school, we were an official couple, and by the time we finished college, we moved out to California together. We started great careers and lived in a beautiful home, and you were such a kind, generous, and patient boyfriend and fiancé. We went on some awesome vacations. I especially loved when we went to the Bahamas and went swimming with dolphins."

She giggled and wiped her eyes before continuing. "Jon, I know we had our issues, and that I broke your heart, but please know you were a great partner. I wasn't perfect, I know this. So I'm sorry for the heartbreak I caused you, but I still love you very much and I always will. Thank you, Jon. Thank you for so many amazing years together."

Just then, Jon's heart monitor began beeping more quickly, and his eyes began to flicker until they opened ever so slightly, his gaze meeting Lisa's. His thumb rubbed against her hand at a faster speed. Lisa's eyes widened, as did Nick's and Jon Sr.'s.

"You see this?" Lisa asked with tears of joy streaming down her face. "He's looking at me! He sees me! Oh my gosh!"

We were all crying tears of joy by that point, happy to see Jon somewhat alert. In that moment, it seemed entirely possible that he would wake up and begin recuperating. I smiled and laughed as I saw him with his eyes open, taking the time to wave and give the thumbs up. Then, just as quickly as his moment of lucidity emerged, it disappeared. His eyes closed once more and his heart rate slowed down again. Our spirits, so high for a few brief seconds, plummeted back down. My lower lip trembled as I did my best to keep my disappointment to myself.

Lisa's face fell, as did Nick's and Jon Sr.'s. We should have known it was too good to be true. Lisa slowly let go of Jon's hand and nodded to me. I nodded back then grasped his hand, clearing my throat.

"Hey, mate," I began through fresh tears. "I have a confession. I'm not ready to let you go. You're my best friend and I want us to have more time together. Part of me hopes you will wake up and begin a miraculous recovery, and that as long as we keep you hooked up to these machines, it's only a matter of time before you open your eyes and get out of bed. But another part of me knows that the longer you lie here, the less likely you are to get better. And I know you don't like being a prisoner in your own body, unable to move, because you're such an active person. Jon, I love you so much. You have made me the person I am today. As hard as this is, I'm grateful to have closure. I have so many fond memories of us. I loved riding our bikes through the streets of London, flirting with girls and showing off our riding skills. And who could forget all those double dates in high school, and sporting events where you and I were always competing with each other. We took so many amazing trips together as well. You got me to do so much, so many things that I was afraid of. I have always loved how fearless you are. Aside from being daring, you've always been compassionate. Whenever I was having a hard time, you were there for me, keeping me company and giving me great advice. There's nobody else like you, Jon. Nobody. Oh, dear god..."

I began to sob as I held onto his hand, which he began rubbing. I saw his eyes flicker once again, trying his best to open them so he could look at me. His heart rate sped up ever so slightly but then returned to normal after a few seconds. It was a blip, but better than nothing. And just as before, my spirits lifted for the briefest of moments.

Jonathan Sr. was the next to speak to Jon, but was only able to cry and hold his son's hand. I decided it was best to leave him alone with his firstborn, so I rose from my seat. Lisa and Nick respectfully followed. The three of us agreed to go outside for a smoke, desperately needing to clear our heads.

The day continued in a fog of tears, with everyone taking the time to say goodbye to Jon. It just seemed that he wasn't getting any better but his parents made the decision to wait one more week before turning off his life support, holding out hope that he might wake up and recover.

Three days later...

I was sitting next to Jon's hospital bed, when he slowly opened his eyes and sat up, flashing me his trademark smirk. I stared back in total shock.

"Hey, bitch," he crooned, as he looked down at his hospital gown and took it off, revealing his chiseled abs. "Not exactly high fashion, is it, mate?" He quipped.

"Jon, you're awake!" I said excitedly, as I leaned over to give him a hug. Tears of joy filled my eyes.

"Of course I am. I just needed a rest, and now I'm ready to get the hell out of this shithole."

He began ripping out his IV and removing his monitors, then began dressing in his usual clothes, which were under the bed.

I smiled and laughed with relief that he was ok. "I'm so happy, Jon."

He smiled at me as he put on a white t-shirt, followed by his jeans and boots, then his leather jacket. "Let's get out of here, mate. Come on."

He got up from the bed and took my hand, and we walked through the halls of the hospital, which were strangely deserted. When we reached the exit, Jon opened the door with a flourish.

"After you," He said with a wink. So I went ahead of him and walked through the door and out into the bright, sunny day.

I took in my surroundings, and my jaw dropped. We were standing at the edge of a cliff, with a steep drop into the water below. However, it wasn't just ANY cliff. In fact, it was the same place that Jon had driven his motorcycle years ago, and had nearly killed us.

He looked over at me. "Let's jump off!" He said excitedly.

I swallowed. "I don't think that's a good idea. We won't survive."

"Yes we will. I can fly." He smiled sexily. "Trust me, mate. Do you trust me?" He raised his eyebrows.

I nodded hesitantly. "Yes, Jon, I trust you."

He smiled broadly. Then he held onto my hand more tightly and, before I could react, he walked us to the edge of the cliff and jumped off. I held on for dear life as we fell towards the water at frightening speed, closing my eyes and trying to scream but being unable to. Just before we reached the ground, I opened my eyes.

That was when I woke up in my bed, feeling relieved to still be alive but disappointed that Jon would soon no longer be.

"You ok, Ken?" Anna asked, as she turned over in bed to face me. Her face was kind. Oh, how I wished I were ready for a serious relationship. But the sadness of the situation, combined with my fear of being vulnerable, kept me from opening up to her as much as I would have liked.

I nodded and smiled, running my hands through her auburn tresses. "Yes," I lied. "I'm fine. Let's fuck."

With those words, I climbed on top of her and began kissing her hard, lining up my rock hard dick with her sopping wet cunt. "Open wide, my little fuck toy."

Anna hesitated, so I forced her legs apart roughly and slapped her pussy several times with my hand, making her gasp in pain.

"Do as I say or I will do more than slap you down there!" I screamed in her face, before lighting the first of at least twenty five cigarettes and three blunts of weed. I chainsmoked for the full duration of our two-hour long sex fest, continually blowing clouds of smoke in her face and mouth as I pounded the shit out of her, and holding in the smoke for as long as ten minutes. Jon had always enjoyed chainsmoking during sex, devouring as many as ninety cigarettes in a row without getting winded or going limp. He also enjoyed holding in the smoke, having the ability to go without air for over eleven minutes, even while fucking vigorously. Lisa was an extremely heavy smoker as well, smoking as many as four packs of full flavor menthol cigarettes a day. Yet, due to Jon's "training," she had incredible endurance, and was able to hold her breath for over seven minutes.

As for Anna's and my fuck session? It continued without incident, aside from memories of Jon popping up in my head at random. At least twice, I had to close my eyes to hide the tears that were forming. I was not ready to let him go.

Later that day, when Anna had left my house to go to work, I called Daryl.

He sniffled before he spoke. "Hey, Ken," he said in a shaky voice. He sounded like he had been crying.

"Hey, Daryl. You alright?"

"I'm struggling, mate," he confessed. "I can't lose Jon. This sucks so badly. I don't know what to do with myself."

I cleared my throat. "Daryl, I think we need to go out. Let's have some fun. Let's take a cab into the city like we talked about, go dancing, get drunk and high as fucking possible, and have wild and crazy sex with some hot girls. Let's do it tomorrow night, mate. It's what Jon would want us to do."

Daryl laughed and sniffled again. "I don't know, Ken. It sounds like a fun time but I don't know if I'm up for it."

"Oh come on, Daryl," I chided. "You need to do something besides masturbate in front of the telly! Don't be a pussy! Bust your slump! You've only shagged one girl in your entire life. It's time to diversify your pussy portfolio!"

Daryl broke down into raucous laughter. "You're crazy, mate!"

"Is that a 'yes?'" I teased.

Daryl groaned and sighed. "Ok, fine. What time did you want to head out? Like 8?"

"Yes, why don't you come over and park at my place and I can get us a cab? We can go to the same club that we took Tracy to for her birthday. You loved that place. We all did."

Daryl sighed again. "Ok."

I smiled broadly. "Great!"

We made small talk for a few moments before hanging up. I was so excited.

The next day...

I spotted Candy in the club before she spotted me and she had a new friend with her, a brunette I didn't recognize. She wore a sexy black dress with a red floral print, and her friend wore blue. I wasted no time and marched right up to her. Daryl sat at the bar, watching.

"Candy, darling!" I crowed, making her spin around to see who was addressing her.

She grinned ear to ear when she saw me, giving me a big hug before introducing me to her friend, whose name was Adrian. We exchanged pleasantries for a few moments before I got to the point, feeling neither patient nor sober. I leaned in close to Candy's ear to talk to her.

"My friend, Daryl," I gesture towards the bar, "needs a good shag." Candy and Adrian giggled. I continued. "He hasn't fucked in over eight months, not since his ex wife left him for another woman. His brother, Jon, is in the hospital after a bad motorcycle accident and is basically brain dead. In fact, his parents are taking him off life support in about five days. Daryl is devastated and depressed and, between losing his wife and losing his brother, who has been trying to get him laid for a while, he urgently needs a fun night out. That said, would you lovely ladies like to come back to my house after we dance and get drunk off our arses in the club? I have enough for cab fare, and plenty of pot and booze at home."

The girls digested what I had just said then burst out laughing. Candy cleared her throat.

"That was the best 'sales pitch' ever," Candy commented with a chuckle, before turning to her friend. "What do you say, Adrian? Want to hang out with Kenny and Daryl after we party here for a bit?"

Adrian nodded. "As long as I get to dance with Kenny first!" She eyed me up and down with a sexy smile and I felt my dick harden immediately. I licked my lips.

"Of course, doll," I crooned at my new dark-haired friend. "Let's make our way over to Daryl and the four of us can get better acquainted."

We marched over to Daryl, who was busy downing several shots of booze. He appeared tipsy already.

"Hello, girls!" He slurred as we stood in front of him smiling. "Wanna dance?"

Candy nodded and took his hand. "This is my friend, Adrian," she said.

Daryl looked over and smiled. "Pleasure to meet you!"

Adrian nodded and smiled, then I took her hand and the four of us made our way to the dance floor.

For the next two hours or so, Daryl appeared to be having the time of his life, taking turns dancing with Candy and Adrian. I felt so happy seeing him so relaxed and uninhibited. The booze continued to flow and before long, Daryl and I had unbuttoned our shirts and were flat-out dry humping the girls on the dance floor. The sexual tension was palpable. I couldn't wait to bring the bitches home and fuck the shite out of them.

"Let's get out of here and go to my place!" I said to Candy, reaching under her dress to grope her crotch. Once again, she wore no panties.

She nodded excitedly, as did Adrian and Daryl. We made our way out of the club and hailed a cab.

I had never seen Daryl so drunk. He staggered to the cab, and the rest of us did likewise. Once we were seated, I wasted no time kissing and fondling Candy, who unzipped my fly and grabbed my cock through the opening in my boxers. I moaned as she gave me an amazing hand job. Meanwhile, Daryl groped and kissed Adrian, who was rubbing Daryl's bulge through his pants.

"Why don't you unzip me, darling?" Daryl slurred out of the blue. "Give my manhood some much needed air? Dust it off a wee bit?"

I burst out laughing, amused by how much Daryl sounded like his brother. Adrian giggled and did as he asked, unzipping his fly and freeing his erect penis from the confines of his blue boxer briefs. Unsurprisingly,

Daryl was well-endowed. He moaned as Adrian ran her hand up and down his shaft. He climaxed within perhaps a minute, letting go a burst of semen into Adrian's hand. Without hesitation, she licked it off.

Daryl panted and smiled, sweat covering his brow. "More where that came from, my dear!" He assured drunkenly.

Meanwhile, Candy lowered her mouth to my cock, deep throating me for several minutes until it exploded with pleasure. She eagerly swallowed my load then raised her head to kiss me hard on the mouth. I held the back of her head and grinded my mouth against hers, opening it wide and biting her tongue hard enough to make her gasp in pain. I backed away from her lips to talk to her.

"You better get used to being in pain," I growled in Candy's frightened face. "My friend Daryl here is just as aggressive as I am. You thought I was a lot to handle on my own? Try doubling that."

"He's right, bitch," Daryl slurred at Candy. "You better smoke a lot of weed and drink a shit ton of booze if you want to endure what we have in store." He looked at Adrian, whose expression was that of amusement mixed with a bit of fear. "And the same goes for you, too. Have you ever been dual-penetrated?"

Adrian giggled nervously. "Um, no."

I laughed at the conversation. "Daryl, what has gotten into you?" I asked with a chuckle. "You're never like this. You're such a proper boy-next-door type. Now, it's as if you're channeling your bad boy older brother. But I like it!" I winked.

Daryl smiled cockily. "Yes well, perhaps I have turned over a new leaf and am ready to stop being such a good boy. It's bloody time I took Jon's advice."

I nodded in agreement. "Good for you!"

Just then, the cab pulled up to my house. We got out of the car and I paid the driver, then we entered my home.

I made a beeline for the kitchen, pouring multiple shots of scotch and tequila for everyone, including myself, then placing the drinks on a tray. Then I grabbed my bong, which I filled with the good stuff earlier that afternoon. The four of us staggered to my couch, alternating shots of alcohol with hits from the bong.

Daryl stood up, ripping off his shirt. It had been a while since I had seen him shirtless, and he appeared more muscular than ever. He probably outweighed Jon by about thirty pounds, and his abdominal muscles popped like crazy. My jaw dropped.

"Holy shit, Daryl!" I exclaimed with a smile. "Have you been doing steroids, mate? You look incredible!"

Daryl laughed, as he unbuttoned his pants and pulled them down. His leg muscles were impressive as well. "Nope, all natural," He crooned. His bulge was visible through his underwear. He walked closer to Adrian until he was merely inches from her, his 6'4 frame towering over her as she sat on the couch. She looked up at him in awe, taking in his chiseled physique.

"Pull down my underpants," he said in a low voice, a sexy smile on his face. "I'm fully erect and I want you to see what I'm working with."

Adrian smiled flirtatiously before taking a hold of his knickers and pulling them down, freeing his enormous cock that was every bit as big as Jon's. Then, while still seated on the couch, she grabbed it with her dainty hand and began sucking him off.

Daryl fucked her face with reckless abandon. I became even more turned on and hastily undressed. Then I forced myself onto Candy, who, by this point, had lifted up her dress to expose her delicious cunny. I pinned her down on the couch as I lined up my throbbing dick with her opening and wasted no time slamming into her like she was a piece of meat. She howled in pain spiked with pleasure as I impaled her ladybits. I fucked the hell out of Candy for a few moments before looking over at Daryl, who was smiling sadistically as he held Adrian's head to his cock, making her choke and gag. In that moment, it was eerie how much he resembled Jon - in both temperament and looks.

SMACK!

Daryl slapped Adrian in the face, making her squeal and pause momentarily. My mouth hung open in shock. This was so out of character for him!

"Keep sucking me, you little bitch!" Daryl growled as he grinded her head against him.

She whimpered as she struggled to take as much of his throbbing member into her mouth as possible. Within a few minutes, he had an orgasm and pulled out of her mouth at the last second, ejaculating all over her exposed cleavage. Without warning, he knelt down and licked her bosom clean then planted an aggressive kiss on her mouth, forcing her to taste his semen. She gagged momentarily before swallowing. Daryl then lifted up her dress, exposing her shaved pussy and petite breasts, and knelt down before her.

"Spread your legs for Daddy," he growled. "I want to taste your cunny before I fuck the hell out of you."

Still breathless from the face-fucking, Adrian opened her legs for Daryl, who wasted no time burying his face in her snatch. As he did this, he began jerking himself off, developing an erection within seconds.

Meanwhile, I pushed on the backs of Candy's thighs, falling onto her repeatedly. My thrusts quickened, and within seconds, I unloaded inside her. Then I knelt down, sucked my semen out of her pussy, and fed it to her with a sloppy, aggressive kiss.

"Wanna continue things in the bedroom?" Candy gasped between kisses. "I've been wanting you to tie me up."

I laughed heartily and nodded. "You don't have to ask twice, sweetheart," I assured as I began to scoop her up in my arms. "In fact, I already have the restraints set up on my bed."

Earlier that day, I had decided to put the restraints on, despite the fact that they brought back an unpleasant memory - specifically of Jon raping me. But I thought of all the other times I had used the restraints and how much kinky fun I'd had with them over the years, so I decided it was time to keep using them, to cancel out the trauma.

I began carrying Candy to the bedroom, briefly turning around to speak to Daryl, whose face was still buried in Adrian's cunt. "Why don't you two join us?" I asked. "Even if it's just to watch. The more the merrier!"

Daryl backed away from Adrian's pussy and nodded with a smile, then proceeded to pick her up and carry her to my bedroom. I couldn't wait to restrain Candy, and push her to the limit of what she could handle.

I flung the blond bimbo onto the bed and had her lie face up with her arms out and legs spread, then I rapidly fastened the restraints. Meanwhile, Daryl ripped off Adrian's blue dress and bent her over the

Goosebumps formed on Candy's skin as the blade made its way down her stomach and her pubic area. Her eyes remained clenched and her chest rose and fell with her rapid breathing. I smirked, knowing she was feeling a lot of fear in that moment. My cock hardened all the more as it remained buried in her arse. My thrusts sped up, as did the motion of the knife over her flesh.

"Open your eyes, bitch!" I barked, causing her as well as Daryl and Adrian to jump. "I want you to see what I'm doing to you."

Candy hesitantly opened her baby blues, staring at the knife as it traveled upward towards her throat. Her body trembled and her eyes filled with frightened tears. The bed shook slightly from the force of Daryl's thrusts as well as my own, making the knife play even more treacherous.

"Want me to cut you?" I growled as I slid the knife over her clavicle area, making her whimper.

"N-no," she stammered. "But I want you to get me my purse. It's on the kitchen counter. My phone is ringing, and it's in my purse. It could be important. My cousin has been very sick, so I want to make sure it isn't bad news. Please?" Her eyes filled with fresh tears.

I glared at her as I continued to thrust, doing my best to avoid getting choked up as I thought of Jon. I slowly put down the knife and withdrew from her, then got up to grab her purse from the kitchen counter.

Surely enough, her purse was on the counter and her phone made an "alert" noise to let her know she had a new voicemail. I picked up the purse and made my way back to the bedroom. She smiled as soon as I walked back in. Daryl continued to fuck Adrian, who was moaning and smiling as she remained bent over the bed.

Mercifully, I took the restraints off Candy's wrists, so she could use her phone. She thanked me and took her phone out of her purse, sitting up and listening to her voicemail. A look of relief spread across her face.

"I feel better now," she said with a smile. "It was nothing important."

Candy placed the phone back in her purse then rapidly fished another item out of it, a mischievous look on her face. What appeared in her hands next scared the hell out of me. It was a handgun!

Daryl jumped as she saw Candy hold the gun in her hands, flashing it around as if she were showing off a prized possession. Adrian, on the other hand, appeared completely unfazed. I did my best to remain calm and in control as I knelt on the bed.

"What the hell do you intend to do with that?" I asked cautiously as I put my hands up.

She raised her eyebrows as she held it out to me, as if she wanted me to take it from her. "It's what YOU'RE going to do with it," she said suggestively. "You ever fuck a girl with the barrel of a gun?"

I swallowed. "No, that's one thing I haven't done. I'm British and guns are more of an American thing." My voice shook. "But I can do that for you." I forced a sexy smile.

Candy smiled sexily and brought the gun even closer to me. "Take it."

I hesitantly took the gun out of her hands, and it was heavier than I expected. What was the harm anyway, I thought. It's not like she was asking me to SHOOT her.

"Lie down, sweetheart," I crooned. "I'm going to gun-fuck you."

She smirked and lay back on the bed. I crouched between her legs and began to ease the barrel into her opening. She moaned as the cool metal slid inside her womanhood. I began to move the gun in and out of her, pretending it was a toy and not a real firearm.

I briefly looked over at Daryl, whose mouth hung open in shock as he thrusted into Adrian. He was as unaccustomed to seeing guns as I was. I winked at him to convince him I was fine, and not the nervous wreck I actually was. He smiled and winked back, appearing relieved that I seemed to know what I was doing with the deadly tool.

The minutes ticked by interminably as I moved the barrel of the pistol in and out of Candy's pussy. Her hips bucked and a sexy smile spread across her face as she approached orgasm. After what seemed like forever, she squirted all over my hand and moaned with pleasure. I gradually removed the gun from her ladybits, wiping the sweat from my brow. I so needed a cigarette, so I grabbed the pack from the nightstand and lit one, inhaling deeply.

"We aren't done yet," Candy said in a breathless voice as she fingered her wet cunny. "I want you to shoot me."

I nearly dropped my cigarette and Daryl stopped thrusting momentarily after hearing what she just said.

"What?!" I asked incredulously.

"Shoot me," she repeated with a sexy smile. "It's not loaded. I just want you to shoot a blank. I find it exciting. Just aim it right here, and pull the trigger."

Candy opened her legs wider as she pointed to her vagina. I couldn't believe what she was asking me to do, but being a true dominant, I was determined to go through with it. After all, I didn't want to look like a wimp.

"Ok," I said, as I swallowed. Then I picked up the gun, put down the cigarette, and used both hands to aim at her snatch, doing my damndest to keep my hands steady as my fingers remained primed on the trigger.

I thought of Jon and what he would do. I imagined him with a cocky smile on his face, confidently holding the gun and pulling the trigger like it was nothing. Then I did my best to picture what he would say to me in that moment.

"Ken, honey," he would begin in his velvety voice. "YOU are in control here, not her. Use your best judgment, mate. Don't hesitate. Don't think too much. Just act from the heart. You're the boss. Do what YOU want, even if it's not the same as what she wants."

My hands shook slightly as I held the gun in my hands, willing myself to pull the trigger but being unable to do so. I had to stay in control, and that meant doing what I wanted. My gut told me not to. Shooting her just felt wrong. I couldn't do it. I WOULDN'T do it. I could feel my heart pounding in my chest. My eyes filled with tears and I dropped the weapon. Then I got up from the bed.

"I can't do this," I said in a shaky voice. Then, before anyone could react, I left the bedroom and went straight to the loo, where I threw up.

I was in there for a long time, kneeling before the toilet and crying. Then I heard a knock on the door.

"Ken," Daryl said in a kind voice. "Are you alright?"

"Yes, I'm fine," I lied, wiping my tears.

"May I come in?"

I rose from the toilet and splashed some water on my face. "Ok."

Daryl came in the bathroom, wearing his boxer briefs. He averted his eyes and handed me a towel so I could cover myself. Unlike Jon, he was generally modest and respected boundaries at all times.

I took the towel and hastily wrapped it around my waist. Then I sat at the edge of the bathtub and began to cry again.

Daryl sat next to me and gently put his hand on my shoulder. "I know how you feel," he admitted in a gentle voice. "Guns aren't my favorite thing, either. I give you credit for even holding it in your hand." He chuckled softly.

I sniffled. "It just felt wrong," I muttered. "I tried to picture Jon, and what he would do. Always so confident and calm. He probably would have shot a blank at her, no problem. But I'm not him. I imagined him talking to me, telling me to stay in control and do what I wanted, not what SHE wanted. So I did just that. I didn't want to shoot her, and if I wanted to be a real 'dominant,' that meant not giving in to her request. I don't like guns, Daryl. Plain and simple."

He nodded sympathetically. "I understand. And I'm sure Jon would have been proud of you for not giving in to her, and for sticking to your guns. No pun intended!"

We shared a laugh. I loved Daryl for his level-headedness and down to earth demeanor. He was truly a bloke-next-door type. I studied him for a few moments, taking in his gentle blue eyes and wavy, dark brown hair, as well as his stubble. The cleft in his chin made him all the more attractive. In that moment, I actually found myself aroused by my strait-laced best mate, who, in so many ways, was Jon's opposite. I cleared my throat.

"Daryl," I began. "I know you're straight and that you have never been with a man, and I don't expect you to have sex. But... may I kiss you?" I swallowed as I awaited his response.

He chuckled and blushed. "Um, on the lips?"

I nodded.

He took a breath then nodded slowly. "What the hell?" He said with a smile. "I'm plastered anyway!"

I chuckled at his comment. Then I slowly leaned in towards him, cupping his chin before locking my lips with his. The kiss was short, but sweet and genuine.

"How did you like that?" I asked with a gentle smile.

Daryl sighed. "Well, it was lovely, but...I still fancy ladies," he admitted wryly. "Nothing personal." He winked and grinned, revealing teeth that were as white and straight as his brother's.

I chuckled. "Speaking of ladies, why don't we rejoin them?"

Daryl nodded excitedly, and we both left the bathroom to join Candy and Adrian, who were hanging out in the kitchen and sipping wine. They were both naked. My cock swelled at the sight of them.

"Sorry about the gun," Candy said with an apologetic expression as she came up to me and put her arms around my waist.

I smiled and dropped my towel, then wrapped my arms around her. "It's quite alright, sweetheart," I assured. "I was just taken aback. I'd never handled a gun before. Not unless you count a B.B. gun I shot once as a young boy."

Candy smiled softly. "Well, I won't make you do that again. But, did you want to go for round two?" She raised her eyebrows and ran her hands up and down my chest as she awaited my answer.

I looked over at Daryl, who was already taking off his boxer briefs again and grinning ear to ear. I laughed and nodded.

The four of us retreated back to the bedroom, and this time we switched partners. I put Adrian in restraints, intent on doing knife play with her. Daryl wasted no time bending Candy over and pounding the shit out of her. Finished with the restraints, I turned to Daryl with a smirk?

"How's Candy's pussy?" I growled as I fondled myself, getting nice and hard for Adrian, who lay panting and smiling on the bed with her limbs forced apart by leather straps.

"Good enough to eat, mate!" Daryl quipped, then withdrew from her and leaned over to eat her cunny for a few moments. Candy moaned as Daryl devoured her snatch, climaxing within a minute. Satisfied, he abruptly reentered her, thrusting harder than before.

Meanwhile I grabbed the knife from the nightstand and slammed my cock into Adrian's tight cunt. She howled and bucked her hips as I thrusted, then began to glide the blade up and down her chest. Her breathing quickened and she moaned in fear mixed with arousal, as she endured the sensation of cold, sharp metal over her tender, olive tinted flesh. She fidgeted several times, and my quick reflexes were the only thing that kept her from being cut.

"You best lie still," I earned as I looked at her intensely, slowing down the movement of the knife.

"It tickles," she said with a laugh.

I smirked. "It won't tickle if I cut you, sweetheart. Now behave."

"Yeah, behave!" Candy piped up from the edge of the bed as Daryl continued to pound her.

Forgetting herself, Adrian giggled and abruptly sat up on the bed to talk to Candy, pulling the arm restraints taut as she did so. Unfortunately, I was unable to lift the knife in time and left a decent size cut on her stomach. It began to bleed right away. She gasped in surprise, as did I.

Taken aback, Daryl stopped thrusting and withdrew from Candy, who also witnessed the mishap. My penis went limp as I entered "emergency mode," so I quickly withdrew from Adrian, put down the knife and grabbed a wad of tissues from the box that sat atop the nightstand and had her hold it to the wound to slow down the bleeding. She appeared frightened.

"You're alright," I assured my new brunette friend as I undid her restraints. "It's luckily not a deep wound. I could have stabbed you. That's why lying still is so important." I smiled gently.

Adrian nodded. "I know that now," she quipped. "I learned my lesson!"

After a few moments, I took her to the bathroom to disinfect and dress the wound. Daryl and Candy joined us for moral support.

The four of us made small talk for a bit and, inevitably, Jon's name came up.

"Jon always loved an adrenaline rush in AND out of the bedroom," I commented as I cleaned Adrian's wound with disinfectant. "Knives, needles, fire, whips, paddles, you name it. Mr. Dominant." My eyes filled with tears as I thought of him.

"I'm still not giving up hope that he might wake up," Daryl said in a soft voice.

I nodded solemnly as I put a bandage on Adrian's cut. A stiff drink suddenly felt like a good idea, as did a good night's sleep.

The four of us washed up in the loo then retreated to the kitchen to pour ourselves some nightcaps. It was nearly 2am and our eyes were getting heavy. Candy and I sat on the barstools at the kitchen counter and sipped our drinks, chatting idly. Adrian and Daryl got comfortable on the couch in the living room, where they fell asleep in front of the Telly within minutes.

"Let's go to bed," I suggested to Candy with a flirty smile.

She nodded and we quickly finished our drinks before heading to my bedroom for some much needed rest.

Around 7am...

My cellphone rang, waking me from a dead sleep. Nobody ever called me this early. I blindly reached over to grab my phone from the nightstand. It was Martha, Jon's mum. Expecting the worst, my heart sped up something terrible.

"Hello?" I asked in a shaky voice.

"Ken, it's Martha. I just tried calling Daryl but it went to voicemail, so now I'm calling you. I have great news."

"Yes?"

"Jon's awake!"

Around 8am...

Daryl, Candy, Adrian and I rode in my car making small talk as I drove the girls to their respective homes, which were about twenty minutes away. Following Martha's call, I had awakened Daryl to tell him the news. He had jumped up from the couch so quickly that I had laughed out loud. Then I had offered to take the girls home, since their houses were on the way to the hospital.

"Hey, Candy," I began as I drove, "Jon used to have a huge crush on a girl by the same name when he was a young boy."

"Is that right?" She asked from the passenger seat. Daryl and Adrian sat in the back, lost in their own conversation.

"Indeed. See, Jon is an actor and a model. The year we moved to the states, he had a very thick British accent. Thicker than mine ever was. So he took acting lessons to help him master an American accent in order to get more parts in plays and commercials. The teacher's daughter was about his age, maybe a year or two younger. And he LOVED her. They spent so much time together that summer, going on little dates to the park and to the beach, as well as the arcade. He told me he taught her how to skateboard, how to do a cartwheel, and helped her get over her fear of heights by encouraging her to go on a rollercoaster when they went to a fair together. He was so crushed when she moved to Connecticut with her family that fall, after her father landed a gig with the theater department at Yale University. Then he lost touch with her altogether."

I smiled as I thought of the memory of him coming back from his first lesson, a love struck expression on his face.

Candy's eyes were wide. "Is Jon's last name, 'Moore?'"

I nodded. "Yes. Why?" My heart fluttered. Could it be...?

"I'm the girl he was talking about! The acting teacher was my father! Oh my god! I knew his face looked familiar when I saw a photo of you two on your refrigerator. So crazy!" She chuckled, her expression appearing more surprised than before.

"The hell you say! Well, maybe we could set up a reunion of sorts."

"He's at County, right?"

I nodded. "Yes, in the ICU."

"I volunteer there twice a week. In fact, I will be there tomorrow evening between four and seven. I can go visit him. He will be so surprised!"

"I think that would be a nice surprise for him. But I want to make sure he feels well enough for outside visitors first. Also, I'm not sure how his mental status will be. And who knows, he might be self-conscious about how he looks since he hasn't been able to shave or properly bathe for a few weeks. I'm sure you understand."

Candy nodded. "Totally understandable. Let me know."

I grinned, excited at the prospect of him meeting his old friend, who was his first big crush, his first kiss, and his first love. He'd had a crush on Lisa around the same time but had kept his distance because, when he first moved to the states and started school, he had wrongly assumed that she was Nick's girlfriend. Of course, once summer was over and Candy moved, he got closer to Lisa...and the rest, as they say, is history.

Later that day...

Daryl and I sat on one side of Jon's bed and Jon's parents sat on the other. Jon was sleeping most of the time and still needed supplemental oxygen, but was able to open his eyes occasionally and smile as well as nod when spoken to. He appeared rather frail and had plenty of weeks of rehabilitation in front of him, but he was at least able to breathe on his own.

Daryl reached out and grabbed Jon's hand, his eyes filling with tears. "I'm so glad you're doing better, Jon," he whispered through tears. "I was so worried. We all were."

Jon's eyelids fluttered for a few moments until they opened and he turned his head to look at his younger brother. He squeezed his hand, then opened his mouth to speak.

"Don't cry, Daryl," he whispered hoarsely, a gentle smile on his face. This was his first time speaking since he had arrived at the hospital several weeks prior. We all gasped and began to cry happy tears as Jon uttered that first sentence.

"Look who's finally talking?" I teased, laughing through my tears.

Jon smiled broadly. "I'm trying," he breathed. "So tired, mate. Everything hurts."

He began to cough, but recovered quickly. It was so great to hear him talk again.

"I've missed you, Jon," Daryl said as he wiped away his tears.

"Even though I've been a dick?" He gasped, a tiny smirk on his face.

We all broken into laughter, including Jon's father, who ordinarily hated when his son was vulgar.

The four of us continued to chat with Jon, who was mostly quiet except for an occasional word or short phrase. I was so happy to see him alert again, and thrilled at the prospect of him reuniting with his old flame.

The following evening...

Jon was more alert and talkative than the day before. We sat and talked for hours, discussing everything from plans for rescheduling the gym's grand opening, to his upcoming physical therapy for his leg. He was now on heavy duty pain meds, which concerned me, given his addiction issues. According to the nurse, his appetite was minimal, and when he did eat, he threw up. This was due to the meds he was on, along with the fact that years of binging and purging had weakened his sphincter, making him automatically vomit after eating. It would be a while before this symptom would dissipate. I did what I could to keep his spirits up, telling him about Daryl's and my latest sexual adventure and making sure to avoid mentioning Candy's name. Needless to say, he was beyond ecstatic for his younger brother.

"It's about bloody time he fucked some horny bitches," Jon said with a chuckle. "I can't wait to get out of here so I can dust off Big Ben again." We both howled with laughter. "You know, I don't think I've gone this long without having sex since I was 14. As for getting it up, I reckon my dick is still in a bit of a coma." He smirked.

"I'm sure it's only a matter of time before all of you is awake," I assured. "Recovery takes time."

Knock, knock.

"Hello," a brunette aide said with a smile before rolling a cart over to Jon's bed, which had a meal tray on top of it. "Dinner time. Today is chicken soup and apple sauce, and some yummy pieces of bread. And I got you some hot tea to drink. Does that sound good?"

Jon nodded. "Better than the green gelatin I had yesterday," he said with a smirk. "I love chicken soup. Thank you, dear."

The cute nurse blushed and smiled. Jon was charming and sexy, even when unshaven and dressed in a hospital gown. "Enjoy!" Then she turned around and left the room.

Jon leaned over to me. "I'd like to enjoy HER," he whispered in my ear. I laughed heartily.

Jon's hands shook considerably as he handled the utensils, doing his best to appear nonchalant. But after a few moments of struggle, it was clear he was getting frustrated. Suddenly, he threw down the spoon onto the tray and began to cry, his face in his hands. I put my hand on his shoulder.

"What's wrong, mate? Do you need me to get a straw so you can eat the soup a little more easily? Or I could feed it to you?"

He shook his head. "I'm just having a moment," he said with a sniffle. "I'm not used to being helpless like this. It isn't ME."

I nodded sympathetically. "I understand. But just think of how far you have come in the past 24 hours. Just yesterday, you barely spoke and today you're talking like it's nothing. You're a fighter, Jon. You're strong as hell. You've got this." I smiled confidently.

He sniffled and looked at me for a few moments before his mouth formed an amused smirk. "You sound like me, mate. All positive and confident, giving little pep talks. I'm so used to the role being reversed. It's weird hearing someone else comfort ME."

"I think you're long overdue for someone to take care of YOU. Speaking of," I said, picking up his spoon and ladling some of the soup

into it, "Eat up. I read somewhere that chicken soup is good for erectile dysfunction." I winked. "Now shall I feed you, or do you want to give it a shot?"

He chuckled. "What do YOU think?" He grabbed the spoon from me and shakily put it to his lips, taking a hearty slurp of the hot soup. "Hmm. Not bad for hospital fare." He helped himself to some bread and dipped it in the soup, savoring the taste.

"I can't wait until you're out of here," I said with a smile. "Life isn't the same without you."

Jon nodded and smiled, sipping his tea and helping himself to a second piece of bread. "Me too, mate. As soon as I get out of here, I'm gonna throw a huge party. I could rent out the banquet hall at that big casino in Norwich, Connecticut...what's the place? Pequot Moon?"

I nodded. "That place is beautiful."

"We can invite all our friends and family and have a big soirée. Black tie dress code, gourmet food, a live band, top shelf liquor, the works. And I will book the most expensive suite they have, complete with butler service, and have an epic 'after party.' Piles of weed, cocaine, pills, expensive booze, and a veritable buffet of cock and pussy. I'm talking an all-out orgy that would make our trip to New York look like a stay at a Buddhist monastery. You best get your dick ready for the fuck-a-thon, mate. Start training now." He winked as he imitated fellatio with a piece of bread, before shoving the rest of it in his mouth.

I laughed hysterically at Jon's words, loving how vulgar he was. Oh, how I had missed my friend. I picked up the remote and put on a funny movie. I watched for several minutes while Jon ate, doing my best to stay nonchalant as I kept my eye on the clock. Earlier,, I had given Candy the ok to visit Jon, and she said she would be arriving shortly after dinner.

"What was it like, being in a coma?" I asked, curious how it felt to be mostly unconscious for two weeks.

Jon sipped his tea and rubbed his beard.. "Well, I would compare it to being asleep, but you're able to hear what's going on in your environment. And you want to respond, but your body won't cooperate. It's like you know that you're trapped, except you're calm, accepting of the fact that you can't control what's happening around you. I would imagine it's a bit like dying; you have a feeling of peace, a feeling of being able to let go and surrender to a state of oblivion. There's no pain. There's just... stillness." He smiled gently.

I nodded. "That sounds rather pleasant, actually. As for hearing things going on around you, I'm guessing that you recall your parents talking to you? As well as Daryl and your extended family, and close friends?"

Jon nodded, taking another sip of tea. "I did. I was impressed that Lisa and Nick flew out to see me, after the way I reacted on social media to the news of their marriage. It was so nice having so many people come by to pay their respects. And I was blown away by what my father said to me. He's never like that. Perhaps he and I can be closer now." He finished the soup with a satisfied smile.

I smiled and patted his arm. "I'm sure you can."

Suddenly, Jon turned red and appeared to be choking. I stood up, ready to intervene.

"Jon! You ok? Are you choking?"

He shook his head no and suddenly threw up all over his dinner tray, getting some of it in his beard and on his hospital gown. I immediately grabbed some paper towels from the sink area and wetted them, wasting no time cleaning him up. He initially winced at my touch and began to cry in embarrassment.

"You shouldn't have to do this," he said through tears, grabbing some tissues to wipe his face clean as I wiped down his gown. "It's bloody humiliating."

"Jon, we have each other's backs," I assured in a gentle voice. "How many times have you been there for me when I was sick as a dog? And I mean, Christ, you were only nine years old when you held Daryl's hand and bathed him after he got sick from chemo. This is the least I could do." I backed away from his hospital gown to see how I did, clean up wise.. "Looks like most of it landed on the tray. At least your aim is good!" I smirked.

Jon looked at me then began to laugh and shake his head, his eyes filling with fresh tears. "Oh, Ken, I don't know what I would do without you."

Knock, knock.

She was wearing scrubs and had her blond hair back in a ponytail, but still looked radiant.. I nodded with a smile and she approached Jon's bed. He hastily wiped his eyes and ran his hands through his hair,, doing his best to look presentable for this lovely lady that just walked in the room. She stood before him with a smile.

"Jon?"

My best mate squinted, trying his best to figure out who she was. It was obvious that he thought she looked familiar. Suddenly, his eyes widened and he gasped, before a huge smile spread across his face.

"Candy!"

Chapter 7: "Like a Flower"

"How do I look?" Amy asked as she stood in my living room, twirling around in her new royal blue dress. It was strapless and went to mid-thigh, flaring slightly towards the bottom hem. Her long black hair was freshly curled and she wore a beautiful shade of red lip gloss. She looked like a doll come to life. My jaw dropped at how beautiful she was. It was official: Little Amy was now 21 years old, and headed to the casino for the first time with Tracy, Daryl, and me.

I walked in close to her, putting my arms around her dainty waist. "You look stunning," I said softly. "Like a princess. And I can't wait to spoil you this weekend."

Amy blushed and smiled as she returned my embrace. "I can't wait," she cooed.

Just then, Tracy emerged from the bathroom. She was decked out in a lovely pink dress that hugged her curves and accentuated her gorgeous, plump breasts. Her blond hair was freshly highlighted and styled in sexy waves. She smiled broadly at Amy.

"Oh my god, you look so beautiful!" She gushed as she took in the sight of her bestie.

Amy blushed again. "So do you!"

I gave Tracy a hug. "Amy's right. You look incredible. Daryl's going to cream his pants when he sees the two of you!"

The three of us burst out laughing, then the door to my bedroom opened. Daryl emerged, dressed in a sharp looking, black button down shirt and matching pants. His eyes widened as he took in the sight of Tracy and Amy.

"Holy cow, you girls clean up nice!" He said with a chuckle.

We all laughed, and I cleared my throat. "Well, is everyone all packed? Because I'm ready to go!"

Everyone agreed enthusiastically before grabbing their respective overnight bags, and then we all headed to my car, which had the top down. It was a beautiful August afternoon, and not too humid - the perfect day for a drive.

Daryl sat in the passenger seat of my Mercedes and the girls sat in the back. I set the GPS and selected some music, then we were on our way to Connecticut for a night of partying for miss Amy.

"I so need to get away," Daryl said as I drove through town. "The past month has been absolute hell."

I nodded. "Yeah," I agreed. "It's been a rollercoaster."

"Do you think Jon will ever be the same?" Daryl asked with a serious expression on his face.

I swallowed, mulling over the events of the past few weeks. "I don't know."

About a day or two after Jon had awakened and had a visit with Candy, the doctors discovered that he had developed sepsis from an infection in his leg. Early intervention prevented him from requiring an amputation but also delayed his recovery. He wound up having to take a variety of strong drugs, including antibiotics, potent painkillers, and sleep meds due to insomnia. The infection, combined with the side effects of the drugs and the stress of being bedridden for an extended period, led to him feeling increasingly depressed and anxious. He became delusional, convinced that the hospital food was poisoned and refused to eat. Because of this, he would only consume nutritional shakes from a can that he insisted on opening himself, or food that his mother brought him. At one point, he couldn't find his wristwatch and accused Nick of stealing it, since, according to Jon, "the bastard steals everything ELSE I hold dear."

Jon's agitated behavior got to the point that his primary doctor at the hospital insisted that he get a consult with a psychiatrist, who diagnosed him with post traumatic stress disorder and major depression. He started meds for these issues, but the side effects included loss of appetite as well as insomnia. So the doctor put him on different meds that seemed to work better, even though Jon said they made him feel "like a bloody zombie." He had a long road ahead of him, and things would unfortunately get worse before they would get better.

I merged onto the highway, doing my best to think about the fun weekend ahead. My goal was to convince Daryl to fuck Tracy, who he'd had a crush on for many years. Adrian, as nice as she was, had gotten back together with her old boyfriend a week or so after we had met up with her and Candy. So this was the perfect time for him to make the moves on Tracy, who I knew reciprocated Daryl's feelings. As for Amy, the birthday girl? I had booked a two bedroom suite and had splurged on a birthday package for her - a balloon and flower arrangement for the hotel room, a pedicure at the casino's spa, and dinner at a fancy Italian restaurant onsite.

The drive was short and pleasant, and we used valet parking when we got to the casino. Then the four of us made our way through the heavy glass doors and into the impressively decorated lobby.

Amy's jaw dropped as she took in the sights. A gigantic glass sculpture adorned the middle of the mammoth sized lobby, and the floor was made of vivid, shiny tile. The ceiling was stained glass, and nothing short of mesmerizing with its kaleidoscope of colors. Piano music played in the background. The air smelled like fresh soap. People of all ages and backgrounds milled about, and they all looked happy. I knew that this was the perfect place to celebrate Amy's 21st.

"Shall we?" I asked with a smile, offering my arm to Amy, who nodded excitedly and wrapped her arm around mine. Daryl did the same with Tracy. Oh how I wanted to see those two fuck the hell out of each other!

We checked in at the hotel's front desk and got on the elevator, making our way to the suite that was on the 35th floor. When we entered the suite, Amy's jaw dropped.

The balloon and flower arrangement was stunning, as was the decor. The view from the window was nothing short of majestic. The property overlooked a lake, and it was possible to see as far over as the next city. Amy quickly dropped her bag and gave me a huge hug.

"Thank you, Kenny!" She exclaimed.

I hugged her back and kissed her gently on the lips. "My pleasure, sweetheart."

Tracy and Daryl began unpacking their bags and got comfortable in one of the suite's bedrooms, admiring the view and decor. I was so happy that those two were spending so much time together after many years of being polite but distant, and had a feeling it was only a matter of time before they would be more than friends. Jon had noticed chemistry between his brother and Tracy many years prior, wondering why they never dated. There WAS a seven year age difference between them, so perhaps that was a factor in the past.

I looked at Amy with lust in my eyes, and before she could react, I moved my hand up her dress until my hand was on her crotch. She wore satin panties. I felt her up for a few moments, making her moan. Then I grabbed the silky material and roughly yanked down the panties until they were down around her ankles, making her gasp.

"You won't be needing these," I growled. "Pick up your feet."

She stepped out of the underwear, which I took the pleasure of throwing across the room, where it landed on the lampshade that sat atop the nightstand. I fondled her for a few more moments, slipping one of my fingers inside her wetness, before abruptly removing my finger and licking it clean. Then I pulled the hem of her dress back down.

"Ready to gamble now?" I asked with raised eyebrows.

Amy swallowed and nodded, her body trembling with arousal. Just then, Daryl and Tracy emerged from their bedroom, appearing flushed. I thought I was able to make out a bit of Tracy's lipstick on Daryl's neck. It seemed they'd had themselves a little fun as well!

The four of us touched up our appearances and we made our way down to the casino, heading straight to the slot machines.

The sights, sounds, and smells of the casino were intoxicating. Everything from the aroma of fresh coffee, to the bass from live music, to gorgeous waterfalls and glass sculptures with color changing lights graced my senses. It was like being in another world. I silently vowed to visit more often.

Amy and Tracy ran ahead of Daryl and me, giggling like little kids as they took in the sights. After walking for a while, the four of us decided on some nickel slots that overlooked a row of blackjack tables.

Three hours later...

In a matter of hours, Amy and I had managed to baptize a slot machine, a quiet corner of the keno room, the sauna and hot tub in the spa, the rollercoaster simulator at the sparsely populated arcade, and an empty food court. It was relatively easy to find places to fuck if you were creative - and horny - enough! The thrill of being in a public place, and the thrill of being caught, made casino sex all the more exciting. I even incorporated popping candy into one of our trysts, filling my mouth with the fizzy concoction before immediately going down on her. She loved the sensation, and made me stop at the casino's candy store for more packets! I was so looking forward to using the popping candy on her AND Tracy later that night.

The sexual tension was palpable between Daryl and Tracy. At one point in the night, I leaned in close to my best mate and asked him a question that I had been curious about for a while.

"Have you and Tracy...fooled around at all?" I asked, as we walked around browsing slot machines. The girls were several yards behind us, talking and giggling.

Daryl blushed and smiled. "Not unless you count kissing as 'fooling around,'" he said with a wink. "I'm waiting for the right moment."

I raised my eyebrows. "I say the right moment is tonight. In fact, I say we put a rush on it by heading up to the night club on the upper level after dinner."

Daryl shook his head and laughed. "Whatever you say, mate! Speaking of dinner, I'm hungry. Is it almost time for our reservation?"

I checked my watch, and nodded. "Indeed it is. We have six minutes. Let's start walking to the restaurant right now." I turned back to the girls and told them it was almost time for dinner.

We arrived moments later, taking in the sights, sounds, and smells of the upscale Italian restaurant, which sported a waterfall and a beautiful glass sculpture. As for the food? It was the best Italian cuisine I'd ever eaten in my life. The waitstaff even sang happy birthday to Amy, who blushed terribly as they came out with a slice of tiramisu, her favorite dessert. Of course, I had to take a video on my phone.

"What are you going to wish for?" I asked Amy, before she blew out the candle.

She squinted and smiled, taking a sip of her second martini. "I wish Tracy and Daryl would have sex already!" She blurted with a giggle and hiccup.

The four of us broke out in raucous laughter at Amy's comment, and Tracy playfully slapped her bestie in the arm. Daryl turned beet red but was laughing along with the rest of us. The mood was so light and I was so happy to see Amy and the others enjoying themselves and letting go a little, especially after such an intense couple of weeks. My mind wandered to Jon, and I couldn't help picturing what it would be like if he were there with us, celebrating. I could see him bringing some foxy blonde as his date and shagging in plain view atop a blackjack table, a sort of impromptu sex show, and only stopping after being approached by a security officer. Yes, that's exactly what he would do. The thought made me laugh out loud.

Daryl smirked at me. "What's so funny?" He asked with a wink.

"Oh, just imagining what your brother would be doing if he were with us right now," I said with a sigh.

"Don't you mean WHO he would be doing?" Daryl asked with raised eyebrows.

We looked at each other intensely for a moment before blurting out the same name at the same time. "Noelle." Then we burst out laughing.

We soon finished dessert and drinks at the restaurant and made our way up to the night club. The bouncer glanced at Amy's ID and smiled, wishing her a happy birthday before letting all four of us through the red double doors. Amy smiled broadly as she grabbed Tracy's hand and confidently ambled her way into the club. The girls were already tipsy from the drinks they had at the restaurant, and it was nice to see my Little Dollies having so much fun.

The bass reverberated off the walls of the spacious night club, which was decorated in sensual shades of burgundy and black. Many of the club goers wore glow sticks, adding an otherworldly touch to the decor.

Amy downed a shot from the bar then insisted on heading to the dance floor, taking Tracy by the hand as she did so. Daryl and I followed behind, admiring the view of the girls' shapely backsides. I turned to Daryl.

"When do you think you and Tracy are going to fuck?" I asked with a smirk.

Daryl laughed. "You sound like my brother!" He teased. "I was planning on tonight, after we finish dancing at the club."

"Why wait?" I asked with a grin. "Just fuck her right here!"

More laughter. "I reckon I need some more liquid courage before shagging in public!"

I dragged him to the bar, quickly ordering both of us several shots of tequila, and a Long Island iced tea for him. We took those shots together, then I ordered him to guzzle the strong drink. Surprisingly, he did.

"Feel more bold now?" I asked.

Daryl wiped is mouth and nodded. "A bit! Let's dance, shall we?"

We made our way onto the dance floor and joined the girls, who were dancing feverishly with each other. I took Amy's hand and began dancing sexily with her, and Daryl did the same with Tracy. Time seemed to fly by as we moved to the music.

Some time later, a waitress walked around the dance floor with a tray in her hand, offering shots that were served in glow in the dark souvenir tubes. I purchased a round for the four of us, intent on finding out how the tube would look going in and out of Amy's pussy. I quickly downed my shot, then got in close to Amy.

"Ready to 'glow?'" I asked suggestively, lowering the glowing tube to her crotch.

Amy giggled drunkenly then nodded, widening her stance as I guided the smooth tube to her opening. Meanwhile, Daryl got in close to Tracy and aimed his tube at her ample breasts, which were barely concealed by her deep-plunging dress. The he poured the booze onto her luscious tits and rapidly sucked the contents with his greedy mouth. She squealed and laughed with delight, grabbing his arse and leading him in an erotic dance.

I turned back to Amy and shoved the round end of the glowing tube up her snatch, making her yelp with surprise. I worked the tube in and out of her wet womanhood as we danced in the sultry light of the club. She unzipped my fly and began to fondle my hardening member as I fucked her with the tube. I used my other hand to hastily free my cock from the confines of my boxer briefs, and she wrapped her dainty hand around it. I moaned with pleasure as she masturbated me. As nice as this club was,

I wanted to go back to our suite and rip off her clothes as well as Tracy's, and encourage Daryl to join in on the fun. The idea of a four-way with the Little Dollies and my best mate was more than a little exciting, and it took all my willpower to avoid climaxing in Amy's hand right then and there.

I looked over at Daryl and Tracy, who were kissing passionately and dry humping each other. Tracy then unzipped Daryl's fly and fondled his member through his boxers. Daryl's hand disappeared under the hem of Tracy's dress and he felt up her ladybits. Per an earlier conversation, Tracy wasn't wearing panties. Just the thought of Daryl fingering her pussy on the dance floor made me want to cream my knickers right then and there. As for seeing Amy's pussy aglow? It only made me more horny. I couldn't wait anymore. I wanted to be naked and stoned. It was time to go up to the suite to continue the fuckfest!

I abruptly removed the glowing tube from Amy's pussy, and leaned in close to her. "Let's go up to the room, birthday girl," I growled. "I want you to eat cake frosting off the tip of my dick before I slam it into your bum. Cream cheese is your favorite, is it not?" I raised my eyebrows.

Amy giggled and blushed, panting with desire. "Um, yes," she conceded. "You want to leave the club so soon? We've only been here an hour."

I looked at my watch. "Actually, it's been two hours. Time flies when you're having fuck. I mean, fun!" I quipped.

Amy laughed and nodded. "Ok! Let's head up!"

We made the proposal to Daryl and Tracy, who agreed excitedly. The four of us exited the club and practically ran to the elevator. My head was swimming with booze and I could tell that Daryl and the girls were pickled as well. I had brought along a baggie of coke for the trip, rationalizing that it was a special occasion.

Once we walked through the door of our suite, we wasted no time ripping off each other's clothes. I grabbed a pouch of popping candy and a bottle of vodka from the TV stand, as well as the baggie of coke, smiling and winking at Amy, who, like the rest of us, was nude and horny as hell. Daryl stopped kissing Tracy momentarily to look at me.

"Mind if I do a line?" He asked, as he rubbed Tracy's bare breasts. "I've never tried coke and I always wondered how it felt. Lord knows, Jon has always loved that stuff. I'm just curious."

I hesitated. "Um, I suppose a wee line won't hurt," I said.

Daryl smiled. "Great."

Tracy piped up. "Can you snort it off my titties?" She asked drunkenly.

The four of us broke into laughter. "That can be arranged!" I said with a chuckle. "Lie on the bed, on your back."

Tracy got comfortable on the bed. I leaned over her, sprinkling a tiny amount of the drug onto her chest and using the room key to cut two little lines, one atop each breast. I turned to Daryl and handed him the straw.

Daryl took it tentatively, then leaned over Tracy's breasts and snorted both lines. He coughed and sniffled for a moment, then laughed slightly.

"I need a drink," he announced, opening the bottle of vodka and taking a swig. He passed the bottle to Tracy, who passed it to Amy, who passed it to me. This charade continued until the bottle was nearly empty, and we were more than ready to fuck each other's brains out.

Daryl got high as a kite, smoking some weed not long after doing the coke and drinking a ton of vodka. What began as a hot and heavy foreplay session with Tracy ended as a bout of nausea and extreme sleepiness for the poor bloke, who had to excuse himself to the couch in the living area. Tracy and I helped him to the couch and got him comfortable with blankets and pillows, placing a bottle of water on the end table next to his head.

"Sleep it off, dear friend," I said softly to my inebriated best mate, who simply grunted in reply before snoring a few seconds later. Tracy kissed him sweetly on the lips then looked up at me with a big smile.

"Down for a threesome?" She asked with a twinkle in her eye.

I nodded excitedly. "Let's go for it!"

Two hours later...

The three of us lay in the suite's luxurious jacuzzi, happy and completely spent after kinky, three-way sex. I had started things by snorting a line of coke off Amy's bum, after which I fucked her doggie-style while she fingered and licked Tracy's pussy, then they switched places. After that, they had gone down on each other while I fingered their arseholes. It had taken a while for me to convince Amy and Tracy to 69 each other but once they got going, they didn't want to stop and eventually climaxed together. It was beautiful to watch.

As for the cake frosting I had wanted Amy to eat off my cock? I had decided on something with a bit more of a kick. Unbeknownst to her, I had packed a jar of wasabi sauce. Her eyes had grown wide when I had slathered my balls in it. She had gagged plenty and had needed a shit ton of water but she managed to lick every last bit of the spicy concoction off my ball sack. Her reward had been an amazing round of oral sex involving several packets of popping candy, and Tracy had even helped. That's right, Amy had received both our tongues at the same time.

The grand finale had consisted of Amy and Tracy scissoring each other with a double dildo, while I took turns arse fucking each of them and whipping them with a belt. Prior to the anal intercourse, I had managed to toss both their salads, going so far as to squirt some canned whipped cream up Amy's bum and eating it out of her.

The clock said 2am, and I had lost count of how much alcohol and weed I had consumed by that point. I was more than ready to go to sleep. I gave Amy and Tracy a kiss and left the two girlies to relax in the tub while I retreated to one of the suite's bedrooms to sleep.

I saw what appeared to be a notebook on the bed and, somewhat curious, I opened it. I quickly discovered that it was a journal that belonged to Amy. A beautiful, hand drawn flower adorned the inside cover, along with some Chinese characters drawn alongside the flower. Mind you, I'm not typically the nosy type, but my curiosity got the best of me and I thumbed through some of the pages. Her handwriting was precise and neat, not unlike Amy herself. Most of the material was rather ordinary, and she talked about school and her family life, as well as things going on with friends.

I turned to the middle of the notebook and came across another drawing of the flower that graced the inside cover. This particular flower was more detailed, and almost vaginal in appearance. I turned to the next page, and that's when I saw THE entry. It was entitled, "Like a Flower." I skimmed the page, and it was clear that she was writing about the time I took her virginity. I got comfortable under the covers and decided to read the entry in its entirety.

August 31

Despite being in some physical pain, I am crying tears of joy. Why? Because yesterday, I, Amy Wong, self-proclaimed "virgin for life," lost my virginity. And I didn't lose it to just anybody. I lost it to the man I have been in love with since I was a little girl. That man's name? Kenny Smith.

I have known Kenny my entire life. He was my best friend Tracy's babysitter, and he occasionally babysat me. And he was only 12 when he started doing that, initially with his sister's help. It sounds so weird, a teenage boy in charge of watching young girls, but he was so mature, so evolved. Maybe it's because he's British? But in any case, he was, and still is, a natural caretaker.

Over the years, our relationship has changed. I have stopped seeing him as a parent figure, and see him as an object of lust. Tracy is just as much in love with him as I am, but she is more outwardly flirtatious. I have always been the quiet one. So I wasn't surprised when Tracy told me that she had asked him to take her virginity on her 18th birthday. She finds him sexy and charming. But despite her attraction to him, she doesn't want to start a serious relationship with anyone right before starting college, and because he has just lost his wife, he isn't ready for a girlfriend. So they agreed to be friends with benefits.

Ken is into some dark stuff, according to Tracy. Over the summer, they experimented with BDSM. He has choked her during sex, hit her, held her underwater, and even whipped her with a belt. Kenny gives her a "safe word" to call out when she wants to stop, and he stops. Tracy is a "submissive" and Kenny is a "dominant." He calls the shots and she has to go along with what he does. But his dominance is all an illusion because Tracy is in control all along, only having to utter a word or phrase to end things. So she's never REALLY at his mercy. When she explained it to me, I was intrigued as well as a little horrified. As thrilling as it sounds, I'm not ready to be choked, spanked, or whipped. For my first encounter, I wanted what they call "vanilla" sex. I wanted to be nurtured and held, to be treated tenderly. I didn't want to "fuck." I wanted to make love.

The weekend started out on a positive but fairly ordinary note. Following a small birthday celebration with my family, Tracy had slept over my house and we had stayed up half the night, talking. The majority of our conversation centered around her convincing me that it was a good idea for me to have sex with Kenny. After all, he was kind, smart, sexy, and very experienced. He would make sure I was comfortable. I reluctantly agreed before falling into a deep sleep at some ungodly hour.

I woke up the next morning to the sound of Tracy shaking me awake with a huge grin on her face. We were heading to the mall to meet Kenny, and he was going to take me on a "date." Since I had never been on a date before and was nervous as hell, Tracy agreed to come along for moral support. We went out to a nice restaurant for lunch then to the movies, where Kenny placed his hand on my leg. He was merely inches from my crotch. I tensed up something awful, because I was wearing a short skirt and I had never been touched like that by a guy before. In fact, up until yesterday, I hadn't even been KISSED. But I went with it, doing my best to play it cool as I felt my face get hot. It's a good thing the movie theater was dark because when I blush, my face turns very red. Pale Asian problems.

After the movies, the three of us headed back to Kenny's house. He put on some music and took out a bong, taking a hit from it before handing it to Tracy, who did the same. I had never smoked weed before but decided to take a hit. I choked something awful but got a nice buzz. Kenny then offered me a drink, and I obliged. He made me a piña colada with 90 proof rum, and it didn't take much for me to feel drunk. After all, I'm barely 5 feet tall and weigh less than a hundred pounds. Tracy and Kenny drank more than I did but seemed fine, and they loved how silly I got after just one drink. To tell the truth, I loved it too. I had never been drunk before and it felt very nice, like I could be just a little less shy.

After a few hours of hanging out at Kenny's house, Tracy convinced me I would be fine on my own and left for her place, which is luckily a mile down the road. My heart sped up but I decided that I was in good hands with him. I will never forget how he looked at me once Tracy was gone. His chocolate brown eyes were so intense and his smile was so sexy.

"Looks like it's just you and me," he said in his charming British accent. He has a voice that is soft as well as deep. His best friend Jonny has a similar voice, but huskier, with an accent that's more "Cockney" than "London." In fact, he sometimes gets mistaken for an Australian. Jonny is even more of a "bad boy" than Kenny, and I would be lying if I said I didn't fantasize about him from time to time, with his intense green eyes, tousled golden brown hair with natural blond highlights, super-white teeth, and perfect body. He is gorgeous, and very friendly, but he's also VERY intimidating. He has a pet snake that scares the hell out of me. Kenny often says that Jonny isn't afraid of anything and I believe him. Jonny is a gifted athlete and taught me how to dive when I was little, assuring me in his velvety voice that it was ok to be afraid, and that we would jump into the water together. He had been so persuasive and confident that I had given in, had taken his hand, and leaped off that diving board with him. I had felt so triumphant after conquering that fear. These days, Jonny was a multi-millionaire - traveling the world, wearing designer clothes, driving expensive cars, snorting cocaine, jumping out of airplanes, and banging hundreds of people. If only I had that level of confidence... and that lifestyle!

Kenny turned on some soft music, then took my hand and gave me an impromptu tango lesson in the living room. My head was swimming with alcohol and weed but my feet were surprisingly graceful, as I let him lead me in a sultry dance across the hardwood floor of the room. He spun me around, dipped me a few times, and even lifted me up. I felt like I was in heaven as I gazed into his eyes. He held me closer, his face merely inches from mine. Then he asked me a question that made my heart race.

"May I kiss you?" He said in a soft voice. His breath smelled like a sexy combination of tobacco and tequila, with a touch of mint.

Completely tongue tied, I simply nodded and closed my eyes. Within moments, his soft lips graced mine. His stubble felt good against my skin, not scratchy. He opened his mouth slightly, and I did likewise. Then he wrapped his arms even more tightly around my waist and I returned his embrace. I felt his tongue enter my mouth, and I opened my mouth wider, gliding my own tongue against his. My breathing quickened and I found myself more aroused than I had ever been in my life.

Still kissing me, he picked me up and carried me to the bedroom, setting me gently on the bed before lying next to me. He backed away from my lips. By that point I was panting. He sat up in bed and lit some candles on the nightstand, then put on some sensual music. A sexy smile spread across his face as he lay back down beside me, and his hands began to travel underneath my skirt until he was caressing my upper thighs and butt. I tensed up slightly, thankful that I had worn the special, silky underwear that Tracy had helped me pick out at the store a few days before. Gradually, his hand made its way to my crotch and I couldn't help but moan. Instinctively, I pressed my legs together tightly.

"Relax," he whispered, as he began to rub his finger along the satin material of my panties. I took some deep breaths and opened my legs slightly. He smiled gently and continued rubbing his hand over my covered crotch. Then he slowly pulled down the front of my panties until the top of my pubic hair was visible.

"May I touch you?" He asked with raised eyebrows. "I will be gentle."

I swallowed and nodded, feeling my face turn red. Kenny smiled and slid his fingers down to my womanhood, first running his fingers through my pubic hair then gently skimming my outer lips. I moaned with arousal. His touch felt so intrusive but so good at the same time. I opened my legs wider and closed my eyes.

After several minutes of caressing my labia, he glided his finger down to my hole. Once again, I tensed up. He slowed down his movement and began kissing me on the mouth. The tip of his finger made its way inside me and I moaned. I was very wet down there so it didn't hurt. His other hand caressed my breasts and butt, and he pulled down my panties some more. His finger went deeper inside me until it was halfway in. It hurt slightly but not terribly, and I did my best to relax.

He backed away from my lips and smiled, then took of his shirt, revealing his muscular body. Next, he pulled down my panties all the way before removing his own pants and boxer briefs. This was my first time seeing his penis up close. I had seen his penis before, when I used to ride my bike by his house at night and spy on him and his wife having sex. He had a habit of keeping the blinds open to the sliding glass door of his bedroom, so I took advantage of this. One time I even saw Jonny have a foursome with his girlfriend Lisa, and his penis was just as big as Kenny's. At one point, I was convinced Jonny had seen me looking at him, because he appeared to look up and smile directly at me, at which time I sped off. I never told anyone I had done that, and it had thrilled me to see them in bed. Kenny and Jonny were huge, at least double the average, and I knew this partly because I did an online search for average penis size (which included pictures), and because Tracy had shown me some online porn, and the most well hung guys tied with Kenny and Jonny, size-wise.

"Touch me," he whispered, taking my hand and wrapping it around his shaft as he continued to touch my vagina with his fingers. His penis felt smooth to the touch and very hard. I ran my hand up and down his member, trying to keep a firm grip. He slid two fingers into my vagina as I did this, pumping in and out. It hurt slightly since I was so tight and slightly nervous, but it still felt good. He once again leaned down to kiss me. We kissed for several minutes before he backed away to talk to me.

"I want to taste you," he said breathlessly. "May I? It will feel very good, I promise."

His brown eyes were kind and his smile was so sexy. Despite my nervousness, I nodded. Then he unbuttoned my shirt and unhooked my bra, exposing my breasts. We were now completely naked. He left a trail of kisses down my front, taking the time to kiss and suck each nipple as he did so. Before long, his face was positioned between my legs. He kissed my mound gently, then kissed the lips of my vagina. He used his hands to spread my lips then licked gently at my clitoris and inner lips, eventually sticking a finger inside me. It tickled a bit at first, so I giggled. But after a while it felt so amazing. His mouth felt so good on my ladybits, and before I knew it, I was having an orgasm. He smiled as he sucked at my juices, once again leaving a trail of kisses up my front and kissing me on the mouth so I could taste my secretions. I looked down at his penis again and noticed that he had put on a condom. My heart began to race.

He looked at me lovingly and caressed my cheeks and lips, then cupped my breasts. "I want to be inside you," he whispered. "I know this is your first time so I would be very gentle and we can go slow. Would you let me?" He rubbed my breasts and vagina gently as he waited for my answer.

I began to tremble slightly but agreed. "Ok," I mumbled shakily.

Kenny smiled broadly. "Wonderful," He said in a sexy voice.

He kissed me sweetly on the lips as he guided the head of his shaft to my virgin opening. Despite being wet down there, and despite the fact that he went slow, it still hurt when he entered me. I tensed up as my eyes filled with tears. I let go a whimper. Kenny stopped thrusting and ran his fingers through my hair. His expression was kind.

"Are you ok?" He asked. "If it hurts too much, we don't have to continue. I can just hold you."

I smiled shyly. "No, it's ok," I insisted. "I want to continue."

"You sure?" He asked, to which I nodded. "Ok. But let me know if that changes. I want this to feel good, sweetheart."

With those words, he very slowly worked the head of his penis into my vagina, and it hurt even more than before. I winced and began to cry again. I apologized to him. He withdrew slightly and kissed me reassuringly.

"We have all the time in the world," he said soothingly. "No need to be sorry, darling. Here, let me wet it some. That should help." He spat on his hand and spread the saliva around my vulva as well as the head of his penis. Once again, he entered me slowly and gently. After a few minutes of gentle thrusting and nurturing words, he managed to get half of his penis inside me. It felt like a knife. Tears rained down my face.

"I'm sorry," I said through tears. "It feels like I'm being split open."

Kenny's face was sympathetic, and he withdrew from me slightly. I had a feeling that I was bleeding down there, and when I lifted my head to look, there was some blood on his penis but he seemed unfazed. "Oh, sweetheart, it's ok. It's your first time. Take some deep breaths for me, ok? It will help you relax. Look into my eyes as you do it. Breathe with me."

I began breathing deeply, gazing into his dark brown eyes. Before I knew it, I felt myself relax. I swear it felt like he was hypnotizing me. In any case, I felt the walls of my vagina give way and he was able to penetrate me more deeply.

He smiled brightly as he looked down, his penis mostly buried inside me. "You just opened up to me like a flower," he said with tears of joy in his eyes. "It's almost all the way in." Then he kissed me tenderly on the lips.

I began to cry tears of joy and wrapped my arms around his shoulders. I spread my legs wider and eventually wrapped them around his waist, allowing him to enter me even more deeply. It still hurt but felt better than before. He got a nice rhythm going, moving his hips sexily as he whispered loving words into my ear. His thrusts quickened as the minutes rolled by and I felt myself getting wetter down there. Slapping sounds filled the air as his body crashed against mine, and we both started to moan. We held each other more tightly and the volume of our moans increased until we both had an orgasm at the same time. I saw stars as he ejaculated inside me, and I felt the walls of my vagina contract, greedily gripping his member. After it was all over, we held each other in bed, satisfied and on top of the world.

"You're a woman now," he whispered as he held my naked body. His muscles were so defined, I couldn't help but run my hands up and down his toned chest and stomach. A smile spread across my face. I was officially a woman.

I felt plenty sore afterwards, and was bleeding as if it were my period, but he assured me it was normal. He was so sweet and kind, and fed me my favorite ice cream before offering to drive me to Tracy's for a sleepover. I accepted, and even let him walk me to her door and kiss me goodnight.

"I want to do this again with you," he said with a sexy smile. I agreed.

Needless to say, I stayed up half the night telling Tracy all about my experience and what I planned to do next. I continued to bleed, so I had to wear a pad overnight but it had luckily stopped by morning. It's weird and I know it's "just" sex, but I feel so transformed, so much more mature. Like I've blossomed into a real woman. Kenny was right. I AM like a flower.

My next goal: to be Kenny's girlfriend.

I sat there with Amy's journal in my hands for a while, stunned by the detail with which she had told the story. I felt like I had experienced that night all over again. It was amazing how much things had changed in three years. She had evolved so much. As for discovering that she had watched me have sex with my wife? I found it arousing to no end! I closed her notebook and placed it at the foot of the bed where she had last put it, and masturbated myself to sleep.

Some time in the middle of the night, Amy had joined me in bed, wrapping her arm around me. I had sweet dreams about her, as well as Tracy, Anna, Daryl, and Jon.

When morning came, we treated ourselves to room service. The girl who delivered our breakfast was an exotic brunette with olive skin and an ample chest. She was just ending her shift, and I decided to be bold and asked if she would join me and the girls for some foreplay. Surprisingly, she agreed. Her name was Deedee, and she had double D breasts to go with her name. Oh, what fun we had with her! Daryl was still indisposed, sadly, but we spared him no details! He vowed to get less fucked up next time around.

We rode home in good spirits, and when we arrived at my place, each of our phones went off within seconds of each other. Jon had left each of us a very heartwarming text message, wishing Amy a happy birthday and saying "thank you for being so supportive and kind." The text he had sent me read almost like a "farewell" message of sorts, as did the text he had sent Daryl, but I kept my suspicions to myself and simply smiled, agreeing that it was thoughtful of him to send us such nice messages.

Later that night...

The four of us sat watching tv when Daryl's phone rang unexpectedly at 11pm. In my experience, nothing ever good happened from phone calls past a certain hour. Adding to the apprehension was the fact that it was Martha, Daryl and Jon's mum.

"Hello, Mum," Daryl said in a shaky voice. "Everything quite alright?"

I wasn't able to hear the dialogue on the other end but Daryl's expression said it all. His eyes filled with tears and he put his hand to his mouth. He got up and walked outside onto the deck to continue the conversation. When he returned, his eyes were bloodshot and it was obvious he had been crying.

"What's wrong, Daryl?" I asked with concern. Tracy and Amy looked up as well, worried expressions on their faces.

Daryl took a deep breath and wiped his eyes. "Jon is back in the emergency room, and he's in critical condition," he said in a quivering voice. "He attempted suicide."

Chapter 8: A Change of Season

I could hear Jon's voice long before I reached his hospital room. Martha and Daryl had warned me before I visited that he would be in rough shape - screaming, throwing things, and crying nonstop. At least twice in a 24 hour period, he had to be held down by multiple people, placed in restraints, and given an injection to calm down.

Two days prior, I had visited him in the ER along with Daryl and his parents, and he was barely conscious after trying to take his own life by swallowing multiple handfuls of sleep meds. The visit had been a heartbreaking experience for everyone, with plenty of tears. It turned out that Jon had been stockpiling the pills for several weeks, only pretending to take them at night and hiding them under his mattress pad. The near overdose had wreaked havoc on his kidneys, which were already weak, and he had needed to get his stomach pumped. He was very lucky to have survived. Once his condition stabilized, he was going to be transferred to a psychiatric facility. In the meantime, he was completely falling apart.

I was about halfway down the hallway when I heard his voice grow in volume. I walked more slowly, afraid of how Jon would react when he saw me.

"Don't fucking tell me what to do!" Jon screamed. "I'm a model and a movie star! I make more money in a year than any of you will in your entire life! I drive a brand new Tesla and I own several boats! I could buy and sell this shithole! Let go of me!"

I had reached his room, and tentatively popped my head in. Jon was surrounded by at least five staff members, one of whom was talking to him in a soothing voice and holding his hand. Jon himself appeared wild and crazy, with his hair scattered all over and bruises on his arms from being put in restraints. His eyes were red and his face was streaked with tears. His lower lip trembled as the nurse did her best to calm him down.

"I just want to go home," Jon sobbed to the nurse. "I've been in this hellhole for SIX WEEKS."

She nodded sympathetically and talked to him some more. Her voice was very soft and it was hard to make out what she was saying, but I could tell Jon was calming down a bit. I decided to take a chance and walk into the room.

"Hello," I began. The staff turned around and smiled. They all knew me by name and greeted me. "May I come in?" Jon's face lit up when he saw me.

Jon's nurse nodded and let go of his hand and motioned for the others to follow her. "Of course, we were just finishing up here," she said with a warm smile. "Have a nice visit."

Jon forced a smile, ran his hands through his hair, and wiped his eyes before we exchanged pleasantries and a warm hug. He felt like nothing but skin and bones.

I sat down next to him, doing my best not to cry. "I'm so relieved that you survived. I hope you won't do something like that again." I patted him on the shoulder. "I'm glad you're here. Not sure what I would do if you were gone."

"I'm glad YOU'RE here, mate," he said in a quivering voice. "They won't let me go home. I want to leave. Would you help me leave?"

I swallowed. I knew that if I was completely honest with him, he would get agitated and upset, so I simply nodded. "Of course."

Jon smiled. "Brilliant. And I'm glad I survived my silly 'escape' attempt as well, because I would be leaving you and so many other loved ones behind. Plus, I have SO much stuff to do. I have to open the new gym, and I have a winter preview photo shoot scheduled in a couple weeks. September is always a busy month for me." His hands shook so badly from his meds, and he appeared so gaunt. As for his speaking voice? What was normally a smooth, velvety, and confident timbre was now a quivering mumble, with a fair amount of stuttering.

My heart sank as I listened to him continue to talk about plans for the future, knowing all too well it would be a while before he recovered - physically OR mentally. At that point, I wasn't sure he would ever be the same again. His physical therapy had been going well and he was steadily regaining his strength and stamina. The scar on his leg was fading quickly and the broken bone was healing well. Unfortunately, this incident set him back, and he was confined to his bed most of the time, sometimes requiring restraints due to his combative nature.

My mind wandered as he rambled. Despite the fact that I was sitting next to him, I missed him. I blinked back tears and diverted my attention to the telly.

"What do you think?" Jon asked me.

I looked back at him with a startled expression. "I'm sorry, mate. I spaced out. What do I think about what?"

"What do you think about sneaking me out of here today? Wait until an hour before dinner, when the shift change happens for the nurses. We can make a run for the exit. Although you might need to carry me since my leg strength is shit at the moment." He chuckled at his comment. His face was full of hope and his eyes were excited with the mere possibility of escaping the confines of what he called a "bloody prison."

I took a breath. "Jon, I don't think that's wise to do today. Maybe tomorrow? You still need to heal some."

Jon's face turned red. He clenched his jaw and shook his head no. "I want to leave TODAY, mate."

My eyes filled with tears of hopelessness. "I'm sorry, I can't."

He leaned forward in his hospital bed until his face was inches away from mine, his expression nothing short of scary. He glared at me with those blazing green eyes, and a vein popped out of his forehead. "Then get out," he growled.

A tear fell from my eye. "Jon..." I began. "Please, try to understand-"

"GET OUT!!!" He screamed. His face was a mask of rage.

I jumped at his words, which echoed throughout the tiny room and got up from my seat, starting for the door. "Ok, ok. I'm going. See you tomorrow?"

Before I could react, he picked up an empty plastic cup and threw it at my head. I ducked at the last second and it hit the wall behind me. The next item he picked up was a portable urinal, which hit my back as I turned away. I began to cry as I walked out of there, feeling completely defeated. He continued to scream at me as I walked down the hallway.

"You were supposed to help me, Ken! You're useless and pathetic! Why do you think I tried to kill myself?! Because I wanted to ESCAPE! I wanted to end this PAIN! Don't fucking come back unless it's to take me home! FUCK YOU!!!"

I sobbed as I staggered down the hallway, wiping my eyes. Jon's nurse saw me and put her hand on my shoulder, assuring me that I was a good friend, and that none of this was my fault. Then she walked into Jon's room to try and calm him down again. His protesting screams were so loud I could hear him from the elevator at the opposite end of the hallway.

I rode the elevator to the main floor and got off, making a beeline for the cafeteria to meet Jon's mum. Surely enough, Martha was sitting in the front booth, sipping tea. I walked up to her, doing my best to appear calm. Her face was concerned.

"How bad was it?" She asked, as I sat next to her on the comfy seat.

I broke into tears and she immediately held me, and we cried into each other's shoulders.

Four hours later...

Just when I thought the day couldn't get any worse, it did. Anna had stopped by for dinner and "activities," but midway between our candlelit feast of steak and asparagus, she dropped a bomb on me.

"Kenny, I need to talk to you about something serious."

I cut into my steak and took a bite, immediately curious. I reached over and placed my hand on hers. "Of course, doll. What is it?"

She sighed. "I've...met someone."

My heart began to race. "Oh?"

"We have been seeing each other for a while and he wants a more serious relationship. I know that when you and I started having sex, you made it clear you didn't want anything serious and I respect that. And I love how much fun we have had together. But this guy is really interested and I want to give it a shot, and have a traditional, monogamous relationship. Which means that I need to stop sleeping with you." She took a breath and had a sip of wine before continuing. "I still want to be friends of course, but I want to give it a try with this man. He's really nice and I think you two would get along. I'm sorry to drop this on you when you have so much going on with Jon, but I couldn't keep it to myself any longer. And you always told me to be up front with you. So, that's it. That's what I wanted to tell you."

I was upset and disappointed at the news, but not terribly surprised. "Thank you for telling me, Anna. I admit, this will be an adjustment for me, and I will miss hanging out with you and our little adventures, but I definitely want to stay friends. You've grown so much since I first met you. I'm so proud of how far you have come, and I do hope things work out for you two."

Anna smiled with relief. "I'm glad you're taking it so well. I hate breaking people's hearts."

I shook my head and took a sip of wine. "Nonsense," I lied. "No heartbreak here. You're still my friend."

We made small talk through dinner, keeping conversation light. Unlike previous visits, however, we didn't end the night with sex. We simply exchanged prolonged hugs and promised to keep in touch. I was able to keep my emotions in check until she backed out of my driveway and drove down the street. Then I barreled into the house, guzzled several shots of scotch, and curled up on the couch, crying myself to sleep.

I dreamed of Amy that night. A lot. The following morning, I made an important decision. I called her right after eating breakfast.

"Hello, Kenny," she said in her sweet voice. "How are you this morning?"

"Hey, Amy, I'm great actually. I have a question for you. Would you have dinner with me tomorrow night? There's that fancy Italian place downtown that I know you love. I thought we could go there."

Amy giggled excitedly. "Uh, sure. Like a date?"

I blushed. "Yes, Amy. A date. A real one."

"I would love to," she said giddily. "Just when I thought you would never ask me out again, you did! Why the change of heart?"

I swallowed. "I decided to take a risk. Remember that conversation we had earlier in the year, where you told me that you still had feelings for me, and how I revealed that I had feelings for you as well? But ultimately decided that I didn't want to risk ruining things? Well, I thought of what advice Jon would give me if he were..." I faltered.

"If he were his usual self?" Amy filled in.

"Right, exactly," I agreed. "He would say, 'fuck it.' So that's what I'm doing. I'm saying 'fuck it' and asking you out on a date. I am ready to test the waters again with you."

Amy giggled again. "Oh, I'm so happy to hear. I was hoping you would come around."

We talked a bit longer and finalized plans for dinner. When I hung up, I felt so much better. The situation with Anna was a sign that I was meant to test the waters with Amy. I had to get over my fear of getting hurt or of being vulnerable, which I'm sure were two reasons Anna became interested in another man in the first place. Besides, Amy and I had a history, and what I believed was unfinished business. I needed to stop being so afraid and take a leap of faith.

The following evening...

I picked up Amy at her house, making chitchat with her mum and playing with Munchkin, her beloved cat. Amy was still getting ready, but emerged from the bathroom within a few minutes. She looked simply gorgeous in her light blue dress and shimmering eye shadow.

When Amy and I first started dating three years prior, her mum had reservations about her dating someone so much older, but I had managed to win her over with my charm. I spoke some mandarin, and was able to have conversations with her, which she loved. Despite living in the United States for more than twenty years, she still had a very thick Chinese accent. She was funny and outspoken, but very sweet. Her late husband, who had died in a car accident, was half Chinese and half Japanese. I had met him briefly when I had first moved to the states. He had been just like Amy in personality - quiet, modest, and soft spoken.

I complimented Amy on her looks and said goodbye to her mum, then we rode off in my Mercedes. It was a lovely September evening so I drove with the top down. I placed my hand on her thigh as I cruised through the streets, making her blush and smile. It had been so long since I had gone on a real date, and I was excited.

We arrived at the restaurant within about fifteen minutes, just in time for our 6pm reservation. I opened the car door for her like a gentleman and held her hand as we made our way inside.

The smell of the food was incredible. I promptly ordered entrees for both of us, as well as an expensive bottle of red wine for Amy and me to split, intent on getting her nice and tipsy. I was feeling horny and extra dominant, and had a new challenge for her. I poured her a glass and made a toast.

"To us," I said in a soft voice, placing my hand on her thigh.

She blushed and clinked her glass against mine, taking a hearty sip. I did likewise, savoring the flavor.

"You look amazing tonight, rag doll," I crooned, and my hand traveled farther up her leg until I was grazing her covered crotch.

She was wearing satin panties, which I loved. She moaned as she sipped her wine. I leaned in closer to her so I could whisper into her ear.

"Take off those panties and place them on the table," I whispered.

Amy blushed but did as I said, folding the blue satin garment into a neat triangle before placing them on the table next to her napkin.

I reached into my pocket and took out a generously sized rose quartz crystal that was shaped like an egg, and handed it to her. She smiled broadly.

"Is this for me?" Amy asked, to which I nodded. "It's beautiful! Thank you!" She rubbed the cool crystal egg against her skin and rolled it around in her hands.

"It's called a 'yoni' egg," I explained. "It's for tightening your vaginal muscles, and also keeps you nice and wet. Shove it inside your pussy now, so you can get used to it."

Amy turned even redder. "Um, ok. Should I do this at the table, in case it falls out when I get up and walk?"

I shook my head. "No. You go to the ladies room and put it in. I expect you to keep it from falling out using your muscles."

Fear spread across Amy's beautiful face as she slowly got up from the table and headed to the ladies room, tucking the egg in her purse as she did so. The ladies room happened to be at the opposite end of the restaurant from where we were seated, so she would have to walk a fair distance with the egg inside her. The thought turned me on.

In the few short minutes she was gone, the food arrived. I had ordered veal parmigiana and Amy had ordered vegetable lasagna. It smelled so amazing. I took another sip of wine when I noticed Amy walking towards the table, her steps tentative. She slowly sat down.

"How does it feel?" I asked, taking a bite of my pasta.

Amy blushed again. "It feels like it could fall out at any second," she said in a shy voice. "I was so scared I would 'lay an egg' in the middle of this nice restaurant."

I chuckled. "It will make you stronger down there," I assured. "Tighter. And wetter. For me. But it will benefit you as well, because you will experience more pleasure with a tighter and wetter pussy." I took a bite of veal.

Amy took a tiny bite of her lasagna. "Isn't mine tight and wet enough already?" She asked sheepishly.

"After three years of fucking at the hands of yours truly, you have loosened up some," I confessed. "And I usually have to spit on my dick before entering you. So this will be good for you." I winked as I took another bite of food.

Amy slowly nodded and averted her eyes, perhaps disappointed at my revelation. She ate more of her lasagna and drank more wine.

I knocked back the rest of my wine and unzipped my fly. Then I roughly grabbed Amy's hand and placed it on my semi-erect dick. I smiled seductively at her as she began to tremble.

"Should we do this right here?" She asked timidly. "We have never messed around in such a nice place. And the lighting is pretty bright. Someone might see."

"Oh yes we should," I assured as I encouraged her to fondle me. "Part of the thrill is the possibility of getting caught, sweetheart."

She played with my cock with one hand and ate with the other, nervously looking around the restaurant from time to time. Her hand felt so good on my manhood, it was hard to avoid moaning.

We ate in silence for a while, soon finishing our meals as well as the wine. I leaned in close to her.

"I want your cunt and bum for dessert," I growled, then I moved my hand down to her crotch and shoved my finger inside her pussy, pushing the egg more deeply inside her. She squealed, perhaps more loudly than she had intended. I abruptly removed my finger from her vagina and shoved it into her mouth so she could taste herself.

By the time the bill arrived, we were both horny as hell, so we paid and rushed off to my house.

The clothes came off the moment we stepped through the door of my home, and I wasted no time bending her over and bum-fucking her in the kitchen, the egg still embedded in her cunt.

"Take it up the arse like a good slut," I growled, as I pounded the hell out of her. That was when I grabbed the long, auburn wig from the counter and placed it on Amy's head. I had seen the wig in the sex shop where I had bought the yoni egg, and it had reminded me of Anna so I had decided to purchase it. The wig was thick enough to cover Amy's natural head of hair completely, and, when fucking her from behind, I felt like I was with Anna. As much as I cared for Amy, I still missed my lovely red haired girl.

"Why the wig?" Amy panted as she remained bent over.

I pounded harder. "Just a little role play," I explained. "Now, shut up and take every inch of me!"

Her arse felt so tight that it was hard to delay ejaculation, but I managed to hold out for an hour before climaxing all over her back. By that time, we were both sweaty and panting and made our way to the bathroom for a soak in the tub. It had been so long since I had taken a bubble bath with my little rag doll, and I couldn't wait to relax with her under the warm and steamy water.

I turned on the bath tub's faucet and turned to Amy, roughly shoving my fingers inside her pussy. She yelped and grimaced as I poked around in there, eventually plucking the egg out. I licked it clean before setting it down on the bathroom sink. Then I gently removed the wig from her head.

Once the water level was high enough, we got in the tub. As per the usual arrangement, we spooned in the water, reveling in the warmth and comfort of each other's bodies. Since the date had gone well, I decided to be even bolder. There was something else I had been wanting to ask. I cleared my throat.

"Amy, I have something to ask you," I began in a soft voice.

"Yes?"

"I know that you've never lived anywhere but your mother's house, and that we've only just started dating again. But if things continue to go well after, say, a month or so, would you be willing to move in with me? I know that we had briefly talked about it the last time we were seeing each other, but I had ended our relationship before it progressed to that point. But I feel more confident now. What do you say?"

Amy turned around to look at me with a huge smile and a glimmer in her eye. "You serious? Like, actually live together?"

I nodded. "Yes!" I rubbed her shoulder and grinned from ear to ear.

"As a couple?" Her voice got adorably high pitched and I couldn't help but chuckle.

"No, as roommates," I said sarcastically. "YES, silly girl, as a couple! Sleeping in the same bed and eating meals together, going grocery shopping, doing laundry, cleaning, all the boring stuff that couples do. I think it would be great, Amy. It's a huge leap for me, because the last girl I lived with was my wife, but I feel ready. I just want you to feel ready as well, which is why I suggested we date for another month or two before taking this big step. Maybe you could start out by just staying here on weekends, or whenever you have a day off from work or school, so it feels more gradual?"

Amy squinted. "I know my mom would be a little sad to see me move out," she said pensively. "I know she wants me to stay at home until I finish my nursing degree next year, at the very least. If it were up to her, she would want me living at home forever. But I want to be more independent. So, if things are still going smoothly with us in two months, and you're alright with me starting out slow and spending just weekends here, then yes."

I smiled broadly. "Yes?"

Amy nodded. "Yes!"

"Brilliant!" I exclaimed, then held her close to me, kissing her and feeling her breasts and womanhood. I developed an erection within seconds. She was so sexy, I needed to be inside her again.

The water splashed around us as we made passionate love to each other in the tub. I loved the way her petite body looked atop mine, with bubbles piling up around her breasts and hips. It was beautiful the way she fell onto me over and over, my cock disappearing inside her repeatedly. When she wasn't bouncing up and down on me, she was grinding against me, her tender clit rubbing along my pubic bone as her hips undulated in sensual circles. The friction of the water made her pussy feel even tighter than usual, and I climaxed inside of her within perhaps ten minutes. She even sucked me off underwater for a few moments, which was a delightful surprise.

The idea of living with Amy as a real couple excited me to no end. I was determined to make things work the second time around with my little rag doll.

After we finished in the tub, I made her reinsert the egg, telling her to keep it inside her overnight. I also made her promise me that she would keep it in continuously for a week straight, including while at school and at her part time job. Her eyes widened at my proposal.

"Shouldn't I at least take it out when I shower, so I can clean my vagina as well as the egg?"

I nodded. "Certainly. You are permitted to wash. But keep it in the rest of the time. I want to see how tight and wet you get after the week is through. And if you follow my orders, you will be rewarded." I smiled and winked.

Amy nodded timidly. I loved how eager to please she was. My cock hardened at the thought of her cunny being dripping wet during her classes, soaking her panties, and her vaginal muscles straining with the effort of keeping the egg from falling out. Perhaps she would experience an orgasm in public? Oh how fucking glorious that would be to witness: prim and proper Amy Wong climaxing in the grocery store or a classroom - panting, red faced, and ashamed, yet aroused...

Many hours later, Amy and I lay in my bed, naked in each other's arms and on top of the world. I began to kiss and fondle her when I heard my phone buzz. I looked at the screen, seeing a text from Jon.

"Hey mate. Can you come visit me tomorrow morning at the hospital? I am being discharged soon, and going to a psych facility out of state. I wanted to talk to you before I go. Please?"

I sighed and texted back. "Yes, I can do that."

Then I fell asleep, thinking about what Jon might have to say to me.

The next morning...

I walked into Jon's hospital room, finding him fully dressed and sitting upright in bed. His hair was neatly combed. He smiled gently when he saw me and motioned for me to come in and sit down next to him, which I did. Then he took my hand and looked intensely into my eyes. His hands were still very shaky due to the meds, but his gaze was as steady as ever.

"Ken, I am so sorry for the terrible things I said to you yesterday." His voice was sincere. "You're a great friend and I love you. And I want to get better, for myself and for you, and everyone else I care about. It's such a struggle right now. I feel so scared all the time. My appetite is shit. I'm not my usual self. In fact, I feel like an empty shell." His eyes filled with tears, as did mine. I rubbed his hand and let him continue. "This place I'm going to is really good. It's in Massachusetts, in the Berkshire mountains. They're well known for treating addictions as well as eating disorders. I want my life back, mate. The past month and a half has felt more like a year. Anyway, that's what I wanted to tell you. I hope you forgive me, and I hope you will visit me when I'm there."

I nodded and squeezed his hands. "I forgive you, Jon. And I will be there as often as I can. I love you. More than you know. And you're going to be ok. I know it."

Jon's lower lip trembled and he began to cry with relief at my words. "Thank you, Ken. Thank you so much."

I got up from my chair and gave him a big hug. Tears spilled down my face as we held each other in a prolonged embrace, neither of us speaking. I so adored my best mate, and wanted him to get better. It killed me to see him so fragile.

While I was hugging him, I noticed his phone light up. I was close enough to the screen to read the text. It was from Candy. She had written, "No need to apologize, Jon. I'm your friend, and I enjoy our chats. I want to come visit you when you're in Mass. Hang in there!"

I backed away from Jon and cleared my throat. "You have a text." I winked, and handed him his phone.

Jon wiped his eyes and took the phone from me, smiling broadly when he read the message.

"Candy, Candy, Candy," He said softly, typing out a quick reply. "That girl has the patience of a saint. She's been coming by to see me at least a twice a week ever since I'd awakened from my coma. We've sometimes talked for hours, and plenty of texting in between. She's seen me covered in puke, covered in blood and bruises, unshowered, unshaved, crying, shaking uncontrollably, and drugged up. Sometimes all at the same time. Yet she still visits, calls, and texts like this is all normal. Like I'M normal.

"The day before I...you know, did that silly thing, I was in horrible shape and during her visit I had lied to her that I thought I was coming down with something, and didn't want her to catch it. I had done that because I had wanted her to leave, so she would be spared the worst of my depressed mood. Of course, she had found out about my near overdose and came to see me as soon as I was coherent enough for visitors. I had snapped at her, telling her to go away. She had appeared heartbroken and close to tears. I had never yelled at her before and felt awful, hence the apology via text. And now, she wants to travel several hours to visit me in a fancy nuthouse?" He smirked.

I chucked and playfully slugged him in the arm. "She obviously cares about you, silly. And she clearly isn't bothered by your imperfections.

It's about time you allow yourself to be vulnerable, and let others take care of YOU. Candy is a nurturer. She's a good person to have in your life."

Jon nodded. "You're right, mate. Maybe one day, when I can get it up again, I can dip my biscuit in her gravy, and bury my face in her cunny. I bet she tastes like candy," he quipped.

I chuckled at his comment, telling him to give it time. I felt bad that his "equipment" still wasn't working, but felt it was a matter of time before the problem resolved itself. The stress of being in hospital, plus being on so many meds, didn't necessarily make it easy to get an erection. If Jon knew that Daryl and I had visited the "Candy" store before he did, he would probably be very jealous. I decided to keep quiet about Daryl's and my sexual experiences with Candy, sharing only when - and if - I felt it was appropriate. Sometimes the cold, hard truth was just too cold... and too hard.

I chatted with him for a while longer, telling him that Anna had ended our friends-with-benefits arrangement for a traditional relationship with another man. Then I told him about the yoni egg I'd given Amy, as well as our plans to live together in my house. He was ecstatic for me, and proud that I was taking such a big step. He had always thought that Amy was the perfect girl for me. I was starting to think the same thing.

A loud, chirping noise emanated from the telly, and we abruptly looked up at what turned out to be an emergency alert. It turned out that a big storm was headed for the northeast. A change of season and turbulent weather seemed to go hand in hand, and there would be several storms ahead - in more ways than one.

Chapter 9: Jon the Baptist

"Do you know what the punishment is for speaking out of turn?"

His deep, velvety voice echoed off the walls of his contemporary Malibu beach house, which sported pristine granite floors, stainless steel appliances, sumptuous furniture, expensive artwork, and sleek, white walls. The view of the ocean was nothing short of stunning, as was the sparkling pool on the property. The landscaping, not unlike the decor inside the house, was impeccable in its beauty. Nothing but the best would do for Master, who was as beautiful as his surroundings. His chiseled, tanned body contrasted with the stark whiteness of the living room, and his green eyes glowed with sensual passion. At six feet, four inches, he towered over his female slave, who was at least eight inches shorter than him and very thin. He could easily kill her with his bare hands, and she knew this.

"Well?" He persisted, picking up the heavy belt. "What's the punishment?"

Lisa shook like a leaf, her naked body curled up into a tight ball. "Getting whipped," she mumbled, trying her best not to cry.

A sadistic smile spread across his face and he ran his manicured hand over the belt. "Yes, that's correct. Now, get on your knees."

Lisa hesitated for a few seconds before getting on all fours. Nick and I looked on in horror, knowing better than to interfere with Jon's role play. The last time Nick had attempted to "rescue" Lisa during intense edge play, he had suffered a broken nose at the hands of the Master, who had slammed a door in Nick's face. He swallowed as he looked on, his eyes the size of saucers.

"On the count of three, you will receive no less than ten VERY hard lashes with the belt. You can expect to bleed. If you scream like you did last time, I will hold you underwater for three minutes AND make you sleep in the cage overnight, with nothing to eat or drink. If you're quiet, you get rewarded. Ready?"

"Yes," Lisa muttered in a shaky voice.

"YES, WHAT?!" Jon shouted in his powerful voice, making all three of us jump.

Lisa whimpered. "Yes, Master."

Jon got in closer to her, drawing his arm back. "Three...two...one."

BEEP! BEEP! BEEP! BEEP! BEEP!

My phone's alarm awakened me from my flashback dream, and I sat up in bed with a jolt. The time read 5AM. My plan was to head to the Berkshires to visit Jon at the treatment center, and participate in group therapy with him. I was going to drive up there with Daryl, and his parents would meet us there.

Jon had been at the center for two weeks, and his experience had been brutal so far. The staff and residents were all very kind and the program itself was great, but the therapy was very intense. Families were encouraged to get involved, and at least once a week, there were group therapy sessions that included family. Jon's father was proving to be a tough nut to crack, and had a way of bringing out his son's worst qualities. Like his father, Jon was very prideful and didn't do well in situations where he wasn't in charge, and expected to express his vulnerabilities to a group of strangers. So, these particular therapy sessions were especially daunting - for both father and son.

"There are only three things I like about this place: the view of the mountains, the fact that I can smoke, and the Olympic size swimming pool." he had told me via text the first week. "You know how I am with water, mate. I'm DRAWN to it. Remember my old nickname in school? 'Jon the Baptist?' Still applies."

"Speaking of liquids, want to see if I can smuggle in some booze?" I had joked. "Or perhaps some weed? A bong full of tequila, perhaps?"

"Not unless you want to get yourself arrested...and ME kicked out, mate. They do random drug tests here, and their security people are very... thorough. I'm talking everything but a cavity search, and even then, I wouldn't tempt fate. Much as I hate it here, I'm not ready to go home yet. 'Daddy dearest' would be knocking on my door at all hours, and until I serve thirty days in this gold-plated gulag, he doesn't trust me worth a shit. Neither does Mum, although she phrases it more nicely. So save the psychotropic goodies for when I get out of here."

I had laughed and agreed to cooperate. His sarcastic sense of humor tickled me so. Despite my nervousness about going to group therapy with him and his family, I was excited to see him and explore the area. I had been to the Berkshire mountains once as a young boy for a ski trip with my family, and recalled enjoying it.

Daryl and I rode up there together, taking his SUV. Jon had told very few people that he was spending a month at a treatment facility, deciding it would be best to keep the info private. In fact, Candy and I were the only friends of Jon's who knew of his whereabouts. Candy planned on visiting him the following week, and Jon was excited but apprehensive, convinced that his frail appearance would be off-putting to her. According to Martha, he looked emaciated, having lost at least ten pounds since I had last seen him.

Despite the fact that he had cut back on purging, Jon's eating disorder was still a huge problem, and, according to his therapist, played an enormous role in his addiction issues. His mum had told me that his eating patterns were indeed very erratic, and he still suffered from the delusion that his food was being poisoned. He now met the criteria for anorexia as well as bulimia, and was consuming just enough to avoid being fed intravenously. Initially, his treatment goal was to gain five pounds in a month, and now his goal was to avoid losing any more weight. At 150 pounds, he was considered underweight for his 6'4 frame, and his treatment team was working with him to improve his eating habits. So far, however, it was an uphill battle.

Meanwhile, things were going great with Amy and me. She was spending more and more time at my house, staying over for entire weekends more often than not. I had purchased several more of the yoni eggs for her to use, ones that were larger in size. I had even bought her a set of crystal beads to put up her bum, making her go to work and school with them embedded inside her along with the egg in her pussy. When I had asked how it felt to have both holes filled at the same time, she had blushed before giving a simple reply. "Distracting." I had laughed, picturing her going about her day full of anal beads and a crystal egg, doing her best to walk normally and use the loo without the objects falling out.

I got a semi-erection as I drove, my thoughts lost in "Amyland." Nothing was quite as effective as depraved sexual fantasies to get someone through a lengthy trip! So despite having been in the car for quite a few hours, the time flew by rather quickly.

After following the road signs, we reached the facility. With its sleek architecture, scenic beauty, and extensive landscaping, it looked more like a high end resort than a mental hospital or rehab center. I parked the car, then Daryl and I headed to the main lobby. Jon was already waiting for us.

"Hey, boys!" He called out with a smile, holding out his bony arms to give us a hug. Between his pallor from lack of sun, dramatic under-eye circles, and his drastic weight loss, he looked more like a dying man than a fashion model or actor. I felt a lump form in my throat as I forced a grin.

His hair was pulled up in a man-bun and he had grown out his beard, perhaps in an effort to camouflage the skeletal appearance of his face. However, his gaunt facial features were nothing compared to his emaciated body, and his designer clothes hung off of him. His smile, however, was ecstatic. I blinked back tears as I embraced him, afraid that if I hugged him too hard he would break in half. Despite the extreme weight loss, his arms were still strong as hell, and he nearly crushed me as we held each other.

"I'm so fucking glad you're here," he whispered into my ear. "It's been a bloody nightmare, mate."

I backed away from him and smiled. "I'm glad to be here. It's great to see you."

Jon and Daryl exchanged hugs and greetings. My mind flashed back to twenty-odd years in the past, when Daryl was recovering from cancer and was a frail young lad. After getting sick from chemo, Jon had given him a pep talk, assuring him that he would one day be strong and healthy, and big enough to kick his arse. Four year old Daryl had laughed, not believing his elder brother. Now, seeing them together, Jon's words had never been more true. There was usually no more than a twenty-five pound difference between the two blokes. Now? The difference was closer to fifty. Despite Jon's strength, I wasn't so sure he could beat Daryl in a fight at this stage in his disease.

After we signed in at the front desk, Jon gave us a brief tour of the facility, which was quite lovely. There was a spacious cafeteria, and a decent sized gym with a huge pool. Even his room was nice, with a beautiful view of the mountains. The patient lounge area was open and welcoming, sporting several televisions, couches, and recliners in addition to tables and chairs for patients to play cards or board games. I was relieved to see that Jon was in a nice place, even if it wasn't home...where he wanted to be.

Jon suggested we go outside for some fresh air and a smoke, and we agreed. The grounds were beautiful. With all the stunning flowers, enormous trees, and intricately trimmed hedges, I felt like I was in a botanical garden. We walked and chatted for a while before finding a bench and sitting down. Then Jon and I took out our packs of cigarettes and lit up.

"Smoking is the only thing that keeps me sane in this shithole," Jon muttered as smoke streamed out of his mouth and nose. He smoked very quickly, lighting a new one with the butt of the old within perhaps a minute or two. His hands shook terribly, worse than when he was in hospital.

"It's a beautiful place," I commented, to which Daryl nodded. "How bad can it be?"

Jon looked down and took several deep drags before answering. "It's just... the therapy is a lot. They make me talk about things that I'm not ready to talk about. And in front of people I don't know. I have no control over anything. And they get mad at me for not eating, but my meds kill my appetite. Plus I'm convinced they drug the food, because every time I eat, I feel ready to throw up. I'm not the only patient who has this problem, either. It's like they're trying to keep me sick. That's why I want to go home, mate. I don't think they want me to get better. They want to keep me here indefinitely. I was signed up to stay for a month, but I doubt they will let me leave."

Before I had a chance to respond, Martha and Jon Sr. walked up to us, smiling and waving. The three of us stood up and greeted Jon's parents. We made small talk for a few moments before heading into the building. Group therapy started in five minutes.

Jon, Daryl, Martha, Jon Sr., and I sat in a large circle with about a dozen other people, some of them residents and the others family or close friends. Most looked rather normal, aside from a morbidly obese fellow whose face looked vaguely familiar, a very skinny 20-something woman, and, sadly, Jon himself.

The therapist was a nondescript, dark haired man who introduced himself as Jim. He announced that the theme of the group therapy session was "eating disorder triggers." Each patient was encouraged to talk about an event from his or her past that encouraged an episode of disordered eating. I saw Jon squirm in his chair and look down. This wasn't going to be easy for him.

The skinny, 20-something girl, whose name was Rachel, went first. She had been chubby as a young girl and was picked on, so she began dieting. Once she lost weight, she felt more accepted by her peers but then began using drugs in high school to keep the weight off. Eventually, she got clean but her bad eating habits continued, and she'd been in and out of therapy for the last five years. This was her first time being in inpatient therapy, however, and she was determined to get well.

The next patient to talk was the familiar-looking obese man, whose name was Scott. He had just arrived at the center the day before. He had begun struggling with his weight after he hurt his knee playing football in college. He had been a star athlete in high school and got a full ride to an Ivy League university. Then he tore his ACL during an important game and was never the same, physically or mentally. He got depressed when he couldn't play ball anymore, and began to eat all the time. His goal was to lose a hundred pounds so he could qualify for gastric bypass surgery.

Jim encouraged Jon to go next but he shook his head, saying he wasn't ready. The other patients told their stories, some of them rather sad. One young man had become anorexic and bulimic after losing his girlfriend of many years to cancer. Another young woman was bulimic, and in an abusive relationship that she couldn't get out of. She also had an issue with self-mutilation.

Before long, Jon was the only patient left. Martha patted her son's leg and encouraged him to share a story. He smirked and crossed his arms defiantly.

"No point," he mumbled. "It was a long time ago. Why bring things up that happened when I was so young? I want to move forward, not live in the past. This is silly."

Jim smiled patiently at Jon. "Sometimes the only way to heal from the past is to talk about it, and see what we have learned from it. Come on, Jon. You're in a safe environment."

Jon sighed before continuing. "I, uh, began making myself throw up at age ten. After I saw my neighbor attacked." Martha grabbed his hand and rubbed it, her eyes filling with tears.

Jim nodded. "Go on."

"I was over my next door neighbor's house hanging out. Then her drug addicted ex boyfriend came by unexpectedly, and he had three of his junkie friends with him. She was polite and tried to get him and his buddies to leave but they insisted on having some drinks. I was getting nervous because the drunker the men got, the crazier they acted. I saw one of them put something in my neighbor's drink when she was out of the room, and he went up to me, telling me not to say anything or he would make me sorry. Then my neighbor came back and finished the drink and within minutes, she fell asleep on the couch. Then..."

Jon began to shake before continuing. Martha put her arm around him. He took a deep breath.

"Her ex jumped on top of her and began undressing her, also pulling down his own pants. I tried to get up to help her but his three buddies restrained me. Two of them held me down while the other pulled down my pants and began touching my penis. I tried to get away but they were too strong. The guy who was fondling me put his hand over my mouth and told me to keep quiet, or I would be killed. The other guy pulled out a gun and held it to my head, telling me to watch the sex show. So I sat there on this man's lap with tears falling from my eyes, a gun to my head, a hand over my mouth and another on my penis, watching my neighbor get raped while drugged. After about ten minutes, it was all over. The men let me go but made me promise not to tell anyone ever. And if I did, they would kill me. So I ran out of the house, leaving my poor neighbor half naked, unconscious, and completely violated.

"Once I was back home, I ran to the bathroom, because I felt sick to my stomach. But I couldn't vomit. So I stuck my finger down my throat and made myself throw up. I did it over and over until there was nothing left in me. I felt so renewed afterwards, so....reborn. Like I'd been baptized. Then I drew myself a bath and cried my eyes out in the tub. I didn't speak for many hours after the incident, I was so traumatized. To this day, I have a fear of food being poisoned. I also still have flashbacks and I fall completely silent when they happen. It's like I lose my ability to speak. Ever since that incident, I have made myself sick when life overwhelms me. I've cut back on purging but haven't stopped completely. Anyway, I've never told anyone that story in its entirety. And I never want to again."

The room was so quiet, one could hear a pin drop. I was in utter shock at Jon's story, as was everyone else. I hadn't known the details of the neighbor's attack, and now I understood why he had always been vague when I had asked.

Daryl, Martha, and Jon Sr. all had tears in their eyes, as did most of the people in that circle.

Jim smiled kindly at Jon. "Thank you so much for sharing that story, Jon. You're a brave soul. And you've been through so much. That's a huge secret to keep, for so many years. It must feel good to get it off your shoulders."

Jon's lip trembled. "I feel so exhausted," he said shakily. "It's so draining to think about. Luckily those bastards all wound up in jail not long after that, for selling drugs."

Martha chimed in. "Why didn't you say anything?" She asked through tears. "I'm so sorry that happened to you. I just wish you had said something. But I understand why you kept it to yourself. Because you were scared. I'm glad you finally shared this. I love you, son." She gave Jon a big hug.

"I was molested, too," Scott said.

Jon broke his embrace with his mum and looked over at him, eyebrows raised. "Really?"

Scott nodded. "By my own father. He wound up leaving my mom for another man. For a long time growing up, I hated gay men. But really, I was just mad at my father...for what he did to me and also for leaving my mom. And uh, I don't know if you recognize me, but we went to high school together. One day in freshman year I shoved you against a locker and called you a 'fag.' And you beat the crap out of me," he said with a chuckle. "I deserved it. I admit it. And I'm sorry I did that to you."

Jon's eyes were the size of saucers, as were mine. No wonder he had looked so familiar!

"Scott Foley!" He gasped, completely dumbfounded. "I can't believe it. It's been fifteen years. Where does the time go?"

Scott got up from his chair and waddled over to Jon, extending his hand. "Do you forgive me, Jon?"

My best mate slowly stood up from his seat and took his former enemy's hand. "I forgive you, Scott. You're a good person."

Then the two men hugged each other, and everyone applauded. It was quite touching to witness - two former enemies on opposite ends of the weight range, but with similar issues in their past, finally reaching a truce after so many years.

48 hours later...

I held a tearful, exhausted, and naked Amy in my arms, whispering assuring words into her ear. Her back was covered in scratches and whip marks after intense play, and she had some bruises on her bum.

Daryl and I had gone hiking and sightseeing prior to heading back home, and it had felt great to be out in nature. The therapy session had been intense, but I had a better understanding of why Jon behaved the way he did. I believed that his love of BDSM was at least partly due to the trauma he'd experienced as a boy. Sometimes the only way to feel like less of a victim was to dominate and control.

I had beaten the shit out of Amy with a leather paddle and a bull whip, while forcing her to wear a slave collar and walk on all fours through my house. Then I made her sit in a cage for hours, taunting her with a bottle of water, only to snatch it away. My intention was to groom her, to train her for the most hardcore BDSM event of her life AND mine, one that was a full week long: Total Power Exchange.

Total Power Exchange, or TPE, involved the submissive being a virtual slave 24/7. Breaks could be permitted as a reward, and punishment could include everything from a slap in the face to denying water, food, and bathroom privileges. The slave would be treated as an animal, forced to sleep in a cage, on the floor, or at the foot of the dominant's bed. Cooking and serving meals for the dominant, as well as general pampering, might be expected of the submissive as well. Eye contact may not be permitted, as was speaking without being spoken to. I had witnessed TPE firsthand while visiting Jon and Lisa in California for Labor Day weekend three years prior, and the experience had horrified and thrilled me. I had never gotten the chance to test it out on my wife, so I decided to do it with Amy.

"You're such a strong person," I whispered in Amy's ear as I held her shaking body. "I'm very proud of you, and I'm going to take good care of you tonight."

For the rest of the evening, I pampered my lovely little rag doll, doing everything from cleaning and dressing her wounds, to brushing her hair, to feeding her by hand, to painting her toenails. I thought of Jon as my inspiration, thinking of how he would spoil Lisa after a brutal session of torture. In a single night he would take a bath with her, cook her a gourmet meal, do her hair and makeup, and give her a full service manicure and pedicure at home. If she was up to it, he would even take her shopping for clothes or jewelry, or anything else she wanted. If she preferred to relax after he fed and beautified her, he would cuddle with her on the couch for hours, serving her wine, massaging her shoulders, and hand-feeding her chocolate while watching movies of her choice. In the morning, he would serve her breakfast in bed, and go down on her afterwards for a solid hour, before making love to her gently for at least another hour. Nothing was too good for his darling Lisa, who he had nicknamed his "Little Lioness."

As aggressive as I could be, I wasn't sure I had it in me to do some of the things that Jon had done. He had pierced Lisa's clitoris while restraining her on the bed with her legs spread wide, given her electric shocks, administered an enema to her then forced her to hold the contents in her bowels for a painfully long time, forced her to chain smoke two packs of cigarettes while fucking, whaled her on the arse with a cast iron skillet, bitten her nipple hard enough for her to require stitches, and held her underwater for so long that she had come very close to drowning at least twice.

Once Amy and I were in bed that evening, my mind wandered back to the night that Jon had threatened to severely punish Lisa if she screamed during a whipping session. He had been such an unstoppable force that evening, and so incredibly savage. My eyes got heavy as I held my rag doll, and I fell into a deep sleep.

Some time in the middle of the night...

The dream picked up where it left off, with Jon towering over Lisa's frail body, belt in hand. He slowly counted down from five in his sultry voice. Nick and I sat frozen on the couch, drunk and paralyzed with fear as we watched our madman friend draw his muscular arm back, preparing to beat the shit out of his fiancée.

CRACK!

We jumped at the sound of the leather slapping against Lisa's tender flesh, a muffled whimper emanating from her mouth as a red welt appeared on her back.

"Don't scream," Jon warned, bringing his arm back one more time.

CRACK!

Lisa whimpered louder as another red welt appeared on her back. She began to tremble.

Jon lit a cigarette before continuing. "That's a good little cunt," he growled as smoke poured out of his mouth. "Only eight more lashes to go."

Lisa began to cry but did her best to be quiet. She knew what Jon was capable of and didn't want to provoke him.

CRACK!

Whip number three was particularly hard, and Lisa cried out. Blood seeped from the welt. Her trembling intensified.

A sick smile spread across Jon's face. The sight of blood excited him to no end, and his erection grew in size. He put his finger to his lips. "Shhh," he warned. Then he took a long drag off his cigarette before drawing his arm back again.

CRACK!

More crying and shaking, as well as more blood. Nick began to squirm in his seat, and I could tell he was tempted to intervene. His nostrils flared and his jaw was clenched. It was obvious that he was pissed, and was protective of Lisa. Normally an easy going bloke, Nick was scary when he did lose his temper. He cleared his throat.

"Hey, Jon?" he said in as calm a voice as he could.

Jon spun around, looking ready to kill Nick. He took a drag from his cigarette and marched several feet closer to where we were sitting on the couch. A vein popped out of his forehead and his hand formed a fist. He bent down and blew a thick stream of smoke in Nick's face. "WHAT?!" He barked.

Nick stood his ground, refusing to be intimidated by him. "Lisa has had enough. She deserves a break."

The corners of Jon's mouth turned upwards until he was smiling broadly. Then he began to chuckle. His laugh grew in volume for a few moments before stopping abruptly. "You're right."

Nick appeared relaxed after hearing Jon say that. But I knew my best mate. He was going to make Nick pay for interfering with the scene.

Before Nick could react, Jon turned the belt around so the buckle side was facing outward. Then he quickly drew his arm back and whaled Nick in the chest with the buckle. Nick gasped in pain and shock as blood dribbled from the wound. I grabbed a tissue and held it to his chest to stop the bleeding. Then I glared at Jon, whose face was as smug as could be.

"Got something to say, bitch?" Jon asked me with raised eyebrows.

I shook my head, continuing to glare at him as I held the tissue to Nick's wound. "No."

Jon smirked. "Good. Now you boys shut the fuck up and let me finish what I started."

He turned back around and directed his attention to Lisa, who was shaking and crying with streams of blood going down her back. He was going to hit her with the buckle. I knew firsthand how much that hurt, as did Nick. My heart raced.

"Get ready, darling," Jon said with a sadistic grin as he drew his arm back once more. "This is going to hurt. I DARE you not to scream."

CRACK! CRACK! CRACK! CRACK! CRACK! CRACK!

Poor Lisa received no less than six hard lashes to her back with the buckle end of the belt, with no chance to recover in between the blows. She had managed to avoid screaming during the whipping session, but had cried out plenty, not that I blamed her. She began to hyperventilate and looked ready to throw up. Her back was covered in blood, which began to drip on the granite floor.

"Please," she gasped. "No more. Can we stop? I need to stop, Jon."

Jon simply stood there, stone-faced. He took a final drag off his cigarette before putting it out.

"Bonus round!" He called out gleefully, before drawing his arm back once more. This was getting to be too much.

Nick was suddenly furious, breathing heavily and undoubtedly psyching himself up to stop Jon from hurting Lisa.

CRACK!!!

Jon landed a horrible blow onto Lisa, who let go a loud scream before collapsing into a heap on the floor and throwing up. That's when it happened.

"Jon, PLEASE STOP!!!"

Nick sprang up from the couch and tackled Jon from behind, knocking him to the floor and putting him in a headlock.

Mind you, Jon and Nick had been on the wrestling team in high school, and Nick had been the only one to have successfully beaten Jon in a match. Back then, Jon had been unable to escape the headlock that Nick had put him in, and he was once again struggling. Years later, Nick admitted to Jon that he had been using anabolic steroids his first year of high school to enhance his performance. However, this time around, Nick's strength was fueled by pure adrenaline and anger.

I rose from the couch and walked over to the men. Jon was flailing around, kicking his legs, and pulling at Nick's arms in a futile attempt at escape. But Nick wouldn't let up. Jon's face was turning a deeper shade of red with every passing second and it was clear he was in distress.

"Nick, back off," I advised as I got closer to them. "You're going to crush his windpipe! Let him go!"

Jon began making choking sounds and if Nick didn't let up soon, he would pass out.

Nick loosened his grip on Jon, who squirmed away from him as quickly as possible, gasping for air and choking as he held onto his neck. I grabbed a bottle of water from the kitchen and gave it to Jon, who began gulping down the water. Nick began to shake and cry, feeling guilty about what he had just done. He inched his way over to Jon.

"Jon, are you ok?" Nick asked tentatively, reaching out to him.

Jon recoiled from Nick. "Don't touch me." Then he directed his attention to Lisa, who was in a state of shock and lying next to a puddle of her own vomit. She cried quietly.

He put his arm around her. "Lisa, talk to me," he said in a soothing voice. "Let me know you're alright."

She slowly lifted her head and began to sob, shake, and hyperventilate. "Please don't make me lick the vomit off the floor again," she gasped through tears. She was really shaken up.

Jon gently ran his hand through her hair and caressed her back. "No, darling," he assured in a kind voice. "I won't do any such thing. You have been through enough and I'm going to take care of you, ok? You're safe with me. I love you very much. You're SO strong. Why do you think I want you to be my queen, and the mother of my children, hmm? Because you're fierce. And you're beautiful. Now drink some water." He held his water bottle to her lips, and she eagerly drank.

Jon then kissed her gently, and encouraged her to let him hold her. After a few moments of hesitation, she did, and began crying into his shoulder. He rocked her back and forth and spoke loving words to her. Nick and I got closer to Jon and Lisa, to provide emotional support for the poor girl. She had endured so much over the past few days - waiting on Jon hand and foot, sleeping in a cage, and tolerating a ton of abuse, both physical and verbal.

"It's ok, love," he whispered. "Just let it out. We all care about you."

I placed my hand on Lisa's shoulder, as did Nick. "That's right, Lisa," I agreed.

"I love you, baby," Jon said, continuing to speak in a gentle voice as he held her. "I'm going to dress your wounds, and give you a bath. Then I'm going to rub lotion all over your body, massage your shoulders, do your hair and makeup, and paint your pretty little fingers and toes. Then I will cook dinner for you, snuggle with you on the couch, and let you watch whatever you want. Then after, if you're up for it, the three of us will make gentle love to you." He turned to Nick and me. "How does a four-way with Lisa sound, boys?"

I nodded and smiled. "Great."

Nick slowly nodded. "Sorry for getting carried away before," he said to Jon. "I didn't mean to choke you so hard. I just got nervous."

Jon smiled and winked. "It's no problem. I know you were just looking out for my little lioness. I got carried away myself, mate. You sure have one hell of a strong set of arms!"

The two men chuckled. Then Jon gently picked up Lisa and carried her to the bathroom to start filling the tub with water, and to dress her wounds. Nick and I got to work cleaning the living room floor, then joined them in the oversized tub.

Jon lit himself a blunt and shared it with the rest of us. Once he was good and stoned, he took some deep breaths and disappeared beneath the surface to go down on Lisa.

While Jon was submerged, Nick and I simply leaned back in the tub and wanked off, watching the show. The minutes rolled by as Jon devoured Lisa's cunny underwater. It was incredible how long Jon was able to hold his breath. Nick and I could manage ten minutes on a good day, but Jon could push twelve.

Lisa panted and moaned as she approached orgasm. Jon continued to eat her pussy from beneath the surface, refusing to come up for air until she came. After eleven minutes, she climaxed. Jon resurfaced, slowly letting go of the breath that he had been holding. He wasn't even out of breath. He kissed Lisa on the lips.

"How was the Cookie Monster's performance this evening?" He cooed with a smirk on his face. He had received the nickname "Cookie Monster" in high school, due to his affinity for cunnilingus.

Lisa giggled. "Ten out of ten!" She said with a huge grin. "Isn't it painful holding your breath for so long?" She asked. "The longest I can manage is five minutes."

Jon shook his head. "Nope. Despite being a chain smoker, I have good lungs. So do Nick and Ken." He turned to us. "What do you say, boys? Care to enter a little contest, to see who can hold their breath the longest?"

I nodded, as did Nick. Lisa agreed to keep track of time.

The three of us blokes took some deep breaths then dipped our heads beneath the surface.

My thoughts ran all over the place as I remained submerged. I thought of Jon's and Lisa's engagement, which had occurred in late April, not long before I'd lost my wife. He had proposed to her after making her his slave for five days straight. He'd told me he had felt like a monster after keeping her in a cage and doing terrible things to her for days on end, and the grace with which she had handled herself was enough for him to want to marry her. The day of the proposal had been an especially romantic event -he had driven her to a nearby park for a picnic, treated her to a day at the spa, taken her out to the movies and dinner at her favorite restaurant, then had convinced her to take a nice walk on the beach to watch the sunset. Just before the sun was dipping below the horizon, he'd found an especially scenic spot. Then he had gotten down on one knee, opened a box with a stunning, 3 carat diamond, and had asked her to be his "queen." She had gleefully accepted. Then they ran hand-in-hand into the water, laughing and splashing around while fully clothed. Afterward, he had taken her on a mini vacation to Las Vegas to celebrate, and they had planned to elope by jumping out of an airplane. On day two of their trip, I had called Jon in tears, to tell him the news about my wife. When I had called, he had been in the middle of sex with Lisa, who, unbeknownst to me, had become very ill with food poisoning during the trip, thus delaying their nuptials. With Lisa's encouragement, Jon had ended their trip a day early, so he could fly out to take care of me. My best mate was, by turns, the cruelest AND kindest person I had ever met.

Nick was the first to resurface, gasping for breath after forcing himself to stay underwater for ten minutes and two seconds. Like Jon and me, he was an experienced free diver and could go a long time without air. I followed shortly after, making it to ten minutes and fifteen seconds. Jon made it to eleven minutes and sixteen seconds, a cocky smirk on his face as he resurfaced.

After the bath, Nick and I assisted Jon with Lisa's beauty rituals. She deserved the royal treatment, so the three of us went out of our way to make sure she felt pampered and nurtured. Once her body was massaged with her favorite lotion, and her hair, makeup, and nails done, we got to work in the kitchen. We cooked up a sumptuous feast of seafood and assorted vegetables, a decadent homemade dessert, and plenty of wine. By the time dinner was ready, the four of us were pleasantly buzzed and decided to eat in the living room... naked.

Jon, Nick, and I took turns hand-feeding Lisa pieces of delicious fish and veggies, taking the time to kiss and fondle her as we did so. She looked like a doll come to life with her perfect hair and makeup, so it wasn't long before we were all horny. The four of us wound up making passionate love to her on the couch, giving her multiple orgasms as she experienced pleasure in all her holes at once. Jon had first dibs on her pussy, intent on making a baby with her. He supplied condoms to Nick and me, so he could be more certain that, if Lisa did wind up expecting, it would be his child.

The chemistry between Nick and Lisa was palpable. The way they gazed at each other with stars in their eyes, the way Nick touched her so tenderly, and the way Lisa smiled at him all suggested that there was something between them, something unspoken. I could see it, and so could Jon. I noticed how my best mate's jaw clenched when Nick entered Lisa's womanhood. He gently penetrated her, kissing her on the lips and cupping her breasts as he did so. His thrusts were loving and graceful, like poetry manifested in the physical.

SMACK!

Jon slapped Nick's arse very hard, breaking his revelry.

"I've been wanting your luscious bum all fucking night," Jon growled into Nick's ear, before getting behind him and lining up his huge cock with our friend's water-tight arsehole. "Get ready for Big Ben!"

water births, and they were fascinated by the concept. My eyes grew heavy as I pictured my incredibly patient best mate climbing into the birthing tub with Lisa - holding her hand, spooning with her, speaking words of encouragement in his sultry voice, and keeping her calm as she gives birth to a perfect baby...

I woke up sometime around 3am with a dry mouth. So I got up and went to the kitchen for a glass of water. Nick joined me a few moments later. We wound up sitting on the barstools overlooking the kitchen, and had a heartfelt discussion. He opened up to me about how much he cared for Lisa, and how badly he wanted to be with her. But he avoided sharing his feelings with her because he didn't want to ruin their friendship, or the relationship she had with Jon. Plus, he and Jon were close friends. I was able to empathize, knowing all too well how heartbreaking it was to long for someone I couldn't be with.

"I know just how you feel," I said to Nick. "I miss my best girl every day. I don't really talk about it too much these days because I'm trying to get over it. And don't worry, I won't say anything to anyone about what you told me."

Nick smiled. "Thanks, buddy."

Then we exchanged a prolonged hug. Out of the corner of my eye, I thought I saw a shadow appear on the wall near Jon's bedroom door, then quickly disappear. Had Jon been listening to our conversation? I shrugged off my suspicions and decided it didn't matter. Only time would tell who Lisa wound up with.

Early morning...

Amy was acting as my alarm clock, and I awakened to her mouth on my penis. Oh how great it was to be back in the present day!

I bucked my hips as my little rag doll sucked me off, then I noticed the light from her phone turn on. She hadn't even noticed, since her head was down and her eyes were closed. Eugene had texted her.

"Looking forward to this afternoon," the message read with a smiley face.

My member went slightly limp and I swallowed hard, electing to keep quiet and to avoid reading into the meaning of the text. I knew that Amy and Eugene took classes together, and that Eugene was an LPN studying to be an RN. I felt quite jealous, almost enraged, at Eugene. I suddenly understood why Jon behaved the way he did towards Nick. At one point, I had considered my best mate's actions to be completely overblown and good old-fashioned bullying, but now I understood. I channeled my anger into my sexual encounter and began fucking Amy's face. My cock exploded within minutes.

Chapter 10: Total Power Exchange

It was a brisk day in mid-October. I arrived home from the pet store shortly after 10am. I had purchased a shock collar, food dishes, water bowls, a leash, and a cage designed for a medium to large dog. However, I hadn't bought these items for a dog. I intended to use them on a person. Specifically, my girlfriend.

Amy's "training" had been going well. If things continued to go well, I was planning on making her my slave the last week in October. She had even requested time off of work

and school for this event, saying she was going on vacation. Not exactly a lie - her cage would serve as her hotel, and she would get room service... even if it happened to be from a "master," who would feed her meals in a dog food dish and no utensils. Wake-up calls would consist of yours truly banging on her cage in the wee hours of the morning, for activities ranging from random sex acts to house work. If she followed instructions and did what was asked of her, she would get rewarded. I would allow her to make eye contact, wear clothes, and eat a meal with me at the dinner table. If she was extra good, I would let her sleep in my bed instead of the cage.

The first time I had briefed her on what she could expect during "slave week," she had cringed and got tears in her eyes.

"I don't know if I can handle all that," she had said in a quivering voice.

I had put my arm around her and kissed her cheek. "Sweetheart," I began in a gentle voice. "Relax. It's ok. It will be just like our usual edge play. You will get a safe word, and whenever things become too much, you just say the word. And all will return to normal. I promise." I smiled sweetly, and gave her a hug.

She had meekly agreed to give it a shot, after reading over the list I had written. This list included all the things that Amy could expect to do - and have done TO her - over the course of the week.

SLAVE WEEK

Overview: The submissive is to spend seven days as a human slave, having no autonomy or decision making ability. She will not be allowed to wear clothes. She is to spend her nights in a cage, and will be fed meals and water in dog bowls. Utensils will not be allowed. She must ask to use the bathroom, and bathroom privileges may be denied by the dominant. When outside the cage, she is to walk on all fours, and is required to wear a collar. The dominant may take the submissive for "walks," using a leash. The submissive is expected to wait on the dominant hand and foot - cooking, cleaning, and personal grooming are all things that can be expected, and at random hours. Sexual favors are expected, and the submissive cannot refuse these favors. The submissive is not allowed to make eye contact, or to speak unless spoken to. A safe word will be provided to the submissive, in case the situation becomes too intense.

Discipline: Corrective behavior may take place if the submissive behaves inappropriately or commits an infraction. Some examples include speaking out of turn, making eye contact, not cleaning properly, not cooking a meal to the dominant's satisfaction, refusing sexual favors, and so on. Punishments might include slapping, scratching, paddling, hair pulling, whipping, choking, cutting, fire play, punching, kicking, being held underwater, refusal of food and/or water, refusal of bathroom privileges, or being locked in a confined space.

Rewards: The submissive may be rewarded for exemplary behavior. Rewards may include "free time," during which the submissive is allowed to wear clothes, walk upright, eat meals at the dining table, watch tv, go for rides, and engage in conversation with the dominant. The submissive may work her way up to earning a "free overnight," at which time she is permitted to sleep in a bed with the dominant, and be treated to a full breakfast in the morning.

Jon had helped me write the document during a phone conversation, and had used his experience with Lisa as a guide. He had been back home for about five days, but I hadn't seen him yet. His mum had filled me in on his condition, and it wasn't ideal.

After Candy had visited him in the facility, he was determined to return home as soon as possible. His goal was to go on a coffee date with her. So he became a model patient, attending and participating in all the group therapy sessions, and gaining five pounds in a week. His doctor was so pleased with the progress that he decided to discharge him several days early. Unfortunately, his drug use resumed the day he got home, and, after having dinner at his favorite restaurant with his parents, Daryl, and myself, he wasted no time rushing to the in-law apartment at his parents', where he "rewarded" himself with pills and cocaine. He had spent the rest of the night blasting music until 3am and taking videos of himself dancing wildly in his living room. He had posted one of these videos on social media, and while his dance moves were impressive, it was obvious to me that he had been high as a kite. According to Martha, his reason for continuing to use drugs was that he had gone to the facility strictly for depression and an eating disorder, and "not a bloody addiction problem." Denial was alive and well, and it would take an especially harrowing experience for Jon to learn that, in order to be truly healthy, he would have to give up the hard drugs.

I got to work setting up the cage in the living room, then once I was done, texted Amy.

"I got you some presents. See you tonight."

She replied with a smile emoji and a thank you. I admired my handiwork, running my hand over the cool metal of the cage. My cock got hard as I pictured my rag doll confined to the tiny space, naked, with a collar around her neck, trying her best to remain calm.

I became ridiculously horny, so I wanked off and took a cold shower before leaving for work at the gym.

Three hours later...

Daryl and I were about midway through our shift at the gym, and I was in the office doing some work on the computer. Martha's number showed up on the office phone's Caller ID. I picked up after a single ring. I so adored Jon and Daryl's mum, who had started taking CrossFit classes several months prior. She was a yoga teacher by trade, but enjoyed trying different things to stay fit.

"Hello, Martha," I crowed. "How are you this lovely afternoon?"

She sniffled and I could hear banging and crashing in the background. "I'm actually rather horrible," she whimpered. "Can you pop by the house? Jon is out of control and you're the only one he will listen to. I snuck into the loo to call you."

"Oh, dear me," I said, my heart speeding up. "So sorry. I can absolutely come by. I will tell Daryl it's an emergency. He will understand. What is he doing?"

"He's in a drug induced rage," she said through sobs. "It's the cocaine, I'm sure. He's throwing things, breaking things, screaming, and crying. He even punched a hole in the wall. He accused me of stealing his antidepressant pills and he doesn't believe me when I tell him I didn't touch them. His father is at work and doesn't know about this. I'm ready to call the police." Her voice broke.

"I will be right over," I assured, them hung up.

I walked over to Daryl, who was working with a client. I whispered into his ear that I was headed over to his parents' house to help with the incident.

"Your mum is having issues with Jon, and I need to diffuse the situation," I explained. Daryl nodded solemnly and swallowed.

I drove the five or so minutes to their house with my jaw clenched, imagining how frightened Martha must have been, trying to calm her son, who was a foot taller than her and unbelievably strong.

When I pulled into the driveway, I could hear the bangs and crashes emanating from the in-law apartment, as well as Jon's shouting and screaming. I got out of the car and rushed to the door, opening it. I walked past the kitchen and popped my head into the entryway of living room. What I saw made my stomach turn.

Jon was shirtless and dripping sweat, standing amidst rubble that consisted of a broken chair, a cracked vase, empty bottles of alcohol, and an overturned coffee table. Books and various trinkets covered the floor as well. Blood dribbled slightly from his nose. His chin-length hair was wild and crazy as he screamed at a horrified Martha, who stood against the wall of the living room with tears going down her face. She was doing her best to soothe him in her sweet voice, but he wasn't having it.

"Shut the fuck up, mum!" Jon screamed, then picked an overflowing ashtray off the floor and threw it at the wall, where it broke to pieces and created a cloud of ashes and cigarette butts. Martha screamed in shock and surprise. I decided to step into the room and talk to Jon.

"Hey, mate," I began tentatively.

He turned his head to look at me, a murderous expression on his flushed, blood smeared face. "Now is not a good time," he growled, wiping his nose. "My prescription pills are missing. SHE stole them from me!" He pointed to Martha, who began crying harder.

I got in closer to Jon. "Mum didn't steal your pills," I assured. "They're probably just missing. I can help you look-"

"'Missing,' my arse!" Jon shouted, as he began to strip out of his jeans and underwear. "I'm burning up! I can't wear clothes right now! It feels like my body is on fire!" He began to hyperventilate as he tore off his clothes.

Within seconds, he was completely naked and began to lunge at his terrified mum, who began to tremble and shrink away from him. I positioned myself behind him, waiting for him to make a move so I could restrain him.

"I need my fucking pills! GIVE ME MY PILLS, BITCH!!!" He shrieked, charging at Martha. That was when I decided to intervene.

I got behind Jon and put him in a wrestling hold that he had taught me in high school, and pulled him away from his mum. He almost broke free, so I held him more tightly .

"Let me go!" He gasped as he struggled against me.

"Promise me you won't hurt your mum and I will let you go," I said through clenched teeth, my muscles shaking as I did my best to keep him restrained. "Look at her, mate. She's so scared. She's your mother and loves you very much. She would never steal your pills, or do anything to hurt you."

Martha looked on at the terrible scene - her firstborn adult son, sweating, naked from head to toe, in a psychotic rage fueled by cocaine, and being restrained by his best mate. Her lower lip quivered as more tears went down her face.

Jon sniffled and began to sob. "I won't hurt anyone, I.... I just want my pills..." he gasped through tears.

I slowly loosened my grip on him. Then he turned around, placed his arms around my waist, and began to cry into my shoulder. I began to cry myself as I returned his embrace. Martha wiped the tears from her eyes and slowly approached us, grabbing a bathrobe from the floor and draping it gently over Jon's shoulders. He looked up to talk to his mother.

"Mum, I'm so sorry," he sobbed. "I didn't mean it. I just feel sick because I missed a few doses of my meds and took too much coke. I love you. Please forgive me."

Her lip trembled and the tears began to fall from her eyes again as she fastened the robe around Jon's front. "Oh, Jonathan. You're my son," she said through tears. "I will love you no matter what. You will always be my baby, and I forgive you. It's going to be ok." She placed her hand on his back, rubbing it gently.

He broke our embrace to put his arms through the sleeves of his robe, then wrapped his arms around his beloved mum, who eagerly returned the hug. They remained locked in a warm embrace for several minutes, crying into each other's shoulders.

I placed my hand on Jon's back. "Shall I draw you a bath?" I offered with a smile.

Jon looked at me with a tear streaked face and smiled gently. "Yes, that sounds great. With bubbles."

I smiled and nodded. "Of course."

I left the living room and went to the loo to start filling the tub with water. The bubble bath was situated at the edge of the tub so I poured a generous amount of it in the hot water. I realized I had a bit of a headache, so I looked in the medicine cabinet to see if there was a bottle of aspirin. That's when I saw Jon's pills. They were a brand of antidepressants that were helpful for anxiety as well as chronic pain, but even one missed dose could cause withdrawals in some individuals.

I took the bottle out of the cabinet and walked back to the living room to show him. Jon and Martha were sitting on the couch and talking quietly, smiles on their tear streaked faces.

"Guess what I found in the medicine cabinet?" I said, holding out the bottle.

Jon's eyes grew wide as he looked at the bottle, then me. "No shit? I must have forgotten that I had put them there. I usually just leave them on the nightstand next to my bed. Coke makes me forgetful, as well as reckless. I shouldn't use coke anymore, not since it made me crazy enough to destroy my home for absolutely no reason at all, make false accusations, and attack my own mother. I'm so sorry, guys. I thought I could handle an occasional line as a 'treat' but clearly that's not the case." He began to cry again.

I sat on the other side of Jon and put my arm around him, reassuring him that it was ok and we both loved him. "We will help you get clean, Jon," I said with a gentle smile. "Do you want to take your pill now?" I asked, handing him the bottle.

Jon nodded and took the bottle from me. His hands shook as he opened the bottle and, once he got it open, his hand jerked and the pills spilled onto the floor. He shook his head and began to sob in frustration.

"Bloody hell. My hands shake so badly all the time," he cried with his head in his hands.

Martha and I assured him it was ok and got to work picking up the tablets and placing them back into the bottle. I had Jon hold out his hand and placed one of the pills in it. He smiled gratefully and put the pill in his mouth. I handed him a bottled water from the end table and he washed down his meds with it. Then Martha and I walked with him to the bathroom, so he could take his bath.

"I feel like a baby," Jon remarked with a laugh as we all walked to the loo together. "You're both pampering me so much."

"You ARE a baby," Martha chimed in with a smile. "MY baby."

I had Jon test the temperature of the water. He gave the thumbs up and thanked us.

"I believe you have both seen enough of my naked bum, so I will respectfully wait for you to exit before taking off my robe and entering the tub." He winked.

Martha and I laughed. "Let me or Ken know if you need anything," she said, before we both left the loo and spent the next half hour cleaning up the living room in relative silence. At one point, Martha began to cry, and I comforted her, assuring her that Jon would be alright. When we were finished tidying up, we checked on Jon, who was dozing off in the tub.

"Wake up, sleepyhead," Martha cooed, gently running her hand through his hair.

Jon opened his eyes a crack and smiled when he saw us. "Guess I was wiped out," he said as he stretched his arms. "I'm STILL wiped out. I feel like I need a nap."

I grabbed a towel off the back of the door. "Shall we escort you to bed?" Martha smiled and nodded.

Jon chuckled. "All this loving attention for a madman?"

Martha and I laughed. "It's really ok, love," she assured. "We knew that the transition home wouldn't be easy, especially after almost three months of being away. I've been where you are, Jonathan. I know the struggles all too well." Jon's mum had struggled with a cocaine addiction by age 14, but managed to get clean two years later, around the time she started dating Jon's father.

Jon's eyes filled with tears as he rose slowly from the bathtub. I held up a towel to protect his modesty, and he took it from me once he stepped out of the tub, wrapping it around his waist. Martha grabbed his robe and draped it over him so he could dry off more, and the three of us made our way to his bedroom.

I turned down the covers and fluffed the pillows. Martha handed Jon a pair of underwear and a pair of silk pajamas, which he quickly changed into, doing his best to avoid exposing himself to his mum as he did so. As indecent as the bloke could be, he had never once swore at his mother or appeared naked in front of her up until that day. They had a very special relationship and got along incredibly well, and I knew this incident made my best mate feel guilty as hell.

I went to the kitchen and grabbed a bottled water from the refrigerator, then returned to the bedroom. Jon had just gotten comfy under the covers. Martha sat at his bedside, talking softly to him.

"Here's something for you to drink," I said to Jon, handing him the water. "I know you get thirsty after a hot bath."

Jon smiled broadly. "Thank you so much, mate. Don't let me keep you, I know you have to go back to work. And again, I'm so sorry this happened." He sat up and took a sip of water.

I shook my head. "It's alright, Jon. I'm your best mate and I love you. I was thinking we could hang out next weekend if you're up for it. Maybe chill out here, watch a movie? We could order a pizza?"

Jon nodded and laid back down. "Sounds great. Thank you both so much." He yawned and his eyes grew heavy.

Martha and I both hugged and kissed him goodnight, telling him to call either of us if he needed anything. She and I left the in-law apartment, feeling exhausted but glad that Jon was safe for the moment. She thanked me, and promised to keep me in the loop regarding the situation. After this incident, it was clear that he would need intensive therapy to help with his addiction issues. I would soon find out that it wasn't just the cocaine he had a problem with. He was also continuing to abuse his old drugs of choice, specifically pain meds, ecstasy, amphetamines, DMT, and, to a lesser extent, marijuana and alcohol.

I drove back to the gym despite wanting to go home and curl into a ball. When Daryl saw me, he knew better than to ask how things went because my expression said it all. He simply patted me on the back and thanked me, promising me that the next time we went out for beers, it would be his treat.

I wrapped up the last hour and a half of my shift at the gym then drove home as quickly as I could. I wanted to make a nice dinner for Amy and me...with good old fashioned BDSM for dessert. I put on clean clothes and got to work in the kitchen, deciding on salmon and grilled asparagus with baked sweet potatoes.

My little rag doll arrived home just as I was finished cooking. I knew she was famished after coming home from her part time job, but I was going to make her work for her food.

"Hi, Kenny!" She said with a lovely smile as she walked through the door. "It smells so good in here!"

Amy's smile faded quickly when she saw what I held in my hand, as well as the new cage that was situated right next to the dining table. My expression was dead serious, and my voice was authoritative.

"Strip naked and put on this collar, then crawl inside the cage."

Amy swallowed and her eyes filled with frightened tears. "Um, I have to pee first." Her voice trembled.

I grabbed my leather belt and slammed it against the nearby counter as a "warning shot." She screamed in surprise.

"You piss when I say it's ok to piss!" I barked. Then I lit a cigarette, took a drag, and blew the smoke in her face. "Now take off your clothes, you stupid little whore."

She bit her lip and nodded, then slowly began removing her clothes. "Yes, Master."

A sadistic smile spread across my face as I watched her undress. It was obvious that she was nervous, and her hands shook something terrible. "Slave training session number three" was off to a great start, and I could hardly wait to test her limits.

Two weeks later...

"C'mon, mate," Jon slurred as he held out the pipe full of weed. "Jus' one more hit. Don' be a pussy."

I sat on the couch in his filthy living room, which hadn't been cleaned since Martha and I had tidied up several weeks prior. When I had first arrived at his home hours earlier, he had tripped over the rubble on his way to the door, beer in hand, apologizing for the place being what he called a "bloody disgrace." Pizza boxes, takeout containers, and beer bottles littered the floor, and the air reeked of cigarette smoke and pot smoke. The ashtray overflowed with butts. On at least three occasions, Jon tripped over the dumbbells he kept next to the couch. I had been trying to leave for the past hour, but Jon insisted I keep him company while he got high on a dangerous cocktail of substances, including weed, booze, opioid pills, and ecstasy. He had given up coke since the incident with his mum, but had increased his consumption of other drugs to prevent withdrawals. So when he needed a boost, he took ecstasy or amphetamines. Perhaps it was a blessing that I hung around, because it was clear he wasn't safe by himself.

"No thank you," I said, trying my best to watch the telly. "Why don't you eat some more pizza?" I grabbed a slice for myself and took a bite. Food would help him sober up a bit, at least I hoped.

"Why don't you eat my arsehole?" He growled as he took a hit from his pipe. After holding in the smoke for a solid minute, he leaned over and blew the smoke in my face.

I glared at him as I ate. "You're being a real jerk," I warned. "Keep it up and I will leave."

"Noooo," Jon whined. "Don't leeeeave, Papa Bear." He put his arm around me. "I've been a good boy, cleaning my plate and everything. Doesn't anybody care that I've been eating? And not throwing up or skipping meals? So, I like to party. Who the hell doesn't?" He smirked and took a swig of rum, straight from the bottle.

I sighed, then grabbed the remote and turned off the TV. It was time to have a serious talk. Jon looked at me with a startled expression.

"Well, your love of 'partying' has gotten to the point that you only leave the house to go to therapy with your mum twice a week. And you haven't made plans to open your gym, or do any other kind of work for that matter. This is not who you are, mate. I'm proud of you for overcoming your struggles with eating, but your issues with drugs are the worst they have ever been. I love you, but you need to get clean. You're not healthy. You're killing yourself slowly." My voice cracked and a tear fell from my eye.

Jon stared at me for a long time before nodding. "I, uh, was going to wait until later to tell you about my plans, but I will tell you now. I'm actually starting a detox tomorrow night. I KNOW I'm out of control, mate. And I want to stop. This weekend was intended to be one last 'hurrah' before sobering up. I was hoping you would spend the night here. Have a little 'bro' sleepover, for old times' sake? No funny business, I promise. My dick hasn't worked since July anyway." He smirked, then burst out laughing. I followed, unable to remain serious.

"Ok, I will spend the night," I said, still chuckling slightly. "As long as you are serious about starting the detox tomorrow."

"Of course. But just so you know, I will be in rough shape for a long time while the drugs exit my system, so I won't want anybody to visit me while this is going on. My mum and I discussed it. She's going to be my caretaker during the process, which may take weeks."

I nodded. "You know I'm here if you need me," I assured. "I don't mind helping to take care of you."

Jon shook his head. "You don't want front row seats to this freak show, believe me. Besides, I need to do this alone. You and others have suffered enough from my drug and booze related antics. I mean for god's sake, I fucking RAPED you!" His lip trembled and his eyes filled with tears.

I got choked up periodically before putting my arm around him. "It's alright, Jon. You've made a lot of poor decisions while drunk or high, and your behavior has caused others a lot of pain, but now you're determined to clean up your act and get your life back. That's admirable. You're so strong. I know you can succeed." I kissed him on the cheek.

Jon smiled and gave me a big hug. "Thanks for having faith in me. I'm tired of feeling so powerless. I had a feeling this would happen when I got home. I should have done the ninety day program at the facility, but I was so fixated on getting out of there and setting up a coffee date with Candy, and living a normal and healthy life. There is no way I can let her see me like this, and especially not when I'm detoxing. My hair might fall out, my tremors will worsen, my skin will look terrible..." His voice broke and he began to cry.

I held him tighter. "It's going to be ok," I assured in a soft voice. "You and Candy will go on that long awaited coffee date soon enough. You just have to take care of yourself first."

Jon nodded. "I'm so glad you're here. I think I WILL have some more pizza!" He grabbed a slice from the box and ate with a goofy smile on his face, savoring the flavor. I laughed as I watched him devour the slice. I turned the telly back on, settling for a funny movie.

We sat and watched TV, laughing as we ate and drank. After several more hours, our eyes got heavy and we fell asleep on the couch, our tummies hurting from laughter and too much food.

Two days later...

I stood above a frightened Amy, who was the embodiment of subservient slave with her meek physicality, timid facial expression, and lack of clothing. It was day two of "slave week," and I had let her out of her cage so she could do housework and cook me breakfast.

"You are permitted to stand upright," I said coldly. "I don't expect you to clean or cook while on all fours."

Amy slowly rose to her feet, avoiding eye contact like a good girl. Then I handed her a broom and dustpan.

"Sweep and mop the floor, then make me pancakes and scrambled eggs with a glass of orange juice."

Amy nodded timidly. "Yes, Master."

Then she got to work cleaning the floor. I got comfortable on the couch and watched her. I couldn't help but get an erection watching her do housework in the nude.

The first day of slave week had gone remarkably well. I had decided it was best to "ease" her into slavery, so I refrained from beatings or verbal abuse for the first 24 hours. She had followed orders very well, and agreed to sleep in a cage despite her claustrophobia. Day two, however, I planned on being more strict.

While Amy cleaned, I texted Jon to see how he was doing. I had cheered him on when I watched him pour his drugs and booze down his toilet less than 48 hours prior. The first few days of withdrawals were the most challenging, and I had a feeling he must have been experiencing them pretty intensely by this point. My feeling was right.

"Terrible," he txted back with a crying sad face emoji. "Whole body shaking and sweating. Everything hurts. Can't get myself to leave my bed but can't sleep worth a shit, either. This is fucking hell. I hate this!"

I stepped out onto my deck to call him. It made me so upset to learn he was in that much agony. He picked up after one ring.

"Hey, mate," he said in a trembling voice. "I'm in a world of pain. This is so much worse than I thought it would be."

"I'm so sorry, Jon. The first few days of detox are the hardest. I know you said you wanted to be alone during this process, but I don't mind bringing you some food, or simply keeping you company if you think it would help?"

Jon sniffled a few times. "N-no, it's alright. I look a mess and feel even worse. My mum is a saint. She's got me covered during this shit show. Isn't that right, Mum?"

Martha giggled in the background. "That's right, love."

I chuckled. "Well, alright. Keep me updated. And don't give up. You can do this. I love you, Jon."

"Love you, too, MASTER," he said jokingly. "Let Amy know who's boss."

I laughed heartily before saying goodbye and hanging up. Then I headed back inside to check on my little slave.

She was sweeping the living room floor, keeping her eyes averted as I walked back inside the house. Her long black hair cascaded down her petite breasts. My cock stiffened. I snuck up behind her and grabbed her tits, making her jump in surprise.

"Drop the broom," I growled, as I let go of one of her breasts to pull down my pajama pants and knickers.

She did as I asked. I picked her up and dragged her to the couch, where I had her bend over the back of it. Then I spit on my hand, wet my dick, lined myself up with her twat, and began pounding the shit out of her. She squealed. I yanked at her collar, choking her slightly. I knew she didn't like air restriction so I was careful to avoid pulling the collar too hard. The idea was to "bend" her, not to cause her to break, at least not so early on in the week.

My dick exploded in her cunt within perhaps three minutes. Then I ordered her to continue cleaning the floor. Tears streaked her face and semen dripped down her inner thighs as she worked. I went to the loo to clean myself then wetted a washcloth and handed it to Amy.

"Clean yourself," I said coldly.

She timidly took the washcloth from me and wiped her face, followed by her ladybits and thighs. I took the cloth from her when she was done, placing it in the hamper.

Once Amy was done sweeping and mopping, she got to work in the kitchen. I watched as she prepped and mixed the ingredients, noticing how graceful her movements were. Then I began to think of what kind of wife she would make. She had been living with me for almost two months, only sleeping at her mother's on occasion. Granted, two months was a short time, but we had an amazing connection and I could see myself being married to her. I pictured myself getting down on one knee, popping the big question...

CRASH!

My thoughts jumped back to present day and I got up from the couch. "What the hell happened?!" I barked, as I walked over to the kitchen area.

Amy shook slightly. "I-I just dropped the dish in the sink and it made a loud noise. Nothing broke."

I glared at her. "Keep it down."

She nodded meekly before returning to her cooking duties. "Yes, Master."

I walked back to the couch and continued to watch her. My mouth watered as the scent of food filled the air. Amy was such a talented cook, as was her mother. I couldn't wait to eat what she made me. My mouth formed a smile as I pictured her cooking Thanksgiving dinner, the sound of happy little children echoing through our home. I wondered what our children would look like - half Asian and half white, irresistibly cute with Amy's dimples and my naturally wavy hair.

BEEP! BEEP! BEEP!

This time, the oven timer startled me out of my fantasy, but I didn't mind because it meant the food was ready. I got up and walked over to the dining table, where Amy rushed over with a plate full of delectable food and a glass of juice. The eggs and pancakes were cooked to perfection and done just the way I liked them. I took a few bites of the food, nodded in approval, and looked up at her.

"Nicely done. Why don't you fix yourself a plate, and sit with me?" I said with a wink.

Amy smiled broadly. "Yes, Master."

She fixed herself a plate and joined me at the table. It would be the last meal I would allow her to have at the table, OR with utensils, for at least 48 hours.

Day three of Slave Week...

Amy had remained in the cage overnight like a good girl, after waiting on me hand and foot all day.

After our breakfast together, I had allowed her to use the loo, then ordered her back into her cage until it was time for lunch. She had made me a big salad just the way I liked it, eating her own salad in the cage, minus utensils. I had screamed at her and slapped her when she had managed to spill some of the water in her dog bowl, but refrained from any more discipline until later in the evening. By the time dinner had rolled around on day two, I was feeling savage. She had made a lovely dinner of chicken and mixed vegetables with potatoes. Midway through her cooking, I had ambushed her for the second time that day, forcing her to bend over the bar stool while I sodomized her. Then when dinner was ready, I had forced her to eat the hot food with her hands. While in the cage, she had dropped some vegetables, so I had dragged her out of the cage and threw her in the coat closet for three minutes. She detested closed-in spaces, so she had cried plenty during the short time she was in there. Once the time was up, I had given her a hug, knowing how upsetting it was for her to have been in there.

Day three started at 6am. I startled her awake by running my fingers along the metal bars of the cage. Then I dragged her out of the cage and into the bathroom, where I had her take a shower with me. I handed her the sponge and the soap and made her scrub me from head to toe, as well as clean and condition my hair. Then I forced her to get on her knees and suck me off. I loved the way the water cascaded over her pretty head of hair as she took all of my ten inches into her mouth and down her throat.

My little slave squealed as I pulled at her hair while she blew me. I climaxed within four minutes. Once we were done in the shower she toweled me off and even groomed my facial hair, doing a respectable job with the electronic beard trimmer. Then she applied lotion to my body, taking the time to rub my shoulders for a few minutes as she did so. After that, she fixed me a lovely breakfast of French toast and fried eggs. She had even taken the time to cut up the food for me, and place the napkin in my lap. She took her own food into the cage and ate quickly, minus utensils, before hurrying to the kitchen to wash the dishes.

Her sweetness, attention to detail, and overall level of compliance made me feel more than a little guilty about making her my slave for the rest of the week. I was very tempted to scrap the whole idea of "slave week" and take her on a real vacation for a few days - let her wear clothes, let her speak without being spoken to, let her eat meals at a table with utensils, let her share a bed with me, let her be NORMAL. Just when I was about to pull the plug and tell Amy to forget the whole thing and pack her overnight bag for a last-minute casino trip, I heard the sound of breaking glass emanate from the kitchen. I jumped up from my dining chair and spun around.

Amy had broken a bowl. Unfortunately, it wasn't just ANY bowl. It had been my wife's favorite - a beautiful, hand painted glass one that I had given her as a gift for Christmas many years ago. I became livid.

"You little cunt!" I screamed, as I marched up to her in the kitchen. "That was my wife's favorite bowl! You can't be trusted to wash the dishes! Go in your cage! NOW!!!"

Amy's eyes filled with tears and she ran to the cage and got inside. "I'm so sorry," she sobbed. "I didn't mean to break your wife's favorite bowl. It was an accident."

"Shut up!" I barked back, throwing the shards into the wastebasket before washing the rest of the dishes. I became tearful as I cleaned, remembering the time I had given my wife that bowl, and how happy she had been when she saw it. Now it was destroyed. I rapidly finished the dishes and wiped my eyes dry. I needed some fresh air, so I grabbed my phone and my cigarettes then headed out onto my deck.

I sat on the chaise lounge, lit a cigarette, then texted Jon to see how he was. "Any improvement?" I wrote.

"Nope. Believe it or not, I'm worse. I have a fever and I'm so weak. And the tremors are even more intense than they were yesterday. Mum has to help me with bathing and meals, like I'm a bloody infant. All I want to do is sleep. If this keeps up I'm paying a visit to the ER."

I swallowed and took a drag off my cigarette. I knew things would get worse before they got better, but I also knew he was in good hands. "I'm so sorry to hear that. Get some rest and let me know if you need anything. I will check in later. Love you, mate."

I finished my cigarette then headed back inside. I could hear Amy crying and sniffling from inside the cage.

"You can come out of the cage now," I said to her in a gentle voice. She had been in there long enough.

Slowly, she crawled out of her metal enclosure, her body trembling slightly. I knelt down before her and held out my arms, letting her know I was no longer upset. She returned my embrace letting her head rest upon my chest. I ran my hands through her hair and whispered loving words to her.

"It's alright, Amy," I cooed. "It was an accident. I forgive you." Then I backed away from her and kissed her gently on the lips, wiping the tears from her sweet face.

The remainder of day three went by rather quickly. After making me a delicious lasagna for dinner, I had allowed her to remove the collar and sit on the couch with me for two hours to watch a movie on the telly.

Midway through the film, I went down on her, which she loved, and made her orgasm no less than three times. I had felt guilty about yelling at her so harshly for the bowl incident, and wanted to pamper her, to give her a bit of a break so she would be ready for the torture-fest that would be day four.

Jon had referred to the halfway point of slave week as the "middle finger" of the week, in the sense that both master and slave would feel tempted to quit and say, "Fuck this." As I have mentioned, Jon had thrown in the towel by Thursday. Aside from being riddled with guilt by what he had done to Lisa, he was also afraid she would wind up needing medical attention. In fact, day 5 had begun with him finding her lying semi-conscious on the floor of her cage - starved, dehydrated, and caked in urine and menstrual blood. He had wasted no time taking her out of the cage and nursing her back to health. Once he had made sure she was hydrated and fed, he had taken a bath with her, then treated her to a day of pampering that ended in a marriage proposal.

I had set an alarm on my phone for Amy, to let her know when the two hour period was up. The moment she heard the alarm, she looked over at me with a gentle smile and kissed me tenderly on the lips, then placed the collar around her neck and got back into her cage. I smiled at her and winked as I felt my cock swell in my knickers. I loved how well she was handling this.

That night, I masturbated myself to sleep, thinking of Amy as well as Anna. It had been several weeks since I had heard from my favorite redhead, and I couldn't help but wonder how things were going with her and the new bloke. As for Daryl? He had started dating Tracy in early September, and they were getting along great. With any luck, Jon would stay off the drugs and go on a coffee date with Candy. Perhaps Jon and Candy would become an item. And everyone would live happily ever after...

Day Four of Slave Week...

I had forgotten to put my phone on silent, as evidenced by a text message at 5am. It was Martha.

"Sorry for the early text, but I wanted you to know that I just called an ambulance for Jon. He is running a fever of 102, and is delirious. I knew this could happen during withdrawals. I will keep you updated as soon as I can."

I sat up in bed and called her back. She picked up after one ring.

"Hello, Martha," I began. "So sorry for what's happening. Do you need me to do anything? Perhaps I could meet you guys at the hospital?"

"No, it's quite alright," Martha insisted in a shaky voice. "I am going to ride with him in the ambulance while his father drives to the hospital separately. I think he's severely dehydrated. He has been sweating and shaking nonstop for several days, and I've been trying to get him to drink fluids but he just wants to sleep all the time. I suspect they will put him on an IV. He's barely conscious and very confused. I feel so bad for him. He's trying so hard to get clean." Her voice broke.

"It will be ok," I assured her. "Call or text me with any updates, ok? And let me know if you need anything."

Martha agreed and we hung up. Then I lay back down and prayed Jon would be alright. The poor bloke had been through so much over the past few months. My eyes filled with tears as I thought of my best mate struggling so badly. After a while, I went back to sleep for a few more hours.

Six hours later...

"Did you just look at me?!" I barked at Amy, as she came over to the coffee table to pick up the dishes from lunch. I had caught her making eye contact.

She stood still, and began to cry and shake. "I-I didn't mean-"

"BITCH!!!" I screamed, then took the empty, wooden salad bowl and flung it across the living room. I was fed up with all the mistakes she had been making all fucking day.

I jumped up from the couch, picked her up, and carried her to the closet. "You're staying in the fucking closet until dinner, you little bitch. I'm sick of your face!"

"No!" She protested through tears. "Please don't put me in the closet again! I'm sorry! I will do better!"

I opened the door to the closet and flung her inside like she was a sack of fertilizer. She landed hard on her bum and grunted. For a brief moment before closing the door, I thought I made out what appeared to be a cellphone on the floor of the closet, but wasn't sure. In any case, I didn't give a shit and just wanted the useless little whore out of my sight for a little while.

"If you stay quiet, I MAY let you out early, but I'm not promising anything. You've been fucking up ALL DAMN DAY! Now sit down and think about what you did! All the little fuckups you made! Spilling food! Making eye contact! Questioning my judgment!" I leaned down closer to her horrified face. "I'm closing the door now," I growled.

"No! Please!" Amy cried out.

I slammed the door on her protests and turned up the volume on the telly. The screen on my phone lit up, so I took a look.

Martha had texted me an update on Jon. He had indeed been severely dehydrated and was being given fluids intravenously. He was also being given medication to help the withdrawal symptoms. The doctor wanted to keep him overnight to make sure he was stable before sending him back home. I thanked her for the update, beyond relieved that my best mate wasn't seriously ill.

"Kenny?!" Amy cried from the closet, her voice muffled.

I did my best to ignore her and turned up the volume on the TV once more. I took a hit off my bong to take the edge off.

"KENNY!!!" She screamed, and began banging on the closet door.

I swallowed and got up, walking over to the door but not opening it.

"What the fuck do you want?!" I shouted through the wood.

Amy sniffled. "I just want some water," she sobbed. "My mouth is so dry. And I have to pee. Please?"

I sighed, then went to her cage and got her water bowl, which was mostly full. Then I opened the door and placed the bowl on the floor of the closet, right in front of her. She eagerly grabbed it and took some sips, being careful not to spill any.

"There," I barked. "Now you have your precious water. As for the toilet, I expect you to hold it. You're lucky I even got you something to drink. Now shut your mouth. If you stay quiet like a good girl, I will let you out early." Then I slammed the door shut.

I could hear her crying quietly as I sat on the couch watching TV. Familiar feelings of regret crept into my mind and I was very tempted to let her out of the closet, have her use the loo, perhaps watch a movie with me, and have a drink from a real glass. But I decided to go outside for some fresh air and a cigarette, to clear my head.

As I sat outside on my deck smoking, I tried to convince myself I wasn't some horrible monster for doing all this twisted shit to a girl I loved. I imagined Jon sitting next to me, appearing the way he did before disordered eating and rampant drug use affected his looks. I could see him, tanned and muscular, slim but not emaciated, and flashing me his confident smile, assuring me I was just an "adventurous bloke."

One of my favorite movies was on by the time I went back inside. I sat down and smoked some more weed, letting myself get lost in the film. During commercial, I got up and approached the closet, checking in on Amy without opening the door or speaking.

She was still sniffling periodically, and I thought I heard a male voice coming from somewhere, perhaps from the cell phone I thought I had seen when I had opened the closet door. It was possible that Amy was watching a video on her phone to distract herself. Yes, that must have been it. The voice was calm and vaguely familiar-sounding, and I had a hard time making out most of the words, but it sounded like a relaxation video. I would occasionally watch meditation videos to unwind at night, and they were quite helpful.

I smiled gently as I pictured Amy sitting in the closet, doing her best to ground herself and stay calm. At that moment, I decided I would let her out of the closet once the movie was over.

My bong sat atop the coffee table in its usual spot, as did a tiny bottle of tequila. So I decided to take a sip of the booze, and I chased it down with another bong hit. I wanted to mellow out for Amy, so she would be less compelled to think of me as an aggressive bastard. In fact, I decided to reward her handsomely for conducting herself so gracefully while confined to the closet.

Before long, the movie was finished. I got up and walked over to the closet, then slowly opened the door. Amy was lying curled up into a ball, half asleep with her phone in her hand. She dropped her phone and sat up with a jolt when she saw me, instantly afraid. I smiled gently and knelt before her.

"Amy, it's ok," I assured her in a gentle voice as I reached out to caress her long black hair. "You're free to leave the closet now. You've been a good girl. I'm so proud of you." I kissed her on the lips. "Would you go out to dinner with me tonight? I will let you pick the place."

Amy's face lit up and she nodded. "Yes, I would love to! Thank you so much!"

My sweet little rag doll eagerly embraced me and I held her back, rocking her back and forth and kissing her pretty little head. "Of course, darling. You deserve a treat after all this torture."

Amy's phone lit up as I held her.

"Hope he let you out of the closet by now. I'm glad you called me, keep me updated on how you're doing," the message read.

My heart sped up when I saw who had sent the text. It turned out that Amy hadn't been watching a video before; it had been Eugene's voice on the phone.

Slave Week, Day 5, around 3am...

I woke up in a cold sweat from a horrible nightmare, one involving my wife. My pillow was wet with tears and I was breathing heavily.

"Kenny, are you ok?" Amy asked from the foot of the bed, where I had permitted her to sleep. She deserved a break from the cage, and I had felt like I needed company that night.

I wiped my eyes and nodded. "Yes," I replied in a shaky voice. "I just had a bad dream. Why don't you join me under the covers? I want to hold you."

Any smiled and nodded, getting underneath the covers with me and cuddling me. Her body felt unusually warm, as did her forehead when I kissed her.

"Amy, are you feeling alright? You're awfully warm."

Amy sighed. "Actually, I feel a little feverish. I noticed it during dinner, but I didn't say anything. Incidentally, thank you. That was the best Thai food I have ever had in my life." She giggled.

I smiled and kissed her on the lips. "My pleasure. But I hope you're not coming down with something. Perhaps you just need a good night's rest."

Amy nodded and wrapped her arm around me a little more tightly. "Yeah, that's probably it. Goodnight, Kenny." We exchanged kisses once more.

I lay there awake for a little while, holding Amy and thinking of my wife and our old life together. I hadn't mentioned to Amy the fact that I knew she had spoken to Eugene, deciding it was best to keep the information to myself. Besides, I didn't blame her for wanting to lean on a friend for support during slave week. Still, I wished it hadn't been Eugene that she confided in. Their close friendship made me jealous. I held Amy more closely to me before falling back asleep.

Later that morning...

"What's taking you so bloody long in the kitchen?!" I barked from the bedroom. "It's just breakfast in bed, not a fucking banquet!"

It was a bright and sunny morning, and I was back in "Master" mode, deciding to channel my jealous feelings about Eugene into my treatment of Amy. I lit a cigarette as I waited for the dumb little whore to bring me eggs and orange juice.

After what seemed like hours, Amy made it through the bedroom door with a glass of juice for me.

"About bloody time," I grumbled, taking the glass from her hand. "I hope the food is almost ready. I'm starving."

"Hey, Kenny?" Amy began in a weak, shaky voice.

I took a sip of juice and put out my ciggy. "Did I give you permission to call me by my first name? Call me 'Master,' dammit!" My nostrils flared.

Amy faltered, appearing very unsteady. Her cheeks were flushed. Suddenly concerned for her wellbeing, I got out of bed and placed my hand on her shoulder.

"Hey. Are you alright, sweetheart? What's wrong?" My heart rate sped up.

Just then, her eyes rolled back into her head and she collapsed onto the floor.

"Amy!"

Chapter 11: Things Happen In Threes

"How's my lovely rag doll doing?" I asked, as I popped my head into Amy's hospital room.

Her face lit up when she saw me. She had been admitted several hours' prior. The moment she had fainted in my bedroom had been so frightening. When the paramedics had arrived, her pulse and blood pressure were very low, and she had a 101 fever. After being admitted to the ER and having a number of different tests done, it was revealed that she had a severe urinary tract infection, most likely from being forced to hold her urine multiple times during "slave week." The repeated sexual ambushes did not help either, nor did the occasional denial of food and water. I was beyond guilty that I was most likely responsible for her illness, and decided I would no longer deny bathroom privileges during role play. It was one thing to be a sadist, and another to be a heartless monster.

"Kenny, I'm so glad to see you," Amy said in her soft voice as she lay in her hospital bed. She had an IV and appeared so tired, but I knew she was getting good medical care. "I've had so many tests done, I feel like a laboratory rat." She giggled.

I sat next to her and squeezed her hand, smiling gently. "I'm glad you're alright, sweetheart. I was so worried when you passed out."

Amy shrugged. "It happens. It could be a lot worse. I could be one of those highway accident victims. Did you hear about that?"

I shook my head, suddenly alarmed. "No! When did this happen?"

"There was a big, multi-car pileup on I-95 south this morning, around 9am. One of the nurses here was talking about it."

My eyebrows raised and I felt a bit nervous, because I knew that Daryl would be commuting to the gym around that time. Instinctively, I took out my cellphone and looked at it. Surely enough, I had a missed call from an unknown number and a voicemail message.

"Would you excuse me for a moment?" I asked Amy. "I just need to step outside to check my phone and make a call. I will stop at the gift shop on my way back and get you something." I winked.

Amy smiled and nodded. "I'm not going anywhere!"

I walked down the hall and took the elevator to the main floor, then exited the hospital so I could play the message and reply.

"Hello, this message is for Ken Smith," a female voice said. "This is Dr. Sarah Jones at County Hospital. I have you down as an emergency contact person for Daryl Moore. Mr. Moore was in a car accident this morning. There was a multi-car pileup on I-95, and he was involved in it. He has a concussion as well as a broken ankle and broken arm. He was brought to the ER earlier today, and he has been admitted to room 331. He's stable, and very lucky to have survived. If you have any questions for me, call the main number, then dial extension 404. Thank you."

My heart began racing a mile a minute and my eyes filled with tears. First Jon, and now Daryl? Poor Martha and Jon Sr. couldn't catch a break with their sons these days. As for me, I had lost count of all the close calls my two best mates had survived over the years. Cancer, severe asthma attacks, shark bites, drug overdoses, near drowning incidents, and car accidents were among the indignities these two poor blokes have had to deal with. I used my phone to send out a mass email to the gym members, explaining that classes and personal training sessions were cancelled for the rest of the day due to a medical emergency. Then I called Martha.

"Hi, Ken," she said after one ring. "I'm in the hospital, in the cafeteria. I assume you heard the news about poor Daryl? The doctor said she called you."

"Indeed I did," I said as I lit a cigarette and took a deep drag, still in a state of shock. "I'm actually at the hospital myself. I'm outside having a smoke. Amy got admitted today for a urinary tract infection. Seems everyone's falling ill lately!"

"Oh my goodness," she gasped. "No kidding. Well you know what they say. 'Things happen in threes.'"

"This is true. I will meet you in the cafeteria in a few moments, Martha. So sorry about all this."

We chatted for a few more moments before hanging up, then I rapidly finished my cigarette and headed back inside towards the hospital cafeteria. I spotted Martha right away and smiled.

"We need to stop meeting like this!" Martha said with a chuckle as she hugged me. Her eyes were red from crying. I sat down across from her at the table.

"Everything will be ok," I said soothingly. "This is just a rough patch."

Martha nodded as she took a sip of tea. "Jon and his dad should be here soon, and we can all visit Daryl. Poor Jon just got discharged from here yesterday and now he's coming back as a visitor. He's still feeling pretty sick but really wanted to see his brother, so he's dragging himself out of the house."

I gave a sad smile, knowing how ill Jon must have been feeling. "Amy's room is on the same floor as Daryl's. I am going to swing by her room before I go see him because I promised her something from the gift shop next door. She has a thing for chocolate." I winked.

Martha winked. "That's so sweet of you. Amy is such a nice girl. You two make a lovely couple."

I smiled and blushed. Just then, Jon and his father approached our table.

"Hello," Jon's father said to us with a tight smile. "Wish we were meeting under happier circumstances."

Jon stood behind his father, looking more gaunt and pale than the last time I saw him. His hair was back in a man-bun and his beard had grown out. There were dark circles under his bloodshot eyes and he was shaking slightly. He looked even worse than when I had visited him in the Berkshires. It had been barely a week since I had seen him last, but the ravages of drug detox made him appear years older. We exchanged hugs and greetings.

"How you holding up, mate?" I asked as I wrapped my arms around his bony waist. I could feel his body trembling, and he was sweaty despite the cool temperature.

"Horrible," he whispered. "I'm on new meds and they're making me feel like shit." His lip trembled.

I smiled sympathetically. "It will get better."

The four of us stopped at the gift shop briefly. I got a bouquet of roses and a box of gourmet chocolates for Amy. Then Jon spotted a stuffed llama and decided to get it for Daryl as a joke, since his younger brother had always made fun of him for resembling one. We made our purchases and stepped onto the elevator, getting off on the third floor.

I made my way over to Amy's room. When I popped my head in, I saw that she already had company. They were talking and laughing like old lovers. My jaw clenched and I forced a smile.

"Hey, Ken," Eugene said with a wave, standing up from his seat. He was dressed in scrubs. "I was on my lunch break and wanted to stop by to say hello and drop off flowers. Now she has THREE bouquets." He said with a smile and a nod as he saw the flowers I was holding.

"Yeah, my mom was here when you stepped out and she brought me daisies," Amy said with a sweet smile. "She's coming back later."

I nodded and grinned warmly as I walked closer to Amy's bed, handing her the candy and putting my roses in a plastic container situated on a nearby table, next to her mother's daisies and Eugene's tulips. Her eyes lit up and she thanked me profusely as she opened the box of chocolate, helping herself to a piece. I turned to Eugene.

"Nice of you to stop by," I said to him, determined to stay polite despite being insanely jealous. "Daryl was in a car accident this morning, and he's at the opposite end of the hall."

Eugene nodded solemnly. "I know. I saw him already. He's in good shape, considering."

Amy's eyes went wide. "Oh, no! Poor Daryl. Is he ok?" She asked Eugene.

"Well, he has some broken bones and he's probably going to be unable to work for about a month, but he will be alright."

I swallowed and fought back tears, knowing how hard it would be for Daryl to stay home and be unable to work. He so loved the gym. As for me? I would have to do the work of two people until he was well enough to come back. I didn't mind. I was just happy that my best mate had survived and would be on the mend.

Eugene headed for the door, but turned around one last time to say goodbye to Amy. "I will stop by later. In the meantime, be good." He smiled warmly at Amy then waved at me. "Later, dude."

I waved goodbye to Eugene then sat down. "I want to visit with Daryl for a little bit, but you deserved flowers and candy first," I said with a wink as I grabbed her hand and kissed it.

"That's so nice of you, Kenny," she cooed. "Thank you so much. You know, I might actually take a little nap in a few minutes. I'm so sleepy. I don't know if it's the meds they have me on or the infection, but I'm wiped out." She yawned.

I kissed her hand again. "You need your rest. I will visit Daryl and let you sleep for a bit. But I will be back. Can I get you anything else?"

Amy shook her head. "I'm ok."

I rose from the chair and let go of her hand. "Very well. I will be back a little later. Sleep well, honey." I kissed her gently on the lips before leaving the room and heading down the hall to visit Daryl.

It was surreal, seeing him lying semi-conscious in a hospital bed, a bandage on his forehead and his arm and lower leg in a cast. Daryl had been so physically robust for many years now. When I looked at him in that bed, I was transported back in time twenty-odd years, back to when he was a fragile boy with asthma and a history of cancer.

"How are you feeling?" I asked Daryl, as I sat beside him. A shaky and fidgety Jon sat next to me, and Martha and Jon Sr. sat on the other side of Daryl's bed.

"Well, I'm glad to still be here," he said in a weak voice. "I love the llama," he commented with a tired smile.

We all chuckled. It was obvious he was on a heavy cocktail of drugs, and would most likely need to spend time at a physical rehab facility before going home. But I was so thankful that he wasn't in worse shape. Several people had either died or suffered horrible injuries in the pileup on the highway, so he was incredibly lucky.

The four of us chatted with Daryl for a bit, who mostly smiled and nodded as he lay there, comfortably doped up on meds. After a while, Jon got up from his chair, appearing unsteady. His face was covered in sweat.

"I'm not feeling so good," Jon said in a quivering voice. "I need to go home. Sorry."

Martha stood up and walked over to him, holding his hand. "It's ok, love. I will take you home. I know you're still recovering from your own sickness and need rest."

Daryl smiled at his elder brother. "Thank you for stopping by, and for my new little pet," he said, referring to the stuffed llama. "I think 'Jon' is a good name for him."

Jon chuckled and smiled, patting Daryl on his uninjured leg. "Of course, little brother. Now, go on and get some rest and heal up quickly."

"You do the same, Jon. You look like roadkill." He smirked at his younger brother.

We all broke down into laughter at Daryl's reference to an inside joke. Around age six, Daryl had decided to play in a mud puddle following a rain storm, and when he had come back in the house, Jon had remarked to him that he looked "like roadkill." Daryl had laughed heartily, often repeating the line at random. From that point on, "You look like roadkill" became a catchphrase in the Moore family.

I gave Martha a hug, then gave one to Jon. His body was trembling like a leaf by this point, and his shirt was soaked with sweat. My heart ached for him.

"Things will get easier," I whispered as I embraced him. "Hang in there."

"I hope so," he whispered back. "I can't stand this torture."

I backed away from his tear-streaked face. "I will call you later. I love you, mate."

"Love you more," he said with a wink as he wiped his eyes and walked down the hall with his mum, his gait slow and unsteady.

I turned my attention back to Daryl, smiling sadly. "Poor Jon has been going through hell with his drug detox."

Daryl nodded solemnly. "He really looks awful. But I'm proud of him for getting clean."

Jon Sr. nodded. "I never realized how bad his drug problem was until recently." His expression was sad.

"None of us did," I said. "He has always been stubbornly independent, and secretive. I'm glad he's finally opening up and getting help. Now I just have to worry about his brother." I smirked at Daryl, who laughed weakly.

"Oh, nonsense," he commented. "I will be on the mend in no time, and so will Jon. AND Amy." He smiled confidently.

I said a silent prayer that Daryl was right about everyone recovering quickly. The weeks to come would reveal otherwise.

Two weeks later...

My head throbbed and my body ached as I slogged my way through twelve hour days at the gym, covering for Daryl while he slowly recuperated from his injuries. I wasn't getting a day off any time soon and had no life outside of work, but it was worth it because my best mate was getting better. I visited him at the rehab facility as often as I could, giving him updates on things and having meals with him whenever possible. In fact, I'd had dinner with him on my 34th birthday and had managed to smuggle beer into the place, much to his delight. What made it even better was that he had insisted I use the gym's expense account to buy the alcohol. It wasn't like him to spend money designed for business expenses on such frivolous things, but had said, "What the hell?" Tracy had even joined us for a while, showing up with a box of my favorite donuts, putting a candle in one of them, and making her boyfriend join in on a hilariously off-key rendition of "happy birthday." My baby girl and Daryl made such a sweet couple.

Meanwhile, Amy had contracted a horrible case of the flu several days after coming back from the hospital. She was spending almost all of her time in bed and, at my urging as well as her mother's, I convinced her to stay at her mother's house so she could be properly taken care of until my work schedule was back to normal. I hated not being able to pamper my little rag doll while she was so sick, but I knew she was in good hands with her lovely mum. I also couldn't risk getting sick while running the gym by myself, so I was only able to leave little gifts on her porch and call, text, or video chat with her. I couldn't wait to have her back home with me. My bed felt so empty without her.

Despite being horribly ill, Amy had made a sexy video for me, one in which she stripteased to erotic music and masturbated with a giant dildo. I had wanked off to that video multiple times on the evening of my 34th. Then, when I had checked my email, Amy had purchased an electronic gift card to my favorite pizza place. I had wasted no time ordering a late night delivery of delectable pizza and washing it down with the leftover beer I had purchased with Daryl's expense account.

Last but not least, there was Jon. He was withdrawing from the world more and more with each passing day, having fallen into a deep depression as a result of prolonged withdrawal from the drugs.

He had sent me a huge gift basket for my birthday, complete with very expensive bottles of wine as well as imported cheese. He knew how much I loved both. It had undoubtedly cost a fortune, but Jon had insisted it was the least he could do since he felt too sick to celebrate in person. There was a short but lovely, heartfelt note included with the basket that had made me tear up. He had briefly video chatted with me on my 34th while I was visiting Daryl, and the three of us had made a virtual toast - Daryl and me with beer and Jon with sparkling water. Jon's room had been so dim I was barely able to see what he looked like during the video call, and he had worn a baseball cap to hide a bad hair day, or, more specifically, "the "monstrosity growing atop my fucking head."

Jon had spent almost every day of his life under the influence of one substance or another since age 10, and had admitted to me during an emotional conversation that he had no idea how to cope with life as a sober person. His long and arduous journey with psychotropic substances began with cough syrup, which he would drink to get a buzz. Then by age 12, it was weed. If it wasn't weed, it was alcohol. And if it wasn't alcohol, it was pain pills. If it wasn't pain pills, it was cocaine. Or psychedelics, or ecstasy, or speed, or anabolic "performance enhancers."

I had offered to pop by Jon's place several times with food, but he didn't want anyone seeing him, because he was embarrassed by how awful he looked. In fact, he was even telling his mum not to come by, and she began to leave meals and other various items outside his door. Candy continued to stay in touch with him, patiently accepting a rain check for their coffee date.

Between Jon's depression, Daryl's injuries, Amy prolonged illness, and my insane workload, I was ready to go on a fucking bender. Despite the danger of substance use, I wanted to just let myself go for a short time, to help get myself through this bad patch. All I needed was one more straw to break the proverbial camel's back. And I got it.

I stopped at the grocery store one night on my way home from another long and horrible day. I spotted the two of them in the produce section, hugging and kissing, looking so happy. I abruptly turned around and went down another aisle, determined not to see them, and not wanting them to see me.

It's not that I didn't want Anna to be happy, but seeing her with the man she had dumped me for bruised my ego and made me jealous. Perhaps I wouldn't have minded so much if I was actually spending time with my own girlfriend, but of course poor Amy was still battling illness while trying to catch up with schoolwork.

The combination of blue balls, overwork, and social isolation can bring out the addict in anyone after a while, so I quickly paid for my groceries and made a detour to the liquor store. I bought a large, expensive bottle of single malt scotch and called my dealer friend, asking for a baggie of coke. I hadn't used that stuff since Amy's birthday weekend almost three months' prior and, despite what it had done to Jon, I was craving it. Besides, I didn't use coke the way my best mate did, so what was the big fucking deal?

That night I got so completely, utterly fucked up that I blacked out, waking up naked on the floor of my kitchen around 4am, with my hand on my cock. The half empty bottle of scotch lay next to my head, as did an empty box of leftover doughnuts that Tracy had given me for my birthday. This incident set the tone for the next few weeks, which would pass in a drug-addled haze.

I started my days at the gym high as a fucking kite, even snorting a line or two at lunch to keep my energy up. Some time over the next few days, I managed to lose my phone charger and then my actual phone. I didn't give a fuck about anyone and wanted to make it through the pre-holiday rush as quickly as possible, so I didn't even bother calling Amy or Jon from my landline or work phone for god knows how long. As for Daryl, I managed to visit him only once in a week and a half, and for only two hours. I had shown up stoned, having smoked a blunt in the parking lot of the facility.

Before long, it was Thanksgiving week. I couldn't recall when I had last spoken to Jon or Amy, or any of my other friends besides Daryl. My charger resurfaced, but my phone was still missing and I lacked the fortitude to look for it or replace it.

The day before Thanksgiving, I snorted a few lines of coke on my lunch break and used the office phone to call my brother Lawrence, talking with him briefly to let him know when I was coming over for Thanksgiving dinner. Then I rang Amy, but it went to voicemail. I left a sweet message for her, wishing her a happy Thanksgiving and asking her to have dinner with me the first Saturday in December. Then I called Jon, but it also went to voicemail, so I simply wished him a happy holiday and told him to call me at the office or landline when he had a chance.

Knock, knock.

Someone was knocking on my office door. It was a quiet day overall, and I didn't have any personal training sessions scheduled for several hours, so I wasn't expecting anyone. I stood up and opened the door. It was Deedee, the sexy, big-busted room service girl from the casino, who had engaged in foreplay with me and the girlies on Amy's birthday.

"Deedee!" I said gleefully, feeling the effects of the drugs. "What a pleasant surprise!"

She smiled and gave me a hug. Her large breasts felt so good against me. I wanted to suck on them.

"So good to see you again," she said. "I was in the area and wanted to know if you had any personal training sessions available? I know it's last

"Take every inch of me, you little bitch," I spat as I pounded the hell out of her. I grabbed her hips and slapped her arse cheeks several times. It felt so great to channel all my pent up frustration into a fuck session, and I sped up my thrusts once more.

Deedee climaxed within ten minutes of being on her knees, the walls of her vagina contracting around my engorged member. Nowhere near done with her, I withdrew my cock, picked her up, and turned her onto her back. Then I pushed on her inner thighs until her legs were spread wide and once again lined myself up with her pussy.

I impaled her repeatedly, reveling in her pained facial expression as I pushed on the backs of her legs and went balls-deep inside her over and over again. Nothing else mattered but that moment. I was like a horny monster, hell bent on achieving a release, even at the expense of another's comfort. In the confines of the gym, I felt like a true "master," running a crash course in "Submission 101." In that moment, my gym went from a place of fitness to a school of carnal pleasures, and I was the dean. I looked down at my reluctant student, lying on her back with frightened eyes, receiving a hard lesson in domination. If she wanted to pass the course, she would have to make me climax.

I abruptly withdrew from her and ordered her to get on her knees again to suck me off. I held her head to my slimy cock and forced her to take every inch. She gagged repeatedly and nearly threw up on my dick as she fellated me, and I laughed at her struggle. After around five minutes, I approached climax. I let go of the back of her head and withdrew my cock from her pretty mouth, ejaculating all over her full breasts. Once I was done, I bent down and licked the cum from her titties, then kissed her aggressively on the mouth so she could taste my load. She nearly choked but managed to swallow what I gave her like a good little slut.

Just then, I heard the gym door open. Luckily, Deedee and I were far enough away from the entrance that we were able to grab our clothes and get dressed without being discovered by the gym member who came through the door. I ran my hands through my hair as Deedee grabbed her shoes and clothes and scurried off to the ladies' locker room with a giggle. Then I greeted the chubby, middle aged man who had come in for personal training.

"Harold!" I exclaimed with a smile as I waved to the balding fellow, who insisted on shaking my clammy hand. I winced inwardly as I just thought of where that hand had been a mere two minutes prior. Ah, well. What he didn't know, wouldn't hurt him.

Who fucking knows how many hours later...

"Ken?"

My elder brother's authoritative voice permeated my drunken thoughts, but my eyes remained closed despite my efforts at opening them.

"KEN?" Lawrence's voice repeated in a louder tone. Then I felt him shaking my shoulder.

I tried to move my body, but felt glued to the floor. I grunted, then slowly opened my eyes a crack and took a look around. I was lying on the floor of my living room and had no idea how long I had been there, or how I even got there. Bloody hell, I could barely recall having arrived home from work.

"Ken, can you hear me? Open your eyes." Lawrence tried to sit me up, but my body was completely limp and I simply fell back down to the floor.

"Ughh!" I grunted as I landed onto the laminate floor with a thud. "What...when...what day is it?" I slurred, realizing how dry my mouth was as I spoke.

Lawrence knelt beside me on the floor. It was at that moment that I realized I was naked, but my brother had had the decency to cover me with a towel.

"It's Thanksgiving night," he said softly. "You didn't show up for dinner and you weren't answering your cellphone or land line. How much have you had to drink?"

Suddenly my head throbbed and my heart sped up something terrible. I slowly sat up. I rubbed my head.

"Oh, Christ," I groaned. "I don't even know. I can't remember much of anything. I'm sorry I missed dinner."

Lawrence patted me on the back. "Hey, you're alive. And I brought you a plate. I even included extra stuffing and a big slice of Diana's pecan pie."

I smiled. "Thank you so much, Lawrence. I'm such a wanker for getting so plastered. But my life has been nothing but crap for the past month."

Just then, I heard my bathroom door open. She was wearing only a towel, which barely concealed her huge breasts. She jumped when she saw Lawrence.

"Oh, hey," Deedee said. "Sorry, I didn't know anyone was coming over. I'm Deedee," she chirped with a sweet smile.

Lawrence blushed and stammered a greeting, before Deedee excused herself to my bedroom to get dressed. That was when I began to recall the events that led up to that moment.

After Deedee's and my little tryst at the gym and Harold's personal training session, I was done for the day and ready to celebrate. My busty, brunette friend had chilled out in the lady's locker room while I worked with Harold, waiting patiently for me to finish the session and close for the day. Once I was done closing the gym, I had asked Deedee to hang out at my place for an "encore," and she had said yes. I was delighted, and she had followed me in her car.

Once home, I had whipped out the baggie of coke and convinced her to do a line. She had never tried coke before and was eager to experience the high. She had wound up doing three lines, and I had done a whopping ten, followed by multiple bong hits and an entire bottle of scotch. Then we had shared one of the bottles of wine that Jon had given me for my birthday. We were soon completely fucked up and decided in our inebriated state that it would be a wonderful idea to fuck on the beach, which, in late November, was completely deserted.

It had been a very mild night, with temperatures in the high 50s, so it was rather pleasant. It had been difficult doing inverted 69 on uneven sand while drunk, but I had managed to avoid dropping Deedee on her head. She was great with her mouth as well as her hands, and her cunny tasted so sweet. I had made her climax countless times before we had headed back inside my house, where I ate apple pie off of her breasts and she ate cranberry sauce off my cock and balls. What better way to ring in the start of the holiday season than with some jolly old food play?

I had opened yet another bottle of scotch, and that was when my brain got muddled and my memories foggy. I recalled torturing her with a turkey baster full of hot gravy, squirting the steamy concoction inside her vagina as well as her bum. Then we had gone into the shower and fucked some more, and I recall having loved the way her back door had felt with the hot gravy acting as lube. We had eventually fallen asleep in the bathtub, waking up hours later in lukewarm water.

She and I had wound up finishing the second bottle of scotch and fucked once again on the living room floor for god knows how long. I couldn't get enough of those double D's. They were the perfect size for tit-fucking, and the plump flesh felt so great against my throbbing dick.

After the shagfest, we had fallen asleep in a drunken stupor for what must have been close to 18 hours.

My entire body throbbed something awful, and I began to feel guilty about what I had done. It's not like Amy didn't know I was polyamorous, but the fact that she and I hadn't discussed the terms of our relationship, along with the fact that she preferred monogamy, made me feel regretful. I so needed to call my ragdoll and speak to her.

Lawrence and I chatted for a while longer before he headed back home, assuring me he wasn't pissed off and was simply glad I was alright. Perhaps he had changed over the years, becoming less uptight.

Once my brother was gone, I picked up the landline and dialed Amy's number, which, once again, went to voicemail. I left a message for her.

"Hello, Amy. I miss you so much, sweetheart. Happy Thanksgiving night to you and your lovely family. I was hoping to reach you but I'm sure you're celebrating, or possibly in a food coma. I know I haven't been around too much lately but I wanted to see you as soon as possible, if not this weekend then the next one for sure. My cellphone is still missing, so try calling my house phone or work phone. If I still can't find it by next week I'm getting a new device. I love you, my little rag doll. Talk soon. Bye."

It would be at least two weeks before I would see Amy again, and it would be an experience that would completely turn my life upside down.

"Hey, Kenny, what do you think of my outfit?"

I looked up and was greeted by a very horny Deedee, who was decked out in a sexy pilgrim costume. I might not have been able to celebrate Thanksgiving with my ragdoll, but in that moment I would settle for stuffing this little slut's turkey. I stood up, towering over her as I came in close, rubbing my hands over her ample breasts as I looked her up and down. A horny smirk crossed my face.

"Bend over, bitch."